My Husband's Wife

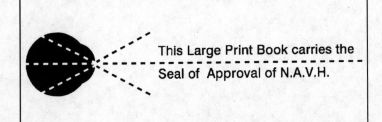

This Large Print Book carries the
Seal of Approval of N.A.V.H.

My Husband's Wife

Jane Corry

THORNDIKE PRESS
A part of Gale, Cengage Learning

GALE
CENGAGE Learning·

Farmington Hills, Mich • San Francisco • New York • Waterville, Maine
Meriden, Conn • Mason, Ohio • Chicago

GALE
CENGAGE Learning·

LIBRARY OF CONGRESS CIP DATA ON FILE.
CATALOGUING IN PUBLICATION FOR THIS BOOK
IS AVAILABLE FROM THE LIBRARY OF CONGRESS

ISBN-13: 978-1-4104-9739-0 (hardcover)
ISBN-10: 1-4104-9739-9 (hardcover)

Published in 2017 by arrangement with Penguin Books, an imprint of
Penguin Publishing Group, a division of Penguin Random House LLC

Printed in Mexico
3 4 5 6 7 8 21 20 19 18 17

*This book is dedicated to my
amazing second husband, Shaun.
Never a dull moment! Not only do you
make me laugh but you also
give me space to write.*

*This dedication is also shared with
my wonderful children,
who inspire me every day.*

ACKNOWLEDGMENTS

I would like to thank my US editor Pamela Dorman and her assistant Jeramie Orton for their warm welcome from across the "pond" and their valuable expertise. It has been a real pleasure to work with them — as well as being an education. Despite having made several visits to the wonderful USA, I hadn't realized that so many of our British words meant something totally different in America! I must also express my heartfelt gratitude to my Penguin UK editor, Katy Loftus, and my agent, Kate Hordern, who championed this book from the very beginning. *My Husband's Wife* and I are immensely appreciative of everything they do.

Books would not reach the reader if it were not for the tireless efforts of sales, rights and publicity teams plus several other departments. Again, I would like to thank everyone concerned on both sides of the

Atlantic.

Meanwhile, old friends are like old novels: always there and always comforting. I was lucky enough to meet Betty Schwartz when starting off on my writing journey. Betty has encouraged many authors over the years and I consider myself blessed to be among her protégés.

Great efforts have been made to ensure that I have described the legal world correctly and also given a fair representation of those on the autistic spectrum. It was very kind of the following to give up their time in this respect: Richard Gibbs, Ian Kelcey of Kelcey and Hall Solicitors and Advocates, the Law Society in London, Peter Bennett, the National Autistic Society and Dr. Elizabeth Soilleux. It should be pointed out that HMP Breakville is not modeled on the prison where I was writer in residence for three years. "My" jail gave me an insight into a world which I could never have imagined without venturing through those daunting gates.

Writers are renowned for needing solitude but they also need like-minded friends. Among these, I would like to single out novelists Kate Furnivall, Bev Davies, Rosanna Ley, the Freelance Media Group and the fabulous Prime Writers. I know how time-consuming this can be and I am very grateful.

Thanks, too, to all my readers. I really appreciate you — especially when you e-mail with lovely comments! I've made some wonderful friends this way.

Finally, I'd like to sign off with praise to the age-old institution of marriage. That wedding ring can lead to some extraordinary situations, as my heroine Lily is about to find out. I hope you enjoy meeting her.

PROLOGUE

Flash of metal.

Thunder in my ears.

"This is the five o'clock news."

The radio, chirping merrily from the pine dresser, laden with photographs (holidays, graduation, wedding); a pretty blue and pink plate; a quarter bottle of Jack Daniel's, partially hidden by a birthday card.

My head is killing me. My right wrist as well. The pain in my chest is scary. So, too, is the blood.

I slump to the floor, soothed by the cold of the black slate. And I shake.

Above me, on the wall, is a white house in Italy, studded with purple bougainvillea. A honeymoon memento.

Can a marriage end in murder? Even if it's already dead?

That painting will be the last thing I see. But in my mind, I am reliving my life.

11

So it's true what they say about dying. The past comes back to go with you.

THE DAILY TELEGRAPH

Tuesday 20 October 2015
The artist Ed Macdonald has been found stabbed to death in his home. It is thought that . . .

■ ■ ■ ■

PART ONE:
FIFTEEN YEARS
EARLIER

■ ■ ■ ■

1
LILY

Late September 2000

"Nervous?" Ed asks with a note of sympathy in his voice.

He's pouring out his favorite breakfast cereal. Rice Krispies. Usually I like them, too. As a child, I was obsessed by the elfin-faced figures on the packet, and the magic hasn't quite left.

But today I don't have the stomach to eat anything.

"Nervous?" I repeat, fastening my pearl earrings in the little mirror next to the sink. Our flat is small. Compromises were made.

About what? I almost add. Nervous about the first day of married life, perhaps. Nervous because we should have taken more time to find a better flat instead of one in the wrong part of Clapham, where both bedroom and bathroom are so small that my one tube of Rimmel foundation and my two lipsticks (rose pink and ruby red) snuggle up next to the teaspoons in the cutlery drawer.

Or nervous about going back to work after our honeymoon in Italy? A week in Sicily, knocking back bottles of Marsala, grilled sardines and slabs of pecorino cheese in a hotel paid for by Ed's grandmother.

Maybe I'm nervous about all these things.

Normally, I love my work. Until now, I've been in employment law, helping people — especially women — who've been unfairly sacked. Looking after the underdog, that's me. I nearly became a social worker like Dad, but, thanks to a determined careers teacher at school, here I am. A twenty-five-year-old newly qualified solicitor on minimum wage. Struggling to do up the button at the back of my navy-blue skirt. No one wears bright colors in a law office, apart from the secretaries. Or so I was told when I started. And the fact that I was advised to wear a *skirt* suit, not trousers — don't even get me started.

"We're moving you to criminal," my boss announced by way of a wedding gift. "We think you'll be good at it."

So now, on my first day back, I'm preparing to go to prison. To see a man who's been accused of murder. I've never been inside a prison before. Never wanted to. It's an unknown world. One reserved for people who have done wrong. I'm the kind of person who goes straight back if someone has given me too much change in the newsstand when I buy my monthly copy of *Cosmo.*

Ed is doodling now. His head is bent slightly to the left as he sketches on a notepad next to his cereal. My husband is always drawing. It was one of the first things that attracted me to him. "Advertising," he said with a rueful shrug when I asked what he did. "On the creative side. But I'm going to be a full-time artist one day. This is just temporary — to pay the bills."

I liked that. A man who knew where he was going. But when he's drawing or painting, Ed doesn't even know which planet he's on. Right now, he's forgotten he even asked me a question. But suddenly it's important for me to answer it.

"Nervous? No, I'm not nervous."

There's a nod, but despite that earlier kind tone, I'm not sure he's really heard me. When Ed's in the zone, the rest of the world doesn't matter. Not even my fib.

Why, I ask myself, as I take his left hand — the one with the shiny gold wedding ring — don't I tell him how I really feel? Why not confess that I feel sick and that I need to go to the loo even though I've only just been? A shiver passes down my spine as I spray duty-free Chanel No. 5 (a present from Ed, using another wedding gift check) on the inside of both wrists. Last month, a solicitor from a rival firm was stabbed in both lungs when he went to see a client in Wandsworth.

"Come on," I say, anxiety sharpening my usually light voice. "We're both going to be late."

Reluctantly, he rises from the rickety chair that the former owner of our flat had left behind. He's a tall man, my new husband. Lanky, with an almost apologetic way of walking, as if he would really rather be somewhere else. As a child, apparently, his hair was as golden as mine is today ("We knew you were a 'Lily' the first time we saw you," my mother has always said), but now it's a sandy brown. And he has thick fingers that betray no hint of the artist he yearns to be.

We all need our dreams. Lilies are meant to be beautiful. I look all right from the top bit up, thanks to my naturally blond hair and what my now-deceased grandmother used to kindly call "elegant swan neck." But look below, and you'll find leftover puppy fat instead of a slender stem. No matter what I do, I'm stuck on the size fourteen rail — and that's if I'm lucky. I know I shouldn't care, and Ed always says he doesn't, but I just do.

On the way out, my eye falls on the stack of wedding cards propped up against Ed's records. Mr. and Mrs. E. Macdonald. The name seems so unfamiliar.

Mrs. Ed Macdonald.

Lily Macdonald.

I've spent ages trying to perfect my signature, looping the *y* through the *M,* but somehow it still doesn't seem quite right. The names don't go together that well. I hope it's not a bad sign.

Meanwhile, each card requires a thankyou letter to be sent by the end of the week. If my mother has taught me anything, it is to be polite.

One of the cards has a particularly flamboyant *look at me!* scrawl, in turquoise ink. "Davina was a girlfriend once," Ed explained before she turned up at our engagement party. "But now we're just friends."

I think of Davina with her horsey laugh and artfully styled auburn hair that makes her look like a pre-Raphaelite model. Davina who works in events, organizing parties to which all the "nice girls" go. Davina who narrowed her violet eyes when we were introduced, as if wondering why Ed would bother with a too-tall, too-plump woman like me.

Can a man ever be just friends with a woman when the relationship is over?

I decide to leave my predecessor's letter until last. Ed married *me,* not her, I remind myself.

My new husband's warm hand now squeezes mine. "It will be all right, you know."

For a minute, I wonder if he is referring to our marriage. Then I remember. My first criminal client. Joe Thomas.

"Thanks." It's comforting that Ed wasn't taken in by my earlier bravado. And worrying, too.

Together, we shut the front door, checking it twice because it's all so new to us, and walk briskly down the ground-floor corridor leading out of our block of flats. As we do so, another door opens and a little girl with long, dark, glossy, curly hair — looking as though it's trying to escape from that ponytail — comes out with her mother. I've seen them before, but when I said "hello," they didn't reply. Both have beautiful olive skin and walk with a grace that makes them appear to be floating.

We hit the sharp autumn air together. The

four of us are heading in the same direction, but mother and daughter are now
slightly ahead because Ed is scribbling
something in his sketchbook as we walk.
The pair, I notice, seem like carbon copies
of each other, except that the woman is
wearing a too-short black skirt (while carrying what looks like a uniform) and the little
girl — who's whining for something — is
dressed in a navy-blue school blazer. When
we have children, I tell myself, we'll teach
them not to whine.

I shiver as we approach the bus stop; the
pale autumn sun is so different from the
honeymoon heat. But it's the prospect of
our separation that tightens my chest. After
one week of togetherness, the thought of
managing for eight hours without Ed is
almost scary.

Not so long ago, I was independent.
Content with my own company. But from
the minute that Ed and I first spoke at that
party six months ago (just six months!), I've
felt both strengthened and weakened at the
same time.

We pause and I steel myself for the inevi-
table. My bus goes one way. His, the other.
Ed is off to the advertising company where
he spends his days illustrating slogans to
make the public buy something it never

intended to. Just before our wedding, he'd presented me with a beautifully designed box of expensive hand cream. I'd thought it was a gift he had picked out for me, but it had turned out to be a "freebie." Now he is tearing a page out of his notebook and handing it to me. It's a sketch of a four-leaf clover inside a heart with the words *Good luck* below. "Thank you," I say, with a catch in my throat. He makes an *it's nothing* gesture.

"You know, it won't be so bad when you're there," adds my new husband before kissing me on the mouth. He tastes of Rice Krispies and that strong toothpaste of his that I still haven't gotten used to.

"I know," I say before he peels off to the bus stop on the other side of the road.

Two lies. Small white ones. Designed to make the other feel better.

But that's how some lies start. Small. Well meaning. Until they get too big to handle.

2
CARLA

"Why?" Carla whined as she dragged behind, pulling her mother's hand to stop this steady, determined pace toward school. "Why do I have to go?"

If she went on making a fuss, her mother might give in out of exhaustion. It worked last week, although that had been a saint's day. Mamma had been more tearful than usual. Birthdays and saints' days and Christmas and Easter always did that to her.

"Where has the time gone?" Mamma would groan in that heavy, rich accent that was so different from all the other children's mothers' at school. "Nine and a half years without your father."

For as far back as she could remember, Carla had known that her father was in heaven with the angels. It was because he had broken a promise back when she was born.

Once, she had asked what kind of promise

he had broken.

"It was the sort that cannot be mended," Mamma had sniffed.

Like the beautiful blue teacup with the golden handle, Carla thought. It had slipped out of her hand the other week when she had offered to do the drying. Mamma had cried because the cup came from Italy.

It was sad that Papa was with the angels. But she still had Mamma! Once, a man on the bus had mistaken them for sisters. That had made Mamma laugh. "He was just flattering me," she'd said, her cheeks red. But then she had let Carla stay up late as a special treat. It taught Carla that when Mamma was very happy, it was a good time to ask for something.

It also worked when she was sad.

Like now. The start of a new century. They'd learned all about it in school.

Ever since the new term had started, Carla's heart had ached for a caterpillar pencil case, made of soft green furry stuff, like everyone else had at school. Then the others might stop teasing her. Different was bad. Different was being smaller than any of the others in class. *Titch!* (A strange word which wasn't in the *Children's Dictionary* she'd persuaded Mamma to buy from the secondhand shop on the corner.) Different was having thick black eyebrows. *Hairy Mary!* Different was having a name that wasn't like anyone else's.

Carla Cavoletti.

Or "Spagoletti," as the other kids called it. *Hairy Carla Spagoletti!*

"Why can't we stay at home today?" she continued. *Our real home,* she almost added. Not like the one in Italy that Mamma kept talking about and that she, Carla, had never even seen.

She stopped briefly as their neighbor with the golden hair walked past, shooting her a disapproving glance.

Carla knew that look. It was the same one that the teachers gave her at school when she didn't know her nine times table. "I'm not good with numbers either," Mamma would say dismissively when Carla asked for some help with her homework. "But it does not matter as long as you do not eat cakes and get fat. Women like us, all we need is to be beautiful."

The man with the shiny car and the big brown hat was *always* telling Mamma she was beautiful.

When he came to visit, Mamma would never cry. She'd loosen her long dark curls, spray herself with her favorite Apple Blossom perfume and make her eyes dance. The record player would be turned on so that their feet tapped, although Carla's weren't allowed to tap for long.

"Bed, cara mia," Mamma would sing. And then Carla would have to leave her mother and guest to tap their feet around the little sitting room all on their own, while pictures of her mother's family glared down disapprovingly from the cracked walls. Often their cold faces visited her in the nightmares that interrupted the dancing and made Mamma cross. "You are too old for such dreams. You must not bother Larry and me."

A little while ago, Carla had been given a school project called "My Mummy and Daddy." When she'd come home, fired with excitement, Mamma had done a lot of tongue-clicking followed by a burst of crying. "I *have* to bring in an object for the class table," Carla had persisted. "I can't be the only one who doesn't."

Eventually, Mamma had taken down the photograph of the stiff-backed man with a white collar and strict eyes. "We will send Papa," she announced in a voice that sounded as though she'd gotten a hard candy stuck in her throat. Carla liked hard candy. Sometimes the man with the shiny car brought her some in a white paper bag. But they stuck to her hand and then she had to spend ages washing off the stain.

Carla had held the photograph reverently in her hand. "He is my grandfather?"

Even as she spoke, she knew the answer. Mamma had told her enough times. But it was good to know. Nice to be assured that she had a grandfather like her classmates, even though hers lived many miles away in the hills above Florence and never wrote back.

Carla's mother had wrapped the photograph in an orange and red silk scarf that smelled of mothballs. She couldn't wait to take it into class.

"This is my nonno," she'd announced proudly.

But everyone had laughed. "Nonno, nonno," one boy had chanted. "Why don't you have a granddad like us?"

That had been just before the saint's day when she'd persuaded her mother to phone in sick to work. One of the best days of her life! Together they had taken a picnic to a place called Hyde Park where Mamma had sung songs and told her what it was like when she was a child in Italy.

"My brothers would take me swimming," she had said in a dreamy voice. "Sometimes we would catch fish for supper and then we would sing and dance and drink wine."

Carla, drunk with happiness at having escaped school, wove a strand of her mother's dark hair around her little finger. "Was Papa there then, too?"

Suddenly her mother's dancing black eyes stopped dancing. "No, my little one. He was not." Then she started to gather the Thermos and the cheese from the red tartan rug on the ground. "Come. We must go home."

And suddenly it wasn't the best day of her life anymore. Today didn't look too good either. There was to be a test first thing, the teacher had warned. Maths and spelling. Two of her worst subjects. Carla's grip on her mother's hand grew stronger.

"You might be small for your age," the man with the shiny car had said the other evening when she'd objected to going to bed early, "but you're very determined, aren't you?"

And why not? she nearly replied.

"You must be nice to Larry," Mamma was always saying. "Without him, we could not live here."

"Please can we stay at home together? Please?" she now begged.

But Mamma was having none of it. "I have to work."

"But why? Larry will understand if you can't meet him for lunch."

Usually she didn't give him his name. It felt better to call him the man with the shiny car. It meant he wasn't part of them.

Mamma turned around in the street, almost colliding with a lamppost. For a moment she looked almost angry. "Because, my little one, I still have some pride."

Mamma's work was very important. She had to make plain women look pretty! She worked in a big shop that sold lipsticks and mascaras and special lotions that made your skin look "beautiful beige" or "wistful white" or something in between, depending on your coloring. Sometimes Mamma would bring samples home and make up Carla's face so that she looked much older than she was.

That's how Mamma had found Larry. She'd been on the perfume counter that day because someone had been sick. Sick was good, Mamma had said, if it meant you could step in instead. Larry had come to the shop to buy perfume for his wife. She "wasn't feeling very well, which made Larry sad." And now Mamma was doing the wife a favor because she was making Larry happy again. He was good to Carla, wasn't he? Didn't he bring her candy?

But right now, as they walked toward the bus stop where the woman with golden hair was waiting (the neighbor who, according to Mamma, must eat too many cakes), Carla wanted something else.

"Can I ask Larry for a caterpillar pencil case?"

"No." Mamma made a sweeping gesture with her long arms and red fingernails. "You cannot."

It wasn't fair. Carla could almost feel its soft fur as she stroked the caterpillar in her mind. She could almost hear it, too: *I should belong to you. Then everyone will like us. Come on, Carla. You can find a way.*

3
LILY

The prison is at the end of the District line, followed by a long bus ride. Its gentle woody green on the Underground map makes me feel safe, not like the Central red, which is brash and shrieks of danger. Right now, my train is stopping at Upminster and I stiffen, searching the platform through rain-streaked windows, seeking familiar faces from my childhood.

But there are none. Only flocks of baggy-eyed commuters like wrinkled crows in raincoats, and a woman shepherding a small boy in a smart red and gray uniform.

Once upon a time, I had a normal life not far from here. I can still see the house in my mind: pebble-dash, 1950s build with primrose-yellow window frames that argued with its neighbor's more orthodox cream. I recall with startling clarity my father telling me that soon I was going to have a new brother or sister. At last! Now I would be like all the others in class, the ones from exciting, noisy, bustling families. So different from our own quiet threesome.

For some reason, I am reminded of the whining little girl in a navy-blue uniform from our block this morning, and her mother with those bee-stung lips, black hair and perfect white teeth. They'd been speaking in Italian. I'd been half tempted to stop and tell them we'd just been there on our honeymoon.

Often, I wonder about other people's lives. What kind of job does that beautiful woman do? A model, perhaps? Maybe for a petite range of clothing. But today I can't stop my thoughts from turning back to me. To the decisions I've made. What would my life be like if I'd become that social worker instead of a lawyer? What if, just after moving to London, I hadn't gone to that party with my new flatmate, something I'd normally always say no to? What if I hadn't spilled my wine on the beige carpet? What if the kindly sandy-haired man ("Hi, I'm Ed") with the navy cravat and well-educated voice hadn't helped me to mop it up, telling me that in his view the carpet was very dull? What if I hadn't been so drunk (out of nerves) that I told him about my brother's death when he'd asked about my own family? What if his arty, privileged world (so clearly different from mine) hadn't represented an escape from all the horrors of my past? What if this funny man who made me laugh hadn't proposed on the second date?

Are you telling me the truth about your brother? My mother's voice cuts through the swaths of commuter crows and pulls me in an invisible towline away from London to Devon, where we moved two years after Daniel had arrived.

I wrap my grown-up coat around me and throw her voice out of the window, onto the tracks. I don't have to listen to it now. I'm an adult. Married. I have a proper job with responsibilities. Responsibilities I should be paying attention to now, rather than going back in time. "You need to picture what the prosecution is thinking," the senior partner is always saying. "Get one stage ahead."

Shuffling in an attempt to make room between two sets of sturdy, gray-trousered knees — one on either side of my seat — I open my bulging black briefcase. No easy task in a crammed carriage. Shielding the case summary with my hand (we're not meant to read private documents in public), I scan it to refresh my memory.

Pro Bono case

Joe Thomas, thirty, insurance salesman. Convicted in 1998 of murdering Sarah Evans, twenty-six, fashion shop assistant and girlfriend of the accused, by pushing her into a scalding-hot bath. Heart failure combined with severe burns the cause of death. Neighbors testified to sounds of a violent argument. Bruises on the body consistent with being forcibly pushed.

It's the water bit that freaks me out. Murder should be committed with something nasty like a sharp blade or a rock, or poison, like the Borgias. But a bath should be safe. Comforting. Like the woody-green District line. Like honeymoons.

The train jolts erratically and I'm thrown against the knees on my left and then those on my right. My papers scatter on the wet floor. Horrified, I gather them up, but it's too late. The owner of the trousers on my right is handing back the case summary, but not before his eyes have taken in the neat typed writing.

My first murder trial, I want to say.

But instead I blush furiously and stuff the papers back into my bag, aware that if my boss were present I would be sacked on the spot.

All too soon, the train stops. Time to try to save a man whom I already loathe — a bath! — when all I want is to be back in Italy. To relive our honeymoon.

To get it right this time.

Whenever I've thought about a prison, I've always imagined something like Colditz. Not a long drive that reminds me of Ed's parents' rambling pile in Gloucestershire. I've been there only once, but that was enough. The atmosphere was freezing, and I'm not just talking about the absence of central heating.

"Are you sure this is right?" I ask the taxi driver.

He nods, and I can feel his grin even though I can't see it from behind.

"Everyone's surprised when they see this place. Used to be a private home till Her Majesty's Prison Service took over." Then his voice grows dark. "Pack of bleeding nutters in there now, and I don't just mean the criminals inside."

I sit forward. My initial worry about putting a taxi on expenses has been dissipated by this rather intriguing information. Of course I knew that HMP Breakville has a high proportion of psychopaths and that it specializes in psychological counseling. But a bit of local knowledge might be useful.

"Are you talking about the staff?" I venture.

There's a snort as we carry on up the drive, past a row of what appear to be council houses. "You can say that again. My brother-in-law used to be a prison officer here before he had his breakdown. Lived in one of those, he did."

My driver jerks his head at the council houses. Then we round another corner. On the left rises one of the most beautiful houses I've seen, with lovely sash windows and a stunning golden-red ivy climbing up the outside. It is Edwardian. It's certainly a complete contrast to the crop of tin-roofed huts on my right.

"You check in there," says the driver, pointing at the house. I scrabble in my purse, feeling obliged to tip him if only for the extra information.

"Ta." His voice is pleased but his eyes are troubled. "Prison visiting, are you?"

I hesitate.

"Sort of."

He shakes his head. "Take care. Those blokes . . . they're in there for a reason, you know."

Then he's off. I watch the taxi go back down the drive, my last link to the outside world. It's only when I start to walk toward the house that I realize I forgot to ask for a fares receipt. If I couldn't get that right, what hope is there for Joe Thomas?

And, more importantly, does he deserve any if there's even the remotest possibility that he's really guilty?

"Sugar? Sellotape? Crisps? Sharp implements?" barks the man on the other side of the glass divide.

For a moment, I wonder if I've heard right. I'd gone toward the lovely house, relieved that prison wasn't that terrifying after all. But when I got there, someone directed me back across the grounds, past the tin-roofed huts and toward a high wall with curled barbed wire on top that I hadn't noticed before. My heart thudding, I walked along it until I reached a small door.

Ring, instructed the sign on the wall.

My breath coming faster, I did so. The door opened automatically and I found myself in a little room, not that different from the waiting area in a small domestic airport. On one side was a glass partition, which is where I find myself right now.

"Sugar, Sellotape, crisps, sharp implements?" repeats the man. Then he looks at my briefcase. "It saves time if you get them out before you're searched."

"I don't have any . . . but why would it matter if I had the first three?"

His small beady eyes bore into mine. "They can use sugar to make hooch, Sellotape to gag you. And crisps as bribes. It's happened before, trust me."

I know his sort. Rather like my boss. The type who relishes making you uncomfortable. He's succeeded, but something inside me makes me determined not to rise.

"If, by 'they,' you're referring to your inmates, then I'm afraid they're out of luck," I retort. "I don't have anything on your list."

He mutters something that sounds like "bleeding-heart defense lawyers" before pressing a bell. Another door opens and a female officer comes out. "Arms up," she instructs.

Again I'm reminded of an airport, except this time nothing bleeps.

"Open your case, please."

I do as instructed. There's a stack of documents, my makeup bag and a packet of Polos.

The woman seizes on the last two as if trophies. "Afraid we'll have to confiscate these until you're out. Your umbrella, too."

"My umbrella?"

"Possible weapon." She speaks crisply, but I detect a touch of kindness that was absent in the man behind the glass partition.

"This way, please."

She escorts me through another door and, to my surprise, I find myself in a rather pleasant courtyard garden. There are men in Robin Hood–green jogging bottoms and matching tops, planting wallflowers. My mother is doing the same in Devon; she told me so on the phone last night. It strikes me that different people from various walks of life might be tending their gardens at precisely this moment all over the world.

One of the men glances at the leather belt around the officer's waist. There's a bundle of keys attached and a silver whistle. How effective would that be, if these men attacked us?

We've crossed the square toward another building. My companion selects a key and opens up. Down another hall. Double doors and also double gates, separated by an inch or so of space. She unlocks and then re-locks them after we've gone through.

"Do you ever wonder if you've done it properly?" I ask.

She fixes me with a stare. "No."

"I'm the kind of person who has to go back and double-check our own front door," I say. Quite why I admit this, I don't know. Maybe it's to introduce a note of humor into this terrifying world I've found myself in.

"You have to be on top of things here," she says reprovingly. "This way."

The corridor stretches out before us. There are more doors on either side with signs next to them: A Wing, B Wing, C Wing.

A group of men in orange tracksuits come toward us.

One of them — bald with a shiny scalp — nods at the officer. "Morning, miss."

Then he stares at me. They all do. I blush. Hotly. Deeply.

I wait until they've passed. "Are they allowed to wander around?"

"Only when it's free flow."

"What's that?"

"When the men are off the wing and on their way somewhere like gym or chapel or education. They are permitted to move in groups then, with only a couple of officers in charge, instead of having a one-to-one escort, which is what happens in other situations."

I want to ask what kind of 'situation' that

might be. But instead, partly from nervousness, I find a different question coming out of my mouth.

"What do the different-color uniforms mean?"

"It's to show what wing they're on. And don't ask them questions like that or they'll think you're interested in them. Some of them are dangerously smart. The next thing, they're getting information out of you without you realizing it, or making you do things you shouldn't."

That's ridiculous! What kind of idiot would fall for something like that? We've stopped now. D wing. Another set of double doors and gates. I step through as the officer closes both behind us. A wide gangway stretches out before us, with rooms on both sides. Three men are waiting, as if loitering on a street. They all stare. A fourth man is busy cleaning out a goldfish tank, his back to us. It strikes me as being incongruous — murderers looking after goldfish? — but before I can ask, I'm being taken into an office on the left.

Two young men are sitting at a desk. They don't look very different from those in the corridor — short hair and inquisitive eyes — except they're in uniform. I'm aware that my skirt band is cutting into my waist, and once again I wish I'd been more disciplined in Italy. Is comfort eating normal on a honeymoon?

"Legal for *Mr.* Thomas," says my companion. She pronounces the *Mr.* with emphasis. It sounds sarcastic.

"Sign here, please," says one of the officers. His eye travels from my briefcase to my chest and then back to my briefcase again. I notice that in front of us is a tabloid, sporting a scantily clad model. Then he glances at his watch. "You're five minutes late."

That's not my fault, I want to say. *Your security delayed me.* But something tells me to hold my tongue.

"Heard Thomas was making an appeal," says the other man. "Some people, they just don't give up, do they?"

There's a polite cough behind us. A tall, well-built, dark-haired man with a short, neat beard is standing at the door of the office. He was one of those waiting in the corridor, I realize. But instead of staring, he is smiling thinly. His hand is extended. His grip is firm. He holds my eyes as if trying to prove he is reliable. This was an insurance salesman, I remind myself. One who was accustomed to persuading others. Old habits die hard.

My client doesn't look like an archetypal prisoner, or, at least, not the type I'd imagined. There are no obvious tattoos, unlike the prison officer beside me, who is sporting a red and blue dragon's head on his arm. My new client is wearing an expensive-looking watch and polished brown slip-on shoes that stand out among the other men's trainers and are at odds with his green prison uniform. I get the feeling that this is a man who is more used to a jacket and tie. Indeed, I can see now that there is a crisp white shirt collar peeping out from under the regulation sweatshirt. Is that allowed? His eyes suggest someone who is wary, hopeful and slightly uneasy all at the same time. His voice, when it comes, is deep. Assured but with an accent that is neither rough nor polished. He could be a neighbor. Another solicitor. Or the manager of the local deli.

"I'm Joe Thomas," he says, letting go of my hand. "Thank you for coming."

"Lily Macdonald," I reply. My boss had told me to use both names. ("Although you need to keep a distance," he'd said, "you don't want to appear superior. It's a fine lawyer/client balance.")

Meanwhile, the look on Joe Thomas's face is quietly admiring. I flush again, although less from fear than embarrassment this time. On the few occasions I've received any kind of attention, I've never known how to respond. Especially now, when it's so clearly inappropriate. I can never rid myself of that constant taunting voice in my head from school days. *Fat Lily. Big boned. Broad.* All things considered, I still can't believe I have a wedding ring on my finger. Suddenly, I have a vision of Ed in bed on honeymoon in Italy. Warm sun streaming in through creamy-white shutters. My new husband opening his mouth, about to say something, and then turning away from me . . .

"Follow me," says one of the officers tightly, jerking me back to the present.

Together Joe Thomas and I walk down the corridor. Past the stares, past the man cleaning out the goldfish tank with a care that might seem touching anywhere else, and toward a small room marked Visits. The barred window looks out onto a concrete yard. Everything inside is gray: the table, the metal chairs on either side, the walls. There's just one exception: a poster with a rainbow and the word *HOPE* printed under it in big purple capital letters.

"I'll be outside the door," says the officer. "Okay with you?" Each word is tinged with a distaste that appears to be directed toward both of us.

"Prison officers aren't very keen on defense solicitors," my boss had warned me. "They think you're poaching their game. You know. Trying to get them off the hook when it's taken blood, sweat and tears on the police and prosecution's part to get them banged up in the first place."

When he put it like that, I could see his point.

Joe Thomas now looks at me questioningly. I steel myself to look back. I might be tall, but he's taller. "Visits are usually in sight of but not necessarily in hearing of a prison officer," my boss had added. "Inmates tend to reveal more if there isn't an officer actually in the room. Prisons vary. Some don't give you the choice."

But this one had.

No, it's not okay, I want to say. Please stay here with me.

"Fine, thank you." My voice belongs to someone else. Someone braver. Someone more experienced.

The officer looks as though he's going to shrug, although he doesn't actually do so. "Knock on the door when you've finished."

Then he leaves us together.

Alone.

47

4
CARLA

Time was dragging. It felt like ages since she'd seen the golden-haired fat woman staring at her this morning. But already her stomach was rumbling. Surely it must be lunchtime soon?

She stared despondently at the classroom clock. The big hand was on the ten and the small hand on the twelve. Did that mean ten minutes to twelve? Or ten o'clock?

Carla's eye traveled to the desks around her. It seemed like each one had a green caterpillar, bulging with pencils, felt-tip pens and fountain pens with real ink. How she hated her own cheap plastic case with a sticky zip and just a Biro inside, because that's all Mamma could afford.

No wonder no one wanted to be her friend.

"Carla!"

The teacher's voice made her jump.

"Perhaps you can tell us!" She pointed to

the word on the board. "What do you think this means?" P U N C T U A L? This wasn't a word she'd come across before, even though she sat up every night in bed, reading the *Children's Dictionary*. She was on the *c*'s already.

C for cat.

C for cold.

C for cunning.

Underneath her pillow at home, Carla kept a scrap of paper so she could carefully write down the meaning of each word and draw a little picture next to it, to remind her what it meant.

Cat was easy. *Cunning* was more difficult. It was in the advanced section.

"Carla!" Teacher's voice was sharper now. "Are you daydreaming again?"

There was a ripple of laughter around her. Carla flushed. "She doesn't know," chanted a boy behind her, whose hair was the color of carrots. Then, a bit quieter, so the teacher wouldn't hear, "Hairy Carla Spagoletti doesn't know!"

The laughter grew louder.

"Kevin," said the teacher, but not in the same sharp voice she'd used earlier on Carla. "What did you say?"

Then she swung back, her eyes boring down on Carla in the second row. She'd

49

chosen to sit there so she could learn.

"Spell it out, Carla. What does it begin with?"

"P." She knew that much. Then "U." And then . . .

"Come on, Carla."

"Punk tool," she said out loud.

The squeals and shouts of laughter around her were deafening. "I've only got to 'C' at home," she tried to say. Her voice was drowned out — not just by the taunts but also by the loud bell. Immediately, there was a flurry of books being put away.

Lunch? Then it must be ten minutes to twelve! The classroom was empty. Carla breathed in the peace.

The boy with the carrot hair had left his green caterpillar on his desk.

It winked at her. *Charlie,* it said. *I'm called Charlie.*

Scarcely daring to breathe, she tiptoed over and stroked its fur. Then, slowly, Carla placed Charlie inside her blouse. She was "nearly ready" for her first bra, Mamma had said. Meanwhile, she had to make do with a vest. But things could still be hidden inside.

"You're mine now," she whispered as she pulled her cardigan down over the top. "He doesn't deserve to have you."

"What are you doing?" A teacher poked

her head around the door. "You should be in the cafeteria. Go down immediately."

Carla sat away from the rest of the children, conscious of Charlie nestling against her chest. Ignoring the usual spiteful remarks ("Didn't you bring your own spaghetti, Carla?"), she struggled through a bowl of chewy meat. Finally, when it was time for recess, she made her way to the far end where she sat down in the corner of the playground by the tall wire fence and tried to make herself invisible. If only there was a tree to hide behind.

Usually she'd feel upset. Left out. But not now that she had her very own green caterpillar who felt so warm and comforting against her skin. "We'll look after each other," Carla whispered.

But what will happen when they find you've taken me? Charlie whispered back.

"I will think of something."

Ouch!

The blow to her head happened so fast that Carla hardly saw the football hurtling through the air. Her vision spun and her right eye didn't feel like it belonged to her at all.

"Are you all right? Carla, are you all right?" The teacher's voice was coming at her from a long way off. In the blurry distance, she could see another teacher telling off the carrot-haired boy. The one who really owned Caterpillar Charlie.

"Kevin! You were told quite clearly about the new rule, this morning. No ball games in this part of the playground. Now look what you've done."

This is our chance, hissed Charlie. Tell her you need to go home and then we can make our escape before they realize I'm missing.

Carla staggered to her feet, careful not to make a sudden movement that might dislodge her new friend. Folding her arms to hide Charlie's shape, she managed a smile. One of her brave smiles that she practiced in front of the mirror. This was a trick she had learned from Mamma. Every evening, her mother ran through a series of different looks in front of her dressing-table mirror before the man with the shiny car arrived. There was the happy smile when he was on time. There was the slightly sad smile when he arrived late. And there was the smile that didn't quite meet her eyes when she told Carla to go to bed so she and Larry could listen to some music on their own.

Right now, Carla assumed the slightly sad smile. "My eye hurts. I would like to go home."

The teacher frowned as she took her to

the school office. "We will have to ring your mother to make sure she's in."

Aiuto! Help! She hadn't thought of that. "Our telephone, she is not working because we have not paid the bill. But Mamma, she is there."

"Are you sure?"

The first part was the truth. Mamma was going to tell Larry about the phone when he came around next. Then he would pay for it to work again. But the second part — about her mother being in — wasn't true. Mamma would be at work.

"There's a work number here," announced the teacher, opening a file. "Let's try, just in case."

Trembling, she listened to the conversation.

"I see." The teacher put down the phone. Then she turned back to Carla, sighing. "It appears your mother has taken the day off. Do you know where she is?"

"I told you. She is at home!" The lie slid so easily from her mouth. "I can walk back on my own," she added. Her good eye fixed itself on the teacher. "It is not far."

"We can't allow that, I'm afraid. Is there anyone else we can ring? A neighbor, perhaps, who can fetch your mother?"

Briefly she thought of the golden-haired

lady and her husband. But she and Mamma had never even spoken to them. *We must keep ourselves to ourselves*, that's what Mamma always said. Larry wanted it that way. He wanted them for himself.

"Yes," Carla said desperately. "My mother's friend. Larry."

"You have his number?"

She shook her head.

"Miss. Miss!" One of the other children in her class was knocking on the door. "Kevin's hit someone else now!"

The teacher groaned. "Not again." On the way, they passed the woman who helped out in her class. She was new and always wore sandals, even when it was raining. "Sandra, take this child home for me, will you? She's only just down the road. Her mother will be there, apparently. Kevin? Stop that right now!"

By the time she turned onto her road with the sandal woman, Carla's eye was throbbing so badly that it was difficult to see. There was a pain above the eyebrow, which was pulsing through her head. But none of this was as bad as the certain knowledge that Mamma would not be in and that she'd then have to go back to that horrid school.

Do not worry, whispered Charlie. *I will think of something.*

He had better hurry up!

Just as she'd expected, there was no answer when they knocked on number seven. It was a lucky number, Mamma had said when they moved in. All they had to do was wait for the luck to arrive.

"Maybe my mother has gone out for some milk," she said desperately. "We can let ourselves in until she comes back."

Carla always did this, before Mamma returned from work. She'd get changed, do a bit of tidying up (because it was always a rush for Mamma in the mornings), and start to make risotto or pasta for supper. Once, when she had been really bored, she'd looked under Mamma's bed, where she kept her "special things." There she had found an envelope filled with photographs. Each one showed the same young man with a hat at a funny angle and a confident smile. Something told her to put him back and not say anything. Yet every now and then when Mamma was out, she went back to take another look.

Right now, though, the key wasn't in its usual place on the ledge above their door.

If only she had a key for the back door, by the rubbish behind the flats. But that spare key was for Larry so he could come in whenever he wanted and have a little rest with Mamma. Her mother joked it was like his private ground-floor entrance!

"I can't leave you." The sandal woman's voice was all whiny, as though this was Carla's fault. "We'll have to go back."

No. Please no. Kevin scared her. So did the other children. *Charlie, do something!*

And then she heard the distinct padding of heavy footsteps coming toward them.

5
LILY

Appeal.
 A peal.
 A peel.

Joe Thomas writes on a piece of paper opposite me.

I push back my hair, normally tucked behind my ears, and take another look at the three lines on the desk between Joe Thomas and me. The charming man I met an hour ago has disappeared. This man has barely uttered a word, as if determined that I should play by his rules.

For anyone else it might be unnerving.

But all that practice, when I was growing up, is now standing me in good stead. When Daniel was alive (I still have to force myself to say those words), he would write words and phrases in all kinds of ways — upside down, the wrong way around, in an odd order.

"He can't help it," my mother used to say. But I knew he could. When it was just the two of us together, my brother wrote normally. *It's a game,* his eyes would say, sparkling with mischief. *Join me! Us against them!*

Right now I suspect that Joe Thomas is playing his own game with me. It gives me an unexpected thrill of strength. He's picked the wrong person. I know all the tricks.

"Appeal," I say crisply and clearly. "There are several ways of interpreting it, aren't there?"

Joe Thomas is clicking his heels together. *Tap, tap. Tap, tap.* "There certainly are. But not everyone thinks that way."

He gives a dry half laugh.

I wonder who put up the purple Hope poster. A well-meaning officer, perhaps? Or a do-good prison visitor.

I could do with a bit of hope myself. I glance down at my paperwork. "Let's take 'peel.' The report says that the scalding bathwater peeled the skin off your girlfriend."

Joe Thomas's face doesn't flinch. He must be used to accusations and recriminations by now. That is what this particular prison is all about, apparently: psychologists talking to prisoners about why they committed their crime. And then fellow prisoners quizzing each other so that, say, a rapist might ask a murderer why he killed a man. And a murderer might ask a rapist why he . . . I can't even say the words.

My boss took great pleasure in filling me in, almost as if he wanted to frighten me. Yet now that I'm here, in prison, I sense an unbidden curiosity slowly creeping over me.

Why *had* Joe Thomas murdered his girlfriend in a scalding bath?

If indeed he had.

"Let's go over the prosecution's argument at your trial," I say.

His face is impassive, as if we're about to check a shopping list.

I glance down at my notes, although my gesture is more to avoid that black stare than to refresh my naturally photographic memory. A useful attribute for a lawyer; not so good if you want to forget the past.

"You and Sarah moved in together, a few months after you met in the local pub. You were described in court, by her friends, as having an 'up-and-down relationship.' Both her parents took the stand to say that she had told them you were controlling and was scared you would hurt her. The police report verified that Sarah actually lodged a complaint against you on one occasion for pushing her down the backdoor steps and breaking her right wrist. But, she then withdrew the complaint."

Joe Thomas gives a quick nod. "That's right. She fell because she'd been drinking even though she'd promised to stop. But she initially blamed me because she didn't want her family to know she was off the wagon again." He shrugs. "Drinkers can be terrible liars."

Don't I know it.

"But a previous girlfriend made allegations against you, too. Said you stalked her."

He makes an irritated noise. "I wouldn't call it stalking. I just followed her a few times to check she was going where she said she was. Anyway, she dropped her complaint."

"Because you threatened her?"

"No. Because she realized I was only following her because I cared for her." He gives me a blank stare. "Anyway, I dumped her shortly after that."

"Why?"

He fixes me with a disdainful stare. "I stopped caring for her because she didn't live by my rules."

Right.

"And then you met Sarah."

He nods. "One year and two days later."

"You seem very certain."

"I'm good at numbers and dates."

He says this proudly. As if I should congratulate him.

I continue. "On the night of her death, your neighbors said they heard screaming."

Joe shakes his head. "That Jones couple? Those two would have said anything against us. I told my lawyer that at the time. We had endless problems with them after we moved in."

"So you think they made it up? Why would they do that?"

"I'm not them, so I don't know, do I? But like I said, we didn't get on. Their television was so loud. We never got any peace. We complained to them, but they didn't listen. And old man Jones didn't like it when I told him off about his garden. Talk about being run-down! Reflected badly on ours, which, I might add, I kept in pristine condition. After that, they got really unpleasant. Started threatening us. Threw litter in our garden." His mouth tightens. "Mind you, accusing me of murder was taking it a touch too far."

"What about your fingerprints on the boiler?" I point to the relevant lines on the report. "The prosecution said you turned up the water temperature to maximum."

Those dark eyes don't even flicker. "I told my defense at the time. Do I need to repeat this? The pilot light was always going out, so I had to keep relighting it. So of course my fingerprints were on the boiler."

"So how did Sarah die if you didn't murder her? How can you explain the bruises on her?"

His fingers begin to drum on the table as though to a silent beat. "Look. I'm going to tell you exactly how it happened. But you have to let me tell you in my own way."

I know that this man needs to be in control. Perhaps if I allow him to think he's in charge for a while, he'll let something slip.

"Fine."

"She was late getting back from work. It was two minutes past eight when she got back. Usually it's six p.m. On the dot."

I can't stop myself from butting in. "How can you be so certain?"

His face suggests I've just said something very stupid. "Because it took her precisely eleven minutes to walk home from the shop. It's one of the reasons I encouraged her to take the job, just after we moved in together. It was convenient."

My mind goes back to Sarah's profile. "Fashion shop assistant." The job title reminds me of a department store clerk who resents being behind a counter. Immediately I rebuke myself. I am no typical lawyer. Ed is not a typical advertising man. And Joe? Is he a typical insurance salesman? He's certainly very precise about figures.

"Go on," I say encouragingly.

"She was drunk. That was obvious."

"How?"

Another exasperated look.

"She could barely stand straight. She reeked of wine. Turned out she'd had half a bottle of vodka, too, but it's difficult to smell that stuff."

He's right. Her blood alcohol level was high. But it doesn't prove he didn't kill her.

"Then?"

"We had an argument because she was late. I'd made dinner, like I always did. Lasagne with garlic, basil and tomato sauce. But it was all dry and nasty by then. So we had a row. Raised our voices, I admit. But there was no screaming like the neighbors said." His face wrinkles with disgust. "Then she was sick, all over the kitchen floor."

"Because she was drunk?"

"Yes, it was disgusting. She seemed better after that, but the vomit was all over her. I told her to have a bath. Said I'd run it, like I always did. But she wasn't having any of it. She slammed the door on me and turned up the bathroom radio. Radio 1. Her favorite station. So I left her to it while I washed up."

I interrupt. "Weren't you worried about her being alone in a bath if she was drunk?"

"Not at first. Like I said, she seemed better after being sick — more sober — and anyway, what could I do? I was worried she'd report me to the police. Sarah could be very imaginative."

"So when did you go and check on her?"

"After half an hour or so, I *did* get worried. I couldn't hear her splashing and she wouldn't answer when I knocked. So I went in." His face goes blank. "That's when I found her. Almost didn't recognize her, even though her face was up. Her skin was purple. Dark red and purple. Some of it was peeled back. There were these huge blisters."

My body shudders involuntarily.

Joe goes quiet for a minute. I'm glad of the break. "She must've slipped and fallen in. And the water was so hot," he continues. "Much hotter than you'd expect after thirty minutes, so I can't even guess the temperature when she got in. I burned myself lifting her up. I tried to resuscitate her, but I've never done a first aid course. I didn't know if I was doing the right thing. So I dialed 9-1-1."

He is saying the last bit in an even, steady tone. Not distraught. But not totally detached either. Like someone trying to hold it all together, even after all this time.

"The police said you didn't seem very upset when they arrived."

His eyes are back on mine. "People show emotion in different ways. Who's to say that the person who wails loudest is the most distressed?"

He has a point there.

"But the jury found you guilty."

I sense a tightening behind the eyes. "They got it wrong. My defence lawyer was an idiot."

The Hope poster stares mockingly down.

"An appeal is generally only launched if there's new evidence. The bones of what you have said is already in the files. Even if what you're saying is true, we have nothing to prove it."

"I know that."

I'm losing patience now. "So do you have new evidence?"

He is staring hard at me. "That's for you to find out." He picks up the pen again. PEAL, he is writing now. Over and over again.

"Mr. Thomas. Do you have new evidence?"

He just continues writing. Is this some sort of clue?

"What do you think?"

I want to snap with frustration. But I wait. Silence is another trick I learned from my brother.

There's the steady sound of ticking from a clock I hadn't seen before. It has a handwritten notice stuck up underneath it: DO NOT REMOVE. Unable to stop myself, I give a short snort of laughter. It's enough to break the silence.

"One of the men stole the last one." Joe Thomas is clearly amused, too. "He took it to bits to see how it worked."

"Did he succeed?" I ask.

"No. He killed it." His face becomes hard again and he draws an imaginary line across his throat. "Kaput."

The action is clearly designed to intimidate me. It does. But something makes me determined not to show it. I look across at the piece of paper on the desk and point to the second word. "What's the significance of 'peal'?"

"Rupert Brooke. You know. That line about whether there is honey for tea. Church bells pealing across the village green and all that."

I'm surprised. "You like the war poets?"

He shrugs, looking out the window toward the exercise yard. "I didn't know them, did I? So how can I say I like them? But I can guess how they felt."

"How?"

His face swivels back to mine. "You haven't done your homework very well, have you, Miss Hall?"

I freeze. Didn't he hear me when I introduced myself as Lily Macdonald? And how does he know that Hall is my maiden name? I have a flash of Ed's warm hand holding mine at the altar. This meeting was arranged before my marriage, so maybe Joe Thomas had been given my previous name. Maybe he wasn't listening properly when I introduced myself. A niggling instinct tells me that it would be safer not to correct him at this stage.

Besides, I'm more concerned with the reference to the homework. What did I miss? A lawyer can't afford to be wrong, my boss tells us all, again and again. So far, I've never missed a beat. Not like one of the newly qualified lawyers who was taken on in the same month as me and sacked for failing to lodge an appeal within the given time.

"It won't be in your notes," he adds, observing my glance down. "But I'd hoped that your lot would have done more digging. Think about it. War poets. What did they go through? What behavior did they display when they came home?"

"Shock," I say. "Many refused to talk because of posttraumatic stress."

He nods. "Go on."

Desperately, I try to dredge up my A-level memories. "Some of them were violent."

Joe Thomas sits back, arms folded. A satisfied smile on his face. "Exactly."

This isn't making sense. "But you weren't in the army."

"No."

"So why did you kill your girlfriend?"

"Nice try. I pleaded innocent. Remember? The jury made a mistake. That's why I'm appealing." He jabs at my notes with a long, slim forefinger that doesn't match his substantial frame. "It's all there. Apart from this extra clue, that is. Now it's over to you."

The chair scrapes on the floor as Joe suddenly stands up. For a moment, the room spins and my mouth goes dry. All I know is that those dark eyes appear to be looking right through me. They know what's inside me. They see things that Ed doesn't.

And most important of all, they don't

condemn.

He leans toward me and I catch the smell of him. I can't put my finger on it — not a pine or lemon cologne smell like my husband's. More like a raw, earthy, animal smell. I feel a strange shortness of breath. There's a loud thud against the window.

I jump. So does he. Outside, a large gray pigeon hovers in the air. A white feather blows gently in the breeze; the bird must have flown into the window. Miraculously, it is now flying away.

"The last one died," says Joe Thomas sadly. "You'd think they'd have more sense, wouldn't you? Perhaps they're curious. Maybe they see the bars on the inside and wonder why they're there."

He seems more upset about the birds than he did when describing his girlfriend's death. There's something else about him that I can't quite put my finger on.

"By the way," I find myself saying suddenly. "Why aren't you wearing the regulation sweatshirts that the other men wear?"

He gives a self-satisfied smile. "I'm allergic to the material. So I got special dispensation."

I get the feeling that this is a man who gets what he wants. But freedom is not so easily obtained.

"I want you to go away and come back next week." The instructions clip out of Joe Thomas's mouth as if we haven't been discussing uniforms or birds at all. "By then, you need to have worked out the connection between the war poets and me. And that will give you the basis of my appeal."

Enough is enough. "This isn't a game," I say shortly to hide the inexplicable mixture of fear and excitement beating against my rib cage. "You know as well as I do that legal visits take time to organize. I might not be able to come back so soon. You have to make the most of this one."

He shrugs. "If you say so." Then he glances at my still-tanned wrists with my silver bracelet and then down to the shiny gold wedding ring, heavy with newness. "By the way, I got it wrong just now, didn't I? It's Mrs. Macdonald, isn't it? I trust you had a good honeymoon. Italy, was it?"

I'm still shaking when the taxi driver drops me off at the station. How did Joe Thomas know that I'd been on honeymoon, let alone in Italy?

As for Joe's "mistake" over my name, I can't help wondering if it was on purpose. To wrong-foot *me,* perhaps? But why?

"Five pounds thirty, miss."

The taxi driver's voice cuts into my head. Grateful for the diversion, I fumble in my purse for change.

"That's a foreign coin." His voice is suspicious, as though I'd intentionally tried to pull one over on him.

"So sorry." Flushing, I find the correct money. "I've been abroad and haven't sorted out my purse yet."

He takes my tip with bad grace, clearly unconvinced. A mistake. A simple mistake. Yet one that could so easily be taken for a lie. Is that how Joe Thomas feels? I'm so flummoxed that I forget to ask for the vital receipt. Now I'll have to pay for the taxi out of my own pocket — something we can't really afford.

I glance at my watch. It's later than I thought. Surely my time would be better spent going back to the flat, rather than the office, and typing up my notes. Besides, it would give me the opportunity to look into Rupert Brooke. My client may have unnerved me with his knowledge about my private life but he also intrigues me.

"Get as much from him as possible," my boss had said. "He was the one who approached us to make an appeal. That means there has to be fresh evidence — unless he just wants some attention. That happens quite a lot. Either way, we might seek counsel advice."

In other words, a barrister would be consulted.

But I'm painfully aware that I haven't gotten very far. On what grounds can we appeal? Insanity, perhaps? Or is his behavior merely eccentric? How many other clients would set a puzzle like this for their lawyers? Still, there are bits in Joe's story that ring true. Drunks do lie. Neighbors can tell lies. Juries can get it wrong.

The different arguments in my head make the train journey back much faster than it seemed this morning. In no time at all, or so it feels, I am on the bus back home. The word sends a thrill through me. Home! Not home in Devon, but our first home as a married couple in Clapham. I'll be able to get a meal on. Spaghetti Bolognese, perhaps? Not too complicated. Change into that mid-blue kaftan my mother bought me for the honeymoon. Tidy up a bit. Make the place look welcoming for when Ed gets home. And yet something still doesn't feel right.

On the few occasions I've left work early, I've always felt like a naughty schoolgirl. And that wasn't me. My reports were always covered with the word *conscientious,* as if they were a salve for more convincing accolades like *intelligent* or *perceptive*. It was no secret that everyone — most of all, myself — was astounded when I got into one of the most prestigious universities in the country through sheer hard slog. And again when I was taken on at a legal firm despite the competition. When you're constantly prepared for things to go wrong, it's a shock when they go right.

"Why do you want to be a lawyer?" my father had asked.

"Because of Daniel, of course," my mother had answered. "Lily wants to put the world to rights. Don't you, darling?"

Now, as I get off the bus, I realize I've thought more about my brother today than I have for a very long time. It must be Joe Thomas. The same defensive stance. The arrogance that, at the same time, comes across as distinctly vulnerable. The same love of games. The same refusal to toe the line in the face of clear opposition.

But Joe is a criminal, I remind myself. A murderer. *A murderer who has gotten the better of you,* I tell myself crossly as I walk up the stairs to our flat, having paused to pick up the post from the mailboxes by the front door. A bill? Already?

I feel a flutter of apprehension — I *told*

Ed we shouldn't have taken out such a big mortgage, but he just gave me a hug and declared that we would get by somehow. There's a disagreement going on between a woman and a child by number seven. I'm pretty sure it's the same girl in the navy-blue school uniform I saw this morning. But the adult is definitely not the mother with those cascading black curls. She's a plain woman in her thirties — at a guess — with open red sandals even though it's not the right kind of weather.

As I draw nearer, I spot a massive blue bruise on the child's eye. "What's going on?" I say sharply.

"Are you Carla's mother?" asks the woman.

"I'm a neighbor." I glance at that terrible bruise. "And who are *you*?"

"One of the teaching assistants at Carla's school. I've just got the job."

She says this with some pride.

"I was told to take her home after an accident at the playground. But Mrs. Cavoletti doesn't appear to be in, and her boss says she isn't at work today, so we'll have to go back to school."

"No. No!"

The child is tugging at my arm. "Please can I stay with you? Please? Please?"

The woman is clearly uncertain. I recognize the feeling. I don't know this child, even though she is acting as though she knows me. But she has been hurt at school. I understand what that's like.

"I think she needs to go to the emergency room," I say.

"I don't have time for that!" Her eyes widen as if in panic. "I've got to pick up my own kids."

Of course this is none of my business. But there's something about the distress in the child's face that makes me want to help. "Then I'll do it."

I take out my business card. "You might want my details." *Lily Macdonald. LLB. Solicitor.*

It seems to reassure the teaching assistant, though, perhaps, it shouldn't.

"We'll get a cab to the hospital," I say. "May I drop you off somewhere?"

She declines, and it occurs to me that it would be very easy to kidnap a child if the circumstances were favorable.

"My name's Lily," I say after the woman has gone and I've slipped a note under the door of number seven to tell Carla's mother what has happened. "You know, you shouldn't really talk to strangers."

"Charlie said it was all right."

75

"Who's Charlie?"

She brings out a green pencil case from under her jumper.

How sweet! I had a wooden one when I was in school, with a secret drawer for the eraser.

"What happened to your eye exactly?"

The child looks away. "It was a mistake. He didn't mean it to happen."

"Who made a mistake?"

But even as I ask the question, I hear voices.

The jury made a mistake, Joe Thomas had said.

There's got to be a mistake, my mother had sobbed when we found Daniel.

Is this a mistake? I'd asked myself as I'd walked down the aisle.

No more mistakes, I say to myself, as I take Carla into our flat to call the local taxi firm. There was no way we could afford a cell phone on our budget.

From now on, I've got to be good.

6
CARLA

"Who made a mistake?" said Lily with the golden hair as they went into number three. Her voice was very clear. Like an actress on television. Posh, Mamma would have called it.

"Kevin. A boy in my class. He threw a ball at me."

Carla nuzzled Charlie's fur. It felt warm and cozy against her skin. She glanced around the flat. It was the same shape as theirs but there were more pictures on the walls. How messy it was, with pieces of paper on the kitchen table and a pair of brown shoes underneath. They looked like they belonged to a man, with those thick soles and lace-ups. Shoes, Mamma always said, were one of the most important weapons in a woman's wardrobe. When Carla said she didn't understand, Mamma just laughed.

"If your mother isn't at work, where do

you think she might be?"

Carla shrugged. "Maybe with Larry, her friend. Sometimes he takes her out for lunch near the shop. She sells nice things to make women beautiful."

"And where is this shop?"

"A place called Night Bridge."

There was a smile as if she'd said something funny. "Do you mean Knightsbridge?"

"Non lo so." When she was tired, she always lapsed into Italian.

"Well, we've left her a note to say where we are. The taxi will be here in a minute."

Carla was still stroking the soft green fur. "Can Charlie come, too?"

"Of course it can."

"*He* can. Charlie's a he."

The woman smiled. "Okay, sweetie."

See, whispered Charlie. *Told you we'd find a way.*

They were nice to her at the hospital. One of the smiley nurses gave her a hard candy that stuck to the roof of her mouth. Carla had to put her finger in to poke it out. Mamma didn't allow her to have sweets at home unless Larry gave them to her.

She hoped the golden-haired woman wouldn't tell. "Be brave," she said kindly as the nurse put something that stung on her eyebrow. "Think of something nice."

Carla squeezed her eyes tightly shut. She'd think about her new friend. Such a lovely name! When Larry came to visit, he sometimes brought lilies. Once, her mother and Larry had danced so hard when she was in bed that the lilies fell onto the ground and stained the carpet bright yellow. When she'd come out to see what had happened, Larry said it was "nothing." He'd arrange for it to be cleaned. Maybe he'd arrange for Mamma's blouse to be mended, too. The top three buttons had lain scattered by her feet like little red sweets.

She told Lily this story as they got into the taxi to go home.

Lily was quiet for a while. "Do you ever see your daddy?" she asked.

Carla shrugged. "He died when I was a baby. Mamma cries if we talk about him." Then she looked out the window at the flashing lights. Wow!

"That's called Piccadilly Circus," said Lily.

"Really?" Carla pressed her nose against the window. It was beginning to drizzle. "Where are the lions?"

"Lions?"

"You said it was a circus. I can't see any lions or ladies in skirts walking on wires."

There was a muffled sound of laughter. It

was like the noise that Mamma made when Larry visited. Carla always heard it through the wall that divided her bedroom from Mamma's.

"Don't laugh like that! It's true. I know what circuses look like. I've seen pictures in books."

Maybe she shouldn't have shouted. Lily's smile had become a straight line now. But instead of being cross, like Mamma's when Carla did something she shouldn't, Lily looked kind and gentle.

"I'm sorry, but you reminded me of some-one."

Instantly Carla's curiosity was aroused. "Who?"

But Lily turned away. "Someone I used to know."

They were going under a bridge now. The taxi grew dark inside. Carla could hear Lily blowing her nose. When they came out the other side, her eyes were very bright. "I like your pencil case."

"It's not a pencil case. He's a caterpillar." Carla stroked the green fur lovingly, first one way and then the next. "Charlie can understand every word you are saying."

"I used to feel that way about a doll I had. Her name was Amelia."

"Do you still have her?"

Her face turned away again. "No. I don't."

Lily used exactly the same tone of voice that Mamma used when she said that there was only enough dinner for one and that it didn't matter because she wasn't hungry. And just as she did with Mamma, Carla stayed silent because sometimes adults didn't want you to ask any more questions.

Meanwhile, the taxi was jolting along through wide streets with pretty shops and then smaller ones with wooden boxes of fruit outside. Eventually, they passed a park she recognized and then they turned into their road. Carla felt her heart beating quickly. Mamma might be home now. What would she say?

Never talk to strangers. How often had she told her that? Yet Carla had not only gone off with a stranger, she had also stolen Charlie.

"I'll explain everything to your mother," said golden-haired Lily, as if she knew what Carla was thinking. Then she handed over a crisp ten-pound note to the driver. How rich she must be! "Do you think she'll be home yet? If not, you can —"

"Piccola mia!"

She smelled Mamma's rich perfume before she saw her. "Where have you been? I am out of my mind with worry." Then she

81

glared at Lily, black eyes flashing. "How dare you take my daughter away? And what have you done to her eye? I will report you to the police. I will . . ."

It suddenly occurred to Carla that Lily wouldn't understand what Mamma was saying because she was speaking in their own language. Italian! Certainly Lily had looked very confused until the word *polizia.* Then her face grew red and cross.

"Mrs. Cavoletti? I'm Lily Macdonald, one of your neighbors. Your daughter got hit by a ball at school." She was speaking very slowly, as if making a big effort to stay calm. But Carla could see that her throat had gone all blotchy. "One of the staff took her home but you weren't in. She was going to have to go back to school but it just happened that I came back from work early and offered to take Carla to the hospital for that eye."

"The teacher, why did she not do this?"

Mamma was speaking in English now. It worried Carla when she did this because she sometimes got the words in the wrong order. Then people would laugh or try to correct her.

"She had to get back to her own children, apparently."

"They rang your work from school," Carla

butted in. "But they said you weren't there today."

Mamma's eyes widened. "Of course I was. My manager had sent me on a training course. Someone should have known where to get me. Mi dispiace." Mamma was almost suffocating Carla with a big hug. "I am so sorry. Thank you for looking after my little one."

Together, she and Mamma rocked back and forth on the dirty steps. Even though her mother's grip was uncomfortable, Carla's heart soared. This is what it had been like before the man with the shiny car had come into their lives. Just Mamma and her. No laughter through the walls that shut her out and danced up and down in her nightmares.

"You are Italian?" Lily's soft voice released Mamma's arms and the old emptiness dived back. "My husband and I spent our honeymoon in Italy. Sicily. We loved it."

Mamma's eyes were wet with tears. Real tears, Carla observed. Not the kind of tears she practiced in front of the mirror. "My daughter's father, he came from near there . . ."

Carla's skin began to prickle. She hadn't known that.

"But now . . . now . . ."

Poor Mamma. Her voice was coming out in big gulps.

Carla heard her own voice piping up. "Now it is just Mamma and me."

"It is very hard," Mamma continued. "I do not like to leave my little one alone, but there are times when I have to work. Saturdays are the worst, when there is no school."

Golden-haired Lily was nodding. "If it would help, my husband and I can look after her sometimes."

Carla felt her breath stop. Really? Then she wouldn't have to stay inside the flat all on her own, with the door locked. She would have someone to talk to until Mamma got home!

"You would look after my little girl? That is very kind."

Both women were flushed now. Was Lily regretting her offer? Carla hoped not. Adults often suggested something and then took it away.

"I must go now." Lily glanced at her case. "I have work to do and you'll want time with your daughter. Don't worry about the cut. The hospital said it would heal fast."

Mamma clucked. "That school, she is no good. Wait until I see the teachers tomorrow."

"But you won't, Mamma! You will be at work."

"Tsk." Already she was being whisked inside.

"We're in number three if you need us," Lily called out. Had Mamma heard? Carla made a mental note just in case.

As soon as they were alone, Mamma rounded on her. Her glossy smile had become a creased scowl. How could adults move from one face to another so fast?

"Never, never speak to strangers again." Her pointed red finger wagged in front of her nose. There was a small chip in the polish, Carla noticed. On the right of the nail. "You were lucky this time to find an angel, but next time it might be the devil. Do you understand?"

Not exactly, but Carla knew better than to ask any more questions.

Apart from one.

"Did my father really come from Sicily?"

Mamma's face went red. "I cannot talk of this. You know it upsets me." Then she frowned at Carla's blouse. "What are you hiding in there?"

Reluctantly, Carla brought Charlie out for inspection. "He's a caterpillar." She had to squeeze the words out of her mouth with fear.

"One of those pencil cases you've been nagging me for?"

Carla could only nod.

Her mother's eyes narrowed. "Did you take him? From one of the other children? Is that why you have a bruise?"

"No! No!" They were speaking in Italian now. Fast.

"Lily told you. Someone threw a ball at me. But on the way to the hospital, she bought Charlie to make me feel better."

Mamma's face softened. "That is very kind of her. I must thank her."

"No." Carla felt a trickle of wee run down her legs. That happened sometimes when she was nervous. It was another reason why the others teased her at school. It had happened once in PE. *Smelly Carla Spagoletti! Why don't you wear nappies, like a real baby?*

"She would be embarrassed," Carla added. "Like Larry. You know what English people are like."

Holding her breath, she waited. It was true that when the man with the shiny car gave them things, Mamma said they mustn't talk about it too much in case it embarrassed him.

Eventually, Mamma nodded. "You are right." Then her pretty nose wrinkled with distaste. "You have wet yourself again?"

"I am sorry." She would be in trouble now. But at least Mamma seemed to believe her story about Charlie.

"Go and wash yourself. And clean your hands, too. Hospitals are dirty places." Mamma was glancing at herself in the mirror, running her hands through her thick black curls. "Larry is coming for dinner." Her eyes sparkled. "You must go to bed early."

7
LILY

Early November 2000

"Sugar? Sellotape? Sharp implements? Crisps?" barks the man on the other side of the glass divide.

It's true what they told me in the office. You get used to prison, even by your second visit. I face the officer impassively. His skin is clean-shaven.

"No," I say in a confident voice that doesn't belong to me. Then I step aside to be searched. What would happen, I wonder, if I succeeded in hiding anything illegal — drugs or simply an innocuous packet of sugar from a coffee shop? The idea is strangely exciting.

I clip-clop across the courtyard in my new red kitten heels. Just to boost my self-confidence, I told myself when I bought them. Today, there are no men in prison uniform, tending the garden. It's a dull day with a nip in the air. I wrap my navy-blue jacket protectively around me and follow the officer through the double doors.

"What's it like?" Ed had asked the evening after my first visit.

To be honest, I'd almost put prison out of my head after the drama of taking the little Italian girl to the hospital and then facing the wrath of her mother until she'd calmed down.

Her reaction was, of course, understandable. She'd been worried. "Thank you from the bottom of my heart for looking after my Carla," she had written in a little note that I found slipped under the door later.

I still doubt my wisdom in stepping in. But that's what happens when you have an overdeveloped conscience.

"It's airless," I said to my husband in reply to his question. "You can't breathe properly."

"And the men?" His arm tightened protectively around me. We were lying on the sofa, side by side in front of the evening television, a little squashed, but in that nice together sort of way.

I thought of the prisoners I'd seen in the corridor with their staring eyes and short-sleeved T-shirts with bulging muscles underneath. And I thought of Joe Thomas with his surprisingly intelligent (if odd) observations and the puzzle he had set for me.

"Not what you'd think." I shifted toward my husband so my nose was nestling comfortably against his neck. "My client could be an ordinary next-door neighbor. He was clever, too."

"Really?"

I could feel Ed's interest stirring. "But what did he actually look like?"

I hesitated. I shouldn't really be discussing personal details about a client, but this was my husband after all. He wasn't going to tell anyone. "Well built. A beard. Tall — about your height. Very dark brown eyes. Long thin fingers."

Ed nodded, and I could feel him drawing my client in his head.

"He talked a lot about Rupert Brooke, the war poet," I added. "Implied that this had something to do with his case."

"Was he in the army?"

It was a tradition that Ed's family went to Sandhurst before enjoying distinguished careers in the army. During our first date, he told me how disappointed his parents had been when he refused to follow suit. Art school? Was he mad? A proper job, that's what he needed. Graphic design in an advertising company was an unhappy compromise all around. People didn't rebel in

Ed's family, he told me. They toed the line. Ironically, I rather liked that at the time. It made me feel safe. Secure. But it seems to have given my husband a chip on the shoulder. At the few family gatherings I've been to with him, he's always felt like the odd one out. Not that he's said so. He doesn't need to. I can just see.

"The army?" I repeated. "No, apparently not."

Then Ed sat up and I felt a breeze of coldness between us. Not just the loss of warmth from his body, but the distance that comes when someone is on another plane. Ed's family may have refused to finance art school, but no one could stop him from doing what he did best, in his spare time. A sketchbook had appeared in his hands and my husband was already beginning to draw . . .

And now, here I am, walking across the courtyard with the answer to my lifer's puzzle right here, in my briefcase.

"Your father was in the army," I say in the visitors' room, sliding a folder across the table toward my client.

Joe Thomas's face goes blank. "So what?"

"So he was discharged. Not honorably either."

My tone is brisk. Clipped. I want to stir this man, make him react. Something tells me it's the only way to help him. *If* I want to help him.

"He tried to protect himself when a man threatened to stab him in a pub, according to his statement." I look down at the notes that had taken me days to put together with the help of a keen junior trainee. "But when your father pushed the man away, he fell through a window and nearly bled to death. I think there's a link between that and your case. Am I right?"

Joe Thomas's eyes darken. I glance around the room.

"There's no emergency button here," says my client softly.

My skin goes clammy. Is this man threatening me? Then he sits back in his chair and regards me as though I'm in the hot seat instead of him. "My father was punished for acting in self-defense. He was shamed. Our family was ridiculed. We had to move. I was bullied at school. But I learned a big lesson. Self-defense is no defense, because no one ever believes you."

I look at this man in the chair before me and then pull a photograph from my file. It shows a slim redhead. Sarah Evans. Joe Thomas's dead girlfriend.

"Are you saying that you acted in self-defense against a woman who barely looks as if she's got enough strength to pick up a brick?"

"Not exactly." His face swivels toward the window.

Two officers are walking past outside, deep in conversation.

Joe Thomas is looking at the men, an amused smile playing on his lips.

I'm growing impatient. "So what exactly do you want to base your appeal on?"

"You've passed the first test. Now you've got to pass the second. Then you'll know."

He's writing something down on the scrap of paper he's brought with him.

101.2
97-3

The list keeps growing.

I've never been great at numbers. Words are more my strength. There are letters next to some of the numbers, but they mean nothing to me.

"What is this?"

He smiles. "That's for you to find out."

"Listen, Joe. If you want me to help you, you've got to stop playing games." I stand up.

He stands up, too. Our faces are close. Too close. Once more, I smell him. Imagine what it would be like to lean forward . . . But this time, I am ready for it.

"If you're to help me, Mrs. Macdonald, you need to understand me. This appeal is everything to me. I want to be satisfied I've got the right person for the job. Until then, I'm not Joe. I'm Mr. Thomas. Got it?"

Every part of my skin feels like it's on fire.

He strides across to the door. "See you when you work out the answer."

The man isn't just being overfamiliar, I tell myself as I make my way to the office and sign out. He's acting as though *he's* in charge instead of me.

So why do I feel a sense of rising excitement as well as annoyance?

"Everything all right?" asks the officer when I sign out.

"Fine," I say. Something warns me not to add any more.

"Bit of a rum one, isn't he?"

"In what way?"

"You know. Arrogant. Cold fish, too. Still, at least he hasn't given us any trouble. Not like the other." The officer is smiling nastily as though trying to scare me.

"What do you mean?"

"Didn't you hear? One of the boys went

for his solicitor the other day. Didn't hurt him, just gave him a fright." His face hardens. "But if your lot are intent on defending murderers and rapists, what can you expect?"

Then the officer hands me a small coin. It's a lira. "You dropped this when you were here last time. Joe Thomas handed it in."

I am filled with relief. So that's how he knew I'd been in Italy! As for the honeymoon, Joe might have just deduced that from my shiny wedding ring. Even so, it's another reminder that I am dealing with a smart — and clearly manipulative — prisoner. Am I up to it?

"What do you do for a living, then?" asks the man who has just sat down next to me.

I'm perched on the edge of a lime-green sofa in Davina's Chelsea flat with its rose-pink walls and soft lighting. Music is playing loudly and my stomach is rumbling. "Don't bother to cook before we go," Ed had declared. "There'll be food at the party." But there are merely mushroom vol-au-vents and wine. Lots of it. My new companion appears pleasant and easy to talk to. It's just that right now the last thing I want to do is talk.

"I'm a lawyer," I reply.

He nods deferentially. It's a gesture, I've noticed, that many people use when I tell them what I do. Sometimes it's flattering. At other times, it's almost demeaning, as if they assume a woman isn't capable of such a job.

Four hours ago, I was in prison. Now I'm surrounded by people chatting loudly and getting drunk. Some are even dancing. It seems weird. "What about you?" Even as I speak, I'm not interested in the answer.

What I want to know is where Ed has gone. I didn't want to come tonight. In fact, I didn't know anything about it until I got home and found my husband at the door wearing his new collarless cream shirt. The smell of pine aftershave was strong. "We're going out."

My heart lifted. The last couple of weeks had been difficult, yes. But my new husband wanted to take me out!

"Davina rang. She's having some of the old crowd over and wants us, too." He ran his eye over my navy lawyer suit. "Better get changed."

And now, here we are. Me in my pale blue M&S dress. And Davina in a clingy, bright red skirt. An outfit that clearly caught my husband's attention — much more than mine — when she welcomed us in. That was over an hour ago. Where is she? And where is Ed?

"I'm an actuary." My companion's voice cut into my thoughts.

"Fascinating," I say out of politeness.

There's a rueful grin. "Not everyone thinks that, but it can be surprisingly exciting." He leans toward me like a keen student. "At the moment, I'm working on a new formula to estimate how many people are likely to choke to death before they're sixty. Cheery stuff, I know, but it's important, you see, for insurance." He puts out his hand. "The name's Ross. Nice to meet you. I know your husband. In fact —"

There they are! I almost leap off the sofa, and make my way toward Ed. His face is flushed and I smell wine on his breath. "Where've you been?"

"What do you mean?" His voice is defensive, abrupt. "I just went out to get some air."

"You didn't tell me?"

"Do I have to tell you every time I leave a room?"

Tears prick my eyes. "Why are you being like this?"

He stares at me. "Why are *you* being like this?"

Because I can't see Davina, I want to say.

But that would be stupid.

"Because I couldn't see Davina," I hear myself saying.

Ed's face hardens. "And you thought she and I were together."

My heart skips a beat. "No. I didn't mean . . ."

"Right. That's it." He grabs my arm.

"Wait — what . . . ?"

"We're going." He pulls me toward the door.

"But I need my coat," I protest.

People are watching us — including Davina, who is walking into the room, arm in arm with a much older man I hadn't seen before.

"Leaving already?" Her voice is silky smooth. "What a shame. I wanted to introduce you to Gus." She gazes up at her companion adoringly. "I must apologize for not being a very good hostess. But Gus and I have been . . . busy."

Ed's hand grips mine so hard that it hurts. Then he releases me and moves away. "Lily's got a headache."

No, I haven't, I almost say. But I hear myself thanking her for a lovely time and am appalled at how easy it is for the lie to escape so smoothly. "You must come to us, next time," I add.

Davina's eyes sparkle with amusement. "We'd love that. Wouldn't we, Gus?"

Then she walks up and nestles her head in the spot between my husband's arm and chest. It's a smooth, natural gesture, reminding me that they had once dated. She smiles at me. *See,* she seems to say, *I had him long before you.*

Appalled, I wait for Ed to move away. But for a minute he just stands there as if weighing his options.

I want to say something. But I'm too scared of the consequences. Thankfully, Gus breaks the uneasy silence that has fallen, despite the music around us. "I think we ought to let the newlyweds go. Don't you? Let me find your coat, Lily."

Ed refuses to speak to me all the way home. It's a one-sided conversation.

"I don't know why you're being like this," I say, running to keep up with him. "I only wondered where you were. I was worried. And I didn't know anyone . . ."

"You're jealous of her."

At least he's speaking to me now.

"No. No, I'm not."

"Yes, you are." There's a click as Ed opens our door.

"All right. I am."

I can't stop myself. "You followed her around like a puppy from the minute we went into that smart flat of hers. You couldn't take your eyes off her. And then you disappeared for ages . . ."

"To get some bloody air!"

I stand back, shocked. Despite his ups and downs, Ed has never shouted at me before.

"You heard her." He's speaking more quietly now, but the anger is still there. "She's got a boyfriend. And we're married. Isn't that good enough for you?"

"But is it good enough for *you*?" I whisper back.

There's a tight pause between us. Neither of us dares to speak.

I finally allow myself to think of our honeymoon and what happened. Or rather what didn't happen. My mind goes back further to the night after Ed's unexpected proposal on that second date in a little restaurant in Soho. To the fumbling afterward on the bed in my tiny shared flat. To my mumbled request that, if he didn't mind, I'd rather "wait" until we got married.

His eyes had widened in disbelief. "You haven't done this before?"

I'd expected him to declare that this was ridiculous. That hardly anyone was still a virgin at twenty-five. I prepared myself to return his ring, admit it had all been a dream.

But instead, he had held me to him, stroking my hair. "I think that's rather sweet," he'd murmured. "Just think what an amazing honeymoon we'll have."

Amazing? More like a complete disaster.

Just as I'd feared, my body refused.

"What's wrong?" he'd asked. But I wouldn't — couldn't — tell him. Even though I knew he thought it was his fault.

The atmosphere became so bad between us that I made myself go through with it on the final night.

"It will get easier," he said quietly afterward.

This is the time to tell him, I think now. I don't want to lose this man. Ironically, I love it when he cuddles me. I like talking to him, too. Being with him. But I know that can't be enough for him, not for much longer. No wonder Ed is tempted by Davina. I have only myself to blame.

"Ed, there's something that I must . . ."

I stop at a strange scratching noise. A note is being pushed under the door. Ed bends down and hands it to me silently.

This is Francesca from number seven. I have to work on Sunday. I am sorry to request. Please could you look after my little one. She will be no trouble.

Ed shrugs. "Up to you. I'll be painting." He turns to go to the bathroom, then stops. "Sorry, what were you about to say just now?"

"Nothing."

I'm filled with relief. Thanks to the timely distraction, the moment has passed. I'm glad. If I'd made my confession, I'd have lost Ed forever.

And that can't happen.

8
CARLA

Mama was happy, observed Carla with a lightness in her own heart. They sang together all the way to the bus stop. Last night Mamma and Larry had danced so hard that the floor had shaken. But Carla had been a good girl and did not get out of bed to ask them to stop, even though it was difficult to sleep. She'd cuddled up to Charlie the caterpillar instead.

Right now, she was jumping. It was essential, Carla told herself, to take even more care than usual to leap over the unlucky cracks in the pavement. She had to make sure that nothing bad happened again.

"We're sorry that you have been bullied," one of the teachers had said — the only nice one — when all the others had gone out to play. "The boy who hit you has hurt others, too. It will not happen again."

Kevin wasn't there. So she was safe to bring Charlie into school! A warm feeling of thanks wrapped Carla up like a woolen cloud blanket. *Grazie! Grazie!* She would be like all the others.

Well, not quite. Carla eyed her reflection in the bus driver's mirror as she and Mamma got on. She would always be different because of her olive skin, her black hair and her eyebrows, which were thicker than anyone else's. *Hairy Carla Spagoletti.*

"Carla," said Mamma sternly, breaking into her thoughts. "Do not wriggle around like that. It will not make the bus start any faster."

But she was looking for Lily. Not long after the bruised eye Mamma's boss had told her she had to work on a Sunday. "What am I to do?" Mamma had said, her eyes round with anguish. "I have no one to leave you with, cara mia."

Then her gaze had fallen on the photograph of the hunched woman in a shawl with a face that looked like lots of little crinkly waves made out of stone. "If only your nonna were here to help."

Carla had been ready with her idea. "The lady who took me to the hospital, remember, from number three. She said she would help anytime."

As she spoke, she remembered Charlie. Supposing Lily with the golden hair told

Mamma that Charlie the caterpillar was not a present after all?

Too late. Mamma had already written a note and slid it under Lily's door. All night, Carla worried in her little narrow bed with the simple cross above, made of wood from the Holy Land. Poor Charlie was scared, too. *I do not want to leave you,* he said.

In the morning, Carla woke to find Mamma's eyes sparkling over her. "The nice lady and her husband are going to take you for the day. You must be good. Yes!" Charlie's heart was beating as they walked down the corridor. Hers, too.

Please don't let us be found out, she prayed.

"I will be back as soon as I can," Mamma was saying to Lily. "You are too kind. I must thank you, too, for the present you bought her."

There was a silence so loud that everyone had to hear it. Slowly Carla looked up and met Lily's eyes. She was wearing trousers that made her hips look very wide, and she did not have lipstick on. Instinctively, Carla knew this was not the kind of woman who would lie.

"Present?" Lily said slowly.

"The caterpillar pencil case." Carla's voice trembled as she fixed her eyes on Lily's while crossing her fingers behind her back.

"You bought it for me after the hospital to make me feel better. Remember?"

Another long silence. Then Lily nodded. "Of course. Now, why don't you come in? I thought we might make a cake together. Do you like baking?"

Mamma's voice sang out in relief. Carla's, too. "She loves cooking!"

No school now, Carla told herself as she skipped inside. It was a wonderful day! She and Lily got flour all over the floor when they weighed the cake ingredients. But her new friend did not get cross like Mamma. Nor did she have to have "a little rest" with her husband, a tall man named Ed who sat in the corner of the room doing something on a pad of paper. At first she was in awe of him because he looked like a film star in one of the magazines that Larry brought Mamma. His hair reminded her a bit of Robert Redford, one of Mamma's heroes.

She was also a little alarmed because Ed asked Lily why she'd moved his paints "again" in a fed-up voice, just like Larry's when he came over and found that she was still up.

But then Ed asked if he could draw her, and his face seemed to change. He looked much happier.

"You have such wonderful hair," he said

106

as his eyes darted from the paper to her head and then back again.

"Mamma brushes it every night! One hundred times. *Cento!*"

"Chento?" said Ed hesitantly, as if he were tasting a strange food for the first time, and she laughed at his accent.

Carla taught Lily and Ed how to make proper pasta instead of the hard sticks they had in the cupboard. It took a long time, but how they giggled when she showed them how to stretch it from the clothes rack that hung above the cooker.

"Stop!" commanded Ed, his hand raised. "I have to sketch the two of you, just like that! Go on, Carla. Put your arm through Lily's again."

"Charlie has to be in the picture, too."

As soon as she said the words, Carla knew she should have kept quiet.

Lily's face grew still. "How did you *really* get your toy, Carla?"

"He is not a toy." Carla hugged Charlie protectively. "He is real."

"But how did you get him?"

"It is a secret."

"A bad secret?"

Carla thought of the other children in the class who had fathers and didn't have to rely on men in shiny cars. Did that not give her a right to take what they had?

She shook her head slowly.

"You stole him, didn't you?"

Something told Carla there was no point in disagreeing. Instead, she silently nodded.

"Why?"

"Everyone else has one. I didn't want to be different."

"Ah." The frown on Lily's face ironed itself out. "I see."

Carla gripped her hand. "Please don't tell."

There was a silence. Ed didn't notice, his head glancing from them to the paper and back to them again.

Lily's sharp breathing was so loud that it sent little prickles down the skin of Carla's arm. "Very well. But you must not steal again. Promise?"

A balloon of hope rose out of that heavy gray puddle in her chest. "Promise." Then she held Charlie up so Ed could get a better view. "Charlie says thank you."

When Mamma came to knock on the door, Carla didn't want to go. "Can't I stay a bit longer?" she pleaded.

But Ed was smiling and had his hand around Lily's waist. Perhaps they wanted to dance. "Here," he said, pushing a piece of paper into her hands. "You may have this."

Both Carla and Mamma gasped.

"You have captured my daughter exactly!" Mamma said. "You are so clever."

Ed pushed his hands into his pockets and looked like Larry did when Mamma thanked him for the perfume or the flowers or whatever gift he had brought that evening. "It's only a sketch. Charcoal, you know. Don't touch or it will smudge."

Carla would not have dreamed of touching it. Was this really her?

"What do you say?" demanded Mamma.

"Thank you." Then, remembering the book they were reading at school about English kings and queens, she bent her knee in a sweeping curtsy. "Thank you for having me."

To her surprise, Ed burst out laughing. "She's a natural. Come again anytime, Carla. I will do a proper painting next time." His eyes narrowed as if he was measuring her. "Maybe acrylic."

And now, here they were on the bus to school, waiting for Lily.

Perhaps she will not come, said Charlie from his place on her lap. *Perhaps she is still cross with us because you stole me.*

Carla stiffened. "Do not ever say that again. I deserved to have you. Just as you deserved to have me. Did you really want to stay with that big bully?"

Charlie shook his head.

"Well, then," hissed Carla below her breath. "Let's not talk about it again."

"Hold on." Her mother put out a hand protectively as the bus lurched forward. "It's starting at last."

Sitting back in her seat, Carla watched the trees go past with their yellow leaves fluttering down to the ground. And then she saw her! Lily! Running down the street. Running as fast as Carla tried to run in her nightmares, even though her feet, in that other world, always stayed glued to the ground.

"Come on!" she called out. "You can sit next to me!"

But their bus went on, gathering speed. On the other side of the street, she could see Ed, waiting for a different bus. Carla knocked hard on the window and waved. Yes! He was waving back. And although Carla was sad that Lily had missed her bus, she also felt warm and happy because now they had friends. Proper friends. It was one more step away from being different.

"I think you were wrong, Mamma," she said.

Her mother, who was examining her face in the little mirror that she always carried in her bag, glanced sideways at her. "Wrong about what, Carla?"

"You said that women who are fat like Lily don't get handsome husbands. But Ed is like a film star."

Her mother let out a little trill. It made the man on the other side of the bus glance at her admiringly. "That is true, my clever little bird." Then she pinched her cheek. "But what I didn't say was that women like Lily might get a husband, but they need to be careful. Or else they might lose them."

How could they lose them? Carla wondered as she prepared to get off. Did they drop them in the street? Or mislay them on the bus like she had mislaid a pink hair tie the other week? Besides, Lily might be big but she was kind. She had kept Carla's secret about Charlie. And she had let her make a cake. Was all that enough for her to keep Ed?

She was about to ask, but Mamma was calling her. Giving her instructions for this afternoon when school finished. "Wait for me, my little one. Do you hear me? Right there by the gate, even if I am late."

Nodding happily, Carla jumped off the bus, waved, scuttled across the playground and made her way into the classroom. After the ball incident the other week, she'd been disappointed to find that the children in her class had still not been very friendly. But now she had Charlie, they would soon come around. She was sure of it.

At recess, she wrapped Charlie up carefully in her jumper so he wouldn't get cold, and left him in her locker. Then she went out to play. "May I join in?" she asked the girls who were playing hopscotch. No one answered. It was as if she had not spoken.

She tried a group of girls who were hitting the side of the wall with a tennis ball. "Can I play, too?" she asked. But they just looked the other way.

Carla's stomach felt like it did when it was empty, even though it wasn't.

Slowly, she returned to her classroom. No one was there.

Excitedly, Carla went to her locker and began to unwrap her jumper. Charlie would understand about the children who wouldn't talk to her. Charlie would make her feel better . . .

No. *No!*

Charlie was dead. Slit from top to bottom in a jagged line, his lovely green fur ripped. And on top of him, a note. In big red capital letters.

THEEF.

9
LILY

I need to run faster or I'll miss the bus. If I were thinner, it might be easier to run. My heavy breasts thud against my chest. The same breasts that Ed had fondled when he'd rolled on top of me unexpectedly last night. Yet afterward, when his eyes finally opened, they expressed surprise to see me beneath him.

I, too, had been surprised. In my half-awake state, I had imagined someone else. His soft hands on my breasts. His mouth on mine. His hardness against my body . . .

"Got to wash," I mumbled before staggering to the tiny bathroom and drying my tears. When I returned, Ed was asleep.

Where had that come from? Why had I imagined Joe in bed with me?

And who was Ed imagining? I can guess. There might not be anything concrete apart from that overfamiliar gesture the other night. But I can smell it. Just as I smelled

Joe. If there's one thing I've learned over the years, it's to listen to my intuition.

While all these thoughts churned endlessly through my mind, Ed slept. He looked so peaceful. Snoring lightly, a growth of fine fair hair on his chin. Quietly, so as not to wake him, I eased myself out of bed, tiptoed into the kitchen and grabbed the mop propped up on the wall by the sink.

The distraction worked. I didn't hear Ed coming in until I heard his voice. "Why are you cleaning the floor at this hour?" He was fastening his tie as he spoke. It bore a drop of blood from the shaving nick on his neck.

I looked up from my kneeling position, not wanting to tell him that I'd been at it for hours. "It's grubby."

"Won't you be late for work?"

So what? I had an almost insane urge to make the linoleum gleam. If I couldn't fix my marriage, I could at least fix the kitchen floor. I remember reading a magazine interview with a woman whose husband had cheated on her. Her first reaction was to clean the house from top to bottom. "At least I could control *that*," she explained. Now I know how she feels.

And that's why I'm running. If I hadn't gone mad with the cleaning, I wouldn't have left the flat fifteen minutes later than normal. Wouldn't be watching the bus disappear up the street. Wouldn't be dreading the excuses I'd have to make to my boss.

As I come panting to a halt, I see Carla, nose pressed against the glass, waving madly at me. "Come on," she mouths. Then she appears to add something else.

Fatty? Surely not. Carla's a sweet child. Although I've seen the way Francesca looks at me pityingly. And I've also seen how the daughter copies everything the mother does.

Besides, it wouldn't be the first time someone had called me fat.

As I sit waiting for the next bus, I can't help thinking about Carla. Carla and her green caterpillar.

"You stole him, didn't you?" I'd said when we'd looked after her. "Why?"

There was a shy yet defiant turn of the head. A discomfortingly mature pose that suggested it was practiced. "Everyone else has one. I didn't want to be different."

I don't want to be different. Just what Daniel used to say. It makes me even more certain that, somehow, I need to help this child.

My boss is waiting in his office. He's about thirty years older than me and has a wife who gave up her job when she got married.

I get the distinct feeling he disapproves of me.

Soon after I'd joined the firm, I was foolish enough to tell one of my colleagues that I wanted to go into law "to do some good."

My boss overheard. "Good?" he scoffed. "You're in the wrong job for that, I can tell you."

I flushed and kept my head down after that. Yet at times, especially when he's barking at me, I want to tell him what happened with Daniel.

Of course I wouldn't really. Even Ed wouldn't understand if I told him the full story. It would be madness to tell Mike, my boss. He's sitting across from me now, a pile of papers between us, and a frosty smile on his lips. "So how are you getting on with Joe Thomas?"

I cross my legs under the table and uncross them again. I'm aware of Ed's imprint from last night, still inside me.

"The client is still playing games with me. I think he might . . . might have mental health issues."

My boss laughs. It's not a friendly laugh. "He's in a prison with a high proportion of psychopaths, Lily. What do you expect?"

"I expect a better briefing." The words are out of my mouth before I can take them back. Fear gives me courage — rightly or wrongly — to stand up for myself. "I don't think I have enough background," I carry on, trying to recover. "Why has he launched an appeal after being inside for two years? And why won't he talk to me properly instead of speaking in riddles?"

I pull out the paper Joe gave me with the strange numbers and letters.

"What do you think these figures mean?" I ask, in a more conciliatory tone. "The client gave them to me."

My boss barely glances at the creased sheet. "No idea. This is your case, Lily. New evidence, perhaps, that he's only just got hold of? That might explain the delay in the appeal." His eyes narrow. "I'm throwing you in the deep end, just as they did to me at your age. It's your chance to prove yourself. Don't let either of us down."

I spend the rest of the week doing what I can, but there are other cases in my workload, too — they pile up with unrelenting regularity. Clearly, my boss is testing me. Just as Ed is doing, with his sometimes friendly and sometimes cold approach to me.

"I'm having problems with a client," I start to say one evening over dinner: an undercooked steak-and-kidney pie that doesn't look quite like the picture in the well-worn cookery book that Ed's mother passed on to me.

"The one who . . . Ed? Are you all right?"

I jump up from the table. Ed's gasping for breath and his face has gone all red. Something's stuck in his throat. Shocked into action, I whack my hand down on Ed's back. A piece of meat shoots out across the room. He splutters and then reaches for a glass of water.

"Sorry," I say. "Perhaps it was a bit under-done."

"No." He's still spluttering, but his hand comes up to reach mine. "Thank you. You saved me."

For a minute, there's a connection between us. But then it goes. Neither of us feels like eating anymore. I scrape the offending meat into the bin, realizing, too late, that it should have been braised before I put on the pastry top. But there's something else, too.

How easy it would have been to let Ed choke to death. To pretend it was an accident.

I'm shocked — no, appalled — by myself. Where did that thought come from?

But it's then that I have my idea.

■ ■ ■ ■

Ross. The actuary I met at Davina's awful party. Hadn't he discussed this very issue with me? *I work out how long people have to live from statistics. How many people are likely to choke to death before they're sixty. Cheery stuff, I know, but it's important, you see, for insurance.*

So I got his number from Ed. And yes, Ross was free the following day. How about lunch at his club?

"These figures," I say, handing the sheet of paper over to Ross as we sit at a table with a stiff white tablecloth and hovering waiter, "were compiled by a client of mine. He's . . ."

I hesitate, wondering how much to reveal. Surely it's all right if I don't mention Joe's name? "He's in prison for murder."

Ross shot me a surprised look. "And you think he's innocent?"

"Actually, you might be surprised if you met him."

"Really?"

We wait as the waiter pours out our wine. Just one glass, I tell myself. Nowadays, I appear to be drinking more than I used to.

"I need to know what these figures refer

to," I say, rather desperately. "My client is good with numbers."

"Really?" His eyebrows rise with interest.

"Apparently, he has some kind of condition. He's very methodical in some areas and yet finds it difficult to speak to people. He prefers to speak in puzzles, and this . . . well, this is one of them."

I detect a gleam of interest in Ross's eyes. "I'll look into it." His tone is so reassuring that I almost want to hug him. "Give me a few days and I'll come back to you."

And he did. "A mixture of water temperatures and makes of boilers, including their age," he says now, beaming. "And, if I'm not mistaken, the implications are pretty big. I showed them to an engineer friend — don't worry, I didn't give him the background. But he said that there's a definite pattern. So I had a hunch and did a bit of rooting around in our resource department."

He hands me a newspaper cutting. It's from the *Times* back in August when I was preparing for my wedding. An exciting time, when I hadn't, perhaps, read the paper as carefully as I normally do.

SCANDAL OVER FAULTY BOILERS

I scan the piece with increasing excitement. "So," I say, summarizing the article in front of me, "a number of boilers, made over the last ten years, are suspected of being faulty. To date, seven customers have made complaints involving irregular temperatures leading to injury. Investigations are currently being carried out, but so far there are no plans to recall the models in question."

Ross nods. "That's seven who have come forward, but there are sure to be more."

"But it's been going on for years. Why didn't anyone realize before now?"

"These things can take time. It takes a while for people to spot a pattern."

Of course it would. Lawyers can miss things, too. But I can't be one of them.

"I've worked out the figures," I say as I enter the visitors' room the following week.

Funny how this is becoming more natural now. Even the double doors and gates seem quite familiar. The same goes for the seemingly casual pose of my client, arms crossed as he leans back in his chair, those dark eyes fixed on mine. This man is thirty. Ed's age — my husband had his birthday not long after we got back from our honeymoon. Yet although he seems older, I also feel as though I'm dealing with a truculent teen-ager.

"Worked out the figures?" He seems slightly annoyed. "Really?"

"I know about the boilers. The lawsuit. You're going to tell me that the boiler company is responsible for Sarah's death. You said the water was hotter than you'd expect after thirty minutes. Your boiler was faulty. It's your defense — or rather your *self*-defense."

He's tilting his head quizzically to one side, as if considering this. "But I told you before. Self-defense can't get you off."

"It can if you have the right lawyer," I shoot back.

"Congratulations." He's gone from disappointed to smiling in just a few seconds. Holding out his hand as if to shake mine.

I ignore it. I'm cross. Unnerved, too.

"Why couldn't you just have told me about the boiler figures at the start? It would have saved a lot of time."

"I told you before. I had to set you the clues to see if you were bright enough to handle my case."

Thank you, Ross. Thank you.

Then he leans back, slaps himself on the thighs and lets out a laugh. "And you did it, Lily. Well done! You're hired."

Hired? I thought I was already hired.

"You still haven't told me exactly what happened." My voice is cool, laying down a boundary between him and me. "I've had enough of messing around," I add. "No more clues. No more games. Why, for example, did you always cook dinner? Why did you usually run Sarah's bath?" I take a deep breath. "Was Sarah right when she told her family you were controlling?"

His face is rigid. "Why do you need to know?"

"Because I think it might help us."

For a while, he says nothing. I let the silence hang between us.

Joe is looking out the window. There's no one in sight, even though it's another beautiful crisp autumn day. Maybe the other men are at work; they all have jobs in the prison.

"The bath, Joe," I repeat. "Why did you run it for her?"

My client's voice is quieter than usual. "So I can make sure that the cold goes in first. It's what I've always done. Means you don't burn yourself." The thump of his fist on the table makes me jump. "Stupid girl. She should have listened to me."

"Fine. The bath was too hot. But that

doesn't matter. They proved you pushed her in."

His face hardens. "Didn't prove. Just argued successfully. I've already told you. I didn't touch her. She must've fallen in. The bruises must have been from that."

"So why didn't she get out again if the bath was so hot?"

"Because . . . she . . . was . . . too . . . drunk."

He says each word slowly, spelling it out for me.

"If she'd let me run the bath for her, it wouldn't have happened," he says again. He seems obsessed with this point. And something about his obsession makes me believe him. About this part anyway.

"And don't think I don't feel guilty, because I do."

My skin begins to prickle.

"I shouldn't have left her there for so long. I should have checked on her earlier. I was always so careful with her. But this one time . . ."

Joe Thomas is clearly a control freak. But that doesn't make him a murderer any more than the rest of us. I've now started to wash the floor every morning before work. It's become part of my daily ritual. A rather sudden one, which is possibly verging on an obsession. Then again, Daniel had to fold his bedsheets in at the corners, just so. My boss always hangs his coat in a certain way by the door of his office. Joe Thomas likes to position his scrap of paper dead center on the desk between us. I see now that such actions are comforting.

"You need to do things your way," I say softly, "because it makes you think that you can control your life and that nothing will go wrong."

He glares. "So?"

"It's okay. I understand."

He stares at me as if willing me to look away. If I do, he will think I've just said this to make him confide in me.

But something's still niggling.

"If the boiler was faulty, why didn't you find out the next time you turned it on?"

"I'd been arrested by then, hadn't I?"

Stupid me.

"And the people who moved in after you? Didn't they realize the water was boiling?"

He shrugs. "They re-kitted the bathroom — boiler and all, apparently. You would, wouldn't you, if someone had died there?"

"So when did *you* realize there may have been a manufacturing problem?"

"A few weeks ago, someone sent me these figures in the post, along with a single word

— 'boiler.' "

"Who sent them?"

"I don't know. I did my research in the prison library and reckoned this was the answer." His eyes shine. "They've got to believe me this time. I'm not the one who's responsible for Sarah's death." His voice shakes as he looks at me.

I consider this. Anonymous tip-offs, we were told in law school, were sometimes given to both lawyers and criminals — usually by people who had a grudge against someone or who wanted to push a particular issue.

I stand up.

"Where are you going?" His voice is demanding. It reminds me of Carla with her thick black curls and knowing gaze that belong, surely, to a teenager rather than a nine-year-old.

"I need to find a barrister who will take on our case."

A slow smile breaks out over Joe Thomas's face. "So you think we have one, do you?"

I have my hand on the doorknob. "We might," I say cautiously, "providing what you're saying checks out. We need to work on this together. Promise?"

Promise, said Daniel, toward the end.

Promise? I said to Carla, when I asked

her not to steal again.

"Promise," Joe Thomas now says.

I find myself walking down the corridor toward the office to sign out, side by side with my client.

We pass a large man in an orange track-suit. "Still on for this afternoon?" he says to Joe.

"Three p.m. on the dot," he said. "In the community lounge. Looking forward to it." Then Joe turns to me. "Table football."

I recall that when I first came here, an officer had described Joe as arrogant, but that exchange had sounded quite friendly. It gives me the courage to bring up something that's been worrying me.

"How did you know on my first visit that I'd just got married?"

He shrugs. "I read the *Times* every day from cover to cover. I have a photographic memory, Lily. Macdonald is an army name. It comes up every now and then."

Even though I introduced myself to Joe (according to my boss's instructions) as Lily Macdonald, I feel the urgent need to put some distance between us here. Tell him to refer to me from now on as Mrs. Macdonald in a bid to stop him getting personal. Despite the thoughts that are coming into my head.

Luckily, unlike sugar, Sellotape, crisps and sharp implements, I can hide them all.

10
CARLA

THEEF.

They had spelled it wrong. Carla knew that because she had skipped ahead to the *t*'s in the *Children's Dictionary.*

If she screamed loud enough, Carla told herself, Charlie would be made whole again. THEEF.

If she continued to scream, that missing black eye would be back where it belonged, and he would wink at her. *Did you think I would leave you?* he would say.

And then she'd hold him to her and his soft green fur would make her feel good again.

But the screaming wasn't working. Not like it did in the flat when she wanted something and Mamma would give in because the walls were thin or because the man with the shiny car was coming by any minute.

"What on earth is going on?"

A tall, wiry woman marched into the classroom. Carla didn't like this teacher. She had a habit of pulling off her spectacles and looking at you as if she knew — really knew — what you were thinking. "Is that what you're crying about?" She pointed with a bony finger to Charlie's remains. "This old thing?"

Carla's gulps spilled out over each other. "It's not an old thing. It's Charlie. My caterpillar. Someone's stabbed him. Look."

"Stabbed? What a melodramatic word!" The glasses were coming off.

"Now stop crying."

"Charlie. *Charlie!*"

Too late. The horrible teacher with the spectacles and bony nose had yanked him out of her hands and walked away. Then the school bell sounded and a tide of children poured into the classroom, including a girl who'd been friendly with Kevin.

"It was you, wasn't it?" Carla hissed, waving the felt-tip note in front of her.

The girl looked at it briefly. "Thief," she said loudly. "That's what you are, isn't it? We know what you did."

"Thief, thief," said someone else.

Then they were all doing it. "Thief, thief. Carla Spago-letti is a thief!"

The chanting made her scream inside.

"What's all that noise?" The bony-nosed teacher was back. "Quiet down, everyone."

"What have you done with my Charlie?" sobbed Carla.

"If you're talking about that broken old pencil case, it's in the dustbins outside. I'm sure your mother will buy you another. Now behave yourself, young lady, or I will give you detention."

Charlie wasn't really dead. Instead, he was mixed up with eggshells and brussels sprout peelings and tea bags. Carla had to dig deep into the bin to find him, and by the time she did, her uniform was stained and smelly.

"Don't worry," she whispered. "It will be all right." Then, very carefully, she held him in her arms while waiting around the corner for Mamma.

It didn't matter that Charlie wasn't speaking. She only had to wait for three days and then he would be all right again. It would be the same for all of them. The priest had said so.

But, the more she shifted from one foot to another, the more Carla began to wonder if she and Mamma had missed each other. All the other children had gone home. Even the teachers.

The sky was dark. It would nearly be

winter in Italy. The cold months there, Mamma often said wistfully, were wonderful! There was always a fire with loved ones sitting around it. Their songs and their arms warmed you up, heated your belly. Not like here where the greedy electric meter gobbled up coins.

Start walking. At first, Charlie's voice was so soft that she hardly heard it. Then it got louder.

"I knew you'd get better," she said, gently stroking his poor torn, stained fur.

But which way should she go? Maybe right at the crossroads. Now where was she? Perhaps she ought to go left. Usually, when Mamma met her, they danced along the pavement so fast that it was hard to keep track of the lefts and the rights. They would chat about their days. ("There is this new perfume, my little one. My manager, she has lent me a brand-new bottle to try it out. Smell it! What do you think?")

And she would tell Mamma about hers while crossing her fingers. ("I got top marks in maths again.")

Carla and Charlie had passed a park now. Was it a different one from the park near their home? Maybe if they went on, she might find the shop where she and Mamma sometimes looked at magazines. "You must buy if you want to look," the man at the counter would tell them. But so far, there was no sign of the man or his shop. Carla felt her chest tighten and her palms sweat. Where were they?

Look, whispered Charlie weakly. *Over there.*

A shiny car! The same blue shiny car that sometimes parked outside their flat.

It is Larry, whispered Charlie again. *See the hat?*

But the woman sitting next to him was not Mamma. Her hair was even blonder than Lily's — yellowy white — and her lipstick was bright red.

Now Larry was pressing the lady's lips hard. The teacher had shown them a film about that. If someone stopped breathing, you had to make your own breath mix with theirs to give them life.

Feverishly, Carla knocked on the window of the car. "Are you all right?"

Instantly, the yellow-white-haired woman and Larry sprang apart. There was red on *his* mouth, too. Carla felt her heart pounding.

"What the hell are you doing here?" he shouted.

It was a loud shout that came through the window even though it was closed. It hurt her ears.

"I'm lost." Carla didn't mean to cry, but now that she was safe, she could admit she'd been scared walking down those roads in the dark. "Charlie made me late and Mamma wasn't at the gate. I think she may have gone home. Or else she is late from work again . . ."

"What's she saying, Larry love?"

Only then did Carla realize she had lapsed into her mother language.

"Wait there."

For a minute, Carla thought that Larry was speaking to her. But then she realized he was addressing the red-mouthed lady. Suddenly, she found herself being marched away from the car, toward the corner of the road. "What did you see? Tell me."

His voice was hard, like old skin on your foot that you had to smooth off every evening, just as Mamma did with a gray stone in the shower. ("Only the English take baths, my little one. Such a dirty habit!")

Carla's mouth was so dry that it took time for the words to come out. "I saw you pushing your mouth against that woman's. Your lips are all red, like hers."

"What do you mean?" His grip on her arm was getting tighter.

Carla felt herself getting more scared.

"Like the stuff on your collar," she whispered.

He glanced down and wiped away the red smear. She could smell whisky. Sometimes Mamma did not eat dinner so that they could afford to buy a bottle. It was important. A man needed to feel welcomed. Whisky and dancing. And in return, the rent would be paid. The heating bill would be sorted. Larry had paid the phone bill again. *It is worth it, cara mia. Trust me.*

His face came close to hers. She could see the hairs in his nose. Ugh! Then he began to march her fast along the pavement. "If you're so clever, Carla, why don't you tell me what little present I can buy you. So we don't have to tell your mother about today."

Remember, whispered Charlie. Remember the film?

Of course. She and Mamma had watched a story on television the other night. The film had been about a young boy who had seen a couple stealing from a shop. The couple had given him money for not saying anything. They had called it "blackmail." At the time, she hadn't understood what this had meant. But now she was beginning to realize.

"Is this blackmail?" she asked now.

Larry's face began to break out in tiny

135

beads of water. "Don't play games. What do you want?"

That was easy. She held out Charlie. "Make him better." He frowned. "What is it?"

"My caterpillar. Someone hurt him."

The grip on her arm started again. "I will buy you anything you want if you keep your mouth shut."

Anything? Carla felt a tingle of excitement.

"This is what we will do." He was marching her back to the car now. "I will take you home. And on the way, we will stop off at a toy shop. I will tell your mother that I found you wandering the streets after school and bought you a present. In return, you won't mention anything else. And I mean anything . . . You don't want to upset your mother, do you?"

Carla shook her head firmly so that her curls swung from side to side.

He opened the car door. "Out." This last sentence was directed at the yellow-white-haired woman in the front seat.

"But, Larry, what —"

"I said *out.*"

Larry reversed so hard that his car hit a stone pillar by the side of the road. Then he cursed all the way home as if it was Carla's fault instead of his own impatience.

"You found her. You found my precious one," her mother wailed when they got home. "I was so worried. She was not there at the school gate so I thought she had gone ahead and . . ."

Quietly, Carla crept into her room. Looking over her shoulder, she could see her mother embracing Larry. Any jealousy was replaced by the smug knowledge that in her bag was a new Charlie to replace the old one.

The priest had been wrong. It didn't take three days for a person to come to life again.

It took three hours.

My head hurts.

My thoughts are confused.

Sometimes I think I am fifteen years younger.

Sometimes I think I am not here at all, but looking down at everything that is still happening.

Perhaps there really is such a thing as resurrection.

But not as we're taught in church.

Maybe it's the chance to do it all again. Right this time.

Or maybe this is just the rambling of a dying soul.

Never to return again.

11

LILY

**BOILING BATH KILLER LAUNCHES
APPEAL FROM PRISON**

Joe Thomas, who was sentenced to life in
1998, is to appeal against his conviction
for murder. Thomas claims that his girlfriend, Sarah Evans, died as the result of
a faulty boiler.

Miss Evans's parents described themselves as "shocked" when they heard the
news. "That man took our little girl away
from us," said Geoff Evans, a fifty-four-
year-old teacher from Essex. "He deserves
to rot in hell."

Mrs. Evans, fifty-three, is currently un-
dergoing chemotherapy for breast cancer.

My boss sucks in his breath as he scans
the story on page two of today's *Times.* "So!
They're baying for your blood already.
You're sure about your brief?"

"Absolutely. Tony Gordon has agreed to

do it pro bono like us. Says it could be a case of national importance." My boss makes a *well, what do you know?* face.

"I don't want a woman," Joe had said firmly. "No disrespect meant. Juries might like to watch a woman strut around and imagine what's under her dress. But it's a man's argument that will sway them."

I swallowed my response to that.

"I've seen him in court a few times," I assured my client. "Tony can play the crowds."

It helps that he's handsome — in some ways, Tony reminds me of Richard Burton — with a gift for making female jurors feel as though they're the only ones in the room, and for making male jurors feel privileged to be entrusted with the life of the accused in the dock.

With any luck, he'll pull the rabbit out of the hat. First, we have to make an application to the Criminal Cases Review Commission, for leave to appeal. If it thinks there are grounds, it will refer the case to the Court of Appeal. If the latter allows the appeal, says Tony, we'll seek a retrial. Meanwhile, he's confident enough to "do quite a lot of spadework" first to save time. The courts are rushing cases through at the moment. We need to be prepared.

I return to my desk to continue my briefing notes for Tony. I'm meant to share the room with another newly qualified solicitor, or NQ (as we're known for short). But my colleague, a young man fresh from Oxford, is ill with stress.

It's common in law. So easy to make a mistake. To let clients down. To let the firm down. And we have the constant fear of being sued hanging over us for inadvertently making a mistake. It reminds me of something that one of my tutors once said to us in the first year: "Believe it or not, the law isn't always just. Some will get away with it. Some will go to prison for crimes they didn't commit. And a certain percentage of those 'innocents' will have gotten away with other crimes before. So you could say it balances out in the end."

I'm aware of all this as I lean over my computer. Yet my thoughts wander back to Ed.

"Why don't we have a dinner party?" I suggested over dinner the other night. My husband of two months looked up from his tray. That's right. We'd started having dinner in front of the television, something Ed's mother certainly wouldn't approve of.

But it helps to fill in the silent gaps. The sweet, kind, amusing man I met less than a year ago appears to have lost his sense of humor. He no longer tries to cuddle me in bed. But sometimes he takes me in the night — when we are both half asleep — with an urgency that makes me gasp.

"A dinner party?" he repeated when he'd finished his mouthful of macaroni cheese. Ed is polite, if nothing else. My latest imitation of a Delia Smith dish is distinctly runny, but he is manfully plowing on. I've "progressed" now from undercooked steak-and-kidney pie to overcooked macaroni cheese. Even with two salaries, our budget is tight.

"Yes," I said firmly.

It had been Ross's idea. "How's it going?" he'd asked when he rang to see how his information had worked out. His voice reminded me, to my shame, that I hadn't even sent him a thank-you note. And the kindness in it made me well up. It's strange what a bit of thoughtfulness can do. Or the lack of it.

"Bit tense," I choked out.

"Because of Ed?"

"Why?" My chest tightened. "Has he said something to you?"

"No . . ."

"What, Ross?" My hands were clammy on the phone. "Tell me. Even though he's your friend, I need to know." My voice was tearful. I was reaching out to someone I'd only recently met but this was one of the few people who could tell me the truth.

"Are you certain? I doubt it's anything really. Just people stirring."

"Ross, tell me. Please." Surely he couldn't fail to hear the note of desperation in my voice.

There was a sigh. "Davina is going around telling everyone that she had a drink with Ed last Tuesday. I'm sure it's nothing."

Last Tuesday? My mind spun as I tried to recall the week. He'd been working late. Suddenly I felt angry. This was my husband we were discussing. We might not have gotten things right yet, but there was still time. I wasn't going to let this woman get in the way of my new start. The one I had planned before even meeting Ed.

"Look, maybe I shouldn't have said anything. But if I were you, I'd do something about it."

"What?" My voice came out like a croak.

"Have her to dinner. Have lots of people to dinner. Show her you're a couple." His voice hardened. "Davina's not a very nice person. You're worth ten of her."

Then, before I could say anything else, he added, "And don't forget to invite me."

■ ■ ■ ■

Quite frankly, a dinner party is the last thing I need now that the case is gathering speed.

"If we can show there was negligence on behalf of the boiler manufacturer, it will have a huge impact on the whole industry," Tony had told me after agreeing to take us on. "But we've got a lot of research and interviewing to do. I'll start with the expert witnesses. Meanwhile, I want you to inter-view this lot." He passed me a list of phone numbers. "They're other people who have reported extreme changes of temperature in their boilers."

"Where did you get them from?"

"It doesn't matter. We just need to get cracking." There's hardly been time for a break. I shouldn't be taking one now, yet here I am. Eight of us squeezed around the little table in our small flat, which I have somehow managed to make rather pretty with paper lanterns and lilies. Lilies every-where. I bought armfuls from the market. The smell is overpowering.

I've also taken great care, on Ross's advice, to use the "our" word at every op-portunity. "Our" new sofa, which we bought together. "Our" plans for Christmas. "Our" wedding photographs. The message is clear: we're a couple now.

It's not hard to see that I've really got up Davina's nose. In fact, she hasn't stopped sneezing from the minute she arrived.

"I'm afraid I'm allergic to pollen," she gasps as I remove the large vase from the middle of the table — just opposite her place setting. Obviously, if I'd known, I'd never have bought them. Probably.

Ed's face is disdainful as he takes in his ex. He's an artist. He likes things to look nice. And right now, Davina isn't fitting the bill.

Even my coq au vin is quite passable.

I am triumphant.

"Thank you for a lovely evening," she splutters before leaving on the arm of the boring man she brought with her. A different one from the last time.

Ross winks at me as he brushes my cheek good night.

"Thanks," I whisper in his ear.

"Anytime." His eyes sweep over me. Surely he's not checking me out? Although for once I think I look rather good. I'm wearing a simple white dress that covers the curves I'd rather not show, while revealing the ones that are more acceptable.

"You look lovely," says Ed, as soon as the

door closes. "At least Ross seems to think so."

The thought occurs to me that a touch of jealousy on my husband's part might not be a bad thing.

"We might have a drink together next week," I say casually as I pull on my washing-up gloves.

"A drink?" His voice sharpens. "Why?"

"He's been helping me on a case." I take a glass, heavily stained with lipstick, and wash it angrily in hot soapy water. "We're just friends, you know. Unlike you and Davina. I'm aware you met up with her for a drink the other night. Don't deny it."

"For pity's sake." Ed flings down the tea towel. "It's you I married in the end. Not her."

"What do you mean, 'in the end'?"

He's not looking at me. "We were engaged," he says slowly. "She broke it off. I didn't tell you, because I didn't want you to feel threatened when you met her."

Threatened? Is he kidding? I feel even worse now.

"When did she break it off? How long before we met?"

"Two . . ." He hesitates.

Two years? Two months?

"Two weeks," he murmurs.

"*Two weeks?* You started seeing me two weeks after your fiancée broke off your engagement, and you didn't think to tell me?"

"I explained why." Ed's face is red. "Aren't there things you haven't told me about your life?"

I go hot and then cold as the picture of the stables comes into my head. What does he know? *How* can he know? Don't be silly, I tell myself. He's just lashing out blindly. Keep quiet. Say nothing.

Ed is moving toward me now. Placing his hands on my hips. "Davina and I had a drink to catch up." His voice is pleading. "There was nothing in it."

Tears are in my eyes. "Did you marry me on the rebound, Ed?"

"No. I married you because . . . because you're kind and caring and beautiful . . ."

"Beautiful? Now I know you're lying."

"I'm not." He holds me by the shoulders. "To be honest, part of the attraction is that you don't know how lovely you are."

"I'm fat!" I almost spit out the words.

"No. You have the shape of a woman. A proper woman. But more important than that, you're a beautiful person within. You care about putting the world right."

If only he knew, I think to myself as Ed

147

kisses me softly.

Doesn't he have a right to know?

Do I believe him when he says there is nothing between him and Davina?

Do I have any right to ask when I have hidden so much from *him*?

The doorbell rings as I am lying in Ed's arms. I almost did it, I tell myself. Honest love between husband and wife. Well, affection, at least . . .

The bell goes again. Wrapping my dressing gown around me and glancing at the clock — ten o'clock in the morning already? — I make for the door. A beautiful doe-eyed woman in a black and orange silk dress is standing there, dark curls cascading over her shoulders. I'm still so caught up with Ed and me, it takes me a second to figure out who she is.

"I am so sorry," says Francesca. "I have to work again and I have no one else to ask."

Little Carla has already burst through our door as if she lives here. She is dancing up and down. "Can we cook like we did before?" she sings.

Of course this is an intrusion. The warning bell in my head tells me that the more I allow it to go on, the more of a habit it will become. And I have work to do. But I am just trying to form an excuse when Ed comes up, the phone in his hand, his face shocked.

"That was Davina's boyfriend. She's been rushed to the hospital with an asthma attack. Brought on by those lilies."

"Is she all right?"

"Yes. But it could have been much worse apparently."

To my shame, I feel a flash of regret along with relief. Then the lawyer in me goes on the offensive. "You should have told me she was allergic to pollen before I put the flowers out. Surely you knew?"

He shrugs. "I forgot until it happened."

The intimacy of last night is fast evaporating. Suddenly we're aware of the little girl dancing and Francesca waiting impatiently at the door.

"Carla's mother needs to work today," I say quietly.

Ed nods. The relief in his eyes matches mine. We both need a distraction from each other. This little girl is the perfect excuse. We can play Mummy and Daddy again.

"That's fine," Ed says, turning to Francesca. "Happy to help out. Carla's no trouble. No trouble at all."

12
CARLA

"May I lick the bowl? Please? Please?" asked Carla, the wooden spoon already midway between her mouth and the delicious-smelling mixture of egg and flour and butter and sugar. Mamma never let her taste anything before it was cooked. But something told Carla she could persuade Lily. Sometimes you just had to know the right way for the right person.

"Pleeease?"

"Of course!" Lily was next to her in a polka-dot pink and white apron. "My brother and I always used to do that when I was your age."

"Mmm. Yummy!"

"Not quite so much or you'll be sick!" Lily put a gentle hand on her arm.

Carla pouted the way Mamma did when Larry said he might be late again. Then she remembered that this sometimes annoyed him. She didn't want to annoy Lily. "What is your brother's name?" she asked in the hope of changing the subject.

There was a tight pause as Lily put the cake into the oven. She could feel it, rather like that beat between the needle being placed on the record and the sound of the music.

Ed, who had been sitting on the floor cross-legged while sketching, laid down his charcoal stick. Lily took a great deal of time adjusting the position of the cake in the oven before coming back to the table.

"He was called Daniel."

Carla knew that voice. It was the one Mamma used when she said something that was very important but that she didn't want Carla to make a fuss about. "Your grandfather does not wish to see me anymore." Or, "One day, perhaps, you might go back to Italy on your own. Your grandmother would like to meet you."

The English language was very strange. But even though she hated school, Carla paid great attention to grammar. She liked it. It was like a rhyme. They were doing tenses now in class. Present. Past. Future. *She walks down the street. He walked down the street. My brother is called Daniel. My brother was called Daniel.*

That meant Lily's brother must have

changed his name. They'd been reading a story at school about someone doing that.

"What is he called now?"

Ed's charcoal stick was scratching quickly again. But Lily had turned back to the oven, her back to Carla. "I don't want to talk about him anymore." Her voice was unexpectedly harsh.

Instantly, Carla's mouth went dry. The sweetness of the butter and flour and sugar had gone. Yet there was a thrill of excitement running through her — the sort you got when something bad happened, but not to you.

"Did someone hurt him?" A picture of poor Charlie with his ripped fur came back to her.

"I think that's enough questions for today." Ed stood up. "Come and look at this, Carla. What do you think?"

The girl on the paper looked just like *her*! She was lifting the spoon from the cake mixture to her lips. Her eyes were shining. But at the same time, there was a hint of something sad. How did Ed know that inside she was still hurting for Charlie? The new one didn't smell the same. He didn't love her as much. She could sense it.

"Where is Lily? She's not in the picture."

There was a laugh that sounded deeper

than usual. Normally Lily had a high, tinkly laugh. "Don't worry about that, Carla. I'm used to it."

A ripple of unease ran through her. Didn't Mamma say such things when Larry was late or didn't turn up at all? *I'm used to it. Used to your wife coming first. Don't worry about me.*

"Stop." Ed's voice was low and growly. "Not in front of the child."

"I am not a child," she started to say, but Ed was pushing his drawing into her hands.

"You may keep this, if you like."

"Really? This is mine?" She tingled with excitement. "Thank you! I will put it in the special box with the first drawing you gave me."

"Good idea. It's better than keeping it here. My dear wife might start to be jealous of that, too."

Lily was washing up angrily. "I thought you said 'Not in front of the child'?" Suds were flying in all directions. One landed on Carla's shoe. Something told her that she needed to make Lily and Ed happy again. "May we go out for a walk?" she asked. Then she remembered something that she had heard Mamma say through the wall, after she and Larry had been dancing. "Please? Pretty please?"

Carla had five more pictures. Carla in the park, on the swing. Carla feeding the ducks. Carla running. Carla thinking with her hand on her chin. Carla eating a Knickerbocker glory with gooey strawberry sauce that Lily had treated her to.

"Why do you not have any pictures of Lily?" she asked Ed one day in the park.

Lily gave a strange laugh. "Because he would rather paint other people."

Ed said nothing. But when Carla returned the following Sunday, there was a new picture, propped up against the wall. It showed Lily looking out of a window. And that's when Carla realized — Mamma was wrong. Lily might be a different shape from her mother, but she was still beautiful. Kind. Caring. Carla's heart swelled up inside. How she loved her!

"It is wonderful," she breathed.

Ed looked pleased. So did Lily. They put their arms around each other and looked much happier than she had ever seen them look recently. It made Carla feel good, too. She couldn't wait to come back. If it were not for Sundays, Carla wouldn't be able to get through the week.

Mamma no longer had to put a note under Lily's door. It seemed to be accepted that on the Lord's day she went to Ed and Lily's, while Mamma went to work.

"Soon," promised Ed, "I will draw you again."

But he wasn't her favorite person. That was Lily. Lily who took her to the swings in the park or helped her with homework or played card games. Ed, on the other hand, just drew all the time.

One afternoon, though, Lily was busy, too. "I need to go through some work papers," she said. "Can you read to yourself for a bit?"

Carla stuck out her bottom lip. This was usually effective in getting her way. "But I've left my book behind."

"Do you have a key?"

"There's one above the ledge of the front door."

"Can you get that, then?" Lily barely looked up as she spoke.

"Okay."

"Thanks." Lily beamed at her. Instantly Carla felt full of warmth again.

"Shall I come with you?"

"You're busy." Carla was keen to please. "I can do it."

As soon as she put the key in the lock,

Carla heard the moaning. Someone was in pain! Was it Mamma sent home ill from work? The sound was coming from her room.

Carla opened the door and then stopped dead. That was Larry's hat on the floor. The rest of him was on top of Mamma. Was Larry hurting Mamma? But then Mamma started to shout. "Yes. Yes. More. More."

Carla turned and ran.

"Where is your book?" asked Lily when she returned.

"I couldn't find it."

"Are you all right? You're very quiet."

"May I just watch television?"

"Of course."

"And could I stay here. For the night?"

Lily gave her a hug. "We've only got one bedroom, sweetie."

Then Lily shut her books. "Tell you what. I'll do this later. Why don't we make some fudge? Then you can give your mother a piece when she comes home from work."

There was the sound of a bell and a voice cooing through the door. "Piccola? It is me."

Carla's heart sank. Instinctively, she knew Mamma was here because Carla had seen her at home when she was meant to be at work. And although Mamma's voice sounded nice, she was bound to be cross when they were alone together.

"In fact," said Lily brightly, "it looks like she's back early."

13
LILY

I'm running after Davina in the park. She's holding something and I need to take it away from her or my marriage to Ed is over. She's slowing down, but every time I speed up, she zips ahead. Then she starts sneezing so loudly that whatever she's holding falls out of her hand. I reach down to get it, but it keeps slipping out of my hand. Finally, in the light of the moon, I manage to pick it up. It's a wedding ring. Just like the one that Ed gave me — the one that had belonged to his great-grandmother. But as I hold it, the ring crumbles in my hand. I try to piece it back together but it's no good. The pieces dissolve into dust. Then Davina laughs. A high-pitched shriek of a laugh . . .

"Can you turn it off?"

Ed's sleepy voice comes from the other side of the bed. Slowly it dawns on me — what a relief! — that Davina's laugh is the alarm clock. The light filtering in through the window is indeed the moon, but even so, it is time to get up. It's six a.m. I need to get an earlier bus because I have a meeting with Tony Gordon. The man who might, or might not, help me set Joe Thomas free.

"Let's go over the facts one more time."

Tony Gordon is the type of tall, imposing man who would be as at home on the cinema screen as he is in his Lincoln's Inn chambers. It isn't just the breadth of his shoulders or the assured way he wears his dark gray suit. It's also his deep, authoritative voice and his stride that suggests an inborn confidence. It's his crisp, expensive-looking shirts and the unhurried way in which he answers the phone.

As I listen to Tony go over the statistics — boiler figures, the timing of the "incident" — I am already dreading going home to my husband. On the outside, we seem fine. We go shopping together on Friday nights, watch our favorite TV shows next to each other on the sofa after work and look after little Carla on Sundays. I make sure I give Ed space to paint in his spare time because that's all he wants to do. How he resents working for his "moronic" bosses during the week. But it's hard not to notice that his two glasses of wine a night have now become three or four. Or that he hardly ever tries to touch me anymore.

I'm aware as I list these complaints that they sound like the disgruntled litany of a long-married couple. In fact, we've barely been married for three months.

"What do you think?"

Suddenly I'm aware of Tony Gordon staring at me. I flush. This is a famous barrister. He could be the key to saving an innocent man. At least, my gut instinct tells me that Joe is innocent, even though I don't like him very much. And here I am, thinking about my failing marriage.

"I'm not sure." It seems a safe thing to say.

"Come on, Lily, stay with me. The additional psychologist report that I asked to be carried out says that our man shows signs of Asperger's and also has obsessive behaviors." Tony Gordon glances down at his notes. "Both are broad labels and mean different things to different people. But in this case, one of our man's characteristics is that he likes everything to be neat and tidy. It disturbs him when objects aren't in their right place. He interprets language literally. He doesn't always respond to situations in the same ways as other people. He has difficulties communicating with people. He also dislikes change of any kind."

"My brother is a bit like that," I hear myself say. Even as I speak, I realize I should have said *was,* rather than *is.* The truth is that I often do that. It makes it easier to pretend Daniel is still alive.

"Really?" Instantly I feel Tony Gordon's interest sharpen. "How does it make him act?"

"When he was younger," I say slowly, "we were just told he was difficult. We weren't given any label. But he could be charming to people one minute and rude or abrupt the next. He didn't like change . . ." Mentally I run my hand over the smooth saddle. Smell the wood. Cradle Amelia in my arms. *No.*

"Are you all right, Lily?"

I look down at my shaking hand. "Yes."

Yes, it made Daniel do strange things. No, I'm not all right.

But Tony Gordon has already moved on. "We've got to watch that," he's muttering to himself. "Got to emphasize the facts and the figures rather than the emotions. In my opinion, the defense didn't do that enough last time. It would help, too, if the jury is made up of people who like statistics: they need to be the type whose heads rule their hearts rather than the other way around. We also need to show that although some people on the autistic spectrum share certain common behaviors and features, everyone is different. According to my research, this cold, unemotional, obsessive behavior that's recorded in his notes is not necessarily a consequence of the spectrum. Tricky. Especially if someone on the jury has personal experience that doesn't fit in with Joe's."

I'm beginning to wonder if I even need to be here. After all, I've briefed my barrister. It's up to him now.

"Please ask your firm to make sure you are with me when I visit the client," he says. "Your experience could be very useful. There'll be a lot of publicity surrounding this case, you know." He gives me another kindly look. Almost fatherly. "No one will like us," he adds. "We'll be the devil, you and I. A murderer is always a murderer in the public eye, even if proved innocent. This case is of huge national importance. If it's allowed to run and we win, it will open the floodgates to all kinds of suits. We've got to be careful."

"I know," I say, although if I'm honest, I'm a bit out of my depth here. But I mustn't show my ignorance. I want to be grown up. I want to be good at my job. I want to be good at my marriage. I just don't seem to know how.

I leave Lincoln's Inn with its beautiful brick walls and rich green post-rain grass to weave my way through the midday tourist crowds. I like walking in London. Besides, it gives me time to think.

I take a right toward Westminster Bridge and pause for a moment to admire the skyline. The famous line comes back to me and I whisper it out loud. "Earth has not anything to show more fair . . ."

Daniel used to love poetry. He admired its order. The way the words fell into place exactly where they were meant to. When he was distressed about something — a missing jigsaw piece or a shoe that was not in its usual place — I would sometimes read to him. It had to be a poet with structure and a certain touch of quirkiness. Edward Lear was always a good choice.

"Sorry," I say as someone bumps into me. Ruefully, I rub my elbow. Typical of me to apologize for someone else's rudeness. I did that all the time for Daniel. Meanwhile, the man hasn't even stopped to acknowledge me. I glance back but he's already disappeared into the crowd.

Then I realize something. My bag containing the papers concerning Joe Thomas, plus

163

the figures he'd given me and the notes made during our meeting just now. It's gone.

As I walk quickly toward the office, Tony Gordon's words come back to me: "This case is of huge national importance. If we win, it will open the floodgates to all kinds of suits. We've got to be careful."

At the time, I'd interpreted his words as meaning that we had to be careful to win. Now I'm beginning to wonder if he was referring to our own personal safety. Was it possible that I had been deliberately targeted? Had the man on the bridge — whose face I can barely recall — bumped into me on purpose? Isn't this a common mugging practice? How stupid of me not to be more careful.

I'm almost running now along High Holborn, the throbbing in my elbow intensifying. I'll have to tell my boss. Tell Tony Gordon, too . . .

Racing up the staircase with its elegant Victorian mahogany handrail, I almost collide with one of the secretaries. "I've got two messages for you."

The first is from Tony. In the short time since leaving him, he's heard from the CCRC. It's referring our case to the Court of Appeal. Great. All we need now is the court's agreement to allow it and then, hopefully, a retrial.

"Not now, please," I say to the secretary as she waves the second message in front of me.

"It's urgent." She presses a piece of paper into my hand. "You've got to ring her immediately."

Sarah Evans.

Why does the name sound familiar?

And then I realize. It's the name of Joe Thomas's dead girlfriend.

14
CARLA

Carla pulled at her mother's hand. Away from the bus stop. Away from the journey that led to school. Away from the nasty looks and the laughs that made her feel stupid.

It didn't help that the new Charlie said nothing.

"You must hurry," said Mamma, her voice edgy. "We will be late."

As she spoke, the bus rounded the corner. "It is there!" Mamma's beautiful face turned old with frown lines. "Quick."

Reluctantly she allowed her feet to be dragged along the pavement. She'd been really bored without Lily and Ed. "You cannot go to them every Sunday," Mamma had said, as if it had not been her who had made the arrangement in the first place.

But Carla was all too aware of the real reason. It was because she had seen Mamma and Larry at home when Mamma was supposed to be working. Mamma felt guilty. This had seemed a good thing at first because it would make her do what Carla wanted. But then it had become a bad thing because she had canceled Sundays with Lily. No baking cakes or licking the bowl! No making pretend people out of conkers and pins. No sitting in front of Ed, feeling special while he drew her. No running in the park.

Just staying at home with Mamma, waiting for Larry even though he hadn't turned up last Sunday. They'd made lasagne specially.

"On you get." Mamma's voice was heavy with relief. They had managed to catch the bus after all. Carla clambered up the stairs and took her usual place at the front.

Recently, Lily had not been on the bus. "I have to leave earlier now for work," she'd explained. But Ed was still there. Waiting on the other side of the road, his notepad in his hand, sketching. Maybe he was drawing *her*! Fiercely, she knocked on the window.

"Carla!" Mamma's voice was annoyed. "I've told you before not to do that."

But Ed had heard! He was waving his notepad at her! Carla's heart grew warm. He liked her. She could tell from the way he observed her face, every detail. He'd made those thick eyebrows of hers look almost pretty! If only the other children at school could see them like that. Then they might not be so horrid.

As Ed's face disappeared out of sight, Carla felt a jolt of emptiness. "Aren't you going to pick up Charlie?" said Mamma, pointing down at the dirty bus floor where Carla had dropped him among the old cigarette ends and a tin can.

"He's not Charlie. He's just a caterpillar," Carla said in the same voice that the other kids used when she said something stupid in class.

Mamma was clearly puzzled. "But you used to love him."

That was the old Charlie, she wanted to say. The one she'd taken from a bully at school and had been so cruelly murdered by another. But she couldn't. This one, which Larry had bought, did not smell the same. It was too quiet. It did not listen to her secrets.

"Here we are!" Mamma's voice was bright as school came into sight. It was as if her mother wanted her to go as quickly as possible so she was free to get to work and laugh and smell nice and see Larry at lunchtime, perhaps.

"Please, Carla. Please."

Her mother was trying to pull her down the bus stairs.

"I will only go if you ask Lily to have me this Sunday."

Her mother's eyes flickered. "You want to be with strangers instead of me?"

"They are not strangers. They are my friends. I want to be with them just as you want to be with Larry."

"Are you getting off or not?" said the conductor loudly. A woman with a shopping bag was staring at them. So were the girls in the brown uniforms who came from the nicer school down the road — the one with no boys and where no one spat or was rude. Mamma said it was a convent school where nuns taught. She had tried to get Carla a place there, but they didn't want her because they didn't go to mass regularly. "Couldn't we start going now?" Carla had asked.

"I said we would do that but the nuns told me it was too late."

Carla only hoped it was not too late to go back to Sundays with Lily and Ed.

"I will ask." Mamma sighed. "But you must go to school this instant. Promise?"

Carla nodded. "Promise."

Mamma held out her face for a kiss but Carla ignored it. Instead, she made her way toward the school gates and another day of misery.

"Eeetalian!"

"Why do you speak all funny?"

"Why have you got hairs on your arm like a man?"

"They're as furry as your eyebrows!"

The taunts came thick and fast, as they did every day now.

"What are you going to steal next, then? My dad says all Italians are thieves. They stole my auntie's handbag in Rome."

This last comment was from a thickset boy with a face like a dog she had seen in the park. A bulldog, Ed had called it.

"I do not steal nothing."

"Anything, Carla." The bony-nosed teacher's sharp voice cut into the conversation. "The correct word is 'anything.' And what is this about stealing?"

"Carla stole my friend's pencil case. I told you. But no one would believe me 'cause he socked her with the football."

It was no good. She couldn't help the burning flush creeping up her cheek. "It is not true."

The teacher's eyes narrowed. "Are you sure?"

She sat up straight. "Very."

"I see." The teacher nodded before moving on to the next table.

"Liar, liar," shouted the children.

If Charlie were here — the real Charlie — he would tell her to ignore them. But instead she had an impostor (she was on the *i*'s now in her dictionary), who just sat on her lap and did nothing.

"Liar, liar."

"If you do not stop, then God will punish you." Carla's eyes flashed at Jean, the girl who was nearest and loudest. "You will die!"

There was a shocked silence. Carla was shocked at herself, too. She was not even sure where the words had come from.

"Carla Cavoletti! Leave the table this instant."

Good. That was exactly what she wanted. Head high, she sailed out of the cafeteria and into the corridor.

"You will sit there for the rest of the afternoon."

Good again. She would not be bullied if she wasn't in the classroom. It was then that Carla had her idea. She knew now just what she needed from Larry next.

"I hate school," Carla declared over and over again that evening. The teacher had, of course, told Mamma about the detention.

Carla had tried to explain her side of the story but Mamma was cross with her.

"I have told you, cara mia. You have to fit in with these English."

For the first time she could remember, Carla wished Larry would visit that night so she could get on with her plan. Mamma was expecting him because she had put on her pink dress and sprayed Apple Blossom down her chest. But then the phone had rung. Larry's wife needed him after all.

The next morning, when she dawdled through the school gates, there was a strange air of quietness in the playground. The others were huddled in groups, shooting her horrible looks.

"What has happened?" Carla asked one of the girls who sat at the front of the class and was not quite as nasty as the others.

But the girl shied away as if Carla were a dangerous dog. "Do not come near me."

When they trooped into assembly, Carla finally understood. "Sadly, we have some terrible news," began the headmistress. Her eyes were red like Mamma's had been last night after Larry had phoned. "Jean Williams was knocked down by a car last night on her way back from Brownies. She is in the hospital and, I'm afraid to say, doing very poorly."

In the hospital? Jean Williams? The girl whom she had told would die?

Carla became uncomfortably aware that the girls on either side of her were moving away. Several people were turning around to look at her warily. That day in the playground, no one taunted her. No one even spoke to her.

By the end of the week, Carla was neither eating nor sleeping. When she did eventually drift off, she dreamed of Jean falling under the wheels of Larry's shiny car. Then she would wake up screaming.

"What is wrong, cara mia?" said her mother, stroking her brow. "Is it because of that poor little girl?"

It was my fault, Carla wanted to say. But something held her back. If she could make Mamma continue to feel sorry for her, she would succeed with her plan.

"The others, they are not nice to me," she said instead. "Jean . . . Jean was the only kind one."

The lie slipped out of her mouth so easily that it felt like the truth.

"My sweet." Mamma's eyes filled with tears. "What can I do to make you feel better?"

This was her chance! "I want to go to a different school. The one where they wear a

173

brown uniform and don't take boys."

"But I have told you, piccola. The nuns will not let us in."

Carla looked up from under her lashes. "Ask Larry. He can do anything."

Mamma flushed. "Even he cannot fix this. But, perhaps, he might consider sending you to a private school . . ."

That night, when Larry came to dinner, Carla did not need asking twice when it came to bedtime. Putting her ear against the wall, she could hear muffled voices. "I know it is a lot to ask, but . . ."

"Impossible! What would my wife say if she found out that such a large sum of money was leaving our account every term?"

More muffled voices.

"There is something I might be able to do, however. That convent you mentioned just now. Our firm sets aside an annual amount for local donations. I can't promise anything. But it might be possible to pull a few strings. Even for naughty lapsed Catholics like you, my darling . . ."

The music finished before Carla could hear more. They were going into the bedroom. Soon, Larry would come out and go to the bathroom.

Quickly, she leaped out of bed and opened her door.

"Larry," she whispered.

Then she stopped, horrified. Instead of his suit, he was wearing a shirt that was open, and underneath . . . ugh! Desperately, he covered himself with his hands. His face showed that he was as shocked as she was. "You are meant to be asleep!" He sounded angry.

Carla glanced at Mamma's closed bedroom door. "If you don't help me go to the school with nuns, I will tell Mamma about the woman in the car."

His face scowled. "You little —"

"Larry!" Mamma's voice called out from the bedroom. "Where are you?"

Carla glared. "I will not tell you again."

I will not tell you again. It was what one of the teachers had said when she'd missed what was being said in class. Now it was her turn to be tough.

The following morning at breakfast, Mamma was all smiles. "My darling, guess what? I told Larry how unhappy you are and he is going to see if he can get you into the convent school. Isn't that wonderful?"

Yes! Yes!

Carla gave Larry a steady look. "Thank you," she said quietly.

"Aren't you going to give him a kiss on his cheek to say thank you?"

Bracing herself, she walked across and brushed her mouth against his skin. It felt old. Dry.

"Mamma," she said sweetly when she sat down again. "Have you thought again about what I asked before? You know. Going to work on Sunday so that I can see Lily and Ed?"

A quick look passed between her mother and Larry. "Is that what you would like?" Mamma's voice had an edge of excitement.

"Yes, please."

"Then I will ask if they mind."

Mind? Of course they didn't. Carla heard Lily's voice from down the corridor. "We love having her here. Just drop her off when you go."

Something had changed. Carla felt it from the minute she entered the flat. Ed was barely speaking to Lily. And Lily, instead of greeting her with a new cake recipe or a ball of wool to make some more pompoms, was sitting at the kitchen table surrounded by books.

"She is working on a case," Ed said as he asked her to sit a certain way on the sofa. "We must not disturb her, mustn't we?"

"Just as we must not disturb you when you are painting," snapped Lily.

Carla began to feel uncomfortable. "I thought a case was something that you carried things in."

Ed took a swig out of the glass in front of him. It had a dark brown liquid inside and smelled like the whisky Mamma gave Larry when he came around. "Believe me, we are carrying enough baggage at the moment."

"I think that's enough, don't you?" The words sang out of Lily's mouth, but her eyes were empty.

"Sure." Ed turned around to face Carla. "Now I want you to sit there without moving and think of something nice."

So Carla thought what it would be like to go to a new school where no one teased her. And she thought of the postcard of a London bus that she and Mamma had written to Nonno in Italy, even though they did not expect one back. And she wondered if —

What was that scratching noise under the door? An envelope! Eager to please, she ran to get it, handing it to Lily.

"Ed?" Lily's voice sounded odd. "Take a look at this."

15
LILY

My first thought, as Ed hands the note back to me, is that it must have come from Sarah. My mind races back to the message that the secretary gave me last week.

"The caller?" I asked at the time. "What did she sound like?"

The girl shrugged. "I don't know. Normal."

Not dead? I almost asked.

Fingers trembling, I dialed the number.

"Sarah Evans speaking."

There was no doubt about it. Sarah Evans was speaking to me. What was going on?

"I'm Lily Macdonald," I began, remembering at the last minute to use my new surname. "I'm returning your call about —"

Angrily, she cut in. "About my daughter."

Relief flooded through me. Sarah Evans must have been named after her mother.

"How can you defend that man?" she hissed. "How could you?"

Relief was soon replaced by a sinking feeling. Wouldn't I feel the same if I had a daughter? Until this point, I'd been more concerned with whether we could get Joe Thomas off.

But the distraught voice reminded me of my own mother's words all those years ago. *How could you, Lily? How could you?*

My fingers began to sweat. Poor woman.

"I'm so sorry, Mrs. Evans, but I can't discuss the case with you."

Then, hating myself, I replaced the receiver and went to tell my boss the bad news about "losing" certain papers that were vital to Joe Thomas's release.

Now, in our flat, as I read the note that has just appeared under our door, I assume it's from her. "How did she find me?" I say, my hands shaking. "How does she know where we live?"

"She?" Ed's mouth is grim. "You know who wrote it?"

Briefly I explain what had happened.

"Why didn't you tell me?"

"Because we don't have that kind of relationship." The words burst out of my mouth in an angry rush. "You never ask me about my day. All you do when you come back is paint."

"Please don't argue, Lily and Ed."

The little voice at my side reminds us that Carla is still here — a child we are responsible for, if only for a day at a time.

"Sorry, sweetie." I put my arm around her. "We need to see if your mother is back home now. I've got an important phone call to make."

"Can't I stay while you do it?"

Those deep brown eyes are imploring.

"Not today." Ed's voice is firm. Then he looks at me.

"Do you want me to call this woman?"

"Why?"

"I'm your husband."

"Ready to go?" says Ed to Carla. I hear them walk along the corridor, Ed's slow measured step next to Carla's little hopping ones. Then I look at the note again. It is typed with several spelling errors. It doesn't seem like the kind of note that an educated-sounding Sarah Evans would write. But then again, you never know.

IF YOU TRY TOO HELP THAT MAN, YOU WILL BE SORY

I try to stop my hands from trembling but it won't go away. Ed's right — I have to report this.

I'm lying in bed trying not to think about my new reality. Someone out there wants to hurt me.

"Tell me one more time what happened," Tony Gordon instructed when I rang the following day. So I did. Just as I had told the police and my boss. A child who was visiting heard the note being pushed under the door. No, we didn't see the person who did it, although I had received a phone call from the victim's mother a few days earlier. On the same day that the vital papers were stolen.

The more I had to repeat it, the more I felt as though I was the accused. There was also the weird temptation to embellish it slightly, to make it more interesting or believable. Was this how criminals felt? Was this how they dug themselves into a deeper grave? Like Daniel?

Of course, no one could do anything about it. How could they trace a typed note from an unknown sender without a postmark? All they could do was warn me to "be careful," as if that might help. Instead, it has done the opposite. Even when I walk to the bus and hear footsteps behind me, I purposefully do not look back.

I will not be scared. I will not be intimidated. That was the whole point of entering

181

the law — I have to believe in something that has power over evil. If I allow myself to be bullied, I've lost.

I turn restlessly in bed, staring at the ceiling as it's lit up by a passing car's headlights.

Then I hear it: "Please. Davina," says Ed. Then, louder, "Davina." He's talking in his sleep.

"I'm not Davina." I shake him. He jerks awake.

"What's wrong? What's happened?"

"You called me Davina."

"Don't be ridiculous."

"I'm not. You called out for her. You still want her. Don't you?"

"For pity's sake, Lily. Go back to sleep and stop imagining things."

But I know I'm not.

This time, it's him who is lying.

Afterward, a new coolness develops between us. We act like the other doesn't exist, trying to squeeze past each other in our tiny flat and sleeping at opposite sides of the bed as though a mistaken brush of skin against skin might kill us both.

I've never had close friends. Always shied away from too much intimacy — too many chances of sharing confidences and revealing something I shouldn't. But now I find myself in desperate need of having someone to talk to. Someone who might be able to give me advice about Ed.

There's only one person I can think of.

I ring Ross during my lunch hour and tell him about what happened last night. Then, because he's so understanding and sympathetic, I find myself telling him about the threatening letter from the unknown sender and how the police had merely told me to "be careful."

Ross listens rather than offering quick-fix solutions. But it helps just to voice my own fears to someone other than myself.

That night, Ed comes home late. "I've been out for a drink," he says.

"With who?" I demand, my heart racing. It had to have been Davina. He's going to leave me after all. Despite his behavior, I'm terrified — now I'm going to have to start again. Who else would ever love me?

"With Ross, actually." He reaches for my hands. "Look, I know our marriage hasn't got off to the best start but I do love you, Lily. And I'm worried about you. This letter . . . that man who took your bag . . . you visiting that criminal in prison . . . I don't like it. I'm scared."

"It's my job."

My words come out harshly, but inside I'm relieved that he seems to care.

"I know it is and I admire you for it. Ross said you're a girl in a million. And he's right."

If only he knew!

"Just talking to him," Ed continues, "reminded me how lucky I am." His hands are gripping mine. They're warm even though it's a frosty night outside. "Let's start again, shall we? Please?"

"What about Davina?"

"What about her?" He looks straight back at me. "I'm over her, Lily. It's you I married. And I want to stay that way. Do you think we could start again?"

By the end of the week, I'm exhausted. It's been full on in the office, with constant phone calls from Tony Gordon. Luckily he has copies of the documents that were stolen — he tells me he always photocopies documents at least twice — even though it's "unfortunate" that someone else has the originals.

And it's full on with Ed, too.

It's as though this time he is finally seeing me. He says my name and not hers. As I slowly start to trust my husband, my body begins to respond to his. Yet there are still occasions when I slip, and imagine Ed is someone else.

It makes me irritable with guilt. And the constant pressure of my work makes us both snappish.

"You need a break," says Ed when I work through another file while eating supper. "I've barely spoken to you this week."

I glance at his sketchbook by the place mat. "At least I get paid for it. It's not a hobby."

A mean jibe provoked by my annoyance at what I'm reading. But it's too late to take it back.

"One day," says Ed in a tight voice, "I *will* be paid for doing what I want to. In the meantime, I am flogging myself during the week in a job that I loathe in order to bring in the bacon."

"I contribute, too."

"And don't we know it."

I want this marriage to work. But despite what's going on in the bedroom, I'm beginning to wonder if it can. Maybe it's just this case with Joe Thomas. When it's been resolved, I'll be able to think straight again. But not now. There's too much going on.

And at the back of my mind that day is looming. November 24. Eight years ago. Every year it comes around all too fast.

"I have to visit my parents," I tell Ed a few days later as we lie entwined in each other's arms. The alarm clock has gone off. We are both steeling ourselves to get out of our warm bed (the flat is like an icebox) and set off for work. But I have to face the thing I've been putting off.

"It's the anniversary of Daniel's death," I add.

His arm tightens. "You should have told me. Should I come with you? I can call in sick."

"Thanks. But I think it's best if I go alone." I think again about the sanitized version of events I gave Ed, back when we first met. We haven't talked about it since. I'd told my parents about this, too. They agreed with my deception.

There are some things that we don't want the rest of the world to know.

I'd hoped Mum and Dad would move after Daniel's death. But no. There they stayed: a rather tired but still lovely Georgian village house, bought years ago by my grandparents, nestled in its spot on top of the cliffs, with its neatly trimmed topiary bushes in the front garden and its footpath down to the sea at the back.

There are the stables, too. And ghosts.

"We don't want to lose the memories," my mother had said at the time.

Memories! Wasn't that exactly what we needed to shed?

As I walk down the gravel drive toward my old home, I find myself wishing Ed were here to hold my hand after all. I'm wishing now that I'd told him everything when I had the chance.

But if I had, he would surely have left me.

"Lily!" My father wraps me up in a bear hug. There is no resisting.

"Lily." My mother's faint voice cuts in. "It's been so long."

"I'm sorry," I begin.

"It's all right. We know you've been busy at work." My father is already leading me into the sitting room. My parents may have inherited this lovely house, but they have little money to run it. The central heating is rarely on. I shiver, wishing I'd brought a thicker jumper.

"I've been reading about this new case of yours," says Dad. "Sounds very interesting."

He flourishes a copy of the *Daily Telegraph* at me and my heart quickens. There it is. A large article on the second page.

MOTHER OF BOILING BATH VICTIM LASHES BACK

I scan it quickly. There are the usual gory

details about the crime, a picture of Sarah Evans that I try not to look at, and a quote from her mother: "I can't understand how anyone can defend this evil monster . . ."

Below are two pictures. Me and Tony Gordon. We each have a smile on our faces. Not very suitable under the circumstances. Great. Where did they get them from? Some official entry in a Law Society document?

"Sounds like you've taken on something very big."

My father's voice swells with pride as he pours me a gin and tonic.

"How do you know this man is innocent?" asks my mother, sitting next to me on the sofa, a glass already in her hand. She's gazing wistfully out the window.

When I was a child, I had been the apple of her eye. I can remember her cooking with me like I bake with Carla. We'd cuddle up together and sing songs. Go for long walks to find chestnuts. But then Daniel had come along and there'd been no time for those sorts of normal things anymore.

How do I know Joe is innocent? My mother's question catches me.

Because he reminds me of Daniel, I want to say. Because he can't help telling the truth even if it's rude. And because my gut feeling tells me that I need to save him.

188

I select the only part that would make sense. "Some new evidence has emerged that shows . . ." Then I stop.

"She can't talk about it. You know that, love."

My father might be retired, but as a social worker he worked a lot with lawyers. He understands the etiquette.

"Are you staying over?" My mother again.

"I can't. I need to be back for Ed."

Their disappointment is palpable.

"Lunch is almost ready." She rises and, en route to the kitchen, tops up her own glass.

The meal is torture. We talk about everything else except the reason I am here. My mother refills her glass far too often. Meanwhile, I pick at the fish pie, my brother's favorite.

Afterward, my mother melts away for her "rest." My father is looking weary from the effort of keeping the peace.

"Mind if I go upstairs for a bit?" I ask.

He nods, gratefully.

The stairs creak, just as they did when Daniel used to come down them in the dead of night and I would follow, to make sure he was all right. His room is exactly as he left it. Toy cars perfectly positioned on the bookshelves along with Palgrave's *Golden Treasury* and old copies of *The Beano,* which he still read in his teens. Posters of scantily dressed models on the wall. Clothes neatly folded in the drawer — jumpers mainly and the odd T-shirt. I pick one up and press it to my nose. At first, it used to smell of him. But the scent has worn away over the years.

Unable to stop myself, I turn to the cupboard where my brother kept his "special things." The pile of sticker albums is stacked in perfect order. So, too, are the Lego models he used to spend hours making. Woe betide anyone who touched them. Once I recall a cleaning lady "having a bit of a sort out." She had to be given a hefty tip in order not to report the bruise on her wrist, courtesy of my brother.

Now, reverently, I take out a sticker book. It's about birds. Daniel used to save up his pocket money to buy packets of stickers. He would spend hours carefully placing each one in exactly the right position within the frame marks. Robins. Thrushes. Blackbirds. Pigeons.

Swiftly, I slip the book into my bag. And another two. Then I glance out the window at the old brown cob horse grazing on the winter grass. I ought to go and see Merlin, nuzzle my face against his. But I don't feel strong enough. My bittersweet memories

always kept me from going into the paddock, let alone the stables, when I visited
my parents.

There's a noise at the door. It's my father.
"I've been wanting to have a quiet word."

My heart sinks. What now?

"How is married life?" he asks.

I hesitate. It's just enough for him to
notice.

"I see." He sighs and pulls me to him. I'm
a teenager again. Raw with grief. "Remember what I told you?" he says. "You have to
start again. Put the past behind you. Otherwise you'll end up like us." He doesn't need
to spell it out. His words take me back to
less than a year ago, when I'd admitted to
Dad that I didn't go out very much and
spent most of my time in the office.

"You need a social life," he'd advised. "A
new century is dawning, Lily. It's time to
move on, Daniel would want that."

And that's when my then flatmate suggested I go to a party with her. The same
one where I met Ed. I could hardly believe
it when this tall, handsome man began to
talk to me and then — miraculously —
asked me out. What did he see in me? I
thought of saying no. I'd only get disappointed.

At the time, it seemed like my escape

route to sanity.

"Crisps? Sellotape? Sugar? Sharp implements?" barks the officer the following week.

I watch Tony go through the process. Prison, said Tony on the way here, can grow on you. It can also, he added with a warning look, be curiously addictive.

We're following the guard across the courtyard, through the set of double doors and gates, down the long corridor past men in green jogging pants, and finally into D wing.

The Hope poster has a big rip on the bottom right-hand corner. Joe Thomas's arms are folded, as if he has summoned us.

"This is Tony Gordon," I say, plastering on a smile to hide my nervousness. After my weekend, all I can see is Daniel sitting there. The same clever face which, at times, looks unsure of itself. That sideways manner of looking at you as if working out whether you're to be trusted or not.

"He's your barrister," I add unnecessarily, because Joe has been told this already.

"What have you got to say to me, then?"

I'm almost embarrassed on Joe's behalf at his lack of social grace. But Tony proceeds to rattle through the defense — the boiler company data, our proposed cross-examination of the Joneses (the neighbors who testified against him last time), the other expert witnesses — before proceeding to ask Joe more questions. Some of them I've wanted to ask, too, but haven't quite dared to. Some of them I haven't considered at all.

"Why did you usually run the bath instead of allowing Sarah to do so?"

There's an *Isn't it obvious?* stare that reminds me of a look he'd given me when we'd first met and Joe was declaring his innocence over Sarah. "I have to. It's what I do."

I'm reminded of the ritual side of obsessive behavior that I've been reading up on.

"Would you say you have some habits that others might find strange?"

Joe glares at Tony challengingly. "What might seem strange to you isn't strange to me. And vice versa. My habits are quite normal in my book. They keep me safe. If someone wants to be part of my life, they have to accept that."

"Did you tell the defense this at the first trial?" Tony glances at his notes. "Because there's no record here."

Joe shrugs. "He thought it made me sound too controlling. Would make me *unsympathetic* to the jury."

"Did you hit Sarah during that row when she came home drunk?"

"No."

"Did you turn up the temperature on the boiler?"

"No. I told you before. But the water was still hot when I found her, which suggests the water was near scalding when she'd turned it on, earlier. That's why I had burns on my hands. They came from getting her out of the bath."

The questions go around and around, as though we are in court already. Vital preparation for the real thing.

If Tony is irritated that each of these replies is addressed to me, he doesn't show it.

"Right," he says, getting up. "I think we have enough now to be getting on with."

"Think?" For the first time since we've arrived, Joe Thomas's keen eyes train themselves on my colleague. " 'Think' isn't going to be enough to get me out of this place. Trust me."

"And trust me, too." Tony Gordon's voice comes out as a low growl.

Daniel had been obsessed with horses, so, after considerable pestering, my parents had bought him one from a neighboring farmer when we'd moved to Devon. This steady, safe, lumbering beast didn't see Daniel as "different" from anyone else. Right from the start, they had forged a special bond. It was my brother whom he would nuzzle first when we went down to the stables in the morning to feed him and muck out. When we took turns to ride him across the downs, Merlin seemed to take special care with Daniel, who visibly grew in confidence as a result. We even rode him along the beach.

Now Joe looks at me. His eyes are nervous. I want to reassure him even though I'm scared myself, still spooked by the message under the door. This was not, Tony had told me firmly beforehand, the right time to mention the note to the client.

"He's good at his job," I whisper to Joe as we leave the room. "If anyone can get you off, he will."

And then I do it.

Reaching into my bag, I take out one of my brother's sticker albums. I've already worked out it will be small enough for Joe to slip into his pocket, although I've also told myself that I might not give it to him. Just show him. As he reaches for it, his hand brushes mine. An electric shock passes through me. So violent I can hardly stay standing. What am I doing? Luckily, Tony's back was to us. I can't see a camera but what if it's hidden?

Even so, I've just crossed the divide that my boss and the officer had warned me about. I have committed an offense. Given a present to a prisoner for the simple reason that he reminds me of my brother. My reasoning is full of flaws. I can no longer comfort my brother, but I can comfort this other man instead. Yet in so doing, I have risked my entire career. My life . . .

As for that brush of the hand, it was accidental. At least, that's what I tell myself. Besides, Joe is looking away as though it never happened.

As Tony and I sign out in the office and make our way along the corridors and through the double-locked doors, I am convinced I'm going to be called back. Someone will tap me on the shoulder. I'll be fired on the spot.

So why do I now, as we leave the front gates, feel a thrill zip through me?

"Thought that went quite well, considering," says Tony Gordon, running his hands through his hair as we finally find ourselves outside in the car park.

I gulp in the fresh air. "I didn't see any cameras in the room. Did you?"

"Didn't you hear the officer warning us before we went in? They're out of action at present until new ones are fitted — part of a security review." Then Tony looks at me sharply. "Why?"

I shrug. "Just wondered."

For the second time in my life, I tell myself, I'm a criminal.

16
CARLA

"Carla! Carla! Come and play! Come and play!"

The little girl bobbing up and down in front of her at the playground had sticking-out teeth with a thick silver band across them, and ears that sprang out on either side of her head as though God had planted them at the wrong angle.

If this had been her old school, thought Carla, this girl would have been teased mercilessly. But instead, she was one of the most popular in the class! More important, she was also really nice to everyone. Including Carla. And she even had a daddy who had come from Italy many years ago. Just like her Mamma!

When she'd started at the convent, Carla had been so terrified that she could barely put one foot in front of the other. Term had started ages ago. Everyone else would already know each other. They'd be bound to hate her. But as soon as she'd walked through the gates with the statue of Our Blessed Mary looking down at her, Carla felt calmer. Carla's new friend made sure she was included at recess. It was, thought Carla happily as she joined in the skipping game, as though all her dreams had come true.

Even the nun-teachers were nice, and they approved of the way Carla knew how to cross herself at the right place in morning assembly. "What a lovely voice," said one nun when she heard Carla sing "The Lord Is My Shepherd" with a little tremor. And when she got stuck on long division, another nun sat down with her and explained exactly what to do.

"I see," murmured Carla. Now it all made sense!

No one told her she was stupid.

There were only two problems. "We're even now," Larry had whispered when he'd come over last night. "I had to ask a lot of favors to get you here. So no asking for anything else. Do you understand me?"

Did a new school equal a woman in the car who wasn't Mamma? Carla wasn't sure. It wasn't the kind of sum she could ask her new teachers about.

The other problem wasn't as big, but

something had to be done about it. After all, *no one* had a Charlie at school! Instead, everyone had kitty pencil cases. Soft furry ones in pink with plastic eyes that rolled and real whiskers made of plastic.

No asking for anything else, Larry had said. But she wanted a kitty! She needed one. Otherwise she'd be different with a capital *D* all over again.

"If my daddy was alive, he would buy me a kitty case," Carla confided to her new friend Maria as they sipped their soup, taking care to tip the bowl away from themselves as instructed. They had a proper dining room at the convent, with wooden tables instead of plastic ones that wobbled. They also had to sit up nicely and wait until everyone was served.

Maria leaned forward, the little gold crucifix swaying around her neck, and crossed herself. "How long has your daddy been in heaven?"

"Since I was a baby." Carla stole another wistful look at her friend's kitty pencil case, which was sitting on her lap. It was even rumored that Sister Mercy had one, too, that she kept in her office.

There was a light touch on her hand. "My uncle gave me a kitty for my birthday without realizing I already had one. I keep it as a spare at home. You can have it if you want."

"Really?" Carla felt a thrill of excitement followed by a heaviness in her heart. "But everyone will think I have stolen it."

"Why should they?" Maria frowned. "If they do, I will say it is a present. When is your birthday?"

"December the ninth," she replied promptly.

"That's not far away!" Her friend with the braces smiled toothily. "Then it can be a present. I got a new bike when it was *my* birthday."

Maria was as good as her word. The very next day, she brought in a brand-new kitty pencil case with soft pink fur and rolling black eyes.

"My very own kitty!" So warm. So comforting against her cheek.

Charlie scowled. That was all very well, but he should have talked more, like the old Charlie. It was time to move on. Now she could be like all the others!

That afternoon, they had Art. There were more paints and crayons at this school. Carla loved it! Maybe, if she listened really carefully to the instructions, she might grow up to be a real artist like Ed.

At the moment, though, they were making

a collage by cutting out pictures from magazines and sticking them on a giant roll of paper. It was going to be part of the Advent display, and all the parents would be coming! Mamma was even trying to get time off.

"May I have a pair of scissors?" asked Carla casually.

The nun — one of the younger ones — handed them to her carefully, holding the blade away from Carla. "Be very careful, dear, won't you?"

Carla treated the nun to one of her prettiest smiles. "Certainly, Sister Agnes."

She waited a little while before putting up her hand. "Please may I go to the bathroom?"

Sister Agnes, who was busy cutting around the Virgin Mary for another pupil, nodded. Now was her chance!

Quickly, Carla grabbed Charlie with one hand and the scissors in the other. Holding her breath, she ran down the corridor toward the bathroom. Then, shutting herself in one of the cubicles, she snipped off Charlie's head. He didn't make a sound, although his face, severed from the rest of his body, stared reproachfully up at her. Then she cut his body in half. Still nothing. Finally, she stuffed his three bits into the bin at the side that read Sanitary. (No one knew what that was exactly, although it was rumored that the older girls placed blood inside as a penance for sins like kissing boys.)

After that, Carla pulled the chain to make it sound as though she had gone, washed her hands and walked back to the classroom, holding the scissors by the side of her swinging, pleated brown skirt. Quietly, she slid back into her seat and began cutting out a picture of baby Jesus in his crib.

Then she lined up at the desk to take another picture from the pile of magazines and papers.

"What does this word mean?" asked the girl in front of her. She was pointing to a picture of a boy and some writing underneath: M U R D E R.

Carla listened intently. She liked the way that questions were encouraged at this school. No one teased you for asking things. You could learn a lot.

"Dear, dear. That shouldn't be there. Let me take it away."

"Murder," piped up another girl who was near the front of the queue. "That's what it spells."

"But what is it?"

"Murder, dear, is when someone takes

away the life of another, just as they took away the life of our dear Lord. It is a sin. A grave sin."

Carla heard her voice rise into the shocked classroom air. "Does it have to be the life of a person?"

Sister Agnes shook her head. "No, dear. It applies to the life of all the dear Lord's creatures. Look at Saint Francis and how he cared for every living being."

Carla felt bile rising into her mouth. Charlie had been a living being. She had murdered the new Charlie just because he was "old-fashioned" and because her friend had pitied her.

"Is there anything people can do to say sorry for murder?" she asked in a small voice.

Sister Agnes's forehead erupted into a field of frowns. "They can pray." Then she crossed herself. "But there are some crimes that God cannot forgive."

The nightmares began again after that. Sometimes Carla saw the new Charlie crawling around heaven in three pieces, his head looking for his other end. Sometimes she saw him staring at her. *You murdered me. You murdered me.*

Sometimes it was the old Charlie, which

was even worse.

"What is wrong, my little one?" Mamma kept asking. "You are happy at school, yes?"

She nodded. "Very happy."

"Your friends, they are kind to you." Mamma picked up the pink kitty pencil case that Carla was about to put in her bag. "And the nuns, they teach you good manners. You must stop dreaming about the old school now. Thanks to Larry, it is a thing of the past."

If Mamma wanted to believe that her nightmares were about the old school, there was no need to tell her the truth. At least that's what kitty told her. *I am your friend now. You must not worry about Charlie.*

So Carla tried. But it was not as easy as it sounded. She'd often noticed before that when she learned a new word, it began to appear everywhere. It was the same with this new word. *Murder.* Carla began to spot it on newspapers in the bus. She heard it on the television. And it kept coming into her dreams, night after night.

Meanwhile, she and Mamma had to get an earlier bus so Mamma could get into work before anyone else and borrow some of the new lipsticks to try out at home.

One morning, Lily got on at the same

time! Carla was beside herself with excitement.

"Do you like my new uniform?" she asked, smoothing down her brown blazer. "It had to come from a special shop and it cost a lot of money. Luckily Larry —"

"Tsk," said Mamma sharply. "You must not bother Lily. Look, she is working."

"It's all right." Lily put down her big pile of papers and gave Carla a lovely smile, which also included Mamma. "It's only homework, like you have to do."

Carla peered at the papers. "Is it arithmetic? I could help you if you like. I didn't understand it at my old school, but now the nuns have explained it and . . ." Her voice trailed away.

"What is the matter?" asked Mamma.

Lily was hastily putting the papers away in her bag. Too late. Carla had already seen that scary word.

Murder.

What was it doing in Lily's homework? Did that mean her friend had killed someone? A real person? Not just a pencil case?

A cold shiver crawled down the middle of her back.

"Nice people aren't always as good as they seem," the Mother Superior had said at assembly only the other day. "The devil can creep into their skin. We must all be vigilant."

Carla hadn't known what *vigilant* meant until she looked it up in the *Children's Dictionary.* Now she edged away. Was it possible that Lily, who helped her to bake cakes and let her lick out the bowl, was really bad? Was that why she was always arguing with Ed? Because he thought she was bad, too?

"What is the matter?" Mamma repeated.

"Nothing." Carla looked out the window toward the park, where the last of the red and yellow leaves had fallen from the trees.

Suddenly Lily didn't seem so nice after all.

Maybe — what a scary thought — she was just being nice to Carla so she could hurt her, too.

After that, Carla always got a tummy ache on Sundays. "I want to stay at home," she told Mamma the first time.

"But Lily and Ed are expecting you."

Carla rolled over onto her side and made a groaning noise. "Lily is always doing her homework and Ed makes me sit still so he can draw me. I don't want to go."

Mamma begged and cajoled, but it was no good. *Stick to your story,* urged kitty, her black beady eyes rolling. *She will have to believe you eventually. Listen! It's working already. Now she is on the phone to Larry, saying she can't see him because you are sick.*

Later in the afternoon, Carla felt well enough to go to the park. But Mamma was not happy. "Your stomachache has gone very fast," she observed.

The following Sunday, though, Carla's stomachache began again. This time, Larry came around, even though she was sick. He sat on the edge of her bed. His face was solemn. "What do you think would help your tummy feel better?" he asked quietly.

Maybe a bike, said kitty next to her. A pink one like Maria's. He still owes you after seeing him in the car with that woman.

"Maybe a bike," repeated Carla. "A pink one. With a bell. And a basket."

Larry nodded. "We will see what happens for your birthday on Tuesday, shall we?"

Carla felt a little catch in her throat.

"You will be ten then, I think."

She nodded.

"Old enough to stop playing childish games." Larry's voice was low but firm. "After this, there will be no more silliness. Do you hear me?"

17
LILY

December 2000

Despite my brave words to my husband — "I can look after myself, thank you" — I am shaken by the anonymous note and everything that's gone on since. Earlier today, I found myself breaking my vow as I walked to the bus stop. Something made me look back. It's dark on these nippy winter mornings, and there is ample opportunity for someone to hide in the shadows of the bushes.

But I couldn't see anyone.

I haven't seen Carla for some time now either. I hope her tummy ache wasn't something more serious. We've missed her, Ed and I. Missed the buffer she has become between us, the distraction that means we don't have to talk to each other. Missed the role she plays as a muse for Ed — his new portrait of her is really coming along — and the permission it gives me to work on the case uninterrupted.

There's little time in my life to do anything else. "The court has allowed the appeal and we have a retrial," Tony Gordon rings to tell me. "The date is set." He sounds excited but also slightly apprehensive. "March 15. Doesn't give us much time, but they're catching up on their backlog. Prepare to cancel Christmas."

I suspect he's not joking. The berries on the holly trees are already out in force when I walk past them every morning.

Red for blood. Red for anger. Red for the jacket that Daniel was wearing that night.

"Christmas is like a battlefield with mince pies thrown in," my brother had told me once. I had the feeling that this was something he'd heard, but he told it as though he'd made it up himself.

Either way, he's right. Ed wants us to go to his parents' for the day. I want him to go to mine. "They don't have anyone else," I point out. We still haven't come to an agreement.

As I speak, I wonder how Joe Thomas will spend the holiday. Will anyone visit *him*? I also wish — too late — that I had never given him Daniel's old sticker album during our last meeting. I'd crossed the line. What had gotten into me?

Today's visit has to be different.

Joe Thomas's eyes are blazing. He's almost snarling as he speaks. "Someone put a threatening note under your door?"

On the way to prison that morning, Tony had declared this was the time to come clean about it. "We've got to squeeze him now that we've got a court date," he says, his mouth tightening. "Get things moving. Provoke him, see if we can get more out of him. If there are any holes."

It's doing that all right. Joe's jaw muscles are jumping. His hands, on the table between Tony and me, are clenched into fists.

"What did the note say?"

"If you try to help that man, you will be sorry."

Tony pronounces each word very clearly.

"I ought to add," says Tony with a half laugh, "that it wasn't spelled very well."

"Leave it to me." Joe's eyes grow darker, if that is possible. I've read about eyes changing color before, but thought it was poetic license. "I'll put out feelers."

Tony nods. "Thank you."

So that's why, I suddenly realize. Tony wants to see if Joe has contacts on the outside. By playing on what my barrister has already referred to as "the client's obvious empathy with you," he's confirming his suspicions.

"How else could your feelers help us win this case?" asks Tony, leaning across the metal table, rocking it so one of the legs comes down against my leg, ripping my tights.

Instantly, Joe sits back in his chair, arms folded. "What do you mean?"

"Those figures that were sent to you in the post," says Tony softly, "they came from a mole, didn't they? They must have. Someone working for the gas people or the boiler company or somewhere in the industry. Are you paying them, or do they owe you a favor?"

Joe's face is set. Suddenly emotionless. I've seen it before on my husband's canvases. An outline. Nothing more. Then Ed fills in the feelings: a curve of the eyebrow to indicate disbelief or amusement, a curl of the lip to imply irritation or longing. Joe's face does none of these.

"Why would I do that?" he asks. "And why do you assume I'll tell you if it's true, even though it isn't?"

"Because," snaps Tony, "you need to help us in order to help yourself. I'm going to give you some time to think about this, Joe. When I come here next, I'd like you to tell me who your mole is and then we might stand a chance of winning your case. And before you start bleating about honor among thieves, I want to ask you something. Do you really want to spend another Christmas inside this place?"

He looks around the bare room with its DO NOT REMOVE notice next to the clock and the torn linoleum on the floor. "Because I wouldn't, in your position."

As we leave the room, I shoot Joe an *I'm sorry* look. I can't help it. His reaction to the note has helped to convince me once and for all that he's innocent. You can't fake that kind of thing.

"Thanks for the pictures," he whispers as I pass him.

I freeze, hoping the officer standing by the open door hasn't heard.

"I don't get many gifts in here."

I don't dare reply.

Then Joe's eyes go down to my legs; he's noticed the rip in my tights. He frowns. "You need to do something about that." And then he storms off down the corridor in the opposite direction as though I have personally offended him.

Nervously, I follow Tony down the corridor, past men staring. I wish I could look as confident as my colleague with his straight shoulders and arrogant air.

As we hand in our passes at security, I'm still trembling. "You did very well," said Tony, placing a hand briefly on my shoulder. "Prison isn't easy. Don't worry. Joe and I have built up an understanding now. I won't need you to come with me on future visits. A secretary will be enough. The next time you'll see him is when we're all in court."

I glance back at the high wall with its rolls of barbed wire still visible through the window. Not see Joe until the court hearing? I feel an irrational rush of disappointment. But there's something else, too. He'll think I don't care about him. And suddenly I realize that I do. Very much.

Joe Thomas represents much more than my chance to save an innocent man.

My actions could also help to make up for Daniel.

The phone rings when I am deep in the middle of a file. Not the ones that I should be looking at: cases that my boss has piled on my already overloaded desk, about fraud and battery and shoplifting. But Joe's.

It's all very well Tony saying that he would take over from here, but I've got to carry on at my end in the office. Surely the more information I can give him, the better? And there is so much. Every day, the post brings more letters from people who've read about the impending case in the papers. A woman who had been burned horrifically when she'd taken a shower. A man whose face is scarred for life. A father who had almost placed his toddler in a bath where he had taken great care to run the cold along with the hot, only to find that the cold itself was boiling.

The case is building up, and with it, the press fever. Time and time again, reporters call, begging for updates — anything that will add fuel to what might become a class action.

I've just hung up the phone on a particularly persistent female journalist. When it rings again within seconds, I presume it's her.

"Yes? What?" I bark down the line, realizing as I do so that I'm beginning to sound like my boss. It isn't a pleasant thought.

"Your Joe Thomas has come up with the goods." It's Tony Gordon's smooth, deep voice. "We've got him. The writer of your note."

My mouth goes dry.

"Who is it?" I ask.

"The victim's uncle."

The victim! I might be a lawyer but the word still seems cold to me. I glance down at the folders on my desk. Sarah Evans smiles glossily up at me. She was a person. A woman who shared Joe Thomas's bed. He may have been a control freak. She may have fallen out of love with him. Or she may not have known exactly what her feelings were for this man. Rather like how I feel confused about Ed.

"Do you mean Sarah?"

Tony Gordon's voice sounds amused. "I used to be like you once, you know." Then his tone hardens. "Let me give you a piece of advice, Lily. Don't get too involved with your cases. Keep your distance. It's more professional."

I glance across the room at my boss in his glass office who's holding the phone and gesticulating wildly at me. "I've got to go," I say.

"The man's been cautioned. But I still want you to be careful. This case could release a flood of lawsuits. We are going to upset a lot of people, including the nutters who are always out there. Do you under-stand? Change your route to work. Lock your flat. Make sure that new husband of yours looks after you."

I'm not sleeping. I'm not eating. I'm hardly talking to Ed.

Our previous intimacy has become lost in this manic buildup toward the case. I'm home even later, especially now that the Christmas lights are up on Regent Street and the traffic is slower because everyone is gawping. Ed and I no longer have discussions about what he might want for dinner. We both take it for granted that he'll sort out his own. At least he seems to have cut back again on his drinking. That's because he wants a "clearer head" when he's painting in the evening. It's for that reason, I tell myself, that I decided not to tell him about Tony's warning. I don't want him worrying, getting distracted.

"Your mother rang," Ed says one evening when I get in just before eleven p.m.

"It's urgent," he adds before returning to our little kitchen table. His sketchbooks are everywhere. Pictures of a young girl twisting her hair. Skipping through the park. Jumping over puddles. Reading a book with a cardigan casually draped around her shoulders. Cooking in the kitchen. Another girl with an expressionless face. All studies for a bigger painting.

An unexpected flash of jealousy shoots through me. I'd like time to have a creative passion, too. But instead, I am stuck. Stuck in a case that is too big. A web of what I suspect is a mixture of lies and truths that I — with my limited experience — am expected to unravel.

Mum picks up the phone immediately. In my mind, I'm back home. She'll already have decorated the hall with tinsel woven around the banisters, mistletoe hanging from the central cartwheel light, holly on the pictures going up the stairs, including the pastel portraits of Daniel and me when we were younger. Pretty bits and pieces on the dining room table to hide the emptiness of the unlaid fifth setting at the table. Christmas decorations waiting for me to come home, because without one child, my parents have nothing.

The weight of my responsibility hangs in my words. "Sorry it's late but I've been working."

I wait to hear Mum tell me, as she has done before, that I am working too hard. That a new husband needs his new wife to be around more. But instantly, I know before I even hear the break in her voice that something has happened.

"What is it?" I croak.

After Daniel, there was a weird relief that nothing awful — nothing worse — could ever happen again. It's a feeling I have heard others voice, too. There was a woman on the radio, not long after, who said that when her daughter died in a crash, she knew she didn't have to worry so much about her surviving son because her worst fear had already happened.

That's how I felt, too, until I hear Mum's voice.

"Is Dad all right?" I manage to say.

For a minute, I have a picture of him at the bottom of the stairs. He's slipped. Had a coronary.

"We're not ill."

Relief washes through me in the form of sweat. Ed, meanwhile, is poring over his subject with the expressionless face, but in such a manner that I suspect he is listening.

"Then what is it?"

"Merlin . . . it's Merlin. He's . . . well, he's dead."

I clutch the edge of the table for support. Ed's hand reaches out for mine. Gratefully I clutch it. "He was old . . . ," I begin.

"The vet says it looks like his food was poisoned," sobs Mum.

"Poisoned?"

Ed's face is startled as I repeat the word. "How do you know?"

My mother's voice is choked. "We found him in the paddock. There was a note on the stable door."

A note. My hands begin to shake. My heart feels as if it's beating in my throat. The hunger I was feeling when I got home has disappeared.

"What does it say?" I ask.

But already I can guess.

"It says, 'Tell your daughter to drop the case.' " Mum's voice rises with anguish. "Is this the one you told us about? The one about the boiler that's been in the papers?"

Ed is leaning forward, clearly concerned. So much so that he drops his sketchbook.

Slowly, I put down the phone. Not just because of the terrible shock over Merlin, who was my last link with Daniel apart from my parents. Nor because of the horror that someone, somewhere, has tracked down my family. Sarah Evans's uncle, perhaps? After all, he'd written the previous note.

No, I'm putting down the phone because Ed's sketchbook is open, revealing the full truth. I'd assumed the girl with the expressionless face was Carla, waiting to be filled in. Instead, Davina is laughing at me from the carpet with that glorious head of hair thrown back in victory. "I've won," she seems to be saying. "I'm the one that Ed loves. Why else would he paint me?"

18
CARLA

Carla didn't have a birthday party like all the other girls at school. There wasn't room in the flat, Mamma said. Instead, look what Larry had bought her!

In the hall outside stood the most beautiful pink bike she had ever seen. It was gleaming: almost as shiny as Larry's car. There was a bell, just as she had requested, and a little basket. And when she rode it in the park, she flew!

"You are a natural," said Larry. But he did not smile as he spoke.

The following Sunday, the phone rang twice in an hour. "When I answer," said Mamma, confused, "I can't hear anything. Perhaps it is broken. You get it next time."

Carla did. At first she heard nothing either. But just as she was about to put the phone down, there it was. Breathing.

Then her tummy ache started again.

Mamma ran her hands through her hair.

"You are just worried about those phone calls. They are probably from silly children playing games. When you get to your friend Lily's home, you will feel better."

She began to cry, thinking of the word *murder* in Lily's work papers. "I don't want to go to Lily and Ed's. I am ill."

Mamma's face grew cross. "You are a naughty girl. Do you know that?"

Carla was still resting on the sofa when Larry arrived. She could hear them whispering in the hall.

"Making it up, I am sure of it . . . always better on Monday . . . only says she is ill . . . no temperature . . ."

How tired she felt. Her thoughts began to drift away. But then a word began to beat in her head as if it had been hidden and was now coming out to upset her.

Murder!
Murder!

That was the evil word she had seen on Lily's papers. The more she thought of it, the more Carla became convinced that Lily was going to hurt her, too.

"What are you saying?"

Opening her eyes, she saw Mamma looking down at her.

"You have had a nightmare, cara mia. But

it is over now. You must get up. Guess who has come to see you?"

"Hello, Carla!"

It was Ed.

She'd forgotten how simpatico his eyes were. After all, it wasn't he who was bad. It was Lily . . .

"I was hoping to begin a new portrait today." His eyes were really shining now. "And I would like to enter it in a competition. With your mamma's permission of course."

"A competition!" Mamma repeated the word reverently. "Do you hear, Carla?"

"But first I need another sitting." Ed's eyes were searching hers. Pleading. It made her feel big. Important. "Do you feel well enough to come over this afternoon?" He turned to Mamma. "I'm afraid Lily has got to go into work again, but I'll take great care of your daughter. Would that be all right?"

"Of course," trilled Mamma. "She was just tired, that's all."

Carla nodded. Her stomachache was not so bad now.

"Wonderful." Ed looked pleased. "Let's get started then!"

The first thing that Carla noticed when she

went into number three was a new rug on the floor of the sitting room.

"What happened to the old one?" she asked, noticing with approval that this one was a pale blue-green and not a boring brown like before.

"Lily got angry and threw coffee over it," said Ed.

"Ask him why, Carla." Lily came out of the kitchen, carrying a pile of papers. Her voice was sharp.

Lily was here after all?

Carla froze on the spot.

Ed laughed, but Carla knew he was nervous. "I thought you were going into the office," he said quietly.

"Changed my mind. I'm going to work in the bedroom instead. I lose time doing that journey." Lily smiled. But it wasn't a smile that danced in her eyes as it usually did. "That all right with you?"

"Whatever suits you best." Ed spoke in that polite way that adults seemed to use when they didn't like each other very much. Then Lily disappeared into the bedroom.

"Why don't you sit down on the sofa, Carla."

Trembling, she did as she was told. "Is Lily going to murder you?" she whispered.

Ed stared at her and then began to laugh. A lovely warm, throaty laugh that almost made her want to join in. Then he stopped. "Why do you ask that?"

Instantly, she felt foolish. "Because . . . because I saw the word 'murder' on her homework papers when we were on the bus. And I was scared . . ." Her voice began to wobble. "I thought she was going to kill me — and maybe you — and . . ."

"Shh, shh." Ed was sitting next to her now, his arm around her. "You've got the wrong end of the stick, sweetheart." Sweetheart? That's what Larry called Mamma sometimes. It felt good. As though she was grown up and not a child at all.

"Lily is a solicitor. She helps to put the world to rights." There was a snort as if Ed was disagreeing with himself.

"What does that mean?"

"It means she tries to help people who have been hurt and to look after people who have been accused of hurting others but haven't really. Do you understand?"

No, but Carla felt she ought to nod anyway so Ed wouldn't think she was stupid.

"At the moment, my wife is trying to help a man in prison who was accused of murder but is really a good person — or so she thinks."

"But why did they put him there, then?"

Ed was back behind his easel now, sketching. Carla felt cold without his arm around her. "Good question. But she is also upset because her brother's horse has died."

Carla made a face. "I'm scared of horses. One tried to bite me when we went to a farm for our school trip." Then she remembered the stain on the carpet. "Is that why Lily spilled the coffee?"

Ed began rubbing out something on the canvas. "No. That's because I . . . well, because I did something I shouldn't have done."

He sounded so sad that Carla wanted to get up and give him a comforting hug like the ones she gave Mamma when she was down.

"Please. Don't move."

So she sat still again. "Can I talk?"

His hand was moving across the page. She couldn't see it but she could hear it. "That's fine."

"I did something I shouldn't, too. I . . . I chopped up the new Charlie."

"Who?"

"My caterpillar pencil case."

"Why?"

"Because I wanted something better."

Ed's hand was moving faster. His voice

sounded like it was coming from far away, as though he wasn't really listening. "Well, we all want something better from time to time, Carla. But if we stopped to appreciate what we've got, the world might be a better place. Now take a look at this."

Jumping up, she ran to the easel. There she was! Sitting on the sofa, a smile playing on her lips. But her hands! They were twisted together, as though something was wrong, despite her happy face.

"It shows another side of you," said Ed encouragingly. "Judges get fed up with chocolate-box paintings. This one, with any luck, might just win."

Win? When that happened on television, people became famous! Carla was so excited that when she excused herself to go to the loo, she couldn't help squirting herself with the perfume on the shelf. She also dabbed on a little of Lily's lip gloss sitting next to it.

"That's a nice smell," said Ed, when she returned to her sitting position.

Carla crossed her fingers. "It's just the soap." Then, feeling very grown up thanks to the perfume and the portrait, she tried to sit up straight like a proper English lady.

The portrait had been sent to the judges of

the big competition that Ed had told them about, but it would take them a long time to pick the winner. "We will know by next year," he promised, giving her arm a quick squeeze.

Meanwhile, the whole world was in a feverish state of Christmas excitement. Mamma had come to the Nativity play where Carla and her new friend Maria were angels. Afterward, Mamma had cried and said that she wished her grandfather Nonno from Italy could see them. Then he might forgive her.

"Forgive you for what?" Carla had asked.

"You would not understand." Then Mamma began to weep.

"Larry cannot be with us at Christmas," she sniffed.

Carla's heart jumped. Good. "Why not?"

Mamma sniffed. "Because he has to be with his wife."

Then the woman in front of them on the bus turned around and gave them both such a nasty look that Mamma began crying even harder.

Maybe, thought Carla as they walked past number three, her friends might come out to see what the noise was all about.

"Can we spend Christmas with Ed and

Lily instead?" she asked. Now that Ed had explained that Lily was not a murderer, Carla liked her again. Although not quite so much. She'd upset Ed after all, and it was he who was drawing her picture.

"They are going to their own families." Mamma's arm tightened around her shoulders. "It is just you and me, my little one."

Mamma had still not run out of tears by the time that Carla had opened door number twenty-four on her Advent calendar. The Christmas tree that Carla had persuaded Mamma to buy from the market leaned sadly against the wall. Bare.

"We must decorate it," she had pleaded. But Mamma had forgotten to buy tinsel, and besides, they didn't have enough money. So instead she had put her biggest white gym sock at the bottom of her bed.

At the bottom of the tree there were now two presents.

"Larry gave them to us," said Mamma when she saw Carla looking.

Then she clutched Carla's hand. "We must go and say thank you to him."

But it was dark and cold outside. Mamma said that didn't matter. She would stop crying — "I promise, my little one!" — if only she could walk past the house where Larry lived. ("I find the address once in his briefcase when he is not looking.") So they walked for miles and miles because the bus didn't come, as it was a holiday and drivers need to celebrate, too. Some of the houses Carla and Mamma passed were so big that they could have fit ten of their apartments inside.

And then finally they stopped at a tall white house that went up and up into the sky. Through the window on the second floor shone a light.

Tears began to stream down Mamma's face again. "If only I could be in there, with Larry."

Carla tried to pull her mother away. "Just one moment," Mamma said. But she wouldn't move. Bored, Carla kicked at some leaves while she waited.

"No!" Mamma was gasping, her hand to her throat. Carla followed her gaze. In the window stood a little girl, looking down at them.

"Who's that?" Carla asked.

"It is his daughter."

Really? "Is she my age?"

"A little older." Mama's tears were flowing faster.

"What happens to her and her mamma on Sundays?"

Mamma's voice came out as a sharp cry

as if she was in pain. "We are his family then. *They* belong to the other days. Come, we will go now."

Together, they made their way back through the streets with the street lamps and the decorations in other people's windows, back to the naked Christmas tree and the two lonely presents.

"What are you doing?" asked Mamma as Carla put hers in the bin without opening it.

"I don't want it." Of course she wanted as many presents as possible. But not his. Larry had to go, Carla told herself silently. He was not good for Mamma. Somehow, she had to find a way to get rid of him. Just as she had done with Charlie.

I'm glad I'm not dying at Christmas.

Bad things shouldn't happen when the rest of the world is rejoicing.

It makes it doubly hard for those who grieve.

And the memories spoil every Christmas after that.

Is there ever a good time to die?

I certainly never thought it would be like this.

A strange layering of pain and reflection. Of accusations against others and recriminations against myself.

And of course fear. Because I suspect, from the small sounds around me, that someone is still here. In the house.

19
LILY

Christmases have always been big at home. "Daniel loves it," my mother always used to say by way of explanation for the ten-foot-high tree and the stack of presents below. We didn't have a lot of money, but my mother would save for Christmas all year. One time, my brother got a Hornby train set, which he proceeded to take apart and then put back together again, "just to see how it was made." It took three days, during which he refused to participate in any family meals, including Christmas lunch, because he was "busy."

No one tried to dissuade him. It was impossible to change his mind once it was set. Maybe that's why, in the early days, Daniel got whatever he wanted. It was only when his wish list became illegal that my parents started to lay down boundaries. And by then it was too late.

What will it be like this year? I wonder as

Ed and I wait at Exeter station for Dad to pick us up. In the past few years, Mum has had a glazed, bright, *it's all right* look firmly fixed to her face from the second she wakes. It fools no one. Then, when she's had her third gin before lunch, she'll start talking about Daniel in the present tense. "He'll love these new lights, don't you think?" she'll inquire brightly, as if my brother is going to come downstairs any minute. Dad will wear a forced air of resignation. At the same time, he'll look after Mum with a tenderness that smacks of guilt. When a couple goes through a tragedy, they either become closer than before or drift apart. I suppose I ought to be grateful my parents finally chose the former.

It's cold here in the station waiting room, with the wind blasting through the door. I shiver. And not just because of poor Merlin, who died because of me. Or because of his unknown murderer. (Sarah's uncle had a firm alibi according to the police, although, as Tony said, he may have put someone up to it.)

No. It's because sometimes I wonder if I'm living up to my name. Lilies stain if their pollen brushes something. The recipient is tarnished with a substance that is difficult to remove. It seems to me that I stain whomever I try to love. Daniel, Merlin, Ed . . . Who's next?

Noticing my distress, Ed tries to put his arm around my shoulder, but I shrug it off. How does he expect me to react when he's been drawing the face of the woman he was once engaged to?

"Do you still care for her?" I'd yelled, throwing my mug in anger and getting coffee all over the rug.

"No." He seemed genuinely perplexed, like a lost small boy. "She . . . she just keeps coming up in my work."

"Work?" I'd screamed. "Advertising is meant to be your work." I waved my hand angrily at his sketch of Davina, her head back, laughing.

I couldn't help myself. "Are you having an affair with her?"

"When would I have the time? But even if I was, would you even care? All you're worried about is this case of yours. Not our marriage." Ed was angry now, too.

Before we knew it, the argument turned into a screaming match — something that seemed to be happening more and more.

Since then, we've barely spoken, save for making Christmas arrangements. The day itself at my parents' in Devon. Boxing Day with his, farther up the motorway in

Gloucestershire.

Ed's warm hand is a peace offering. But I'm too wound up in my own thoughts. Daniel. Merlin. The note.

"Here's your father," Ed announces, relief in his voice because we will no longer have to stand silently in the cold wind.

"First Christmas as a married couple, eh?" says Dad, beaming, opening the doors of his old Land Rover for us to get in.

I can't even look at Ed as we exchange pleasantries. All I know is that my parents will be using our sham marriage as an excuse to be cheerful themselves — to forget the empty place at the table and the saddle still hanging on the rack in the boot room because no one can bear to throw it away.

Part of me longs to tell them how miserable I am. But I can't. I owe it to them to make up for what happened in whatever way I can.

"Darlings!" My mother is at the door. Her eyes are unnaturally bright. The glass she's put down on the hall table is half full. "How lovely to see you."

"Great tree," says Ed, taking in the monstrosity behind him that reaches up through the circular staircase to the third floor. "How did you get it in?"

My mother beams. "Daniel helped us.

He'll be down in a minute. Now come on in and make yourselves at home."

"What's going on?" I hiss to Dad as soon as I get a chance.

He looks miserable. "You know what she's like at this time of the year."

"But she's getting worse, Dad. Surely she should be getting better?"

Ed, to his credit, is every inch the gentleman. When Mum gets out the photograph album showing Daniel and me down the years, he appears genuinely interested.

But his questions — "And where was this taken?" — are directed toward my mother. He ignores me.

At midnight mass in our small village, people I haven't seen for ages come up to embrace me and shake hands with Ed for the first time. Thanks to my mother-in-law's insistence that "all Macdonalds" get married in the small family chapel on their estate, there had only been room for immediate relations. "So this is the lucky man," says one of the old boys who used to prop up the bar at the local every night when I lived at home. "We all love Lily, you know." Then he claps Ed on the shoulder. "Mind you take care of her."

This time it's me who can't look at him.

Instead, we trudge in silence behind my parents toward home, breathing in the salty air. When I was a teenager, I'd itched to get away from this place, scorning it for being so "parochial." Only now do I realize how precious it is, how touching the concern for everyone in the flock. And how this little town represents real, solid values. Not outright lies or half-truths or games — whichever way you see them.

Joe Thomas seems another world away.

"Now, who's going to check on Merlin?" asks my mother brightly as Dad fumbles for the backdoor key under the stone wall. "Someone needs to make sure he hasn't knocked his water bucket over again."

"Mum," I begin gently. "Merlin's . . ."

But Dad steps in quickly. "I will, love. You go off to bed. Nothing to worry about. The turkey's already in the oven and this young couple will want to go to bed."

I shiver. It's not just Dad's lies or our couple charade. It's also fear. I told Dad to be careful about security after the note. Yet here he is, still leaving the key in its usual place. Where anyone can get it.

In the morning I'll talk to him, I tell myself as I get into bed while Ed is still in the bathroom. By the time he is finished I have turned off the lights and am pretending to be asleep.

"I'm sorry." My husband's voice clearly indicates that he isn't fooled by my turned back and pretense of even breathing.

I sit up, my back against the pillow. "I presume we're talking about Davina here. But are you sorry you're in love with her? Or sorry that you married me? Or sorry that . . ."

"I'm sorry about Daniel. It must be very hard for you all."

Ed's words sink into the silence. Would he say that if he knew the full story?

"I don't want to talk about it," I say now, turning away from him.

Then I sleep. Easily. Deeply. The best sleep I've had for years. I dream that I'm running along the sand after Daniel. He's still young. Laughing. Jumping in and out of the water. Picking up shells, which he organizes in precise order on the windowsill in his bedroom. Then someone in my dream moves them. Daniel is screaming because they are spoiled. He's throwing the shells out the window and now he's collecting new ones all over again . . .

I wake with a start. It's night. There's a strange scratching sound on the roof. A seagull, perhaps. I wonder what Joe Thomas is doing now. Is he awake? Going over those figures again and again? Deciding whether to reveal the secret source who sent them to him?

And Tony Gordon. What might he be doing? Is he in bed with his wife? He rarely speaks about his personal life. Only once has he mentioned a child, and that was when he had to take a call from his wife about a school play that he'd missed.

Tony Gordon, I suspect, is a man who can compartmentalize quite easily.

My restlessness wakes Ed. He reaches over and strokes my back. Then his hands reach lower. I don't move. Tears begin to run down my face. I don't know if he thinks it's me or Davina. Self-respect dictates that I should move away, waiting until we are both awake so we know what we are doing. But my dream about Daniel has disturbed me. I am lonely and sad. And so I find myself allowing Ed inside me. But when I arrive on a wave of illicit excitement, it is not him in my head.

In the morning, I wash my husband away in the old-fashioned bath, which has a crack in the enamel from where Daniel once removed the plug-hole strainer and stuffed a giant blue and silver marble down the pipe "to see if it would go through."

It had cost a great deal to unblock the system.

"Happy Christmas," says Ed, handing me a shiny red package.

Does he even remember making love to me in the night? Does he feel consumed with guilt for imagining Davina?

The only way I can justify my own fantasy is that I am so wrapped up in my guilt over Daniel that I cannot allow myself to be happy. Self-destruction. Therefore I imagine someone I am forbidden, professionally, to have sex with. I unwrap the red paper, and open the box inside. A pen. I'd been secretly hoping for more perfume. My honeymoon bottle is almost empty. How is it that an artist can be so observant one minute and so blind the next?

"You're always writing. Thought it might come in useful."

"Thank you," I say, handing over the package I had hidden in my case. It's a box of oil pastels. Ed picks them out, one by one. His face is like that of a child. "This is great. Thank you."

"You can paint some more Davinas now." I just can't stop myself.

His face darkens. "We need to leave early tomorrow," he says coldly. "Otherwise we'll

242

be late for my parents."

My childhood home is lovely. But when I first saw Ed's family seat, shortly before our wedding, I couldn't believe it. It was virtually a mansion.

"It's actually not as big as it looks," he said as I sat in the car, willing myself to get out while staring in awe at the Elizabethan stone, the turrets, the family arms over the front door, the mullioned windows and the lawns that extended as far as the eye could see. Who was he kidding? Himself? Artists, I was beginning to learn, were good at deception. Then again, so are lawyers. Both have to act. To play the part. To get inside someone else's soul.

The truth is that a large part of Ed's home is sectioned off for the public; its visitor fees go toward the upkeep. The other part — the finger-numbingly subzero one — is where his parents live, as well as a brother and his wife. Another brother works in Hong Kong and couldn't come back for Christmas this year.

I'm grateful. This lot is more than enough. Ed's mother is a tall, angular, aloof woman whom I haven't seen since the wedding, and has, so far, failed to invite me to call her by her first name. Artemis. It suits her.

The brother is equally pompous, although Ed's father is polite enough, asking me about my case "with that murderer." He's clearly read up about it.

"Consorting with criminals? What an awful job you have, dear," shudders my mother-in-law over predinner drinks in the library — another freezing cold place, where the leather spines are peeling off the backs of the books. "Didn't you want to do something nicer? In my day, if we had to work, we taught or did nursing before we got married. Of course, many of my friends' daughters are in what I believe they call 'public relations,' or 'events management' . . ." Her voice trails off at Ed's look and she moves smoothly on to another topic, but the damage is done.

"I need some air," I murmur to Ed as I grab my luxurious cashmere wrap — a present from my in-laws — and make my way to the terrace overlooking the gardens. They're beautiful — I give my mother-in-law that. She spends all her time out here, apparently.

"Artemis didn't mean it."

I turn at the gentle voice behind me. It's Sophie, my sister-in-law, with a compact, snuffly toddler in her arms. Of all Ed's relatives, she is the one I like best. She seems more normal than the others and has slightly grubby fingernails, possibly because she works as a freelance garden designer. "She just says what she thinks, I'm afraid. You'll get used to it."

Little Henry is grinning at me. He has a wide gap in his front teeth.

"I'm not sure I want to get used to it," I say.

Sophie frowns. "What do you mean?"

"I don't know why Ed married me." I know I'm being indiscreet but I can't stop. Maybe it's the prelunch sherry I gulped down in a desperate need for warmth as well as to curb my nerves. "He clearly still has feelings for Davina. So why did he choose me instead of her?"

There's a short silence during which I see a distinct look of uncertainty flitting across my sister-in-law's face. The toddler struggles to get down. Sophie gently deposits her son on the ground.

"You know about the trust?"

"What trust?"

"You're joking, right?" She takes in my face. "You're not, are you? Shit. He told us you knew . . ." She seems genuinely concerned.

"Please," I beg, "tell me. Don't I have a

right to know?"

There's a quick glance over her shoulder. No one is there. The toddler is now sitting at her feet, eating clumps of frozen earth from a plant pot, but she hasn't noticed and I don't want to stop her now. "Ed was heartbroken when Davina dumped him to get engaged to some banker she'd been seeing on the q.t. for ages. Poor old Ed really loved her — sorry — but it wasn't just that. Time was running out. Henry, spit that out or . . ."

"Time was running out for what?"

"I'm trying to tell you. The trust. Henry, spit it out *now.* It was set up by the boys' grandparents. They all have to get married by the age of thirty and stay married for at least five years or they won't get their inheritance. Sounds totally ridiculous, I know, but apparently Artemis's father has a thing about men who don't get married. His brother was the other way inclined, if you get my meaning, and it brought terrific scandal on the family in those days. I knew about it, but Andrew and I would have got married when we did anyway, trust or no trust."

I can't believe it.

"We got married just before Ed's thirtieth birthday," I say slowly. "I thought it was fast, but I was flattered that he was so keen . . ."

"And he *was*, I'm sure of it."

"Well, I'm not. I was always amazed that Ed had fallen for me. I'm all wrong for him. Why didn't he go for someone more suitable?"

"Have you been listening to that mother-in-law of ours? Honestly, Lily. You've got to have more faith in yourself. Anyone can see Ed loves you. You're just what this family needs. Someone normal."

Normal! Hah! The irony almost makes me miss what she says next.

"When Ed first told us about you, we were shocked, of course. Especially with the wedding coming so soon. But when we met you, we saw why he'd chosen you. You're just the kind of girl he needs. Reliable. Attractive without being a floozy. No offense meant. I said that if it didn't work out — Henry, stop that!"

"You said what?" I say urgently.

She has the grace to look embarrassed. "I said that if it didn't work out, he could always divorce you when the five years were up. It's a bit of a joke among us trust wives."

"Right." I am so stunned I don't know what else to say.

"Come on." She pats me on the arm as we turn back to the house. "You've got to see the bright side."

"Are you joking?"

"Not entirely. Let me put it another way. It means we all stand to inherit quite a bit when the grandfather dies. He's in a home now, by the way. Dementia, poor man. And don't blame Ed." She says the latter more seriously. "He was up against the wall. You should have heard how Artemis was going on about losing all that money if he didn't get a move on. Mind you, I agree he could have told you."

If he had, I wouldn't have accepted his proposal, as he'd have been well aware. The whole thing sounds insane in today's world. But then Ed's family doesn't come from my kind of background. I've always known that. I just didn't realize how far apart we were when it came to telling the truth.

Or how close.

"Of course," continues my sister-in-law, "it was a real setback when Davina broke off her engagement to the other chap . . ."

My skin breaks out into goose pimples. "When?"

"Henry! When you were on honeymoon . . ."

Now, finally, it's all falling into place.

"I see," I say numbly.

"What do you see?"

248

It's Ed, coming up from behind. Looking every inch like a former public schoolboy in his navy jacket, crisp white shirt and beige chinos. But inside, he's no better than a criminal. He's deceived me.

"You married me so you didn't lose out on your inheritance," I whisper. "But you really wanted Davina. No wonder you were so upset when we came back from our honeymoon and you found out she'd canceled her marriage." Alarm is written all over his face. For one minute there, I had hoped this ridiculous story was a pack of lies. Yet my husband is disconcertingly quiet; he makes no attempt to deny the charge. Like all good lawyers, I've got to the truth. But there's no pleasure in it.

"And now, clearly," I continue furiously, "she wishes she'd waited for you — and you for her."

He takes my arm. "Let's walk."

Sophie has gone, along with her son. We pick our way along the gravel path by the early snowdrops. Ed's voice is raw. "She shouldn't have told you."

"Yes. She should." I shake off his arm. "You married me for money. But I could have been anyone who was around, just as long as it was before your birthday."

He looks away, down toward the lake. "It

wasn't like that. No, I didn't want to lose my inheritance. I knew when it came it would allow me to give up my job and let me paint. Maybe start my own gallery. But at the same time, I was genuinely attracted to you. There was something about your face when you told me your brother was dead and . . . and how he'd died. I tried to draw it, after that first night, but I couldn't do it. It was as if your grief was too deep."

"You married me out of pity?"

He is pleading now. "That's not what I meant. I married you because you intrigued me and because I could tell you were a good, kind person." His face crumples. "Look how you insisted on mopping up your wine instead of pretending it wasn't you who had spilled it. Davina would just have left it. You're a much better person than her. Honest."

Honest? I'm tempted, as I've been on so many occasions, to tell him everything. The guilt lies like a heavy stone inside me. But if I'm upset about the trust, how would Ed feel if he knew what I had done?

I try to take a step back, but before I can do so, Ed's hands are cupping my face. "You're a beautiful person, Lily. Inside and out. And the most amazing thing is that you just don't see it. That was another reason I fell for you. You're also brave. Loyal. Clever. I know I haven't been very nice about you working so hard, but I'm actually really proud of you for helping the underdogs in life, like this prisoner of yours."

You've got it all wrong, I want to scream out.

"So why have you been so horrid to me?"

"Because . . . because I was hurt when you clearly didn't want me. You know. Physically. It made me feel rejected. And then Davina made it clear she was still interested and I was . . . well, tempted. Nothing happened. I swear it. Then there's the case. It seems to be all you think about and . . ."

There's a dullness in my chest. The number of divorced solicitors in my practice alone bear testament to the fact that law takes its toll on family life.

He runs his hands through his hair. "The thing is, Lily, maybe we did get together fast. But I've gotten to know you better now and . . . well, I want to be with you. I really do. I love you."

Does he? Or is it the money that's talking? Five years of marriage to get the inheritance.

"Tell me," he says, pulling me toward him, "that you love me, too?"

Love? What is love? Surely I'm the last

person to answer that one.

"We could try again," he says slowly. Gently he tilts my chin so I have to look straight at him. It feels important not to look away. "What do you think?"

We've said this to each other before. Each time we've ended up fighting again. But right now, a pair of brown-black eyes comes into my head. *Go away*, I want to scream.

"I don't know," I say miserably to Ed. "I can't think properly. Not with this case going on."

It's true. If anything, seeing my parents this Christmas and revisiting the empty stable have made me more determined than ever to go ahead with this case. To win. To play my part in delivering justice. It's more important than my own personal life. After Daniel, it *has* to be.

Then I look down at my husband's hands, which are now holding mine. And I drop them.

"I'll give you an answer when it's over. Sorry."

20
CARLA

Carla watched Mamma cry all through Christmas Day. She cried when she unwrapped Larry's present and she cried when her fingers couldn't put it on.

At first, Carla tried to comfort her. "Let me help you with the clasp."

But then, when Mamma looked in the mirror at the silver locket around her slim neck, she cried even more.

Carla gave up. *I wonder if the queen cries,* she asked herself as she sat cross-legged in front of the television, watching Her Majesty's Christmas message.

Carla wouldn't have bothered changing channels for the queen's speech if it wasn't for her new friend at school. "We always watch it," Maria had told Carla when they were tucking into the toffees after the end-of-term carol service.

Sometimes Carla guiltily found herself wishing that she belonged to Maria's family. But at least, thanks to her friend, she now had a kitty. She had the right television program on. Now all she needed was a mother who didn't have a red, blotchy face from weeping. If Larry didn't make Mamma so unhappy, everything would be all right, Carla told herself as she watched pictures of the queen's reassuring face.

She was sure something would happen soon. She just had to be patient.

"Do you think Ed and Lily will be back now?" she asked Mamma.

Her mother shook her head.

"They are still with their families," Mamma said. "Just as we should be with ours."

Carla thought of the sparkly Christmas card of baby Jesus that they had sent to Italy and the much-hoped-for card that had not been sent back in return.

Mamma burst out into fresh tears. "It is all my fault . . ."

"Why, Mamma?"

"It just is." Then her mother's eye fell on the second package under the tree. "Are you not going to open Larry's present to you? I took it out of the bin, just in case."

Part of her didn't want anything to do with it. But another part now wondered what was inside . . .

"Go on," urged Mamma. Her eyes grew brighter. Carla knew what she was thinking — if it was a good present, it meant Larry loved her mother more than his wife and the girl they had seen through the window.

The paper was hard to undo. But eventually, she wiggled out the thing inside. It was a long, slim box. And inside that was . . .

"A watch," gasped Mamma. "How kind of Larry!" Now there was laughter through the tears. "It is expensive, yes? What does the card say?"

Carla looked at it and then put it in her pocket.

"What was on it?" persisted Mamma.

"Nothing. Just 'happy Christmas.' "

But inside, Carla felt a flush creeping over her. The words had been carefully written in black pen so there was no mistake.

Be a good girl.

Larry was warning her to behave. But it was he who needed to be careful.

"The phone!" gasped Mamma. "Quick! Before it stops. It will be Larry. You go. Please. I need to calm myself. Talk to him first. Thank him for your watch. Then I will speak."

Reluctantly, Carla moved toward it and picked up the receiver. "Yes?"

"Is your mother there?" Larry's voice was soft.

"Don't ring again," she whispered so Mamma would not hear. Then she slammed down the receiver.

"It was not him?" Mamma's voice rose in a mournful crescendo.

"I think it was the same person who has rung before," said Carla shakily, looking down at the carpet. If she stared closely enough, she could make a lion face appear in the maroon pattern.

Mamma shivered. "The one who says nothing?"

"Yes."

The face in the carpet stared up at her. *Liar! Liar!* it mouthed.

Mamma put her arm around Carla. "You must not be worried, little one. This is my fault. Next time, *I* will pick up the phone."

But it didn't ring again. Not for two whole days. Two days when Carla thought she might have gotten away with it.

And then it happened.

"Why did you lie to your mother?"

Larry's eyes were shiny and hard.

Larry was standing right in front of her, next to Mamma. It was the two of them against her.

Carla's throat caught in her breath. "I told you. I thought it was that strange person. The one who makes calls and says nothing."

"It is true," burst in Mamma, anxiously. "I have had these calls myself. They scare us."

Larry's eyes flickered. "Then you must tell the police."

Mamma let out a shrill laugh. "What do they care? They cannot even stop the kids from breaking windows. This place, it is not good. Even Ed says so."

Larry's face jerked as if someone had attached a line to the end of his long thin nose and pulled it up tightly. "Who's Ed?"

Carla's voice was cut with scorn. "He is the neighbor who looks after me with his wife while Mamma *works.*" She stressed the word *works* so there was no doubt about her meaning. *Mamma does not really work on Sundays. She spends time with you instead of with me.*

But Larry's gaze was sliding to her wrist. "Are you not wearing your watch?"

"It doesn't work."

"Is that so?"

Why did he sound amused and not cross?

Anger made her reckless. "Did you buy your daughter one, too?"

Perhaps it was just as well that Mamma had now gone into the kitchen to put on the kettle. Larry's face came very close to hers. She could smell the whisky.

"You think you are very clever, don't you, Carla?"

Instead of replying, she focused on a mark on his neck that looked like ketchup. If she did that, it might stop her from speaking again.

"No comment, eh?" Larry stood back as if appraising her. "I approve of that. You think you are clever because you *are* clever, Carla. Believe me. You might not think it, but it's true. One day you'll go far."

Then his eyes narrowed. "I just don't know *which* way. Up or down. It's up to you."

Two weeks later, Carla came back from school beside herself with excitement. "My friend Maria has asked me to her house for tea," she sang.

Mamma was at the door. They had agreed that now that Carla was ten, she should be allowed to come home from school on her own providing that she never, ever talked to strangers. And this school was much closer, so Carla never got lost.

"That is such an honor!" Mamma was

flushed, and for a moment Carla wondered if Larry was here. Mamma always got redder when he was here.

But no. The flat was empty.

"Next Wednesday! Her mother, she will pick me up from school. Then she will bring me home again. We're going to play with her Barbies."

"Her mother drives?" Mamma's eyes grew envious. Carla nodded. "All the mothers do. Please, Mamma. Please say I can go."

"But of course." Her mother was all smiles again. "It is good that you have new friends. Nice friends at this new school. A mother who drives herself must have a lot of money, don't you think?"

It was true. Maria lived in a huge house with a garden that actually had a swing!

The food was delicious. It was definitely a change from pasta.

Maria's mother noticed how she was tucking in. "You like the steak?"

Carla nodded, not wanting to speak with her mouth full. She also took care to hold the knife and fork in the same way that her friend and mother did. Afterward, she offered to clean up.

Maria's mother beamed. "I can see you have been well brought up! Actually we have a dishwasher, but you girls can help me load it."

What a clever machine!

"The plates slot in sideways. That's right!" She handed Carla another plate while continuing to chat as if she were a proper grown-up. "Maria tells me that your mother comes from Italy like my husband. Where is she from?"

Carla hesitated, not wanting to seem stupid. Mamma always got so upset when she asked questions about her family that she didn't like to ask too much. "I am not sure, but I know there is a valley surrounded by hills and mountains. I've heard her say it's near Florence up a very steep, twisty road."

"Really? I must ask my husband if he knows where that is. He comes from the center of Florence, you know. It's where we met." Her eyes went dreamy. "Have you ever been?"

"No." Carla shook her black curls. "But Mamma says that we will visit one day."

This wasn't strictly true, but it seemed to be the right thing to say, because her friend's mother then invited them to help themselves to ice cream from the freezer. One day, Carla told herself, she would have a freezer and a dishwasher and a pretty dressing table like the one in her friend's bedroom.

Later, Maria's mother dropped Carla off outside the entrance to the flats. Home seemed so much smaller!

"You had a good time?" Mamma called out from the kitchen.

Carla nodded. "Can we ask Larry if he will buy us a dishwasher? Maria's mother has one."

"But that is because she has a husband, piccola mia. Maybe . . ."

She stopped as the phone began to ring. "I will go," said Mamma.

But Carla was there first. She would ask Larry about the dishwasher for Mamma and the dressing table for her.

"Hello?"

This time, there really *was* someone breathing but saying nothing.

Quickly, she slammed down the receiver.

21
LILY

Late January 2001

Everything that's been going on since September last year has been heading toward this. Not that long to go now.

Even if I'd wanted to see more of Ed after the Christmas break, it wouldn't have been possible. From the second I returned to my desk, it was full on — even more than it had been before. Phone calls. Letters. Prison visits. "It seems," says Tony with a sharp note in his voice, "that our client still will not see me unless you accompany me."

So I went, with a mixture of excitement and apprehension. I barely even noticed the crisps, Sellotape and sharp implement routine.

Telling myself that I must be mad, I handed Joe a pile of legal papers to sign. Under the second folder was one of the other sticker albums from my brother's collection.

"Thanks." Joe's eyes drilled into mine.

So easy! Yet the buzz was instantly followed by a crashing sense of terror and self-recrimination. Why did I keep doing this?

Luckily, Tony was too busy scribbling down notes to spot the handover. He'd been distracted since the holidays, I'd noticed. Every now and then he asked Joe the same question twice. "I'm not going to push our man any more about how he got those boiler stats," he had told me before the meeting, in what seemed to be a complete U-turn. "I think we'll get more out of him by being less confrontational. Besides, I've had the stats checked out again and they definitely stand up. We could be onto something really big here, you know."

As he spoke, he ran his hands through his hair — a frequent habit of his. I couldn't help noticing, too, that there was a blue-mauve mark on the side of his neck. Did couples who'd been married for thirty years (one of the few facts I'd gleaned from Tony) still give each other love bites?

After the case, I told myself, I'd address my own marital issues.

"You do realize what a key case this is, don't you?" said my boss the other day. Like the secretaries, he has finally begun to treat me with more respect. "If we win this, everyone is going to want to come to us. No pressure, Lily. But this might not just be the making of the firm. It could be the making of you, too."

The press and my boss aren't the only ones who are getting excited. So, too, is Joe Thomas, however hard he tries to disguise his emotions. "Do you think we have a chance?" he asked on our last visit — our final one before the retrial.

Tony nodded tightly. "As long as you do what we've rehearsed. Look the jury in the eye. Remember that one of our key arguments is that you've been officially diagnosed as having Asperger's, as well as having a need to check things and stick to certain rituals and patterns. It's also why you came across as cold and unemotional when the police arrived. One in four people in the UK have some kind of mental health issue at some point. It's likely at least some of the jury will be sympathetic. And the rest we win over with the boiler facts, pure and simple."

But Joe is frowning. "I don't see my checking as a problem. And I wasn't cold or unemotional. I just told them what happened. You make me sound like some kind of freak."

"He doesn't mean to," I break in quickly. "Tony just wants you to tell the truth. Explain that Sarah was late for dinner, which you always had ready on time. That she vomited because she'd had too much to drink. You hate mess. So you suggested she had a bath. But she wouldn't let you run it for her like you normally did, as part of your rules. It made you upset, so you went and did the washing up, to get control. After half an hour, you got worried when you couldn't hear her splashing. You went into the bathroom to make sure she was all right. You saw her in the water. She was all blistered . . . It was a terrible accident."

I stop. Both men are watching me.

"It's almost as if you were there," says Tony slowly.

A picture of the stables comes into my head: the smell of hay, the frost on the rafters, Merlin's hot breath on my cold neck. Mum's agonized cry: *No! This can't be true. There's got to be a mistake.*

"Let's move on, shall we?" I say sharply.

March 2001
"This case, as Your Lordship knows, is of some importance and sensitivity: not only for the defendant, who has consistently maintained his innocence, and of course for

the family of the deceased, and for the wider public; but also for a member of my defense team, who has been subjected to a campaign of serious harassment. The Crown Prosecution Service has been made aware of this, and should anyone present in this courtroom have any contact with those who are responsible, they should know that any repetition will have grave consequences."

Tony Gordon pauses to allow the full force of his words to sink in. I have to hand it to him. He's quite the defender of justice, striding around, waving his hands and eyeballing each member of the jury in turn. I'd be convinced if I were one of them.

The prosecution has already had its say. The opposition put a strong case against Joe, claiming he was a controlling abuser and a cold-blooded killer. But it ran out of luck when it came to the ex-girlfriend who had once accused Joe of stalking her. Turns out she had died a year ago from lung cancer. So young! I'm shocked to feel relief. But that's the law for you. Someone else's misfortune can strengthen your case. "In addition, though it may have nothing to do with this case, a member of my own team has been harassed. Threatening letters have been sent. A bag, containing vital documents, was grabbed in the street. But, worst of all, a horse belonging to one of my colleagues was poisoned in an attempt to make us drop the case."

My name isn't mentioned but it's clear who the "colleague" is from my red face and Tony's swift but meaningful glance in my direction.

There's a collective gasp. From the dock, Joe Thomas's eyes swoop down to catch mine. There's a compassion that I have not seen before, not even when he was talking about poor Sarah.

How dare Tony flag me up in this way? Then I realize he has done this on purpose. He intends to show the jury the tears in my eyes — to see the hurt that's been caused by those who don't want this case to come to court. The jury might not be swayed by Joe Thomas with his cool manner, but their sympathies might well be aroused by a young woman. Like me.

For a while, all I can focus on is regaining my composure. This is Joe Thomas's future we are talking about — a man who is a victim rather than an aggressor.

As my embarrassment dies down, I find myself looking around the court. It's bigger than any I have been in before. Almost church-like. Joe Thomas is above us behind a glass partition. His hands are gripping the shelf in front of him. It strikes me that the court's ordinary municipal exterior appearance does not do justice to the excited circus and theater that is going on around us.

I begin to sweat even though it is frosty outside.

Joe Thomas is mopping his face as if he is perspiring, too.

We watch Tony and the prosecution examine and then cross-examine boiler experts, statisticians, health and safety officers, and the attending policemen from the night of the murder. Then he throws a grenade. He calls to the stand the man who moved into Joe's flat after Sarah's death. After asking a series of innocuous opening questions, he gets to the point.

"Can you describe your new neighbors Mr. and Mrs. Jones?" Tony asks.

The young man sighs audibly. "Difficult. We complained about the noise of their television. First to them, but when they ignored us, we wrote to the council, but nothing's changed. It's become completely unbearable. We've put in for another place."

"Would you believe their claims of hearing screaming from the deceased's home?"

"Frankly, I'd be surprised if they could

hear anything above the sound of their television."

I knew Tony was good. But not this good.

Then Sarah's old boss takes the stand. She hadn't wanted to give evidence, because she'd been a "mate." But under oath, she admits that Sarah had a "drinking problem." It turns out that Sarah had been given a final warning for being drunk while at work.

Then comes another medical expert. Yes, she confirms, it's quite possible that someone who had excess alcohol in their system might get into a hot bath without realizing and then might be too drunk to climb out. And yes, the resulting self-inflicted bruises from falling and then trying to escape might be difficult to distinguish from bruises delivered by someone else.

A second set of neighbors are called in, too. A pair of elderly sisters — a clever move on Tony's part. These two testify, one after the other, that they often saw Joe "acting in a very gentlemanly manner" toward Sarah. Always opening the car door for her. Carrying the shopping. That sort of thing. "We often thought she was a very lucky young lady," simpers the older sister.

A friend of Sarah's is then called. She's what we call a "hostile witness": someone who doesn't want to give evidence but is compelled to do so by court order. Yes, she admits, Sarah did have a drinking problem and it made her do stupid things. How about the Friday before she died? Her friend reluctantly reveals that Sarah had nearly been run over by a car when drunk on a night out. Another colleague must have reported it. And was it possible Sarah might have fallen into a too-hot bath when drunk? Another unwilling yes.

Why weren't such experts called up during the first trial? Like I said before, there are good lawyers. And some not so good. And of course it takes time and resourcefulness to get the right experts.

Tomorrow we'll hear from some medical specialists in autism spectrum disorders. Joe will hate every bit of it, but he knows he needs it for his defense. Apparently, one in a hundred people are affected. So maybe there'll be someone on the jury who will be sympathetic.

And finally, we'll bring to the stand those families whose loved ones were also scalded but survived. "Save the best for last," as Tony so tactfully puts it.

Yet the joy of all this is that ever since the retrial started, I haven't once thought about Ed.

After the case. After the case. The most

difficult decision of my life is looming.

But deep down, I already know what I have to do.

The crowds outside the court, after the case, were thick with cameras, shouting and flashing lights, a wave of journalists pushing microphones in front of us. Tony made a short speech: "This is a day of reckoning not just for Joe Thomas, who has finally been proved innocent, but for all the other victims, too. We expect more developments shortly."

Then he steered us with practiced ease into a waiting car and took us to this pub in Hampstead where the locals are well-heeled members of the public rather than the press. I looked for Ed in the crowds, but he was nowhere to be seen.

Time to think about him later. Right now, this is our moment.

"The jury was only out for fifty-five minutes! You reckoned it would be several hours!"

Joe's face is different from the one he wore inside prison. It is lit up. Exalted. Exhausted, too.

"They knew I was innocent." Joe's upper lip bears a froth of beer. It was, he said, the first thing he wanted: a pint in a pub "with freedom for company and the two people who made it happen."

I've never heard him sound so emotional before. But he was looking at me when he said it. Right now I'm on a high, as if I have been acquitted myself. Tony feels the same. I can see from the flush on his face that says, *We won.*

"Law is a game," he had told me at the beginning. "If you win, you're king. If you don't, you're a loser. You can't afford to be the latter. That's why it's addictive. It's why you're in the dock alongside your client."

That's why, I could now add, a lawyer feels the need to win arguments in his or her private life, too. Because if you can't do that, there's an implication (rightly or wrongly) that you can't be any good at your job.

That's why I'd have expected a thanks from Joe for our part in liberating him. But Daniel hadn't done thank-yous either.

"What next for you, then?" asks Tony now, draining his glass and glancing at his watch. I can tell from the way he speaks that he's hacked off at the lack of gratitude and also — tellingly — that he doesn't really care for our client, who technically isn't our client anymore.

Joe Thomas shrugs. "I'll use the money to

start again somewhere else."

He's referring, of course, to the well-wisher donations that came in during the case when Joe declared he didn't want any compensation — only that his name be cleared.

"I rather fancy a different kind of job, too," he adds.

My mind flicks back to the client profile I read on the train all those months ago. It seems like a lifetime ago.

Joe Thomas, thirty, insurance salesman. Convicted in 1998 of murdering Sarah Evans, twenty-six, fashion sales assistant and girlfriend of the accused . . .

"Do you know where you'll go next?" As I speak, Tony sends me a warning look. Don't get too personal.

"To a hotel, I suppose. Or a bed-and-breakfast. It's not as though I've got a home to go to tonight."

Once more, I am struck by the literal way in which he perceives my question.

"What about the future, in general?" I ask gently.

"I'm still thinking about it." Joe's eyes are steady, looking into mine. "Any suggestions?"

My throat is tight. "If it was me, I would probably go and live abroad. Italy maybe."

Goodness knows why my honeymoon location comes into my head.

Joe wipes his mouth clear of the froth with his sleeve. "Wouldn't that look as if I was running away?"

Tony rises to his feet. "I don't want you to think I'm doing the same, but I've got to be somewhere." He shakes my hand. "It's been good working with you, Lily. You'll go far." Then he looks at Joe and seems to hesitate. I hold my breath.

At times, I've wondered if Tony actually believes Joe is innocent. Or whether it matters to him.

"Good luck for the future."

Inwardly, I breathe out a sigh of relief as Tony finally shakes Joe's hand and then walks away. But our client has noticed the delay.

"He doesn't like me." Joe states it as a fact.

I stay silent.

"But *you* understand me." Joe looks at me again before glancing down at the bag of possessions he's been given — his belongings from prison. I wonder if they contain Daniel's sticker albums. Not that I want them back. Too many memories.

Maybe it's the double gin and tonic Tony bought me, despite my asking for a single.

Maybe it's the relief that we've won. Maybe it's because Joe reminds me so much of Daniel. Whatever it is, I find myself talking. "I had a brother once." My eyes wander out over the street — did I mention we are sitting outside? Even though it's late afternoon, the weather is remarkably mild. Besides, by unspoken agreement we all needed some air after the courtroom. A couple walk past, arm in arm, and I can smell the woman's expensive perfume. But then it turns to a different smell in my head. The smell of straw. And death.

I discovered Daniel was doing drugs when my mother sent me into his room to get him down for dinner, the week before his seventeenth birthday. He was chopping up white stuff with a kitchen knife.

"That's dangerous!" I'd seen some of the sixth-form girls do something similar in the loos at school, though I'd never done drugs myself.

"So what?"

"What's dangerous?" Dad was behind us.

Swiftly, Daniel shoved the evidence into his jeans pocket. *Don't say,* his eyes pleaded.

"Doing fifty miles per hour when you should be doing forty." I picked up the *Learner Driver Handbook* from the desk.

"Of course you can't, son. If you don't understand that, you'll never pass your driving test. Although, frankly, I don't think you should be taking it at all."

"Why not?" Daniel's dark eyes were glaring.

"Because, as your instructor says, you drive too fast."

"At least I'm not doing what you are."

A beat of silence. "What do you mean?"

Daniel's eyes narrowed. "You know what I mean. I've heard you on the extension. More than once, in fact. And I'm going to tell Mum."

Dad went very still. "I don't know what you're talking about."

Nor did I.

"It's nothing," said my brother when I questioned him. One of Daniel's lies, I told myself, to cover his own behavior and move the spotlight onto someone else. It had happened enough times before.

That night, Daniel refused to come down to dinner.

Instead, he stayed in his room, playing loud music that reverberated through the ceiling and made our heads ring.

"Turn that down!" yelled Dad, hammering at the door.

Daniel didn't bother to reply. As usual,

he'd put the bed against the door so no one could get in.

Later, as I passed my parents' closed bedroom door, I heard them having an almighty row. There'd been others of course. Always about Daniel. *What is wrong with that boy? How can we cope anymore?* That sort of thing.

But this one was different. This one sent a chill down my bones.

"I heard Daniel. Who were you on the phone to? Who is she?"

This was my mother.

"No one."

"You swear? On the children's lives?"

There was a silence. Then a low voice, which meant I had to press my head against the door to hear the rest. ". . . your fault. Don't you realize? . . . lavished all your attention on Daniel . . . looked elsewhere."

Mum's distressed voice was all too clear. "So it's the truth? How could you? Do you love her? Are you going to leave us?"

I couldn't hear the reply. Only the desperate sound of weeping. On the other side of the door, I was doubled over. Almost sick. Dad had been having an affair?

Then I saw him. Daniel walking up the stairs. Daniel grinning as though there was nothing wrong. Daniel with huge black pupils.

I rushed up after him to the bedroom. "Mum and Dad are splitting up. And it's all your fault."

He shrugged. "She needed to know."

His lack of concern made me boil. "If you weren't so horrible, Mum and Dad would be all right."

Daniel looked shocked. Hadn't I always protected him? Loved him? Looked after him?

But the shock of my father's affair had made me see red. And that's when I said something else.

"We should never have adopted you. Then you couldn't have hurt me, too. I hate you."

Daniel's face crumpled. Instantly I knew I'd hurt him. No — I'd destroyed him.

I put out my hand to try to make up with him. He threw it off. Then he seemed to change his mind. He took my hand again, but this time he squeezed it, crunching my knuckles with his fingers. The pain made me cry out. Then he pulled me toward him so that his eyes — mad with blackness — looked down on me.

My heart pulsed in my throat. Words lay on the edge of my tongue, ready to be spoken. Words that would change our lives forever.

"You're a bad person, Daniel. Everyone else says it, and they're right."

Then he laughed as though this was a compliment. That's what really did it. Before I could stop myself, I slapped him. Hard. First one cheek, then the other. "You know what? I wish you had never been born."

"What happened then?"

Joe's hand is on mine. Our heads are bowed together — mine with grief, his with empathy. I can feel the same electric shock that passed through me in the prison when I gave him the sticker albums.

I'm certain he can feel it, too.

That's the thing about people like Joe and Daniel. They might not seem to show the "right" kind of emotion at the appropriate time, but if you push them far enough, they bleed. They cry. Just like the rest of us.

"I went out," I mumble. "When I got back, Mum was frantic. Daniel had left a note just saying 'I don't want to live anymore.' We searched everywhere. But it's . . . well, it's a big house. We have a few acres. And . . . and we have stables. That's where I found him. He often went there.

We often went there . . . but this time he was . . . hanging. From a rope wound around a beam." Joe's hand tightens on mine.

My words are blurting out now along with the tears. "I tipped him over. He wasn't well . . ."

Joe's voice is gentle. "What exactly was wrong with him?"

I shake my head. "What they used to call 'willful disobedience,' possibly brought on by a difficult childhood. That's what the so-called experts said." I laugh hoarsely. "He was never officially diagnosed, but some-times I do wonder if . . ."

I stop, not wanting to cause offense.

"If he was on the autistic spectrum, too?"

"Possibly." I twist my hands awkwardly. "But there were other things he did that didn't fit."

Joe is looking thoughtful. "So that's why you understand me." It's not a question.

I nod, embarrassed. And yet also grateful that this man gets how I tick.

"I'm so sorry about your brother." Joe's voice has a softness I've never heard before. "And your horse."

"Actually," I add, searching in my bag for a tissue, "he was Daniel's. That's what made it so difficult."

"Let's go for a walk," says Joe. And as we stand up, it seems quite natural for him to take my hand in his.

22
CARLA

Not long after Carla's visit, Maria had put up her hand at roll call and asked if she could be moved to another desk in the classroom.

"Why?" whispered Carla, even though her sinking heart told her the answer.

Maria ignored her. It was as if she hadn't spoken.

"Who would like to sit next to Carla?" said the nun with the missing teeth.

No one volunteered. Instead, everyone shuffled away. One of the girls — the one with pigtails who usually invited her to play hopscotch — cupped her hand around her neighbor's ear to say something quietly. The other one let out a little gasp.

It was like being at the old school all over again. Carla was so upset that she could not complete her maths exercise. The figures hung in the air with giant question marks.

"They have sent you to Coventry," said

another girl — the most unpopular one in the class, whom the nun had sent to fill Maria's place next to Carla's. She had greasy hair that her mother would only allow her to wash once a month because, as she had told Carla, it was better for the "natural oils." This girl was always last to be chosen for teams; to be placed next to her was one of the gravest insults.

"Coventry?" Carla did not understand. "Where is that?" The girl with the greasy hair shrugged. "It's where they don't speak to you." Then she held out her arm. "It will be much nicer now that there are two of us."

But Carla didn't want to be friends with the girl with the greasy hair. She wanted to be friends with Maria, whose mother had invited her back for tea in their lovely big house on the road with the wide pavement, where no one kicked beer cans in the street.

At snack time, Carla sought out Maria in the playground. "Tell me what I have done wrong," she pleaded.

For the first time that day, Maria raised her face and looked at her. Those beautiful blue eyes were cold. "Papa has an uncle who lives in the same town as your grandparents." Maria was talking as if Carla smelled of something nasty. "He knows them. And he says your mother is a loose woman."

What is that? It didn't sound good. Suddenly all Carla wanted to do was cuddle Mamma with her kind, warm smile and breathe in her lovely Apple Blossom scent. Mamma would explain the confusion. Carla knew she would.

"Maria! Maria!" It was one of the nuns, striding toward them with her crucifix necklace swinging and her lips tightening. "I am under instructions from your mother not to let you talk to that girl."

Carla's eyes welled with tears. "Why?"

The nun crossed herself swiftly across her large breasts. "You will find out soon enough. Be sure to collect an envelope addressed to your mother from the school office before you go home this afternoon."

Mamma wept when she read the letter. "The Mother Superior wants to see your birth certificate," she sobbed, head in hands on the wobbly kitchen table. "She wants proof that you had a papa. This is my fault for sending you to a Catholic school. The old one wouldn't have cared."

Carla put an arm around Mamma. "Perhaps it is under your bed where you keep your special things?"

Mamma's lip curled. For a moment, she reminded Carla of the wicked witch in one of her favorite books from the library. "How dare you go looking there?"

Carla thought of the handsome man with the funny hat whom she looked at every now and then when Mamma wasn't home. He always smiled at her so kindly!

"They are only pictures, Mamma. I was curious."

Mamma let out a groan. "Perhaps you deserve to know. That man is your papa."

Her father! So that is what he had looked like. "Maybe," said Carla, trying to be helpful, "he has taken these papers with him to heaven."

"No. He has not!" Mamma rose to her full height, tossing back her glorious black hair. She was angry now instead of sad. "If you had not opened your mouth to Maria's mother, none of this would have happened."

The sob burst out of Carla's mouth like a giant hiccup. "But I didn't know I was doing anything wrong."

It was no good. Mamma took herself to her bedroom and — for the first time that Carla could remember — locked her door.

"Please, please open it," she begged from outside.

But all she could hear was Mamma sobbing.

Maybe, Carla told herself, Mamma's mood would pass, like it had after Christmas. Perhaps on Monday the girls would start to be nice to her again.

But she was wrong. It got worse. Then Mamma received another letter from the Mother Superior. She did not have long to produce the birth certificate. Otherwise, Carla would have to leave. It should have been "presented" when she started school, but there had been an oversight.

No one wanted to play with her at recess. Maria had already found a new best friend, a pretty girl whose uncle had given her a silver cross that she showed off to everyone. Even the greasy-haired girl moved away from Carla when they had to crowd into the gym because it was too wet to play outside.

"I heard someone say you were a *bastard*," she said quietly.

Carla ran the word through her mouth all afternoon and until she got home. How strange. It wasn't in the *Children's Dictionary*. "What does 'bastard' mean?" she asked when Mamma returned from work, with her uniform poking out of her bag.

"Is that what they are calling you now?"

Then her mother placed her head on the kitchen table and beat her fists so hard that the crack in the wood split and cut her hand.

Another day passed. And another.

"The certificate has not come from Italy yet?"

"No, cara mia."

Even when Mamma eventually admitted there was no such certificate, they still both waited for the postman. "Then we can honestly say that we are waiting for it to arrive," explained Mamma, brushing Carla's hair as she did every night. "If only I could tell Larry. He could help."

That was another thing. Larry was working very hard. So hard that he didn't have time to visit them. "He is an important man," Mamma often said. "He helps the queen decide what is right and what is wrong."

Then, one evening, when Carla was already in bed, she heard his voice at the front door. Usually he came in through the back. Besides, it was a Wednesday! Larry came here only on Tuesdays and Thursdays and sometimes on Sundays. Something had happened, she could tell. Creeping out of bed, in her pajamas, she saw Larry twirling Mamma in his arms right out there in the corridor for everyone to see. Ugh!

"Love you . . . We won the case . . . Wanted to tell you before I went home."

Words drifted out. Words she didn't understand. Then there was another voice.

"Tony?"

It was Lily!

"That's not Tony." Carla came running up, keen to make it all right. "This is Larry. He is my mother's friend. The one who sees her on Sundays while you have me . . ." Then she clasped her hand to her mouth because, of course, Lily thought Mamma had been working. Not lying in bed with Larry.

Now Mamma would be cross with her again. But instead, she seemed confused. "What do you mean?"

Meanwhile, Lily was staring at Larry with a strange look on her face. "Tony, what are you doing?"

Mamma started to sound scared. "This is no Tony. You have made a mistake. Larry! Tell her."

But Larry pushed her hand away and was moving toward Lily. His neck was very red. "I need to talk to you," he said.

It was difficult to hear exactly what he was saying in the corner, although she caught words like *appreciate* and *confidential,* both of which she could spell perfectly because they had been at the beginning of the dictionary.

"You want me to keep quiet about your sordid affair?" Lily was shouting now. Then she turned to Mamma. Carla had never seen her friend's eyes flash like that. "How could you go off with someone else's husband? Don't you have any shame? As for you, Tony, if I see you again with this woman, I will tell your wife."

Carla had a sudden picture of the curtains closing in the house they had walked past at Christmas.

"It's none of your business."

"There's a child involved here, Tony. I'm warning you. I meant what I said just now."

Then Lily stormed back into her own flat, slamming the door behind her.

"Why is she angry?" asked Carla as Larry pushed them into their own flat.

"How do you know Lily?" Mamma frowned, pulling at Larry's sleeve.

Larry wasn't red anymore. He was white. "She," he said, pointing at Carla, "needs to go to her room."

"No." Mamma stamped her foot. "My daughter hears, too. You tell lies to me? Then you tell lies to her, too. We deserve to know the truth."

We? A lovely warm feeling ran through Carla. For the first time since Larry had come into their lives, it felt as though she and Mamma were a team again.

Larry's face had its angry look on. "As you wish. You know I have another family. I made that clear at the beginning."

Mamma hung her head as if hearing something she didn't want to.

"I work with Lily. She doesn't know about . . . about my life at home. She doesn't know about us. Nor does anyone else. I told you my name was Larry because I needed to keep my other life separate." There was a deep sigh. "But my name is really Tony."

"Tony Smith like Larry Smith?" whispered her mother.

The angry look had gone. Instead there was a sigh. A big, tired one. "No. Tony Gordon."

Mamma's lips were moving as if she was repeating all this to herself. Or maybe she was saying her Ave Marias.

"I understand," she said at last. "We will have to be more careful."

Tony took her in his arms. "Francesca, listen to me. We will have to have a break until this blows over. I can't risk Lily telling my wife . . ."

As he held her, he looked at Carla. She knew what he was saying. Knew it as clearly as if he was speaking. *Go away. You are not wanted right now.* This was her chance.

"What about the woman in your car?" she burst out. "The woman you were kissing before my birthday. Do you love her, too?"

There was a terrible silence. Her mother took a step backward, falling against the kitchen table as she did so and knocking the telephone directory out of place. Larry opened his mouth and roared, "You conniving little —"

"Get out!"

At first Carla thought Mamma was screaming at her. But no — it was at Larry. "Get out, get out!" she yelled. Horrified, Carla watched as Mamma hurled a tin at him. A tin of baked beans. It missed. Just. Then another. This time it was a tin of Italian tomatoes.

Larry's face was so angry that Carla thought the tomatoes had broken out of the tin and painted his cheeks. "You've made a big mistake, young lady," he said, bending down to her level. "You will see."

Then he stormed out, leaving Mamma to weep, kneeling on the floor with her head wrapped up in her arms.

"I am sorry, Mamma," Carla whispered.

"I should not have mentioned the lady in the car. I promised Larry I would say nothing. That was why he gave me the new Charlie . . ." Mamma lifted her face. It was red and blotchy, just like Larry's had been. "He bribed you?"

Then Mamma cried even more. She cried so loudly that Carla's stomach began to hurt. The pain grew worse and worse so that it became a knot that throbbed inside her. When the phone rang, they both ignored it.

"I've got a tummy ache," said Carla quietly.

Mamma was still lying on the floor. "Do not expect me to believe you," she sobbed. "I will believe no one. Ever again. Not even myself."

That night, Carla's pain grew worse. In her dreams, it became a red-hot stick, lashing against her body.

"Maria!" she called out. "Please stop. Let me play!"

"It's all right, little one." Mamma's voice floated over her. "The doctor is coming."

23
LILY

By the time I come back from Hampstead, it is nearly seven o'clock. Ed is sitting at the dining room table, working on a sketch.

"We won," I say.

He starts, and I can see that he's been so involved with his work that he'd forgotten today is verdict day. Then he collects himself. "Wonderful," he says, leaping up and throwing his arms around me. "We must celebrate! Open a bottle." His face tightens. "Then we can have that talk you've been promising."

My hand shakes on the fridge door at the thought of the conversation ahead. Then my heart sinks. The Pinot that had been there at breakfast time is gone. No guesses as to who drank it. But I don't feel up to having an argument.

"We're out of drink," I say shortly.

Ed leaps to his feet. "I'll go round to the off-license." He's trying. I'll say that for him.

"Let me." Even though I've only just returned, I'm already feeling claustrophobic. My heart is juddering so badly at what I must do that I simply have to get out of here.

As I turn to leave, I see a man through the window, striding toward the front entrance. His hat is firmly down over his forehead but there's something about that walk that looks familiar.

I close the front door behind me and step into the corridor.

My eyes struggle to understand what they're seeing.

The man who was heading for our apartment building and who is now twirling Francesca around and around in the air is Tony.

"I love you," I hear him say as he puts her back down. "We won the case! Wanted to tell you before I went home!"

Coincidences are one of those things that sound contrived until they happen in real life.

Like Tony and my neighbor.

I am disappointed. And fiercely, overpoweringly angry. How can someone uphold the law when he is acting immorally himself? What a hypocrite.

Perhaps it's also because I can still remember my mother's grief when she found out about my father's affair. An affair that must have been quickly extinguished, because after that row, my parents appeared to carry on as they always had. After Daniel's death I doubt either of them had the energy for love, or for fighting. But it marked my mother. She never spoke to my father the same way again. Part of me thinks she somehow blamed his infidelity for Daniel's death. Since then, I've tried to forgive my father. But sometimes you can never put all the pieces back together again.

That's one of the reasons I let rip. "How could you go off with someone else's husband? Don't you have any shame? As for you, Tony, if I see you again with this woman, I will tell your wife."

Of course I wouldn't really tell Tony's wife (who I've never actually met). That would only cause more hurt. But I'm so angry, I don't really think about what I'm saying.

"What was all that noise out there?" asks Ed when I return.

I tell him what happened.

My husband looks up from his sketch. It's a nose. A cute, pert, turned-up nose. Just like Carla's. "You don't think you should have stayed out of it?"

"No." I turn away. "It's not right — either

295

on her or Tony's wife and children. Or Carla. Tony was carrying on with Francesca when we were looking after her. Her mother choosing a man over her child! And how on earth did he meet her?"

"You seem more bothered about them than us." Ed looks nervous. I know he wants to talk, and I owe it to him. "Shall we open that bottle?"

"I forgot to get it."

"Then I'll go." He lays a hand on my shoulder. "I think we both need a glass, don't you?"

As he shuts the door, something Tony said during the case comes back to me: "There are times when you'll find yourself swearing that blue is black. You'll truly believe it yourself. We all do it. It's not that lawyers lie. It's that they twist the real facts to make another world that everyone else believes in, too. And who's to say that won't be a better world?"

When Ed comes back, I am in bed. Pretending to be asleep.

In the morning, I wake before my husband and leave a note.

Talk tonight. Promise. Sorry.

It is a relief to get back to the office the next day, where I can attempt to block out the confused look on Carla's face, which is preying on my mind. The phones are ringing off the hook. People are rushing everywhere. PRISONER'S RELEASE OPENS GATE FOR MORE BOILER LAWSUITS screams the headline on the corner newsstand.

"Well done," says one of the partners who's never bothered to give me the time of day before.

"You did a good job," concedes my boss who rarely gives praise.

There are balloons on my desk. A bottle of champagne. And a stack of messages. None from Tony. How will I ever face him again? Yet he is the one who should be ashamed.

"We've had a flood of calls from potential clients who want you to take them on," adds my boss. Then he pats me on my back, a laddish pat. "But we'll talk about that later. Why don't you have the rest of the day off to make up for all those extra hours you put in?"

Coming home from the office at lunchtime is virtually unknown in law unless you've been let go. But I don't feel like celebrating. There'll be no getting out of the talk with

Ed this evening. Everything, I think as I turn the key, is such a muddle.

"Ed?" He's in his jeans instead of the usual office suit. A half-eaten bowl of mushy cereal is on the table, surrounded by charcoal sticks and sketches. His feet are bare. "Have you come home early from work?"

"No."

There's a slur to his speech, a smell to his breath. At the same time I notice the half-full bottle of Jack Daniel's on the side.

"I've been sacked."

Sacked?

For a minute, all kinds of possibilities flash through my head. Upsetting a client? Having an argument with his boss?

"They found me working on this when I should have been doing *proper* work."

He says the word *proper* with finger gestures, making sarcastic apostrophes in the air.

I glance down at the drawing in front of him. Little Carla smiles up at me. It's always little Carla smiling. Or dancing. Or riding her bike. He's lost in a world of make-believe.

"For God's sake," I explode. "How on earth are we going to manage without your pay? Do you have any idea what you've done?"

"I need to know what our future is," Ed continues as if I haven't spoken.

"I don't know." I want to scream. "I can't think after what you've just told me."

"You said we'd talk about it when the case was over. We could have thrashed it out last night, but you were more interested in trying to redeem our neighbor's love life before our own."

What can I say? It's true. I brush past him, making straight for the bathroom. You'll get a low after the case, Tony had warned me. It's like coming off a drug. "Sorry. I just need to freshen up." After locking the door behind me, I sit on the edge of the bath and turn on the taps. Hot. Cold. Hot.

After Sarah Evans, I'm never going to look at a bath in the same way again.

Just as I can never look at Ed in the same way.

Or myself.

Desperately, I force myself to consider the options.

If I leave Ed now, I will be alone. Scared. With an uncertain future.

But if I stay, we might be able to start again. Providing Ed really means it about not caring for Davina anymore. But can I trust him? And can I trust myself?

A decision has to be made. One way or

the other.

A coin. Daniel used to toss a coin when he didn't know what to do. I pick up a magazine that I've left by the side of the bath. If I open on a page with an odd number, I'll leave.

If it's even, I'll stay.

I open the magazine at a feature on how to make Sunday family suppers. There's a picture of a happy family sitting around the table. The picture and the print swim before my eyes. Sunday suppers. Everyday life. The kind we could have had if Daniel hadn't come into our lives.

I glance at the page number of the magazine in my hand.

Then I walk out the bathroom door. Ed's not sketching anymore. He's simply staring into space with blank, empty eyes.

"Do you want to start again?" I ask.

He nods. There's hope in his eyes. Fear, too.

I feel exactly the same.

Then I take my husband's hand and lead him into our bedroom.

During the next month, I try to get back into a routine but it's not easy. My workload seems dull after the thrill of getting Joe Thomas released, even though everyone in the office, including my boss, regards me with a new level of respect. And still the work comes pouring in.

"They want Lily to do it," says the secretary when my boss allocates himself to one of the meatier cases.

Yet instead of being jealous, as I feared, my boss nods. "You'd better have a room of your own if you're going to be so popular."

People ring to ask if I can represent them. A woman whose elderly father was burned by a boiler wants me to take on her case. Solicitors I've never heard of ring to congratulate me on being part of "such a high-profile case." A women's magazine wants to interview me as "a rising lawyer." Questions about health and safety are being asked in the House of Commons.

But inside my head, it's hell. Ed and I may have agreed to start again but it was never going to be as simple as that. I have to force myself to believe him when he says he's "having a quick drink with Ross." Ed resents me getting back late, laden with files, but then, out of the blue, he will bring me a cup of tea when I'm working into the small hours and kindly tell me not to "overdo it." And now that he's at home during the day, he's started doing the housework while searching for a new job — something I'm sure his traditional parents would be shocked at. He doesn't do it as well as I would, but I appreciate the gesture.

The guilt over Carla is getting worse. I've been hoping to go over and apologize, but there's no answer to my knocks. One of our other neighbors said she heard "some kind of commotion" on the night I last saw them. Is this my fault? Have they moved away because of what I said? The worry actually makes me feel sick.

"Forget it," says Ed. "You've meddled enough."

"Aren't you concerned about little Carla?" I say.

He shrugs. "You can't help everyone, Lily. She's not our child."

It's amazing how an artist can take such care and compassion over a piece of work, while ignoring his subject's well-being.

Yet isn't that the same as the relationship between lawyer and client? You're together for hours, talking endlessly about a case. But when it's over, your relationship is finished. Just like that. Or at least that's how it's supposed to be.

To be honest, I can't help wondering where Joe Thomas is, what he's doing.

And then, one evening, he's there. Hovering by the entrance to the office as I emerge after a long day's work. How incredible that someone can change so much in a few weeks! Gone is the beard. Gone are the prison scrubs. Gone, too, are the brogues and shirt. This clean-shaven man in a moss-green tweed jacket looks more like an estate manager than an insurance salesman.

"I came to say good-bye."

We fall into step beside each other, just as we did before.

I don't know where we're going and I don't care. In some ways, this man is more real to me than Ed. After all, I've spent more than half a year of my life trying to save him.

"You've got a job?"

"Yes." He speaks briskly. "I took your advice. Remember you talked about working in Italy? Well, I've gone for France instead."

His arm brushes mine as we cross the road together.

"A friend in Corsica wants me to help out with a renovation." He looks down at his hands. "I'm quite good with these. And it'll be a change."

"Will there be a problem with the language?"

There's a grin. "No, thanks to the prison

library. I taught myself to speak French and Spanish."

It doesn't surprise me.

We're going into a restaurant now. A smart one. "This is a thank-you." He speaks as though this has all been arranged beforehand. Doesn't he realize that I'm expected home? The presumption both irritates and thrills me. Yet I go along with it, allowing the waiter to take my coat.

"You did a lot for me," he adds, handing me the menu. I use it to hide my blush.

"I did my job." Then my questions pour out as though he is an old friend I haven't seen for years. "How are you? What are you doing? Where are you living?"

"The same friend in France has a place in Richmond. It's rather nice."

Richmond? I compare it in my mind with Clapham. The tiny kitchen where Ed is still drawing, unpaid, with job application forms around him.

"What about you?" His voice is direct. "How is married life?"

"Okay."

I'm tempted to tell him about Ed and Davina, but I said enough the last time we met. I'm no longer drunk on too much alcohol and that excited flush of having won the case. I have to remind myself that I have a position of responsibility here. Confidences are not appropriate. "Only okay?"

I manage a smile. "It's great. We might be moving actually." I made that last bit up, but perhaps we will.

"Sounds lovely." Joe Thomas sits forward in enthusiasm. "I can see it now, Lily. A country cottage. A horse like Merlin . . ."

"Merlin?" I say slowly. "I never told you the name of Daniel's horse."

"Didn't you?"

His smile is less certain now.

I go cold.

"You had something to do with it, didn't you?"

I expect him to deny it. Despite my question, I don't believe it. There has to be some kind of plausible reason.

"I had to." He rearranges his cutlery neatly around him. "I needed to keep you onside. If a lawyer doesn't believe his client, he or she won't try hard enough."

Bile is flooding my mouth. "You poisoned Daniel's old horse to get me 'onside'? How?"

There's a shrug. I've never seen him like this before — not with me. "I arranged for someone to slip something into his feed when your parents were out. I wanted to make you angry enough to believe my story."

I stagger to my feet. His cunning is unbelievable. His honesty is sickening.

"And my bag? The one that was taken on Westminster Bridge?" I am beginning to see it now. How stupid I've been! "You got someone to do that, too, so everyone in court thought someone in the boiler industry was trying to bully us?"

He shrugs. "It was the courts that messed up. The water was too hot. If they're going to play dirty tricks, they have to expect the same."

Tony Gordon, I suspect, might just agree. But not me. One wrong does not justify another.

Another thought strikes me. "Who helped you?"

A smug grin. "When I was in prison, I advised a lot of people on their financial affairs. Gave them advice on insurance and other stuff. I didn't take any money. But they knew I'd call in favors."

"But if they were inside, how could they help you?"

"Some have been released. Others have contacts on the outside to do things for them. Prison life is like that. Not that I'd recommend it, mind you."

This is unbelievable. Yet my mind goes back to when Joe agreed to meet a man for "table football" in the prison. "Three p.m. on the dot," he'd said. "In the community lounge." At the time I thought it friendly, albeit a bit out of character. Was it really a business appointment?

"I could report you."

"If you do, I'll have to say what happened the last time we met."

"What do you mean?" I stammer.

"Come on, Lily. Don't play games. Not with me. Those sticker books you gave me in prison are nothing compared with the last present. I can still taste you in my mouth. It was worth all the lies."

His voice might sound firm but his hands are shaking. A sickening thought hits me like a sledgehammer. "You did it, didn't you? You *did* kill Sarah. You murdered your girlfriend."

An older woman with large emerald-green drop earrings is looking at us now from the neighboring table. Joe's eyes grow hard. "Be careful what you say."

"But you did." My instinct is certain.

Joe is now talking in a low voice. "Why do you think I arranged to bump into you this evening? To tell you what happened. But remember: when you've been cleared for something, you can't be retried for the same crime. I felt you deserved the truth, Lily."

My heart starts to beat hard. He seems tense as well. Tapping his fists against his knees as though playing a drum.

"She came in pissed, like I said. Late, too. Then she was sick, but she didn't want me in the bathroom. I knew she was trying to hide something. When she was shutting the door, I noticed a mark on her neck."

I have a flash of that mark on Tony's neck from earlier. "A love bite?"

"Love?" He seems to weigh this up. "That depends on how you define love, doesn't it? A bite can also be made in anger."

I'm losing patience at Joe's literal-mindedness. "How did she get this mark?"

"Now that's more relevant." He nods as though I'm a child in class who has finally asked the right question. "When I confronted her, she said the mark was mine. But she was lying. I don't do that sort of thing." More drumming of the knees. "I said we'd talk when she was clean, but she wouldn't let me run her bath like I usually do. Kept calling me a freak. So I went and turned the boiler up. Thought I'd teach her a lesson. But she was still screaming at me. Said she'd found someone else, someone normal. That's when I lost it. How could I

308

let Sarah leave me for someone else? I pushed her. She was so drunk that I hardly needed to touch her. So simple, really. She just fell into the water."

There's a shocked silence. On my part. He doesn't seem fazed at all.

"You didn't try to get her out?"

A shrug. "She hurt me. She was leaving me. So no, I didn't try to get her out. I walked out. Then I made a cup of tea. Cleaned the floor because it was sticky from her vomit. I told myself I'd give her thirty minutes to pull herself together. I didn't mean to kill her. Just teach her a lesson. When I went back in, I found her staring up at me. Purple and red. I've never cared for those colors. That's when I rang 9-1-1 and told them the story I originally gave you. If it hadn't been for that bastard of a neighbor, and Sarah's stupid made-up stories, I would have been all right."

I can't quite believe the way he's talking. He's so unemotional — just like the police said.

Joe continues. "But then I found out about the boiler problem — real stroke of luck — and realized that if I hired the right person, I might have a chance on appeal. Wasn't sure about you at the beginning, to be honest. So I set you a test and, I have to say, Lily, you proved your worth."

I'm stunned. "But the mole who sent you those figures? Who was that? And why didn't you use the evidence sooner?"

Joe snorted. "You're not getting it, are you, Lily? The mole didn't exist. Or the figures. I saw the newspaper stories that had just started to come out, and made them up. No one could prove my boiler *hadn't* been faulty."

"Why not?" I asked.

A smug look flits over his face. "It's easier to prove a positive than a negative. There's some very useful textbooks in the prison library, you know. Plumbing and all sorts."

There is a long silence. I am too shocked to speak. Joe, by his own admission, really is a murderer. When he "tested" me at the beginning to see if I understood the meaning of those figures, it wasn't to see if I was up to the job. It was to see if I was gullible enough to believe him. Not only that, but he played up his idiosyncrasies to me. Did he already know then about Daniel through looking me up and finding the old coroner's report? Was he trying to endear himself to me? It wouldn't surprise me.

No wonder he told the court that he didn't want compensation, only "justice." It was just another way to fool the jury into believing his innocence. Just as he fooled me.

"Come to France with me," he says suddenly. "I know you're not happy. We'd make a good team. You're bright. You earn a living by arguing people out of a hole. That's a great skill."

No. It isn't. The truth is that I allowed the facts to twist me, because I saw Daniel in Joe. I then moved my mind to accept the facts, insubstantial as they were, to make it true.

"You understand me." Joe takes my hand. Part of me wants to snatch it away. Part of me wants to stay in this position forever. His grip is tight. Is it threatening or reassuring? I'm no longer sure. With a sinking heart, I can't help asking myself the question I've been avoiding.

Can I believe anything this man has ever told me?

"Lily . . ."

And now I'm running out of the restaurant. Down the street. Back home. Past Carla's silent front door. Retching as soon as I reach the bathroom. Oblivious to Ed's knocking on the bathroom door to ask if I'm "all right."

Four weeks later, I am still being sick. And

just in case there is any doubt, the evidence is now in front of me, courtesy of the long, thin packet I bought from the chemist.

I am pregnant.

■ ■ ■ ■

PART TWO:
TWELVE YEARS
LATER

■ ■ ■ ■

My head is still throbbing.

When I put up my left hand — the one that's not hurting — to touch it, it feels sticky.

Blood.

My sight is blurred.

Yet I swear I can see something around the corner. What is it?

A shoe.

A red shoe.

A siren roars by.

I hold my breath with wild hope.

But the siren goes past.

If only I could turn back the clock.

But hindsight, as the three of us might say, is a fine thing.

What's that I can hear?

My blood runs cold.

She's still here.

24
CARLA

Autumn 2013

"Excuse me, but I believe you are in my seat," said Carla. She flashed a smile at the business-suited man next to the window, two rows from the emergency exit. It was a carefully cultivated smile. Exactly the right combination of charm and *don't mess with me.*

"I'm sorry. I don't understand what you're saying."

She should have guessed. No Italian would wear such a terrible tie.

Carla repeated her sentence in English with the same smile.

There was a brief flash of annoyance on the man's face, followed by a softening as he took in her smooth black bob, her full glossy lips, her flawless skin and her smell. Chanel No. 5. Her favorite perfume since borrowing Lily's all those years ago.

"I do apologize," he said, leaping up and

almost bumping his head on the overhead lockers as he did so. Then he glanced at his boarding pass. "You're right. I should be in the middle seat."

He said it in such a way that Carla knew he had deliberately made the "mistake" to get the window seat on this flight from Rome to Heathrow. She also suspected that if she had been less attractive or less determined, her fellow passenger might have achieved his goal.

The plane was only half full, she noticed, as it began to taxi slowly down the runway. There was no one on the aisle side. On her row it was just her and the man who had tried to take her seat, who was now reading the *Times*. She glanced at the page he was reading.

NEW PLAN FOR REFUGEE CRISIS

Meanwhile, the flight attendant was doing a safety talk about life jackets and oxygen masks. Then there was a roaring noise that bellowed in her ears, followed by a sudden rush forward.

Carla's hands gripped the sides of her seat. Her second flight ever.

"Nervous?" asked the man.

"Not at all," said Carla smoothly. Mentally

she crossed her fingers. Another old habit from the past whenever she told a lie.

They were already up in the air! Through the window, she watched the tiny houses down below them. *Arrivederci, Italia,* she said silently. Self-consciously, she touched the back of her newly bare neck. How odd it felt without her usual long black curls. "Your beautiful hair!" Mamma had exclaimed when she'd returned from the hairdresser. But Carla had wanted a fresh look to go with the new life ahead. She was nearly twenty-three! About time she made something happen.

Two stewards were pushing a trolley down the aisle in their direction. Carla's stomach rolled. She hadn't been able to eat anything for breakfast and it was now early afternoon.

"Would you like a drink, madam?"

"Red wine, please."

"Small or large?"

"Large."

"Please, let me pay." The man next to her laid a hand briefly on hers. "It's the least I can do for making a mistake over the seat."

"It was nothing," she said.

"Even so."

Men had been flirting with her for so long that Carla had grown to expect it. Even so, it was only polite to show her appreciation.

Graciously, she dipped her head to one side just as Mamma used to do for Larry. "That is very kind."

"Are you going to London for business or pleasure?"

"Both." Carla took a large sip. The wine was not as good as that in Nonno's cellars, but it helped her relax. "I have just finished my law degree in Italy and now I am going to do a conversion course in London. But I am also going to look up some old friends."

"Really?" The man's eyebrows rose. They were sandy-colored, stirring distant memories of Ed's head tilted over his sketchbook. "I'm in the pharmaceutical business myself."

Carla could see where this was going. She'd already said too much, partly out of nervousness. It had encouraged him. If she didn't take steps now, he would drone on for the rest of the journey. "I am so sorry," she said, draining her glass. "But I have a headache. I think I must sleep."

His disappointment gave her a flash of pleasure. Not that she needed any proof that she could turn heads. The real test was whether she could turn the *right* heads.

Carla took out the silk sleep mask from her soft brown leather handbag. Adjusting her seat into the reclining mode, she closed her eyes. Just as she was starting to relax, there was a lurch followed by a ping and an announcement. "This is the captain speaking. We are entering a period of turbulence. Please return to your seats and fasten your seat belts."

Silently, Carla began to recite her Ave Marias. Then, in a bid to further distract herself, she allowed her mind to slip back over the years to the first time when she had flown, when she had been a scared, uncertain child. Not like the new Carla whom she had worked so hard to become.

She'd only just recovered from her appendix operation when it happened. Gossip traveled fast. After Maria's mother discovered that Mamma came from her husband's birthplace, she had promptly gotten in touch with her mother-in-law. If it had not been a small town, it might have been all right. But in a place where everyone knew everyone, news spread like wildfire. Nonno's daughter was not the successful London career woman he had claimed, or a "widow" as Francesca had maintained, but a struggling single mother with a child, working in a shop. Fancy that!

Meanwhile, it appeared her grandmother Nonna had been looking for them. She eventually traced them through information but every time Carla or Mamma had answered, Nonna had been interrupted by Nonno and had quickly put down the phone. But, when Nonno heard that everyone knew the truth about his daughter, Nonna admitted she had found them and Nonno had been shamed into ordering them home. And, because Mamma could no longer pay the rent in London, they had had no choice but to return.

From the minute they arrived, both she and Mamma found themselves firmly under Nonno's thumb. Her grandfather would not even allow Mamma to work. She must stay at home and look after Nonna.

"How I miss Larry," Mamma would tell Carla when they were alone in their shared bedroom.

"But he was a bad man," she would reply.

"He loved me."

Instead, Mamma blamed Lily. Lily had forced him to stay away. Lily and her interfering ways.

Try as she might, Carla could not make Mamma see sense — Larry was as much to blame as Lily. Her mother's hair grew lank. It lost its bounce, and strands of gray crept in. She grew thin. And she kept going over and over that last night in the flat. "I should have called the doctor earlier for you," Mamma kept saying. "You might have died."

"No, Mamma," Carla had reassured her. "You were sad."

Mamma had nodded. "Perhaps you are right. If Lily had not threatened Larry, none of this would have happened." Was that true? Carla wondered. After all, she had planned to get rid of Larry. But after Lily had done it for them, she realized it hadn't been such a good idea after all.

Already their lives were regulated by Nonno. She was never allowed out late, even when she became a teenager. She was banned from parties that her friends were invited to. "Do you want to end up like your mother?" he always demanded.

"Shh," Nonna would say.

But Carla already knew the truth. One of the neighbors had let the cat out of the bag, as the English would say, soon after they had moved in. "Your poor mamma." She said the *poor* bit with a sneer, as though she wasn't to be pitied at all. "To have been betrayed by that man. To think he was already married with a child of his own."

"How do you know about Larry?" she had demanded.

The old woman had frowned. "Your papa's name is Giovanni. He used to live in Sicily, but I heard he has now gone to Rome."

So her father was not dead at all? Carla felt she should be shocked. Yet something inside her had suspected this all along. After all, it wouldn't have been the first lie Mamma had told her. Giovanni must be the man with the funny hat under Mamma's bed. The neighbor's remark prompted Carla to take another look at the box, which Mamma had now hidden at the back of the wardrobe behind her clothes. Sure enough, tucked inside an old envelope was her birth certificate. There was a blank space in the section for the father's name.

Despite this, Carla knew that she must not ask Mamma about it again or she would be even more depressed. So she talked to Nonna instead. "Do you have his address so I can write to him?" she asked. "If he knew I was here, he might want to see me."

"Hush, child." Nonna put her arms around her. "I am afraid he wants nothing to do with us. You must let the past be the past."

Carla reluctantly did as she was told. What choice did she have? No one would even tell her what her father's real surname was. Cavoletti was of course her mother's maiden name, something she'd never thought of when they sent those postcards to Nonno and Nonna.

"I should have said nothing," added the neighbor. "And don't press your mother or grandmother. They have been through enough."

But that didn't mean she couldn't plan for the future. "Don't worry," she would say, holding her mother in her arms when she wept every night. "We will be all right in the end."

"But how?" her mother had sobbed.

Her fists clenched. "I will think of something."

Before long, Carla showed the natural aptitude at school that she had just started to discover back in England, before it all went wrong. Nonno began to boast about his granddaughter who got such excellent grades. He even began to listen to the teachers who said she should consider a career in the "professions." How about becoming an *avvocata*? Carla showed great skill during school debates.

And that's when the idea began to form. She would go to university to study law. It was a five-year course — a commitment — but it would be worth it. But the real reason that Carla wanted to take the course was because Lily had proven that the law gave you power. A right to decide other people's future. The Lily she'd seen in the corridor that last night was full of it. It might also make her rich enough to rescue Mamma from the claustrophobia of Nonno's home.

In hindsight, Carla realized that Mamma had not behaved as well as she might have in England

Maybe she should not have had an affair with a married man. But she had been a vulnerable single mother. Now it was up to her, Carla, to protect her in the future. No point in living in the past.

For the next six years, Carla concentrated on working and studying hard. Then, during her final year at university in Rome, she came across a legal precedent which referred to a case which Lily had handled. It even credited her name. Lily Macdonald! Carla's heart had given a quick skip. Within seconds, she found herself Googling both Ed and Lily.

So! Lily was a partner now. How unfair that she was doing well while Mamma was almost a prisoner in Nonno's home as a result of Lily's actions. The headshot on the firm's website showed that she had cut her hair into a bob. Lily looked almost glamorous — nothing like the Lily she once knew.

As for Ed, she could find very little about him apart from the odd small exhibition here and there. But then a picture jumped out at her from an obscure art site. Her heart started pounding. It was of a little girl with black curls and a smile playing on her lips that was somehow both innocent and knowing. The colors were dramatic — a crimson dress against a sky-blue background — but it was the way the child looked out of the frame that really got you. It was as if she was there in the same room with you.

Which, of course, she had been. Because the child was her. The dress had in fact been black. But an artist, Ed had said at the time, was "entitled to change things."

"Artist sells acrylic painting to anonymous art collector for a five-figure sum," announced the text below.

A five-figure sum?

Stunned, she read on.

Ed Macdonald has given hope to all up-and-coming artists everywhere after a collector made him an offer he couldn't refuse. "I actually painted *The Italian Girl* some years ago and entered it for an award where it won third prize, though it didn't find a home. I was stunned when a buyer, who has asked not to be named, recently walked into a gallery where I exhibit and bought it on the spot."

It wasn't fair! If it were not for her, there would have been no painting. So Carla wrote to Ed. She had not been paid for her services as a model, she pointed out. Perhaps Ed might like to share some of the money.

After three weeks, there was no reply. Maybe they had moved. So she sent a second letter to the gallery mentioned at the end of the article. Still nothing. How dare he not acknowledge her? The more she thought about it, and the more phone calls she had from poor, housebound Mamma, the more Carla became convinced that she was owed something. Her bitterness grew.

Then a chance remark from a tutor gave her an idea. "You are fluent in English, yes? Perhaps you should consider a conversion course in the UK. It will increase your earning power."

It would also bring her closer to the people who had hurt Mamma, including Larry. She would claim what was rightfully hers. And have what Lily had: money, a good job, a new look — maybe a bob would suit her, too.

■ ■ ■ ■

There was a gentle touch on her arm. Carla started. "We are about to land," said the man with the terrible tie. "I thought I ought to tell you."

Peeling off her eye mask, she smiled at him. "Thank you."

"Not at all. Where are you going to stay in London?"

"King's Cross," she said confidently, thinking back to the hostel she had found on the Internet. It had looked so nice, and it was reasonably priced, too.

"Have you been to London before?"

"Of course. But many years ago."

"Things have changed." He took a business card out of his pocket. "Here is my number in case you feel like a drink sometime."

She glanced at the silver wedding band on his left hand. If Mamma's experience had taught her one thing, it was that married men were not worth it. "Thank you but that is not necessary."

His lips tightened. "Your call."

There was a bump, followed by a high screaming of brakes. They were hurtling forward so fast that she wondered if they would be able to stop. This time, there was no comforting pat on the arm. Instead, her companion was keen to get up and grab his bag. If she'd taken his card, Carla told herself, he might have taken her out to dinner.

But nothing must be allowed to distract her from her plan.

EU ARRIVALS THIS WAY

Heathrow was so busy! Bewildered, Carla stared at the various signs. Taxi? The tube would be cheaper. Nonno had given her some money for the course and her living costs, but it was not very much.

It took a long time to reach King's Cross station after taking the wrong train twice. "Excuse me," she said to the man selling newspapers outside, "but can you tell me where Black Street is?"

He ignored her to serve the customer behind. It was getting dark now and she'd forgotten how much colder England was than Italy. Shivering and hungry, she asked directions from person after person in the crowds swarming past.

Eventually she found it. Carla stared with distaste at the dirty concrete building with peeling green paint on the door. Two girls came out, arm in arm, wearing tights with big, glaring holes in them. Over the tights were denim shorts.

Smoothing down the neat cream linen jacket that Mamma had made specially for the trip, Carla went in. "I have booked a room," she said politely to the woman at the desk.

"Name?"

"Carla Cavoletti."

The woman sniffed and handed her a key. "Third floor. First on the right. Lift's out of order."

The steps smelled of pee. Someone had scrawled rude words on the wall in red paint. Carla's heart sank. This room was like a cell! The bed was narrow with a scratchy gray blanket. There was a desk, but the lighting was so poor that it would be hard to study. The "en suite" bathroom was a cupboard with a washbasin. The notice on the wall informed her that the toilets on this floor were not in use. PLEASE USE THE FACILITIES ON THE SECOND FLOOR.

Carla sat down on the edge of the bed and flicked on her phone. "Ring when you arrive," Mamma had said.

"Hello? It is me. Yes, the flight was wonderful and the hotel, she is beautiful. You *know* what my plans are, Mamma. I've told you so many times. Tomorrow, I register at the college. Yes, Mamma. I told you. I will also find Larry to tell him where you are. I love you, too."

As Carla ended the call, a cockroach scuttled out from under the bed. Ugh! She swiftly ground it into the floor with her stiletto heel. There was a crunching sound. Ick! Yet also strangely satisfying.

Kicking the dead insect under the bed, she took out a cigarette, despite the no smoking sign on the wall, and inhaled deeply. That was better. Then she walked to the window. Outside, London glittered with lights and roared with the hum of traffic and possibilities.

Somewhere out there were three people she needed to find.

Whatever it took.

25
LILY

"No. *No!* You have moved my shoes. Now I can't wear them. Why did you do that? *Why?*"

Breathe, I tell myself. Breathe. Don't shout. Don't snap. Don't try to reason. None of it works. It only serves to make me feel temporarily better, and then the guilt will set in. Guilt that I'm leaving all this — yes! — in ten minutes to get the London train. Guilt that I'm leaving Tom with Mum to escape back to my job and my home with my husband. Guilt at the thought that, perhaps, we shouldn't have had him in the first place . . .

No. That's not right. Of course I love my son. Love him fiercely with every inch of my body. The second I had him I knew I'd never go back. But we didn't know what we were doing. And it's hard when your eleven-year-old behaves like a toddler at times and an intellectual, with a reasoning worthy of a genius, at others. It's why we've never had another child.

"I'll sort it, darling. Don't worry." Mum's smooth, reassuring voice cuts in as she re-arranges the offending shoes, which had been moved out of line from Tom's precise positioning of the evening before. It's one of his "little things," as Ed calls it. A ritual that appears to give our son a security that we're unable to provide ourselves.

"I see this sort of thing all the time," said the specialist. He gives a little sigh. "And no, it's not your fault. The autistic spectrum has probably always been around, but now we have a label for it. It can be hereditary. But it can also come up right out of the blue without any family history." My mouth was dry as he continued. "Usually it starts to reveal itself from the age of eight months or so. But some mothers say they suspected from the beginning that something wasn't quite right."

I thought back to Tom's birth. His eyes had darted from side to side as if to say, *Where the hell am I?* He'd been much quieter than the other babies on the ward. But when he did cry, it had been a shrill, unhappy cry that scared me rigid. Or was that because I was scared myself? Terrified of being a new mother at a time when my career was just taking off. When Ed and I were still clumsily trying to start our marriage over again.

From the minute I had shown my husband the blue line on the pregnancy result kit, it had become an unspoken agreement that we would no longer "keep trying" to make our marriage work. We would *make* it do so. My mind had gone back to my teenage days when I had overheard my mother accusing my father of having an affair. I had been terrified they would break up, and so relieved when they stayed together. Many children grow up perfectly well in a single-parent family. But then Carla and Francesca had flashed into my head. Did I really want to end up like them?

And anyway, Ed was a changed man. "A child," my husband had said, placing a hand on my belly. His eyes had shone. "Our child. It can be our new start."

"But how will we manage?" I'd demanded. My voice had sung with guilt, anger, resentment and downright fear. "Everyone wants to hire me now after the case. I've been promoted. You haven't even got a job."

If that sounded cruel, I'm ashamed to say that I intended it that way. I was livid with Ed because I was livid with myself.

"Then I'll work from home and look after

him at the same time."

I have to admit it. Ed was a natural. He doted on Tom. My sister-in-law's words proved true — at least at first. Fatherhood grounded him. He even gave up alcohol for a while, although he now just tries to drink in moderation. Even when our son screamed blue murder as we tried to lift him out of his cot, my husband showed patience I had never seen in him before. Later, when Tom refused to play with the other toddlers in the postnatal group and even bit a little girl when she tried to take his precious red toy train, Ed merely declared he showed "character." "He's much brighter than the others," my husband would say proudly. "This morning he actually told one of the other kids to 'give me space.' Can you believe it? It's almost as if he's a mini-adult. And he can count to ten on his fingers. I bet not many two-year-olds can do that. Just imagine what he will be like when he's older!"

But then Tom's behavior began to get more extreme. He asked one of the other mothers why she had a "hairy moustache." He threw his green plastic cup at another child because it wasn't the usual yellow color, causing a big bruise on his cheek. Ed was asked to find another playgroup.

At home, it was just as difficult. "No,"

snapped our son when I tried to make him put on a soft blue velour jumper which Ross, his godfather, had sent him for Christmas. "I don't like the feel on my skin."

Even Ed began to worry. "What's the matter with him?" he asked when Tom refused to go to bed because his duvet had been washed in a new soap powder and smelled "wrong."

"The mothers at the new playgroup are giving me the cold shoulder now. They seem to think it's my fault."

My parents had once been accused of poor parenting, too.

"There has to be an answer," Ed insisted.

Through our GP, we found a specialist who eventually gave his opinion. Asperger's. An autism spectrum disorder, as well as obsessive behavior. By then, Tom was six. Back in 2008, such experts were few and far between and their understanding of the condition was not what it is now.

"I'm afraid there are no quick-fix cures," said the consultant. "You could try cutting out certain foods but it doesn't always do anything. On the plus side, these children are usually very bright." His eyes flickered with sympathy. "But I won't pretend it can't be a great strain on everyone concerned."

Tom, I told myself in my darkest moments, was my punishment for something so terrible that I could barely admit it to myself, let alone anyone else.

As Ed wept on my shoulder ("I'm trying, Lily, I really am"), I wanted to tell him this. Yet how could I? He would surely leave if he knew what I had done. A child like Tom needed two parents. We were bound together now, just as my parents had been.

"Let us help," my mother finally said when she had come up to London for her monthly visit. (By then, she'd stopped drinking: Dad had said that Tom's birth had made her decide that she'd had enough, once and for all.) Ed and I now lived in a three-bedroom Victorian terrace house in Notting Hill, thanks to his grandparents' deaths, which had finally released the trust fund money. Meanwhile, my healthy salary had meant that Ed could be a stay-at-home dad while trying to make it as a freelance artist. That was great in theory, but in practice it was proving impossible for Ed to work while looking after a child who could do complicated long-division sums in his head one minute and then jump up and down screaming that his hands were "dirty" from play clay the next.

"We could look after Tom during the week," Mum added, looking around at the untidy sitting room, strewn with toys and half-finished sketches where Ed had clearly been trying to work. This led to some frustration all around, as my husband was meant to be caring for Tom at the same time. Only a few days earlier he had trapped his finger in the window "to see how it shut."

"It will give you some time to yourselves."

Mum was always a bit nosy when she came around. In the years after Daniel's death she'd become more interfering, as if his absence had left a hole she needed to fill by playing a more active role in my life. But it intensified when Tom was born. Had she noticed the telltale signs in the spare room? Ed's clothes in the pine chest of drawers. The half-empty bottle of wine in the bottom of the wardrobe. (Not mine — I'd given up drinking as soon as I was pregnant.) All clues that this was the room that my husband usually occupied at night.

"It's easier for my back," he had said when first suggesting separate bedrooms. I was hurt initially. But the more Tom yelled when I tried to brush his hair or when someone moved his "special cup," the more irritated Ed and I became with each other. Sometimes it developed into full-blown rows.

"I can't cope with two kids having tantrums," I snapped during one particularly nasty argument when Ed had told Tom to "get a grip."

Tom's face had creased into confusion. "But where do I find one?" he had demanded. Language had to be crystal clear. "Pipe down" got confused with my father's pipe at home.

Anger or tears on our part did nothing. Tom seemed to have a problem in recognizing other people's emotions. "Why are they crying?" he asked one day when seeing a stream of refugees on television.

"Because they don't have homes anymore," I explained.

"So why don't they just get some new ones?"

Some of these questions might be normal in a very young child. But as Tom grew older, they became increasingly inappropriate. It was exhausting. But Mum's suggestion saved us. Tom moved to Mum and Dad's in Devon by the sea. There was a school down the road where my brother and I had gone. They'd had more "special children" like him since then, the head told us brightly. We mustn't worry. And Ed and I would come down every weekend to see him. Since Tom had been born, my mother seemed to mourn Daniel less. She had another mission now: her grandson. "It's amazing," said Dad gratefully, "to see the effect that Tom has had on us all. I mean, I know he's not easy but he seems to have brought us all together."

Much as I hate to admit it, Tom's absence also gave Ed and me a chance to be a couple again. There was time to talk over meals. To lie on the sofa in the evenings, my legs wrapped around his in companionable silence. To rediscover each other's bodies in one bedroom. I can't say it was — or is — wildly passionate. But it's comfortable. Loving.

Meanwhile, Ed was still trying to make a name for himself. We'd both hoped it would actually happen sooner, especially after coming third in that award. But the market was slow, or so he was told. Every now and then he persuaded a gallery to let him display some of his work. But it was hard going until an anonymous buyer bought *The Italian Girl.* Finally Ed got enough money to achieve his dream — starting his own gallery.

Ironically, my career has blossomed since Tom's birth. To my delight, I was made a partner on the back of my continued success after the Joe Thomas case, which led to a cluster of settlements throughout the

341

country and a change in the law on health and safety. Our contribution has gone down in the law reports.

Just as important, in my mind, was the fact that Davina was now safely married to a Yorkshire landowner. We declined the wedding invitation. Ed insisted that he had never been unfaithful to me with her, but I still felt awkward in her presence.

Still, Ed and I have become much stronger as a couple.

They say that when you have an ill child or one who presents certain challenges, you either grow apart or together. Surprisingly we have done the latter.

"My shoes! I can't wear them now that you've touched them!"

My son's anger brings me sharply back to the present. If I don't catch the early morning train to Waterloo, I'll miss my meeting.

"Please," I beg. Part of me wants to tell Tom not to be so stupid. The other part wants to hug him out of sympathy because he is trapped in his own world. I choose the latter, holding him to me and stroking his head.

"No," he howls, pushing me away. For a split second, I'd forgotten. Tom doesn't like affection unless it's on his terms.

"I'll sort out the shoes," says Mum firmly. Every now and then, I'm convinced she's taken Tom on in order to get it right this time. "Here. I almost forgot. This letter came for you during the week."

And so I go, coward that I am. I leap into the car where Dad is waiting, and I lean back, closing my eyes with relief.

"Ed meeting you at the other end?" he asks.

I shake my head. Unusually, my husband hasn't come down with me this time. He was invited to attend a Sunday showing in an elite gallery off Covent Garden that is displaying a reproduction of *The Italian Girl*. (The original, of course, had already been sold to a private anonymous buyer.) There is something about that painting — the vibrant, almost harsh, colors, and the half-knowing, half-innocent look — that unsettles me every time I see it. Or is it just because I still feel irritated about Francesca using us as babysitters so that she could be with Larry? Or rather Tony Gordon. How could someone live two lives like that?

Now, as the train jolts through Sherborne, I turn over the envelope in my hand. I'm not going to let Joe Thomas touch me. Not even mentally. I'm not going to allow myself to think about my part in helping a guilty man to walk free.

And that's why, as soon as I get to London, I'm going to tear up this envelope, with my former client's distinctive capital-letter writing on it, and drop it in the nearest bin.

When I reach my office, there's the usual urgent, steady, controlled panic. I love every minute of it.

It's not just my career that's on the up. It's my body, too. Some women age badly, like Davina — I can't stifle my grin of triumph — whose picture in *Tatler*'s Bystander column the other month showed her looking decidedly jowled. Others, like me, appear to improve. "Middle age suits you," Ed told me the other morning as he gazed down at my flat stomach and slim thighs.

I'd tickled him out of mock indignation. "Middle age? Forty is the new thirty, I'll have you know."

The ironic thing is, after Tom was born, I was too busy to comfort eat. Dealing with Tom was far more effective than any diet. I also began to run before work. Just puffing once around the block at first, but then farther. Running, especially at six a.m. when the world was just waking, helped me to escape the demons of my dreams.

As the weight fell off and my cheekbones began to perk up, I found myself able to slip into size tens and then eights. I went to an expensive hairdresser in Mayfair and had my long blond hair cut into a "take me seriously" bob. People watch me now as I stride purposefully through the office in my new red stilettos. Power shoes. Clients do a double take, as if one isn't capable of winning a case *and* looking good. Once, in court, the opposing lawyer slipped me a note, asking if I'd like dinner that night. I turned him down. But I was flattered.

Court. That reminds me. I need to be there in precisely one hour. Ever since "that case," I've specialized in serious cases like murder and manslaughter. Watching Tony Gordon strut across the floor all those years ago lit something inside me. Solicitors can gain an extra qualification to take on cases that would normally be handled in court by a barrister. It's another string to your bow and it increases your earning power considerably. So that's what I did.

Now, however, I will only take on cases if I'm convinced of my client's innocence. Any qualm on my part and I will pass him to someone else, claiming that I am "too busy." I have no doubts about this afternoon's case. A teenage girl. Knocked off her bike by a lorry driver.

Justice has to be done.

"Ready?" I glance impatiently at our latest intern: a young boy fresh out of Oxford whose father is a friend of one of the other partners. I don't like it, but what can you do? Nepotism flourishes when it comes to law. The boy is still fiddling with his Old Etonian tie as we stride along. "Aren't we going to get a taxi?" he whines.

"No." My stride is long and measured. Walking is another way I continue to stay slim. And besides, the fresh autumnal air helps me to think as I run over the details of the case.

"Do you get nervous in court?" The boy looks up at me and I feel a touch of compassion.

"I don't allow myself to be." We scale the stone steps into the court. It's not as big as the Old Bailey but it's imposing enough, with its stone pillars and clusters of black gowns, flapping as they walk. Unfair as it is, men still outnumber the women.

"Lily?"

I stop as a gray-faced, gray-haired man pauses beside me. Swiftly, I search my memory. I know him, I'm certain, yet I can't quite place the face.

"You don't recognize me." This was said

in a rasping tone that was a statement rather than a question. "Tony. Tony Gordon."

I'm shocked. I haven't seen him for months, and then only in passing; just a small nod in recognition, as if we never spent all those hours together, heads close, poring over papers that would eventually result in a grave injustice. I've tried as hard as I can to forget those hours ever happened.

"How are you, Lily?" As he speaks, he touches his throat. And then I see it. An unmistakable lump rising from above the top of his collar. "Throat cancer," he rasps again. "They've done what they can, but . . ."

His words are almost swallowed by the busy, echoing voices around us. Beside me, my Oxford intern is shuffling from one foot to the other in embarrassment.

"I saw your name on the list and wanted to catch you." Tony's eyes — one of the few things that haven't changed about him — fall on my companion.

"Can you wait over there, please?" I tell the young man firmly.

My old colleague's mouth twists as if in amusement. "You're different. But I knew that already. Your reputation is spreading."

I ignore the compliment. "How can I help you?"

"Joe Thomas."

My mouth dries. My body freezes. The sounds around us fade.

"What about him?"

My mind goes back to the conversation I had with Tony all those years ago. The panicky phone call I made after Joe Thomas had proudly admitted his guilt. "What do we do?" I had begged.

"Nothing," Tony replied. "He's free and that's it." His lack of surprise was all too clear.

"You knew he was guilty?"

"Suspected it. But I wasn't sure. Besides, that doesn't matter."

"Yes, it does."

"Look, Lily. When you're older, you'll realize that this is a game. One that we have to win even if we're dealt a bad card. There wasn't enough evidence against our client. Besides, it would have jeopardized all those other cases on the back of it. Just get over it. Move on." And that is the real reason I've tried not to cross paths with Tony Gordon again. It isn't just the double life he led and the consternation on poor little Carla's face as she tried to work out why her mother's Larry was really called Tony. It's

348

because I don't want to be a lawyer like him. My principles are higher. Or they should've been.

But now, here we are. "What about him?" I say, glancing at my watch. Just ten minutes until we're due in the courtroom.

"He's written to me. Wanted me to pass on a message." I think of all the unsigned birthday cards that I've received over the years. All sent to the office. All bearing the same handwriting in capital letters. All bearing foreign stamps from countries as far afield as Egypt. Including the latest one, which now lies in bits inside a Waterloo bin. At least, I presume it was a birthday card. My mind briefly flickers back to the low-key birthday dinner I had last week with my husband. No fuss. No fanfare. Just a quiet celebration of beating the odds. Of staying married.

"He needs to speak to you, Lily." Tony pushes a piece of paper into my hand. "Said it was urgent."

Then he's gone. His black coat flapping. No hat. He's striding through the open arched hallway before I have a chance to express my sympathies about his illness.

Meanwhile, I have my work cut out for me. An innocent lorry driver, whose life was ruined when a teenager cycled across the road in front of him without warning.

One might expect the cyclist to be the victim. But that's the challenge in law. Nothing is as it seems.

Right now, I have to get the poor man off. Have to maintain my record of more wins than anyone else in the office. It's the only way to prove that I'm not such a bad person after all.

Then, against my better judgment, I stuff Joe Thomas's number into my pocket and walk on.

26
CARLA

Carla woke early in the morning to a series of shouts and a loud clattering. Flinching with cold as her bare feet touched the freezing floor, she saw men emptying bins into the lorries in the narrow street outside her window.

Then, as she stretched out her arms, one of the men looked up and whistled.

Ignoring him, Carla returned to bed and huddled down under the thin duvet (there wasn't even a radiator in here!) before switching on her computer and clicking on the link she'd saved under "Favorites: Tony Frederick Gordon. Lincoln's Inn."

And then another article:

The Honourable Society of Lincoln's Inn is one of four Inns of Court in London to which barristers of England and Wales belong and where they are called to the Bar. It is recognized . . .

Carla had of course looked all this up back in Italy. But what she still hadn't worked out, despite her assurances to Mamma that she would find Larry, was whether she could simply go to this place in the hope of surprising him. Or whether she should make an appointment, posing as a client.

As she pondered, yet another cockroach crawled out from under her hostel bed. She would make an appointment, Carla decided. That way, she would be certain of seeing him. But, she wouldn't ring. She would turn up in person.

Getting out of bed, she slipped into the pink silk dressing gown that Nonna had bought her as a good-bye present, and carefully tiptoed around the cockroach. It wasn't a matter of being soft, she told herself as she headed for the shared toilet down the corridor. It was a question of being practical. She couldn't kill every cockroach in the room.

But she could make Larry see what he had done.

Half an hour later, she was ready. She wore a slim beige pencil skirt that showed off her figure, and a black skinny-knit jumper with a wide belt to accentuate her waist. Perfect! Especially with yesterday's cream jacket and a squirt of Chanel from the sample bottle she'd swiped at the airport. No one had seen her.

At the hostel reception desk was a pile of London Underground maps. Carefully sidestepping a young girl with a tattoo on her neck and slashed jeans, Carla helped herself. She stared at it, puzzled.

"Where do yer want to go, then?" asked the girl.

"Holborn," answered Carla primly.

"Get the Red line." A dirty finger jabbed the map. "Want to buy a cheap Oyster card?"

"Please, what is that?"

There was laughter from behind her where another girl was hovering. They reminded Carla of the school in England where everyone had been horrid to her.

"You use it to get on buses and tubes. Just twenty quid. It's a bargain."

"I have only euros."

"Then give me forty."

Carla handed over the money and headed for King's Cross station. She could just about remember the way from her journey last night. When she held the Oyster card against the barrier like everyone else, there was a loud bleeping.

"You ain't got no money on that, love," said a man in a neon jacket.

"But someone sold it to me for forty euros!"

" 'Fraid you've been done, then. Only get your Oysters from a proper station or online." He jerked a finger toward a machine and a long line of people.

Furious, Carla bought another. These English! Robbers! All of them.

Still, Lincoln's Inn was even more beautiful than the pictures online. For a moment, Carla stood and marveled at the tall buildings with their big sash windows and wide window ledges. Despite being in the middle of London, it felt like the countryside with those beautiful squares and neatly clipped hedges turning gold with autumn's approach.

To her relief, she found Larry's chambers quite easily.

"May I help you?" asked a woman at the desk.

"I would like to make an appointment with Mr. L — I mean, Mr. Tony Gordon."

The secretary gave her a questioning stare. "Are you a solicitor?"

"Not exactly. I used to know Mr. Gordon and would like to get in touch again."

The stare grew cooler. "Then I suggest you e-mail one of the clerks. He will pass on your message." She pushed across a

354

compliments slip. "Here are the details."

"But I need to see Mr. Gordon now. It's important."

"I'm afraid it's impossible. Now I am going to have to ask you to leave."

The voice was no longer cool. It was angry and firm. Determined not to show her embarrassment, Carla walked out, her head high. Then she found a café with Wi-Fi and composed a brief message.

Dear Tony,
You might remember me from some years ago. I am in the UK now and have a message to pass on to you from my mother Francesca.
Kind regards,
Carla

Polite and to the point. Personally, Carla didn't share her mother's hopes that Larry, or rather Tony, might miss her. But with any luck, he might agree to see Carla. If nothing else, she might be able to extract some guilt money from him.

Now for the next two tasks on her list. Registration at the college was far more successful. Lectures would start tomorrow. Did she have the reading list that had been e-mailed out during the summer? Yes?

Good. There was a freshers' drinks party tonight. It would be a way to meet people.

But, Carla told herself as she headed for the tube again, she had more important things to do.

27
LILY

I wait until after the "innocent" verdict before making the call. The lorry driver case was tight. The other side had produced film of the "victim": a happy, laughing teenager on her bike. It had almost swayed the women on the jury, most of whom had children.

But not quite.

"Thank you." The lorry driver's wife flings her arms around me outside the courtroom. "I thought we were going to lose at one point."

So did I, although I'd never admit it. Drugs. Drink. It's usually one or the other that leads to the cells or death. That memory of the Hampstead pub still haunts my mind. It's why I don't touch alcohol anymore.

"We're going to go out now and celebrate," says the lorry driver's wife, glancing up adoringly at her husband. "Aren't we, love?"

But the lorry driver, like me, is looking across the marble-floored foyer at the middle-aged couple who are silently holding each other. As if sensing our gaze, the mother turns and shoots me a disdainful look.

I'm sorry, I want to say. *I'm sorry for your loss. Most of all I'm sorry that your memory of your daughter has been tainted forever. But it's the law.*

Then she walks up to me and I brace myself. This is an intelligent family. Much was made of this in court. The father is a professor. The mother spent her life bringing up her children. Luckily there are three more. But loss makes human beings into animals, as I have discovered.

The lorry driver's wife gasps as an arc of spits hits me straight in the face. It's directed not at the lorry driver but at me. "You should be ashamed of yourself," chokes out the bereaved mother.

I wipe the spittle off my cheek with the handkerchief that I keep especially for this purpose. It's not the first time this has happened. The woman's husband is taking her away now, casting me a baleful look.

"I'm sorry," says the lorry driver. His eyes are wet.

I shrug. "It's all right."

But it's not. And we both know it. Thanks to an anonymous tip-off (you'd be surprised how often this happens), I was able to name the dealer supplying drugs to the teenager who had ridden her bike into the lorry driver's path. If it weren't for that, we couldn't have established that the cyclist was a regular user, which in turn contributed to her degree of culpability.

Justice has been done. It doesn't always look like you'd expect. But there is always a price to be paid.

I walk down the steps and into the bracing wind outside. It's another world out here, I remind myself as I cross the road toward the park, narrowly avoiding a cyclist without a helmet. A world where I can choose to toss Tony's piece of paper with Joe Thomas's number on it.

Or ring it.

We have to have closure. It's a phrase I hear again and again from my clients. Even if the verdict is guilty, they need to get rid of the sword hanging over their heads. I thought I'd gotten rid of mine. But every time I receive those birthday cards I realize I can't escape. And now I have a phone number.

If I don't ring, I will always wonder what he wanted to say. If I do, I am pandering to him. I take a fifty-pence piece out of my bag and throw it in the air. Heads I don't ring. Tails I do.

Swiftly I catch it before it hits the damp grass.

Tails.

I should go back to the office. But I need time to think. My conversation with Joe has unsettled me. So I head for the National Portrait Gallery. It always calms me down.

Emotions don't change through the centuries. Fear. Excitement. Apprehension. Guilt. And, when I snuggle up to Ed at night, relief that somehow we're all still together. A family unit. Marriage has its ups and downs, my mother has always said. It's true. It's all too easy to throw in the towel. But I'm not going to allow Joe Thomas to do that to me.

I'm staring at a picture of Thomas Cromwell when my mobile goes. "Sorry," I mouth to a disapproving couple wearing matching scarves.

Swiftly, I head for the foyer, where a tourist is questioning the price of the exhibition ticket. "Where I live, our museums are free," I hear her saying.

I fumble in my bag, but my mobile is right at the bottom and I don't get it out in time.

Missed call.

Ed.

My mouth goes dry. My husband never rings during my working day unless there's an emergency with Tom. We haven't had one for a while. It's about time for another. It's how it works.

Fingers shaking, I call him back.

28
CARLA

Carla had been expecting something grand. Not like the Royal Academy, of course, which she was looking forward to seeing. But something that was, well, significant. Yet this narrow building was wedged between a shoe shop and a newsstand. If you didn't know what you were looking for, you might walk straight past.

She entered and then stopped. All around her were white walls. And on those walls was . . . her.

Carla, as she used to be. The small Italian girl who always felt so different.

Some of the paintings she recognized. But there were new ones, too: laughing, frowning, thinking, dreaming. In big frames. Small frames. In bold strokes of red and raven black.

She gasped. There, in the corner, with a stick of charcoal in his hand, was Ed. Older than she'd remembered, with more lines on his forehead. He had glasses, too, which she didn't remember. But it was definitely him.

Sit still, Carla. Please. Think of something nice. Your new pink bike, perhaps. Your friend at school. What is her name again?

Maria! That's right. His words came filtering back to her as she approached him.

"Mr. Macdonald?"

Reluctantly his head rose up to meet her gaze. She could see he was annoyed at being interrupted. His eyes hardened. Then they softened. He made to stand up but sat down again. "Carla?" he said in a choked voice. "Carla? Is it really you?"

She'd been prepared for all kinds of reactions. But not this. Not this genuine look of pleasure. There was no shame. No embarrassment. No attempt to hide.

"I wrote to you," she said, looking him straight in the eye. "But you didn't reply."

Those bushy eyebrows rose. "Wrote to me? When?"

"Last year. And then I wrote again."

"You addressed it to the gallery?"

"Yes — no, not this one." Carla felt a tremor of doubt. "I sent the first to the flat and the second to a different gallery where you had an exhibition."

Ed ran a hand through his hair. "Ah. We moved a while ago. But the people who

363

bought the flat from us are still very good at sending on our mail. Gallery post, mind you, can be a bit hit-and-miss with so many artists coming and going."

Did she believe him? He sounded truthful enough. Carla looked up at this still rather handsome man with warm creases around his eyes. There was real care there. And admiration, too. No doubt about it. A hot feeling rippled through her. This was the man she had idolized as a child. But now she was all grown up.

Perhaps there might be another way . . .

"The letters were to tell you I was coming over. I have done my law degree in Italy. Now I am here to do a conversion course in England, and thought it would be nice to look you up."

"Wonderful!" Ed's hands took both of hers. He was squeezing them tight. Surely for longer than was necessary. "I can't tell you, Carla, how good it is to see you! Welcome. Welcome back!"

29
LILY

Ed's cell phone goes straight to voice mail.

I'm really scared now. Stepping back so someone else can go in front of me in the queue, I try again.

"Lily?"

Thank heavens. He's answering. "What's wrong?" I blurt out.

"Nothing!" His voice is bubbly with excitement.

I'm filled with relief.

"Are you busy?" he asks.

It's a strange question because he knows I'm always busy. The Portrait Gallery is a rare act of rebellion on my part. I should be in the office.

"Actually, I'm taking an hour out after the case."

"You won?"

Nowadays, Ed takes a keen interest in my work.

I feel a flash of pride. "We did."

"Well done." He pauses. "Can you come on down here, then?"

"To the gallery?"

"I've got a surprise."

"A nice one?"

"Definitely."

I feel childishly excited. "I can spare an hour," I say, walking out the doors and back into the street.

Ed's new gallery is in an old basement. It has definite potential, he assured me, especially with that wonderful curved Victorian pillar in the middle.

Quite a lot of people came to the opening. The anonymous buyer (even Ed wasn't told who it was, since it was all conducted through a dealer) had really helped to stir interest in his work. When clients started to ask me if I was related to Ed Macdonald the artist, I felt a burst of pride at telling them he was my husband. But now, after less than a year, this interest is fading. His acrylic style with garish colors and wide dramatic brushstrokes is not, apparently, to everyone's taste.

The hurtful press reviews have gotten to Ed, making him feel insecure again. The other night, he came home with three bottles of red. "I won't drink them all at once," he said defensively. I said nothing. I know my husband has flaws, but then so do I. Instead, we had a relaxed supper together, something we now frequently enjoy during the week with no Tom screaming because someone has tainted his plate by adding a pea by mistake. ("I told you. I don't like green!")

It doesn't help that the trust money had not been as much as we'd hoped, thanks to the stock market. There's nothing left now after paying for the gallery and house expenses. Ed desperately needs another big sale for the sake of his self-esteem and to pay the new business bills. Maybe, I tell myself, edging down the narrow stone steps, that's why he's summoned me here. Perhaps another buyer has turned up!

As I enter the gallery, I see the back of Ed's head.

"Lily!" He swivels around, saying my name as though it is fresh in his mouth. As if I am an acquaintance he hasn't seen for a long time instead of the wife he kissed good-bye this morning. "Guess who walked into the gallery an hour ago?"

As he speaks, a petite woman with a sleek black bob slides out from behind the pillar. Her hairstyle, apart from the color, is almost identical to mine. But she's young. Early twenties, at a guess. Big, wide, sunny smile and a wide, smooth forehead. She's stunning without being conventionally beautiful. Her face is the sort that makes you stare. I twist my silver bracelet — the one I always wear — with inexplicable nervousness.

"Hello, Lily!" she sings. There's an unexpected kiss on both my cheeks. Then she stands back. I feel suddenly cold as if someone has walked on my grave. "You don't remember me? It's Carla."

Carla? Little Carla who used to live in the same block of flats all those years ago, when Ed and I were first married? Carla, alias *The Italian Girl*? Is it really possible that the confident young woman who stands before me now with her immaculate complexion, her sharp, catlike eyes accentuated with just the right touch of eyeliner, is Carla?

It has taken me years to achieve a confidence like that.

But of course it's Carla. She's a mini-Francesca, minus the long curls.

"How are you?" I manage to say. "How is your mother?"

She dips her chin and then tilts her head to one side as if considering the question. "Mamma, she is very well, thank you. She is living in Italy. We have been there for some time."

Ed breaks in. "Carla's been trying to get

hold of us. She wrote to us."

I breathe steadily, just as I do in court when I need to be careful. "Really?" I say.

It's not a lie. Just a question.

"Twice," says Carla.

She is looking straight at me. Briefly I think back to that first letter with the Italian stamp, which was sent to our old address last year but forwarded to us by the current occupants.

My first instinct had been to throw it away like all the other begging letters we received around that time. People assume, rightly or wrongly, that if an artist has one big success, he or she is rich. The reality is that even with the portrait sale and Ed's trust money and my salary, we are still not that well off. Our mortgages on both the gallery and the house are huge. And of course we also have Tom's expensive therapy and his unknown future to think of.

I want to help people in need like any other decent person. But if you give to one, where do you stop? Yet Carla was different. She was right. In a way, we did owe our success to her.

I would talk to Ed, I had decided. But a critic had just written yet another snide review, questioning why anyone would want to pay so much for a "brash acrylic work that was worthy of a Montmartre street artist." My husband had been hurt. It was all I could do to assure Ed that this reviewer was wrong. Better to leave Carla's letter, with its thinly veiled request for money, until things were calmer.

Then came the second one, sent to the gallery where Ed had been exhibiting temporarily before it was forwarded to our home. Luckily, I happened to bump into the postman on the way to work. Recognizing the handwriting and foreign stamp, I slipped it in my briefcase and opened it in the office. The tone was angrier this time. More demanding. I sensed Francesca's hand behind it. If we gave them some money, I thought, they might ask for more.

So I put it away, pretending to myself that I would deal with it at "some point." And then I conveniently forgot about it. It wasn't the right thing to do. I can see that now. But if I had written back to Carla explaining our financial situation, she might not have believed it.

"We were worried when you left so suddenly all those years ago," Ed is saying now. "Why didn't you tell us you were going?"

His question takes me back to the last time I saw Carla. That awful row between Tony, Francesca and me. On top of that, I was trying to work out if Ed and I should stay together.

"Yes," I say, gritting my teeth, "we *were* very worried about you." Then my eye falls on the painting behind her. It's hard not to. There are paintings of Carla as a child all over the room.

"What do you think of your portraits?" I ask. Might as well play devil's advocate, I tell myself. Try to draw Carla out. It would also make me look more innocent in the matter of those unanswered letters.

The young woman in front of me flushes. "They are lovely." Then she flushes again. "I do not mean that *I* am lovely, you understand —"

"Oh, but you are," breaks in Ed. "Such a beautiful child. We both thought so, didn't we, Lily?"

I nod. "Remember that portrait of you that he entered for an award all those years ago? It got third prize. And although it didn't sell then, it was recently bought by a collector."

I watch her intently. She had mentioned both the competition and the sale in her letters. So I knew that she knew about them. But now she gasps as if in surprise, placing fingers to her mouth. Both are exquisitely painted in matching rose. The nails are a perfect oval. Not one chip on the polish. "Incredible!" she says reverently.

Perhaps she's embarrassed about the demanding tone of that second letter she thinks we didn't receive. I can understand that.

"That's why I was trying to find you," adds Ed eagerly. Really? If so, that's news to me. Sometimes Ed says things just to please people.

"I got quite a lot of money," my husband babbles on. He's getting wound up, almost high. I know the signs. It means he is capable of behaving recklessly. I touch his arm, hoping to slow him down, but he continues. "It helped me get a gallery of my own!"

There's a slight pause as my husband and I both think the same thing. That happens quite a lot nowadays. Maybe it's the same for all couples who have been married for a long time. "We ought to thank you," I say, reluctantly accepting that this would indeed be the honorable thing to do, even though we can't afford it.

"We should, indeed," agrees Ed. He's looking away from me, but I know his mind is going around. How much should he pay? What could we afford?

"Where are you living?" I ask, to buy time.

"In a place called King's Cross. In a hostel." She sighs. "There are cockroaches everywhere."

Suddenly that confident woman is no longer there. I see a young girl who has just left her native country and is now finding her feet in a city that has probably changed a great deal. I stop wondering about how much we owe her and how her presence makes me feel nervous because it reminds me of the past. Once more, I want to help. Partly out of guilt.

"You must come over for dinner."

"Yes." Ed is glowing with an almost schoolboy enthusiasm. I know why. Already he is painting her in his head. It's a great angle. I can see that. *Italian Girl Grown Up.* No more curls. A bob instead. A new look. Maybe pastels instead of acrylic. He's been talking about changing his style. It suddenly occurs to me that Carla's reappearance in our lives could be exactly what my husband needs.

"Come over tonight," Ed says.

No. Not so soon. We need time to talk. "Tonight isn't so good," I say, reaching into my bag for a pen. "Give me your number and I'll call you."

Carla scribbles it down eagerly. "I start college soon, but I am sure I will have some free time." Then she stands up straight. "I have done a law degree in Italy and now I am going to take a conversion course and then qualify as a lawyer in England. Like you, Lily!"

Why is my chest tightening? Why do I feel as though this beautiful girl is creeping onto my territory? It's *my* patch. Not hers.

"It's a very competitive world," I find myself saying. "You won't find it easy."

"You were my inspiration!" Her eyes are bright. "I always remember that famous boiler murder case you were working on when Ed was painting me. I studied it at university. What was the man's name — Joe Thomas? 'This man is innocent,' you kept saying. 'I am going to make the rest of the world see that.' "

Why do I feel this is a prepared speech? That there's another reason for her coming here? Or is it me, being neurotic because the girl has mentioned the man I have tried so hard to forget?

I do my best not to think about my phone call earlier today.

"Lily will be able to help you with your assignments," Ed bursts in. He's trying to compensate. I understand why. He feels guilty. After all, he's built a career on this girl.

"We will be in touch to arrange dinner at our place." I press a card into her hand. "Meanwhile, here are our details."

"Take this, too." My husband is pressing a twenty-pound note into her hand. "Get a taxi from the tube station."

"Ed," I say, trying to stay calm. "Can you be back early tonight? There's something we need to discuss."

He pauses, his eye catching mine. *Something we need to discuss.* Every time we have used that phrase in our life, it's been to do with something big. Our marriage. The pregnancy test. Tom's diagnosis. And now how much we should pay Carla.

"Sure," he says uncertainly. "I'll be there if you are." He laughs. "My wife's really important now, you know. Practically lives in the office, she does. Keeps a duvet there."

He hasn't been sarcastic like this for ages. I obviously don't have a spare bed in the office, but I do often get back late.

"There's something else we haven't told Carla," I add.

Ed frowns. "There is?"

That's the other thing about being an artist. You can block yourself out. Hide. When you're not being a caretaker, that is.

"We have a child. A boy." I falter as I often do when telling strangers I have a son. "He's called Tom."

"Really?" Carla's eyes soften. "I can't wait to meet him." I glance at Ed.

"He's very special," I add. And then I turn to one side to hide my tears.

30
CARLA

Perhaps it was best that they hadn't received her letters. It could, Carla told herself, make things easier, provided she played her cards right.

Now, as she made her way back to the hostel, all Carla could think about was the admiration in Ed's face. The crisp autumn leaves and the cold early morning air that caught in her throat reminded Carla of the first time she met Lily and Ed. In her child's eyes, they had seemed so grown up! Yet Lily had probably not been much older than she was now.

How her old protector had changed! Carla had always remembered her as being very tall and plump. Her only asset had been that lovely long blond hair. "I would like to teach that English woman how to dress," Mamma was always saying. "You do not need money for style. It is a question of putting together the right things and then wearing them with pride."

Well, someone, somewhere, must have taught Lily, because she had style now. Carla had hardly recognized her when she had appeared in the gallery. She was much thinner and was wearing an elegantly cut jacket that looked like a Max Mara. The blond bob looked even better in person than it had in the picture. By framing Lily's face, it accentuated her cheekbones. The older woman had become almost beautiful.

Ed might have changed, too, but he still had that aura of kindness and that manner of speaking as if he knew exactly what you meant. You were also aware when talking to him that he was taking in your nose, your ears, your bone structure. It was what a real artist did. And how flattering that it was *her* portrait that had been bought by this unknown buyer!

"We will be in touch," Lily had promised, "to arrange dinner at our place."

Perhaps by then she would have heard back from Larry.

Do not worry, Mamma, she told herself, nodding a thank-you at the good-looking young man who had invited her to go through the main doors first. *I will make sure that we get our revenge.*

31
LILY

Ed is true to his word. He is not only back early from the gallery for our "little chat," but he has also cooked supper. Our signature dish, we call it. Salmon en croute. It was the first meal we ate after my pregnancy test: the beginning of our new life together.

How long can you pretend? How long will it be before someone comes from the past to bring it all back?

Carla. Joe.

Maybe that's why I made such an effort to be back early myself. "No more tonight," I told the eager young intern who was still poring over the papers I had given him. "We all need a break."

"But it's only seven p.m.!"

He might as well have said four p.m. Late nights aren't just expected of you when you're a lawyer; they're one of many sandbags between you and being "let go." Long hours show you're committed. They help protect you from the constant threat of being pushed out.

"That smells good," I say to Ed. My husband produces the dish with a flourish, then places it carefully on the table. On the wall opposite, a picture of Tom looks down on us. His face is serious. Like Daniel, he rarely smiles. How I yearn to make him laugh like other children his age.

"So what is it that you need to talk about? Something so urgent that we couldn't afford to share our time with the girl who has made our money?"

"She made *your* money. Not mine. I make my own."

"But don't you see?" Ed's eyes are shining. "Carla has come back. If she allows me to paint her again, it will kick-start my career. The publicity will be great."

"Maybe," I begin. And then the phone rings.

"You'd better get it," says Ed, tucking in. "It will be work again. Always is."

Reluctantly I pick up the phone.

"Darling?"

My heart freezes. I tried to ring Mum earlier, as I do every day. A quick call to see if everything is all right. A guilt call because my mother is dealing with a situation that I'm no good at. But there wasn't any reply.

Then work took over and I forgot. Yes, I know.

"What's happened?"

My mother's voice is tight. "It's Tom. He's in trouble."

What we want and what we need in life are two very different things. But it takes death to put those two contenders into perspective. Right now, there's only one thing I really want. To live.

32
CARLA

October was almost halfway through already, and she had waited weeks now for Lily to call. Carla had begun to feel foolish and not a little annoyed. Clearly Lily and Ed were the kind of people who said one thing and did another. They had no intention of "thanking her" as promised. They just wanted her to go away! Frankly, she expected this of Lily. But it was Ed who had disappointed her.

If they thought this was over, though, they were mistaken. She would, Carla told herself as she stared at her law books in her cold hostel room, give them two more weeks and then turn up at the gallery again.

Just as disappointing was the e-mail reply from Tony Gordon's clerk.

Mr. Gordon is not available at present. Your message will be passed on to him at the earliest possible opportunity.

"Go around to his house," Mamma had pleaded when Carla had told her in a rushed phone call. But Mamma couldn't remember the name of the street, apart from that it was "somewhere in a place called Islington." Even Google hadn't come up with his address.

Determined not to be beaten, she spent hours walking around Islington one Saturday, hoping that something would trigger a childhood memory from that terrible Christmas when Mamma had been hysterical because Larry couldn't be with them. But all she could remember was a tall building with big windows. There were so many of these that it was like looking for a needle in a haystack, as the English said.

There was nothing for it but to plow her energies into her demanding studies. Everyone at college was so clever. Yet she had an advantage. There was only one other Italian girl there, and she lacked the natural assets that Carla had. Beauty as well as brains. Everyone (the boys, that was) wanted to help her. She was asked out for coffee and dinner so many times she couldn't count them all.

Each time she turned down the request with a smile and the excuse that she needed to work instead. But, she would say with a slight turn of the head, it would be very kind if they could just explain something about the last assignment.

Then, one evening, her mobile rang.

Lily!

"I'm sorry it's taken so long to get in touch." The voice was uncertain. "The truth is that since we saw you, we've had some . . . some problems."

There was a short silence during which Carla felt that Lily had more to say but was holding back. "You are not ill?" she asked quickly.

"No." There was a short laugh. "Not me."

Carla felt a quickening of fear. "Not Ed?"

"No. Not him either."

That was good. Of the two, Carla definitely preferred Ed, with his appreciative eyes. Lily, Carla told herself, was not to be trusted. It was true that she had once idolized the woman who had taught her how to make Victoria sponges and looked after her when Mamma was "working." But look how she had stepped in between Larry and Mamma. Then there was her job. Carla allowed herself a half smile as she recalled how she'd thought Lily had committed murder herself because she'd seen the word on her files. But even so, it took a certain kind of person to defend someone like Joe

Thomas. Carla shuddered. Criminal law wasn't for her. Employment law, said her tutors, was the way forward. It would also suit her natural talent for getting on with other people. Especially those who might prove useful.

Meanwhile, Lily was still going on about her son. "Tom . . . well, Tom got into trouble at school. But it's all sorted now."

"That is good." Carla knew she should sound more interested, but the truth was that she wasn't.

"I had to take some time off work," Lily continued. "But I am now back in London. Ed and I wondered if you would like to come over next week for supper."

Ed and Lily's home was beautiful. Before walking up the steps, Carla stood and stared up at the gracious, tall house with white bricks and late geraniums flowering on a balcony above. A rustle in the hedge running along the front of the house startled her. Just a bird. *Calm down,* she told herself. *You're only nervous because you're finally here.*

Tentatively she raised the silver knocker on the glossy black door, tucking the flowers she had brought under her arm in order to do so. When Ed opened it ("Come in!

Come in!"), she marveled at the black-and-white tiles in the hall. Every room was like a page in a magazine. White everywhere. White and glass. Glass coffee tables. White walls. White counters in the kitchen.

They must have a great deal of money to afford all this. Yet it was almost as if Lily had banished color.

"Roses!" Ed buried his face in the bunch that she'd bought, at half price, from a street flower seller about to shut up for the night. "What a wonderful smell. And such an amazing pink. Now why don't you sit here? Lily will be down in a minute."

If it were her, Carla told herself, taking a seat at the glass table in the kitchen, she would put a rustic pine bench there and a scarlet rug there . . .

"Welcome," said Lily, suddenly appearing.

Carla air-kissed her hostess's cheeks, taking in her cream trousers and the stylish beige pumps. If only she had the money to dress like that instead of buying secondhand or relying on Mamma's sewing skills! "Thank you for having me."

"Thank you for coming. Like I said on the phone, I'm only sorry it's taken us a while. Ed? Is dinner ready now?" Their "dinner" was fish pie from a packet. At home, that would have been considered a disgrace. Meals had to be made from scratch; the process took hours. It was a mark of respect for their guests.

The atmosphere was tense. Everyone, it seemed, was making small talk, which made it worse. "Your home," said Carla, in desperation, "is very minimalist." Since coming back, Carla had made a point of learning a new English word every day. This was one of them. She'd been waiting for an opportunity to use it.

Lily dug the serving spoon into the dish so the juices flooded over the edges. "It's so that all my husband's paintings will stand out."

All? But there were only two that she could see.

"I seem to have lost my creative mojo," said Ed drily, topping up his and Carla's wineglasses but not Lily's. She had sparkling water. "I've been trying all kinds of things but nothing works."

Something had happened to this couple since she had last seen them in the gallery. They looked empty somehow. "I don't understand."

Ed picked up his knife and fork. Carla followed suit. Lily, she noticed, didn't even bother. It was as if the food in front of her wasn't there.

"I have run out of inspiration. It's partly because of Tom. He hasn't been . . . well."

He stopped as Lily flashed him a warning look.

Aware the atmosphere was getting worse, Carla tried to choose her words carefully. "But he is better now?"

"Better?" Ed took another large slug of wine and laughed hoarsely. "Tom will never be better."

"But I thought —"

"Ed." Lily's voice carved through the air. "We must not inflict our troubles on our guest. Now tell me, Carla. How is law school going?"

She braced herself to look directly at the woman opposite. "Very good, thank you."

Somehow, Carla told herself, as she spoke lightly about the past, how she'd loved cooking with Lily as a child, and then described the various lectures she'd been to recently, she had to find a way to bring Larry — no, Tony — into the conversation.

As she finished talking, there was silence. Ed and Lily both seemed completely absorbed in the table in front of them. *Fine,* Carla thought, *I'll just launch straight in.*

"Actually," she said quickly, "I was wondering if you could tell me how I could find Mr. Gordon. My mother, she has a message for him. I've e-mailed his clerk but received a reply to say he is 'not available.' "

As she spoke, Carla noticed a distinct shadow passing over Lily's face.

Ed had almost finished half a bottle now. "You can say that again," he spluttered.

"The truth is that Tony is very ill," said Lily slowly, pushing her plate to one side even though she had barely touched her food. "In fact, he's in a hospice, not far from here."

"A hospice?" Carla felt a catch in her throat. An excited catch that knew it ought to be shocked instead.

"He has cancer. The poor man doesn't have much time."

"Poor man?" Ed snorted. "That's not what you've said about him to me." Then he turned to Carla. "The two of them had some kind of fallout over a case. But my wife here can't go into details because it's confidential." He tapped the side of his nose knowingly. "That's the law for you."

Lily looked furious. "Don't drink if you can't control yourself," she said coldly.

"It's not me who can't control myself." Ed was rising unsteadily to his feet.

"That's enough."

They were arguing as if she wasn't here! Carla felt her chest skip. Yes! If you wanted to get one step ahead in court, her new tutor had said, it was always better if your opposition was divided.

"I'm sorry." Lily touched her arm as Ed stormed out of the room. "Things are difficult at the moment." Then she pressed an envelope into her hand. "This is a small thank-you from us. It's the award money that Ed won all those years ago, as well as a little extra." She spoke fast. Sharply. Without warmth. As if this was a payoff rather than a proper present.

"Thank you." Part of Carla wanted to throw it back. Their "gift" made her feel dirty. Humiliated. It was clear Lily just wanted to get rid of her. "That's very kind. But there's just one more thing."

Alarm flashed across Lily's face. Her eyes grew stony. She thought Carla wanted extra money! The knowledge gave Carla power. Of course she did. But that would come later.

"Could you please," continued Carla, brazening out the hostility in those eyes, "write down the name of Tony's hospice?"

Lily's face softened. "Of course." She reached for a pen. "Here it is. I will ring you soon, Carla. I'm so sorry about this. Like I said, we've had a few problems. Ed isn't quite himself."

Outside, Carla tipped open the envelope. A thousand pounds? If those two thought that was enough, they were very much mistaken.

33
LILY

"I wasn't sure that you'd come."

We're sitting outside an Italian restaurant just off Leicester Square. I'm still shaken after our dinner with Carla, not to mention everything that's been going on with Tom. After all, that's partly the reason I'm here.

It is unseasonably sunny for this time of year. I'm not wearing a coat, but I do have my sunglasses on. The ones with the red frames. They let me observe my companion without allowing him to make that eye contact he was always so good at.

Joe Thomas, it has to be said, looks like any of the businessmen walking past. Respectable in that dark blue suit. Clean-shaven. Tidy hair. Shiny, black, pointed shoes. And a tan.

"What do you want?" I'm keeping my tone deliberately level. Act normal, I tell myself. It's why I suggested this place in full view of the world.

His fingers position the cutlery so that they are perfectly in line with the edge of the place mat. His nails are clean. Well kept. "That's not very polite."

"Polite!" I laugh. "What do you call perverting the course of justice, then?" I lower my voice, even though it's quite low anyway. "You killed your girlfriend and then made me believe you were innocent."

"You *wanted* to believe I was innocent." My companion leans forward so I can smell his breath. "You thought I was like your brother."

Is he still trying to manipulate me? I sit back. It was a mistake to come here. I see this now. Yet I, too, have my questions to ask. "I don't want you to send cards anymore. How did you know when my birthday was?"

"I looked it up. You can look almost anything up." Joe Thomas smiles. "You should know that. I wanted to remind you that I was still thinking of you. But it's Tom I'm here about."

I freeze. "What do you mean?"

"I think you know already. It's why you're here. I would have come earlier, but I've been working abroad until recently. And when I came back, I found out you'd had a child."

He leans across the table toward me again. "I need to know, Lily. Is he mine?"

My body goes cold. Numb. My legs begin to shake as if they have a mind of their own. Words are about to tumble out of my mouth, but I manage to pull them back and replace them with better ones. "Of course not. Don't be so ridiculous. I don't know what you're talking about."

Gripping the edge of the table, I stand up.

"I'm talking about us." Joe's voice is pleading. His former arrogance has been replaced by a note of desperation. "Don't go. I must have the truth."

"The truth?" I laugh. "What do you know about truth? You've allowed your imagination to run wild, Mr. Thomas."

I stop myself. It's not his fault he has "behavioral issues," as we argued in court. But that doesn't explain everything he's done. "You were my client twelve years ago and I've lived to rue the day I helped you get off. It's something I will never forgive myself for." Tears blind my eyes. "Poor Sarah . . ."

Joe is clutching my hand now. "I do have some feelings, you know. I made a mistake, and I'm sorry. But it helped others — all of those other victims."

I pull my hand out of his. People are looking at us from the adjoining table. I throw down a twenty-pound note to cover our drinks and walk off through the square.

"It's Tom. He's been in trouble." Even now, some weeks later, my mother's taut voice, sprung with fear, haunts me. I hear it in my dreams. I hear it when I wake up. And I hear it when I'm meant to be concentrating in meetings, even though I know that that particular "Tom emergency" has been sorted.

Until the next one.

Ed and I had rushed down to Devon just after that shocking encounter with Carla at the gallery. I left quick, sharp messages of instructions to my secretary and junior partners while Ed drove, his mouth set in that thin line that said, *For God's sake, can't you forget about work while we sort out our son?*

And I get it. I've told myself the same thing over and over again, especially when I see another woman with a son of Tom's age walking past us in the streets or lining up for Madame Tussauds.

But Tom would never stand like that in a line. He would be worried about whether our feet were in the "right" position. He would be asking the woman behind us why she had a mole on her chin and how long it had been there and why she hadn't had it removed. Children like Tom don't always realize when they're being rude.

It would cause an awkward explanation on my part and a stepping away on the part of the imaginary woman with the mole. Naturally it's difficult having an almost-teenager who behaves like a toddler. But I can deal with that.

It's the violence that's not so easy. Take this scar on my forehead. It's from where Tom once accidentally hit me with a sauce-pan. I hadn't put the offending item back in its "proper" place in the kitchen, so he charged past me to put it right. And that mark on Ed's arm? That's because Ed once tried to play football with his boy, but Tom's poor spatial awareness skills made him frus-trated.

So he bit Ed.

We'd been trying our best to "put strate-gies of structure in place to address chal-lenging behavior" (according to one rather useful piece of online advice). But as he'd gotten older and bigger — even taller than me — he got worse. More violent. And now the time had come to do something about it. That much was clear when, after a five-hour trip to Devon that night, we had an emergency meeting at our son's school the next morning.

"He flew at the teacher with a pair of scissors."

The head's exhausted tone — usually more sympathetic — made me realize we'd reached the end of the line. Tom had been allowed to go to the local school, despite his special needs, partly because I'd gone there, too, and partly because we'd argued that we wanted him to be in mainstream schooling. If he was with others "like him," Ed and I had argued, Tom wouldn't have any role models to help him improve.

"We've tried, but we simply can't cope with this behavior anymore." The head spoke as if Ed and I had picked up the scissors ourselves.

"But she's all right, yes?" Ed was just about controlling himself.

"That depends," said the head curtly, "on whether you count five stitches as being acceptable."

"Tom was hurt, too," snapped Ed.

"That was self-inflicted."

I'm used to arbitrating between clients, and between clients and barristers, too. But when it comes to my own family, my skills seem to fly out the window. Stick to the facts, I told myself, just as I told my clients.

Stick to the facts. Yet my heart goes out to my son, who is misunderstood time and time again for no fault of his own.

"Can you tell us exactly what happened?" I asked. "Mum told me there had been an argument in Geography."

Those disapproving eyes swiveled back to me. "The children were asked to cut out maps. Tom was fussing about his outline. He said he needed more time to get it right. His teacher told him that his was perfectly acceptable and that they needed to finish before recess. There was an argument, during which he picked up the scissors and nearly stabbed her. Luckily she stepped to one side and they went into the desk."

"Hang on. You said she needed stitches!"

"She did." The head was regarding Ed as though he was no better than Tom. "She fell in her attempt to avoid the scissors and hit her nose."

"He didn't cut her, then? It was an accident."

"That's not the point. It could have been fatal."

"So that explains it!" My relief sang out. "It wasn't because he wanted to hurt her. He was hurting inside because his outlines weren't right. Don't you see?"

There was a shake of the head. "No, Mrs.

Macdonald, I don't."

"You *know* Tom needs to get everything right. It's part of his condition."

"That's as may be, but I won't accept any kind of abuse toward my staff. You're lucky we didn't call the police." Standing up, she indicated the interview was at an end. "I'm sorry, but you must remember what the educational psychologist said the last time this happened."

Briefly, I thought back to the day Tom had gotten too near a girl in the playground. (Problems with personal space again.) She'd pushed him away and he'd pushed her back. She'd fallen awkwardly and cracked her wrist. Full blame, rather unfairly in my view, had fallen on our son.

"It's another example of his behavior." The headmistress was sounding weary now. "We can't keep Tom here anymore. It's time to consider a special school. One that can deal with his . . . his issues. In the meantime, Tom is suspended."

Of course, Mum stepped in. She'd been through "challenging behavior" before with Daniel. This time she would get it right. "We'll look after him at home until they sort something out," she insisted when we returned, drained and worried after the meeting.

"Where is he now?"

My mother bit her lip. "Upstairs. He's pushed something against the door so I can't open it. But he's talking, so I think he's all right."

A cold shaft of terror caught at my heart. I could see him climbing out the window. Cutting his own wrist with scissors. Hanging from the ceiling . . .

Together Ed and I raced up the stairs. "Tom, it's Mum. Are you all right?"

No answer.

"Tom." Ed tried again. "We understand what happened at school. Just let us in."

He could try all day, but Tom wouldn't give in.

"I don't want to talk."

Ed tried again. "Do you know that your teacher has had to have stitches?"

"She didn't have to," he retorts quickly. "She shouldn't have fallen."

Her fault for falling. My fault for upsetting Daniel at the end. Ed's fault for not telling me about his parents' trust. Joe's fault for killing Sarah.

Who knows where blame really lies? It's never as simple as it seems.

Desperately, Ed and I attempted to keep our lives together while sorting out Tom's educational future at the same time. It wasn't easy to find a school that could deal with Tom's needs. But, once more, an online help group, along with the consultant, pointed us in the right direction.

There was a good school about an hour from my parents. It offered flexible boarding, which would take the strain off us all, yet also made us feel guilty. But something had to be done, so we both went down to visit. There were children like Tom, but many were more challenging. One teacher was wiping feces off the wall of a corridor as we passed. The smell clung to us, suffocating us in the knowledge that this was the world we were condemning him to.

"How can we send him to a boarding school?" Ed wept on the way back. The traffic on the snarled-up motorway appeared to reflect our own personal impasse.

"*You* went to one."

"That was different."

"Yours was posh, you mean."

"If you like."

"We're sending him to a boarding school because we can't cope and because they have specialized help," I said, tapping my fingers on the wheel.

"You sound so cold. Emotionless."

It was the only way I could manage. Better than Ed's method, which was to start drinking vodka as well as wine. Ironically, when I went down to visit him the next weekend, Tom seemed far more enthusiastic about seeing me than usual.

When I suggested a walk along the lower cliff path, he readily agreed and took great delight in telling me about the rock formation of the Jurassic Coast.

"Look!" he exclaimed in delight. "This is a brachiopod!"

Then he proceeded to spout a stream of facts and figures. "That's amazing," I said and he glowed with pleasure from the praise. As we returned to my parents' house, I reflected that this was one of the best afternoons we'd ever spent together. Was that because Ed had been detained in London for a commission? Or was it because I was finally, after all these years, learning how to communicate more easily with my son by tapping into the things he was good at — and not the ones he wasn't.

A few weeks later, I finally picked up the phone to Carla and apologized for not having returned her calls. "We had some important issues to deal with, regarding Tom's school," I said before inviting her over for dinner.

I still felt tense, but the occasion went better than I'd expected, apart from some awkward bits about Ed's paintings and when my husband said too much about Tom. At least my husband didn't let slip that Tom now refuses to speak to us on the phone.

The three of us talked about when Carla was a child and we were a newly married couple. It reminded me of our difficult start and, at one point, I reached under the table for Ed's hand to squeeze it. *I'm sorry*, said my squeeze, *that I'm on edge. It's not just the current case I'm working on. It's Joe Thomas, too.* But of course, Ed didn't hear any of that because I didn't have the guts to say it out loud.

Meanwhile, Carla chatted away about her studies. And we talked about poor Tony Gordon and how Carla needed to give him a message from her mother. Really? What had happened to that unlikely pair after our awful row in the corridor? Had Francesca and Tony kept in touch? But I didn't like to ask Carla. Besides, part of me still feels bad for having interfered at the time.

So, slightly against my better judgment, I gave Tony's contact details to our guest.

And then I couldn't sleep all night, wondering if I'd done the right thing.

34
CARLA

November 2013

Carla had been to a hospice only once before. A friend of Nonna's had been in one, just days before she died. Mamma had taken her to visit. It was disrespectful, she said, that her friend's family couldn't look after her at home themselves. But the daughter-in-law was English. What could you expect?

"I am here to visit Tony Gordon," she said firmly to the woman at reception.

The woman glanced at a sheet of paper in front of her. "I'm afraid I can't find you on the list."

Carla summoned up one of her most charming smiles. "I am an old friend, visiting from Italy, and I do not have long. Please. I would be very grateful."

The woman returned her smile. Smiles were catching, Carla knew. Mamma had taught her that many years ago. "Tony is resting at the moment, but you can go in for a few minutes. You might not get much sense out of him, mind you. One of our volunteers will show you the way."

Gingerly, Carla walked down the corridor. As she passed open doors, she glanced in. And then the volunteer stopped. "Just here," he said.

Was that really him? Larry with the shiny car? Larry who had been so tall and imposing?

Carla stared at the gray man lying on his back in the bed. He had no hair and there was a strange boxlike thing attached to his throat. His eyes were closed, but as she approached they snapped open, then froze.

"Larry," she said grimly.

"This is Tony," whispered the young man behind her.

Carla whipped around. "Please leave us," she said firmly. "I need a private conversation."

The young man nodded and closed the door.

Carla fixed her gaze on Larry again. His eyes were frozen, she realized, with fear. *Good.*

"Yes, it's me." Slowly she forced herself to touch the box on his throat. "You cannot talk, I hear. Throat cancer. That means you will have to listen."

Her voice felt like it belonged to someone else. Someone cruel. Like the bullies who had tormented her in school. "You promised a future to my mother, Larry. But you did not deliver. Do you know what that meant?"

His ill, milky eyes were staring up at her, scared. "It meant she had to go back to Italy because she had a child and not a husband. Mamma wasted the best years of her life waiting for you to leave your wife. But you did not do that, did you? And why? If you ask me, it was not just because she was sick. But because you wanted to have your cake and eat it, too."

She said the last part in a mocking tone. Then waited.

There was a small movement, so small that it was barely noticeable. But Larry's eyes were still rigidly fixed on her. Carla could almost smell his fear. But it didn't give her the satisfaction she thought it would. Instead, she almost felt sorry for this curled-up, shriveled shell of a man.

"My mother has sent me here with a message." Her hands clenched inside her jacket pockets. "I am to tell you that she still loves you. That she would like to see you again, if you were to come to Italy. But I can see now that this is not possible."

A silent tear began to roll down from Larry's left eye. And then his right.

Carla swallowed hard. She had not been expecting this.

"I just hope you regret your behavior," she said quietly.

Then she turned on her heels and walked fast down the corridor. Past the dozing young woman. Past the lady at reception. And out of this hellhole as fast as she could possibly go.

Four nights later, her mobile rang.

Lily's voice at the other end was quiet. "I thought you ought to know, Carla. Tony Gordon died last night. Did you manage to see him before he went?"

"No." Carla began to tremble. What if they tried to blame her for upsetting him? "No. I didn't."

"That's a shame." Yet Carla could tell that Lily was relieved. In fact, she was surprised when Lily had given her his details so easily. "Tony Gordon wasn't a saint, but he had his troubles."

"What do you mean?"

"His wife has had multiple sclerosis for years. It couldn't have been easy for him. Ironic that she's outlived him, really. Poor woman is in a wheelchair. It will be hard for her without him."

Something faltered inside Carla. Larry had needed something his wife couldn't offer. Laughter and company. Yet he couldn't leave his wife. Not if she was an invalid. Had her mother known that?

"The funeral is next Wednesday, if you would like to come."

35
LILY

"Live each day as if it were your last."

The words of the hymn reach out to me. It's a salutary reminder that the past is only a second ago. The present merely exists for a brief second before becoming history itself.

Tony apparently chose the hymns himself. I look around the church at the other mourners. From the outside, it's a rather lovely gray building that rises with a calmness of its own next to a busy street. I've walked by a few times but have never been inside before. Now I wish I had. It's surprisingly peaceful, with a beautiful stained-glass window of the Virgin Mary. I find myself praying for Tom, and for Daniel, and for Ed, and for me. Only then do I realize I've forgotten Tony, so I hastily add him.

Somehow I never had my old colleague down as the churchgoing type. But according to the vicar's eulogy, he went every

Sunday. Was generous, too, to local charities. Especially one for multiple sclerosis.

Silently, we all watch the pale ash coffin pass by. Is it really possible that inside is the body of the keen-minded barrister I once admired so much? Who made such an impression on me when I was still young and naive? The same man who had been seeing Carla's mother on the side?

Tony's widow greets us graciously at the reception afterward. It is being held in the hall adjoining the church. Julia is sitting in her wheelchair, back straight and head held high as though she is a queen on a throne. "Thank you for coming," she says, as if welcoming me to a party. She has tiny features, I note. Her complexion is pale and translucent, the kind you might see in an "over sixty and still beautiful" magazine feature. On her knees is a fuchsia silk shawl; the invitation had clearly said "No black." I, myself, am wearing a navy dress suit with wide white lapels, which I'd recently found in a secondhand designer store.

A young woman is leaning over her protectively. I presume she is Tony's daughter — there's definitely something about the eyes.

"Go and look after our guests, darling, would you?" Then Tony's widow turns her face to mine.

"I'm Lily Macdonald," I say. "I used to work with your husband."

"I know. He told me all about you." Her eyes go hard. She looks around. People are keeping a respectful distance. Then she leans toward me. "I am aware my husband had his indiscretions," she whispers. "He told me about that Italian woman on his deathbed. She wasn't the first, you know. But he stayed with me. And that's what counts. I'll thank you to keep any gossip to yourself."

I am shocked by her directness. It's as if she has been waiting for a meeting with me so she can fire this warning shot.

"Do you know, he did everything for me," she continues.

She holds out her hands and I see that the fingers are tightly closed like claws. "When I could no longer cut up my food, he did it for me." She leans forward. There's a smile on her lips, but her eyes are icy. "He dressed me every morning. He ran my bath every night and helped me into it."

I am taken back through time to the visitors' room and Joe Thomas, who liked to run Sarah's bath. I remember thinking at the time that Tony Gordon wasn't the sort to do the same for his wife.

How wrong can you be?

"I understand," I say. And as the words come out of my mouth, I realize it's true. Marriages go through all kinds of ups and downs. But you can make them work. Just look at Ed and me.

"Thank you." Then she nods and the daughter appears, as if silently summoned to her mother's chair. Tony's widow is being wheeled away to mingle with other guests. Thanking them graciously. Wondering, perhaps, how many others know of her late husband's hidden life. Yet, at the same time, believing utterly in her own version of Tony's loyalty.

How can we deceive ourselves so easily?

I turn, about to leave, when I bump into a tall man in a dark suit who's standing just behind me. A cold chill passes through me. The brown-black eyes. His hair is shorter than last time.

"What are you doing here?" My voice is abrupt with surprise. And fear.

"Why shouldn't I be?"

Joe Thomas's voice bears a slightly rougher edge than the highly polished accents around us. "Tony and I were good friends."

I make to move away from him, but the crowds are too thick. The whole world, it seems, has come to pay its respects. "He was your barrister. He got you off for

413

something you should have stayed inside for. That was all."

"Please." He lays a hand on my arm. "Not so loud."

I try to shake him off, but the hand is tightening around my arm and I find myself being taken firmly outside. "How dare you," I manage.

Joe is grinning.

"Just want to get a few points straight, that's all. It's for your benefit, Lily. I'm sure you don't want that lot in there to know."

"Know what?"

We're standing on the church steps now. Traffic is rushing past. I want to run away. Hide.

"I helped Tony a lot after my release. It was my way of saying thank you."

"I don't understand."

Except I do. Or at least I am beginning to.

"I gave Tony extra information for his cases." He taps the side of his nose. "It's one of the reasons why he tried so hard to get me off. Told him I could help in the future, you see. And I did. Picked up quite a lot when I was inside. Turned out that some of those things were useful."

"What kinds of things?"

"I can't go into details, Lily, you must know that. And don't go getting all high and mighty. You've benefited, too."

"Me?"

"Come on. What about the tip-off over the lorry driver?" I go cold. We hadn't been sure we were going to get the poor man off until that envelope arrived anonymously. No postmark. Just the name of the dealer who had supplied drugs to the teenager. Crucial evidence that helped me win. I told myself that anonymous tip-offs happened every now and then. It could be someone completely unrelated to my past.

"How did you know what cases I was working on?"

He taps the side of his nose again. "Maybe I've been dating one of the secretaries."

"Which one?"

He seems to misinterpret my question for interest. "Does it matter?" He shrugs. "She means nothing. It's just a means to an end."

"But you've been abroad."

"Not all the time."

I stare at Joe. "Why are you doing this?"

"Because you got me off. So I want to help you, too. Express my thanks. I've been keeping an eye on you. Heard you were having problems with that case, so I thought I'd try and give you a helping hand."

"*How* did you hear?"

"I won't say."

Not *can't*. But *won't*.

"And there's Tom, too, of course," he continues. "If I'm helping you, it means I'm helping him as well."

"I don't want your help." But even as I speak, I feel the same crawling sensation from the past. That pull — that magnetic pull toward a man I despise.

"I think you do." His face is so close that we are almost touching. "Admit it. We have something between us, Lily." I can smell his breath on mine. I can smell his skin. I want to move away. But my legs won't obey.

"I need to know, Lily." His mouth is hovering over mine. "How is our son?"

Our son?

"I've already told you," I say, pulling away. "He's not yours."

Then I'm off, walking as fast as I can in my heels down the street, past the supermarket and the cinema where ordinary lives are being lived. Putting as much distance between Joe Thomas and me as possible before I do something stupid.

Again.

36
CARLA

OBITUARIES

Barrister Tony Gordon passed away on 22 November after a brave fight. Loyal and doting father and husband.

Darling Mamma,
  There is something I have to tell you.

No, that wasn't right.

Dearest Mamma,
  I need to tell you that I found Larry . . .

No. That might raise her hopes.

Dearest Mamma,
  I have some news that you might find upsetting.

At least that might warn her gently.

Tony Gordon — whom we knew as

Larry — has died. I went to see him before he passed away and gave him your message. He was not worthy of you, Mamma. God has made him pay through an early death. Now we can put him out of our lives.

Tucking the obituary clip from the newspaper inside the envelope and sealing it hastily, Carla dropped it into the postbox on the way to the church.

"The funeral is next Wednesday if you would like to come," Lily had said when she'd called.

"Thank you, but no," Carla had replied, and she'd meant it. But at the last moment, her lecture on tort had been canceled. There was just time to get to the service and back for her next tutorial. It had seemed almost like fate.

As Carla stood at the back of the church, the priest's words rang out around them on the microphone.

"Wonderful family man . . . respected pillar of the community . . . unwavering in his fight for justice . . ."

What a hypocrite!

"Makes you sick, doesn't it?" said a tall man, squeezing in next to her. He had very short hair and a rather abrupt manner of speaking.

Carla started with surprise. But although he appeared to be talking to her, his eyes were fixed on a figure two rows in front — a woman wearing a beautifully cut suit that set off her blond hair and slim figure perfectly.

Lily! Did this man know her? Or was she merely a symbol of everything that he clearly despised?

"What do you mean?" she whispered.

Those dark eyes now turned their focus to her. "I think you understand perfectly."

He was speaking as if they were old acquaintances.

"But —" she began, mystified.

"Shh," someone whispered.

"Going to the reception?" he asked.

Carla shook her head.

"I am." He grinned. "Wouldn't miss it for the world."

"What are you doing for Christmas, Carla?"

"What am I doing for Christmas?" she repeated for effect. "I was hoping to go back to Italy, but my mother is visiting her old aunt in Naples and says it would be better if I stayed here."

Carla didn't have to fake the note of sadness in her voice. Indeed, she had felt a pain in her chest when Mamma had written about her plans. Never before had they spent Christmas apart! Her mother's loopy writing made her feel homesick. She so desperately wanted to feel Mamma's soft cheek against hers, to speak her own language every day, to eat Nonna's bread, which she baked herself. Besides, Carla barely had enough to pay the hostel fees, let alone eat dinner at night.

"Then you must come with us to my parents' home in Devon."

Yes! Yet there had been something in Lily's tone that made Carla feel the invitation was slightly reluctant. Ed, she was sure, would have been warmer.

"There's just one thing," Lily added. "Tom, our son. He's . . . different, as I said before. We never quite know how he's going to behave in front of strangers. So be prepared." Different? Carla understood "different." Had she not felt different for most of her life at school in England, even when she had tried so hard to be the same?

And now here she was, on a train heading out of London. Unusually for English people, the other passengers were chattering away, asking her where she was going for Christmas, and didn't she think the lights in Oxford Street were beautiful?

In her bag, she had some small presents. An embroidered purse for Lily, an artists' notebook for Ed and a plane kit for Tom. All clever buys from a charity shop in King's Cross. She was particularly pleased with the plane kit. It had been hard finding a present for a boy. Besides, she couldn't remember exactly how old he was. Still, even if he didn't like it, it was a gesture. Carla sat back in her seat and watched the green fields roll past. "We are by the sea," Lily had said. "You will love it."

"You must ask them for more money," Mamma had reminded her in another letter, which had arrived just before she left.

But that would be so awkward, thought Carla as she opened her law books and began to study, despite the rocking motion of the train. How was she to just come out with it? *You'll think of something,* sang the train as it rocked along. *You'll think of something . . .*

"But why can't it fly?" demanded the tall, skinny boy, waving his arms around in frustration.

"I've told you, Tom. It's only a model."

"But the picture on the box shows it in the air."

"That's to make it look exciting," Ed

groaned.

"Then they shouldn't show it like that, should they? We ought to report them to the Advertising Standards Authority."

Carla was impressed. "You have a point, Tom! You'll have to be a lawyer like your mum."

"Heaven forbid." Ed grimaced. "One in the family is more than enough. Sorry, Carla, no offense intended."

She flashed him a smile. "None taken."

Up until Tom's outburst, her present of a model plane set had been a great success. The boy had assembled it in ten minutes flat, even though it was much more complicated than she'd realized. But it was afterward that was hard. All these questions! It was exhausting for them all, including Lily's parents, who had been so kind to her.

When she'd arrived at their beautiful house, Carla had been astounded. She'd thought the house in London was lovely, but this was extraordinary, with its huge sash windows, a hall that was big enough for a whole family to live in and a large airy conservatory facing out over an expansive lawn! Just the kind of house she would love to own.

"My grandparents used to live here," Lily had explained.

They must have been very rich, thought Carla, to have afforded such a palace by the sea. It stood high on the cliff overlooking the water; the view from her bedroom was amazing. The lights from the town twinkled below, just as the lights would be twinkling in the Florentine hills right now. But Carla had forced herself to bite back the home-sickness and concentrate instead on the tall Christmas tree in the hall — what a wonder-ful smell — with the presents at the bot-tom. There was even a small pile with her name on it.

The drawing room, as Lily's mother called it, had a rather colonial feel with its soft sage-green carpet and old mahogany furni-ture, hinting of lavender polish. There were paintings hanging on the walls; not Ed's, but older ones, showing scenes of fields and setting suns.

"Copies," Ed had said dismissively when she'd admired them, although he'd spoken in a low voice so no one else had heard.

There were photographs everywhere, too: on the mantelpiece, on the side tables — pictures of Lily as a child and others of a boy who was taller than she was. "That's Daniel," Lily's mother had said in a bright voice.

Daniel? Dimly, Carla remembered a conversation she'd had with Lily about her brother, all those years ago when she'd first lived in England.

I don't want to talk about him.

"Is he coming here for the holiday?" Carla had started to ask, but her question was drowned out because Tom had suddenly started ripping open his presents, even though they hadn't been to midnight mass yet.

And now there was all this fuss about why the model plane couldn't fly. Tom was getting increasingly upset, tugging at his own hair and pulling out strands. Lily was really edgy, although she'd been like that since she'd picked Carla up from the station. She didn't remember Lily being so irritable when she was younger. Lily's mother — who looked just like her daughter, with the same height and hair color — was apologizing profusely.

Different, Lily had said. *Tom, our son. He's . . . different.* When people said that, they usually meant they were embarrassed by the difference. What they didn't consider was how it affected that person.

The only thing that would help was to make him feel good about himself, to reassure him. And since no one else was doing that — Lily constantly had her nose in files — the task clearly fell to Carla. "Actually," she said, "Leonardo da Vinci got his models to fly."

Who is Leonardo da Vinci? she expected Tom to ask. But his face had begun to clear. "The artist? The man who drew Christ like a clock?"

"Exactly." That was the way she had seen the picture as a child, too. Jesus, spread-eagled at quarter to three. "He designed one of the early airplanes. Did you know that?"

Tom shook his head. "I haven't got that far. I've only just got the book out of the library . . ."

"I didn't know you were studying Leonardo at school, darling," said Lily, emerging unexpectedly from the study. Her expression reminded her of Mamma's all those years ago when she was trying to help her understand her maths homework.

"I'm not. I just liked the picture on the cover." He frowned. "If Leonardo could make his models fly, why can't I?"

"It's a different kind of model." Carla was kneeling down next to him now. "Tell you what, in the morning we'll see if we can make our own design."

Tom frowned again. "How?"

"We can use paper."

"That's not strong enough for us to fly in."

We're not going to get in it, Carla almost said. *It's just a model.* But already she could see that Tom didn't reason like any of the children she'd known in Italy.

"Then I will teach you Italian instead," she said suddenly.

"Italian?" Tom's face brightened. "Cool! Then I could tell the man at the pizza place that I don't like tomatoes. He will listen to me if I speak his language. I'm teaching myself Chinese as well, you know. I bought a book on it."

"How fantastic!"

"Thank you," said Ed as they made their way into the dining room with its big oak table, gleaming silver cutlery, red cloth napkins, cut-glass wine goblets and a circle of holly in the middle for decoration. "It's kind of you to put yourself out."

A warm glow spread through her, and she gave him her best smile.

"I enjoy being with Tom," she replied, allowing Ed to pull out a chair for her. "I understand how he feels."

"How?" Ed was watching her. She wondered if he was thinking of sketching her again.

"Because I felt different as a child, too,

and I know what it's like."

His eyes were still on her. "I love it when the passion crosses your face like that." His fingers were fiddling with his cutlery as if he were nervous. "I wonder, would you mind if . . ."

"If you painted me again?"

His face jerked as if he'd woken up suddenly after dozing off. "Exactly."

She flushed with excitement. Of course she didn't mind. "I'd be honored."

He grasped her hands. "Thank you."

From the corner of her eye she saw Lily watching. "Who's for a walk along the beach tomorrow before Christmas lunch?" asked Lily's father from the other end of the table.

"Me. *Me!*" Tom was leaping out of his seat. "Me and Carla."

She could see Lily wincing and couldn't help feeling a sense of satisfaction.

Then Tom's face creased with anxiety. "But I don't want to build a sand castle." He shuddered. "I don't like how the sand feels."

Poor child! "I'm not keen on wet sand either," she said. "It makes you mucky, doesn't it?"

Tom nodded — so hard she feared he might hurt his head. "Exactly."

Carla glanced at Lily's face. Carla knew

that look. It meant she felt shut out. Carla should be pleased. Yet part of her actually felt rather sorry for Lily.

That night, she couldn't sleep. If only she could ring Mamma to wish her a happy Christmas.

Restlessly, Carla got out of bed and wandered toward the window. Perhaps she would go for a walk. Pulling on her coat, she tiptoed along the landing. All the lights were out apart from a low line under the door of Ed and Lily's room. Unable to stop herself, Carla paused to listen.

They were arguing.

"You should have given Carla money for Christmas," Ed was saying angrily.

"How, exactly? It would have made us even more overdrawn."

"A thousand wasn't enough and you know it."

"It's more than she deserves. Her letters were so pushy . . ."

Carla almost let out a gasp but managed to stop herself.

"So she *did* write?" Ed's voice rose with indignation. "You said you hadn't received anything. Why didn't you tell me?"

Lily was pleading. "Because you were in no fit state. And because, as I keep trying to say, we can't afford it. Tom is our priority.

Perhaps you should sell some more paintings."

"How can I when you've dried up all my inspiration?"

"Ed! That's not fair!"

She heard a tinkling of broken glass followed by Ed's angry voice: "Now look what you made me do."

Carla shrank back into the darkness as Lily came flying out the door. Swiftly, she slunk back to her room, shaking. So her first instincts had been right. Lily *had* received the letters. She had lied. As for being overdrawn, she didn't believe it. Not with a house like that.

If she'd had any qualms before, they were gone now.

37
LILY

What a relief to be back! London. Work. It may be that strange, half-asleep time between Christmas and New Year's, but for us, there is always work to do. Finally I can breathe. I'm all right when I can work. It's a welcome distraction from everything else. And it helps to soothe the hurt I'd felt seeing Carla with my son, who clearly adores her.

I'd been edgy the whole time I was in Devon — short with everyone, including our guest. I was aware of it before Ed pointed out that I was like a cat on a hot tin roof every time the phone rang or someone knocked at the door. I'm still kicking myself for telling Ed about Carla's letters, which resulted in one of the worst fights we've ever had.

Hardly surprising that I let it slip out. My mind was still whirling after that encounter with Joe at Tony's funeral.

There I'd been, all those years since his case, basking in the glory of being a criminal lawyer with a ninety-five percent success rate. But it was all down to the help I'd received from a criminal.

Yet what's really had me jumping at shadows this holiday are Joe's continued allegations about my son. I kept expecting my old client to ring or — even worse — just walk in through the door and insist that Tom is his child. This is all quite possible. After all, he knows where my parents live.

No wonder I was tense. On the verge of hysteria, more like. Time and time again, I almost told my husband but managed to stop myself. He wouldn't understand. No one could. If my poor mother didn't have enough on her plate, I might even have confided in her.

But one look at her worn face — exhausted with looking after my son, who should be *my* responsibility — stopped me. This was one I had to sort out for myself.

In a way, it was a relief having Carla there. A stranger in the midst of a tense, wobbly family makes everyone behave themselves at a time of year when the whole world is meant to be happy. In fact, that's why I'd invited her.

Ed had jumped at the idea and I knew why.

Hadn't I realized at our reunion in the gallery that she could save us? Ed needed to paint her. It would revive his career. Then, at Christmas, I watched him from across the table as he thanked her. "I didn't even have to suggest it," he'd said excitedly later on. "She brought up the idea herself. We're going to arrange a sitting in January. Don't you see, Lily? This could be the start of a new phase in my life!"

He was so buoyed up that we almost forgot to argue about Tom. And work. Of course I'd had to check my e-mails ("Yes, Mum, even during the break"), but that was par for the course. And there were a few sticky moments when Carla kept asking about Daniel.

"Why don't you just tell her he's dead?" Ed finally demanded.

I wanted to scream at him then. Couldn't he understand? Daniel was mine. He was none of Carla's business.

And then there'd been that hideous fight about Carla's begging letters, where Ed accused me of killing his inspiration.

"Did you have a good Christmas?" asks my secretary as I settle into my desk.

"Yes, thanks," I answer automatically.

Then I glance at the sparkling diamond on her left hand. "Do I gather that congratulations are in order?"

She nods excitedly. "I couldn't believe it. He put the ring in the Christmas pudding! I almost swallowed it when —"

And that's when the phone goes. It's a woman. A frantic mother. Her son has been arrested for drunk driving. He's in the cells right now. Can we help?

Thank goodness for work. It shuts everything out. It helps me to forget that Mum is, right now, helping Tom to prepare for his first week back at school, where he will go to bed every night without my bedtime kiss or Mum's.

"Oh, and one more thing," says my secretary. "It was in the in tray when I arrived."

A photograph. It's in an envelope bearing just my name and the word PRIVATE in handwritten capitals.

The picture clearly shows a junction without any road marks.

The night porter, who is just finishing his shift, confirms my worst fears. A man with a short haircut gave him the envelope last night.

Slowly, I rip the page of figures into little bits and then hand them to my secretary. "For the shredder," I say.

"You don't need the information, then?"
"No."
From now on, I win cases on my own.

38
CARLA

Not long after Boxing Day, Carla got up to find that Lily had already gone back to work on the 6:05 a.m. train. "A client needs her attention," Ed had muttered.

After Lily's departure, everyone seemed so much more relaxed. No more snide comments. No more, "Please, Tom. Just sit still for a moment, can't you?"

Yet even without Lily's prickly presence, Carla still felt there was something wrong in the Devon house. Lily's mother had been nice enough to her but had worn a sad smile throughout the celebrations. She felt sure it was to do with Daniel, the son no one wanted to talk about. If he were dead, wouldn't someone have said so? She wasn't sure. Or maybe there'd been some long-standing family feud.

Carla spent her last day in Devon walking with Ed and Tom along the beach. She paid particular attention to Tom, teaching him some Italian phrases, and noted with pleasure that he seemed to like her already. He was a quick learner, too, even though he had to hit his knee with his left hand every time he got a phrase right. "One of his rituals," Ed whispered, as if he knew she'd understand.

Carla had also been careful to endear herself to Lily's parents. "Tom's at a special school during the week, you know," his grandfather said to her just before she left for the station. "We all find it very difficult. You, though, seem to have the knack."

"Come back again," Lily's mother said, pressing her cheek against hers on one side. Such an odd English tradition not to do the second cheek! "You are good for us."

When the time came to leave for the station, Carla didn't want to go. On the train she was buzzing. She and Ed had arranged to meet to discuss the sitting. "I can't wait," he'd said, squeezing her hand as she'd left.

The hostel had seemed even colder and lonelier when she returned. Despite knowing many of the girls by sight, she hadn't made any friends. They weren't her type with those ugly tattoos and nose rings. As if sensing the same, no one had asked her to join in the hostel New Year's Eve party.

Instead, she had huddled up under the duvet and caught up on some new precedents.

She'd rung Mamma earlier. It was a big expense, but Carla needed to hear her voice. The line had been faint, though. "I love you, cara mia," she had barely made out.

"I love you, too, Mamma."

Now, lying back on the narrow bed, Carla lit up a cigarette and exhaled deeply as she took stock. It was already January! Yet she still hadn't achieved what she had hoped to by now. Something needed to happen to move things along.

As she thought through her next step, loud music began to vibrate through her ears. The girl in the room next to hers always had it on so loud! How could she possibly think with that racket? Maybe she'd have a shower to get some peace. Grabbing her sponge bag and dressing gown, Carla locked her door and stomped off down the corridor. She'd only been there five minutes or so when there was a hammering on the door.

"Fire! Fire! Quick. Get out!"

I can still smell.

They say it's the last thing to go.

So all is not lost.

Not yet.

That's the good news.

The bad news is that something is burning.

Even worse, the red stiletto shoe is no longer there.

39
LILY

It's New Year's Day. Ed and I are spending a quiet evening in. Somehow, neither of us could muster up the energy to go to the lunch party we were invited to by one of the partners. It wouldn't look good, but there are times, I tell myself, when you have to put family first.

The table is covered with sketches. Carla laughing. Carla bending over Tom. Carla widening her eyes. Carla in thought, her hands around the stem of a wineglass.

The phone rings. "Can you get that, please?" I call out.

A pan on the oven is boiling over. I turn it down. The green beans look overcooked. I turn to Ed, who is, I now realize, clearly trying to calm someone down. My mother. Tom must have done something. Again.

"How awful," he's now saying.

My heart tightens. I knew it. We shouldn't have left. I should give up work and —

"You poor thing."

Ed doesn't usually call my mother "poor thing." I hover by the phone, wondering what is going on.

"But of course you're right to ring. You must stay with us. Wait there. I will come and fetch you. What is the address again?"

My husband grabs his jacket. "It's Carla. There's been a fire at the hostel. She's outside in the street right now in her dressing gown."

"Is she hurt?"

"No, thank heavens. Just scared."

"I'll go if you like."

"It's okay." He's already at the door. "Maybe you can make up Tom's bed."

Of course, it's the right thing to do.

When Carla arrives, her beautiful olive face is drawn. She is shivering in a pretty pink dressing gown and her hands are gripped together so tightly that her knuckles are white. "It was so frightening. We had to run down the emergency staircase outside. I thought I would fall . . ."

News of the fire had been briefly on LBC. No one, apparently, had been hurt. Meanwhile, the police were investigating.

Ed hands her a tumbler of whisky. "Take this. It will help a bit."

Any excuse to have one yourself, I almost say.

"Sit down. Please." I remember my manners. "You're safe now."

"But I have nothing, no clothes," sobs Carla, cradling the whisky with those elegant hands. "And my books are gone, too."

"They can all be replaced," I say soothingly, taking her hands. Although I had plenty of opportunity to examine her at Christmas, I am reminded right now that she really is very beautiful. Those dark, almond-shaped eyes and thick black eyebrows would look masculine on a pale Englishwoman, but only make her look even more gorgeous, even in her distress.

Perhaps having Carla stay will be a good thing. Ed and I will no longer be able to argue with someone else here. Our guest will be a buffer — just as she was as a little girl.

"It will be all right," I say.

Carla lifts up her downcast face. For a second, I see the distraught look of the little girl I found outside her mother's flat with the big bruise on her face. "It is so kind of you to give me a home. Thank you."

A sudden shiver goes through me.

It's only temporary, I want to say. But that would sound churlish.

And I tell myself that this strange beat of premonition is nothing. Nothing at all.

Besides, it is Joe Thomas I need to worry about.

"Don't take it so badly," says one of my partners when I return from court a few weeks later.

But I do, I think. If I had used the photograph that Joe Thomas had sent me, I might have been able to prove that there hadn't been any yield markings on the day that my client had failed to stop at the T-junction. There were lines there now, of course, but that's the name of the game. He'd have been done on the drunk driving, but his sentence might not have been so heavy if I could have proved that those yield lines hadn't been there at the time.

But road markings are allowed to fade. Accidents happen. And then miraculously the council lorry turns up and paints those lines in. Ask any lawyer. The problem is that you can't always get photographic evidence to prove it.

So much for my being able to sort out cases on my own. Maybe that's why I'm not surprised when a two-line note arrives the following day.

YOU COULD HAVE WON IF YOU'D USED MY PHOTOGRAPH. HOW IS TOM?

I sit and stare at it for some time before picking up the phone.

"Do you have time for a drink?"

Ross sounds both pleased and surprised at the same time. "Love to."

We meet at one of my favorite Italian bistros off Covent Garden where our firm sometimes entertains clients. Good food. Authentic music in the background. And a pleasant view out onto the busy street. But today I'm in no mood for any of this.

"What's up?" Ross asks.

I look at our old friend across the table in his tweed jacket and jeans. He'd started out as Ed's friend but soon became just as much mine — especially when it came to giving guidance about my husband, who, as Ross often said, was a complete idiot at times. An idiot whom we both loved.

"I've got a problem," I say. My hands twist with anxiety under the table. How I've been wanting to confide in someone about Joe and the "helpful information" he keeps sending me. But now the time has come when if I don't share it with someone else, I'm going to burst. Of course, I can't tell Ross everything.

"Wow," says Ross when I finish telling the story. "You poor thing. What an impossible position."

I want him to tell me that it will be all right, that there's something I can do to stop all of this.

"For what it's worth," he adds, "I think you did the right thing, tearing up that photo."

"Really?"

"Absolutely." He sounds firmer now. "You can do this on your own, Lily. You've been doing it on your own for years. Yes, this man might have helped you now and then. But don't let that suck away your confidence. You're a good lawyer."

I want to tell him about the other thing. But I can't. Instead, my mind goes back to the pub in Hampstead. The time when Joe took my hand. That charge of electricity. That attraction that should never have been there. The amount of wine I had consumed.

The real reason for my vow not to drink again.

"You won't tell Ed? Or anyone else?"

I'm panicking now. Terrified in case Ross's allegiances are divided. Of course I'm talking about the anonymous tip-offs. I can't tell anyone about the Heath.

"Promise." He glances at his watch.

"Afraid I've got to go back now."

That's the other thing about Ross. When I first met him, he was an actuary. It had been his knowledge of figures that had helped me to crack Joe Thomas's code games. But after Tom was born and we asked Ross to be godfather, he changed jobs. He said that our experience had made him see life differently. Now he heads a big fund-raising company that helps charities. He's a good man. At least he seems to be. After Joe, I'm beginning to wonder if anyone is as they seem. Have I been foolish to trust Ross? What if, despite his promise, he goes straight to Ed now and tells him everything?

By the time I get home, Ed and Carla have eaten. They're sitting at the table, Ed's sketchbook in front of him.

"I am sorry," says Carla apologetically. "I wanted to wait, but . . ."

"It's my fault." Ed is smiling at me — grinning in a way I haven't seen him do for years. And I know why.

"Your meal is in the oven, darling." He hasn't called me *darling* for a long time.

"It should still be edible. Now, Carla, I want you to put your head slightly to one side. Chin down a bit. Eyes to the left. Perfect."

Ed is happy because he is painting Carla

again. Her idea, he keeps reminding me, as if he is flattered.

Frankly, I'm relieved. It will give me space to figure out what to do about Joe.

40
CARLA

February 2014

Carla woke, as she had done every morning for the last month, in her cozy bedroom overlooking the back garden. It was so much nicer here than in the hostel! Despite what Lily had said about being overdrawn, she must be earning a lot of money for them to afford a place like this. And it wasn't even rented. They actually owned it — although Ed was always referring to the "outrageous mortgage payments."

That was one of the constant refrains she heard between Ed and Lily through the wall that divided her bedroom from theirs. "You're just pissed off because I don't earn as much as you" was one of his favorite phrases.

"When are you going to get rid of that chip on your shoulder, Ed?" That was Lily's.

When she'd simply been a dinner guest, Carla had noticed the odd tense remark.

But now that she was living here, it was like picking her way across enemy lines. The smallest thing would make either of them cross — especially Lily. "Please put the milk back in the fridge," she had snapped at Carla the other evening. "Otherwise it will go off like it did last week."

Ed had rolled his eyes to make her feel better. "Don't worry — she's working on a big case," he'd explained after Lily had stomped back to her study. He took off his glasses as if they were suddenly annoying him. "She lost the last one, so it's *essential* for her to win this one."

He had said the word *essential* in a slightly mocking tone. Then he put his glasses back on and picked up his brush again. "Can you cup your hands around that cup of coffee and stare into the distance? As though you're thinking hard about something. Perfect!"

That wasn't difficult. The inquiry into the hostel fire was about to take place. Everyone who had been staying there had been sent an official form asking if they had been smoking in their bedrooms on that night.

Of course, she'd ticked the box that said "no."

Had she caused the fire? It was possible. But there was no point in owning up to something she wasn't certain about. Far better to put it out of her mind.

"Would you like to grab a coffee after the lecture?"

It was the boy with the floppy hair who kept asking her out to dinner, Rupert. His auburn eyelashes were unnaturally long for a boy, and he was rather shy for one so tall and good-looking. It was as though he didn't realize how attractive he was, not just in looks, but in the way he listened — really listened.

Perhaps it was time to make an exception.

"I'd love one," she replied, looking up from her book. "Thanks."

"Shh," someone whispered from the other side of the library, and they smiled at each other in complicity.

"What did you get for your last essay?" he asked over a skinny latte in the students' union café.

"Seventy-five percent," she answered proudly. The tutor rarely gave anything over sixty-five.

His eyes widened. "Fantastic."

"What about you?"

He groaned. "Don't ask. Actually, maybe you could help me with this awful essay on torts! We could talk it through over dinner."

"What dinner?"

"Come on, Carla. I've asked you enough times. I won't bite."

He took her to a small Italian restaurant off Soho Square. She'd expected him to falter over the order in the way that the English did when speaking her language. But instead, his accent was flawless.

"You are familiar with my country?" she asked as the waiter walked away.

He shrugged, pleased. "My parents believed it was essential that we spoke both French and Italian fluently. We were always being packed off abroad during the holidays to improve ourselves. Frankly, I think it was to give them some peace, even though we were away at school during term time."

Just like poor Tom. Somehow, Carla found herself telling this good-looking, intelligent boy about Tom and Lily and Ed.

"You live with Ed Macdonald? The painter?"

"Yes. Do you know him?"

"Doesn't anyone who loves art? He painted *The Italian Girl*."

She flushed.

His eyes widened. "Don't tell me that the model was . . . it *was* you, wasn't it?" She nodded, embarrassed and yet flattered, too.

"I'd love to meet him one day." Her companion was getting quite flustered. "But only if it's not too much trouble."

"I'll see what I can do," she promised.

Carla let a few weeks go by, not wanting to bother her hosts. Ed was too busy with her portrait — it seemed to take up all his time, even when she wasn't there to sit for him. And Lily was working so late that sometimes Carla heard her come in long after she had gone to bed.

But eventually she summoned up the courage to talk to her hostess, who was surprisingly enthusiastic.

"Lily wondered if you'd like to come to dinner one night next week," said Carla as they sat over their lattes in what had become their favorite coffee shop.

Rupert's face shone. "I'd love that. Thanks."

The pleasure was all hers. Rupert could be just what she needed.

When Carla got back that day, there was a letter waiting for her on the hall table. It was a copy of the report on the formal fire investigation. The hostel had sent it to all former inhabitants. The cause of fire, it informed her, was probably due to a cigarette. It had been impossible, however, to pinpoint the culprit due to the extent of the damage and the fact that so many inhabitants had admitted to smoking in their rooms.

What a relief.

Even better, her travel insurance would now pay out for her clothes and books. The letter also informed her that the hostel would remain closed until further notice.

Things were definitely looking up.

"He's just a friend," Carla had told Lily, shyly. "Someone who's been kind to me at school." But from the minute that Carla walked through the door with Rupert at her side, she sensed Ed's hostility.

"So *you're* the Rupert that our Carla has been talking about?"

Carla flushed at the way Ed had accentuated the word *you're*. And the "talking about" suggested *she* was keen rather than the other way around. What would Rupert think? Suddenly, Carla began to wonder if this dinner was such a good idea.

"That's good to hear, sir," said Rupert, shaking Ed's hand with a sideways glance at Lily.

Thankfully, Lily seemed to pick up on Carla's distress. Smoothly, she changed the subject, but all through dinner Ed was prickly. It wasn't just that he was particularly snide when it came to his wife ("We're lucky to have the pleasure of Lily's company, you know. She's usually working at this time"). But he also took a nasty jab at Rupert and his old school ("One of my cousins went there when he flunked Eton").

Ed didn't like their guest, she was beginning to realize. Poor Rupert. He could sense it, too.

Afterward, they went downstairs to the basement to see Ed's paintings. "Carla tells me that you appreciate paintings." Ed crossed his arms.

"I do, sir. These are wonderful."

"They're crap." Ed glanced dismissively at the pictures of old women, young women, the florist, the tobacconist, a mother in the park. "None has done anything. The only thing that worked was my painting of lovely Carla here."

Ouch! Ed was squeezing her shoulder so hard that it hurt. He stank of wine: at dinner, he'd gone through an entire bottle on his own. She knew Lily had noticed, too. "But now I am painting her again. Has she told you that?" Ed's face was close to Rupert's. Part of her felt triumphant. Yet she was also crawling with embarrassment.

"No, sir. She hasn't told me."

"So you aren't privy to everything that goes on in our Carla's pretty head, then."

It was clear that all these "our Carla's" were said in a proprietorial manner, designed to make Rupert feel like an outsider. What was going on?

"That's enough, Ed." Lily was next to him now, taking his arm. "Time to call it a day, don't you think?"

"Nonsense. I expect you'd like to see the painting, wouldn't you, young man?"

Rupert was as red as she was now. "Only if it's not too much trouble, sir."

"Well, it is. And you know why? Because, like many artists, I never show my paintings to anyone until they're ready."

And with that, Ed stomped up the stairs, leaving them alone in the basement.

"I am so sorry." Lily shook her head. "He's tired and he's hoping for a break with his new portrait of Carla."

"I understand." Rupert composed himself quickly. "Artistic temperament and all that. Thank you so much for a lovely evening."

But it hadn't been lovely and they all knew that. That night, Carla listened as Ed and Lily had a heated discussion.

"Why were you so rude? Almost as if you were jealous of him for being head over heels with Carla."

"Rubbish. I just didn't like some pup looking at my paintings and making patronizing comments."

"He wasn't. He was being entirely polite."

"I know what he was being. Anyway, what would you care? You're never here."

"Maybe it's time for Carla to leave. There are other hostels she could stay at. I don't know why you asked her to stay on. It was meant to be temporary."

"So now you want to throw out my model just when I've gotten my inspiration back? It's like you *want* me to fail."

It's happening, Carla told herself, hugging her knees in bed.

Yet in the morning, it was as though the argument had never taken place. "Would you like to come down to Devon this weekend with us?" asked Lily.

Carla shook her head. "I'll stay here if you don't mind."

Ed looked disappointed. "Really? Tom will be sad not to see you. He might not say so, but I just know it."

So will I, said his eyes.

Good.

"I'm afraid I need to work on my next assignment."

"Sure." Ed sounded put out. "When I'm back, Carla, I'd appreciate some more of your sitting time for the portrait."

She flushed. "Of course."

41
LILY

Weeks and then months are passing. Easter shoots past with its nodding yellow daffodils. (Tom loved the dinosaur chocolate egg that I ordered specially for him.) Early summer roses have already come into bloom in our little patch of ground at the back. And so, too, has Carla's portrait.

I watch with increasing amazement and respect as our "lodger" takes form on Ed's canvas. My husband's hand, which had been so unsteady over the last few years, partly due to lack of confidence — and sometimes, let's be honest, due to drink — has taken on a new self-assurance.

Carla's beautiful almond-shaped eyes follow me whenever I glance at the easel. She is there now all the time — a living fixture in the studio that faces the garden at the back of the house, where there is more light. A living fixture, too, in our house, where she takes my coat when I come in from work and announces that dinner is almost ready.

And she's exciting a great deal of interest.

"Your agent said that you're painting the same Italian girl again?" asked a journalist who came around to interview us for an "at home" feature for a minor magazine.

I'd been standing by the canvas that Ed had, quite purposefully, left out rather than putting away as he usually did with a work in progress. "Yes," my husband said in a casual way, which of course I could see right through. "Carla — the little girl whom my wife and I used to look after when we were first married — has come back into our lives. She's in her early twenties now — training to be a lawyer, actually — and has been kind enough to allow me to paint her again."

Word spread like wildfire when the article came out. The phone began to ring. Of course, it isn't just that the art world (and the media) see this as a good story. It's that my husband's painting is amazing. Carla looks as though she could step out of the canvas any minute. Her sleek hairstyle — so different from those childhood curls — declares that this is a woman of style. Her lips look like they are about to speak.

Here I am. Back again.

And sometimes she appeared to be leveling accusations at me. *Why are you such a bad wife? Why doesn't your son live with you?*

Yes, that's right. For the last few weeks, I've had a growing feeling that she doesn't like me, despite the careful way she takes my coat and cooks dinner every evening (her suggestion). I can tell she disapproves of Tom living away from us. "Don't you miss him when you leave him on Sunday nights?" she has remarked on more than one occasion.

"Very much. But he has special needs, needs that his school is better at providing than we are." She wasn't the only person who asked that question. Only a parent of a child like ours can understand the excruciating agony of not being able to cope and wanting to do the right thing.

Ed never says anything to back me up, as though he agrees with Carla. Which, of course, he does. Even though Tom is flourishing at his weekly boarding school, and even though there have been no more incidents, my husband doesn't like the idea of his son being in what he calls "a military dorm" during the week.

Yet it's not really like that. I've seen the cozy room with its comfy beds and teddy bears proudly displayed. (One of his roommates won't go anywhere without his, even though he's nearly thirteen. He's obsessed with them and has them lined up along the wall. If anyone touches them, he has a full-on meltdown.) My husband's reaction, I know, is because of his own time at school, when all he wanted was to be at home.

Carla's disapproval is ironic, given how much I am doing for her. "Carla needs a training contract now that her conversion course is almost over," Ed announces one night at dinner. "I said you'd be able to help."

We're eating an Italian dish, a delicious mixture of white beans and salad that, if I threw it together, would taste like mush. Carla's hand has transformed it into something different entirely. *So he thinks I might be able to help?* I might be one of the partners, but it is still presumptuous of my husband to assume that I can pull strings like that when I have a stack of e-mails from other hopeful students. "We've had lots of applications," I begin. "But I'll see what I can do."

It's won't be easy, because my own record at work has not been so good recently. So far this year, I've lost more than a third of my cases. These include the ones I argued myself and also those where I used a barrister. It's tempting to blame the latter but it wouldn't be true. If I don't give counsel the right information or enough details about the case, he or she can't strut the stuff in court.

I tell myself that my poor performance has nothing to do with the anonymous tips I've received in the post and ignored. I try not to even look at them, but I can't help checking to see if they're from him. How would I know? Because they're always accompanied by a final line: *How is Tom?*

Useful as these tips might be, I force myself to put them into the shredder, telling myself that I can do without Joe Thomas's help. I don't even want to think about how hard he must be working to get these pieces of "evidence." But I do wonder how he has gotten them. Which secretary is he dating? Or maybe he was lying. Perhaps he's getting his information somewhere else. Either way, the idea that Joe is watching me from somewhere makes my skin crawl.

So when Ed invites Carla to Devon for the weekend, and she turns him down, I can't help but feel a wave of relief. A chance to be on our own. For me to get Ed back again.

42

CARLA

May 2014

"What are you doing this weekend?" Rupert asked.

"Working."

Ever since the embarrassing dinner at Ed and Lily's, she'd been avoiding her friend. But here he was, waiting for her outside the lecture hall.

"All weekend?"

She looked up at him. "All weekend."

"That's a shame." He fell into step with her. "Your friends were . . . not quite what I expected."

"Lily can be a bit cranky but she isn't too bad. I'm afraid Ed was rude. I'm sorry."

"Don't be." Gently he touched her arm as they rounded a corner. "Like I said, it's being an artist. To be honest, though . . . well, I thought you were trying to keep out of my way. So I thought I'd just take the bull by the horns, as it were, and hang around for

461

you, to check everything is all right with us."

Carla couldn't help being flattered. But she also felt the need to make things clear. "Of course it is. You're a very good friend."

" 'Friend'?" He was looking at her quizzically, as if hoping for more. "Then may I take you out to dinner over the weekend?"

It was tempting. But wasn't life complicated enough as it was? "Sorry, but I've got two essays to do. Ed and Lily are away until Sunday night, so I was planning on some quiet time."

Carla was as good as her word. She spent the entire weekend poring over her books. But on Sunday lunchtime there was a knock at the front door. Lily and Ed hadn't told her they were expecting anyone. Maybe it was one of those cold callers or a neighbor, perhaps.

But Rupert was standing on the step. "I was just passing." He handed her a bunch of flowers, prettily wrapped with an artful bow. Freesias — her favorites.

"That's very kind."

"How about a walk? Come on, it'll be good for your brain to have a break."

"Well . . ." It was a beautiful day. Why not? "Just to the park and back."

It was surprisingly good to have the

company. There were lots of other couples out, too. Laughing. Holding hands. With a strange feeling in her chest, Carla realized she'd never gone for a walk in the park with a man she liked before.

"I love being with you, Carla." Rupert's hand reached out for hers.

No.

Deftly she put her hand in her pocket. "I like being with you, too, Rupert." There was a brief pause while she counted to five. "But as I said before, I like you as a friend."

Either he didn't notice the rebuff or else he chose not to. "You're different from the others, Carla. You're focused. As though you have a purpose. Most of the other girls I know just want to have fun."

Carla thought fleetingly of the flightier female students who were always chasing Rupert and others like him. "I don't have time for fun."

"Really?" There was definite disappointment in his voice.

Carla shrugged as they wandered out of the park, back toward Ed and Lily's house. "My mother, she is on her own. It is up to me to make money for us so we can live the lives we should have done."

"Wow. I admire the way you look after her."

"In fact, I must return now. Or I will be behind with my work."

"Surely you have time to make me a cup of tea first?"

"I'm not sure . . .."

"Come on." His eyes twinkled. "It's what *friends* do."

They were on Ed and Lily's steps now. It seemed rude not to agree.

Inviting Rupert to take a seat, Carla swiftly cleared away her books to make room at the table in the huge kitchen, which acted as a casual sitting room, too. The sofa, she noticed with irritation, was a mess of cushions and blankets.

"What do you think of . . . ," she started to say.

But suddenly Rupert moved toward her and boldly, but so very gently, began to trace the outline of her lips with his forefinger. "You're beautiful, Carla," he murmured. "Do you know that?"

He drew her toward him.

For a minute, she was tempted. Rupert was so good-looking. So charming. Such a gentleman. But she must not allow him to distract her. Just as she was about to step away, there was the sound of the key in the lock.

It was Ed! Horrified, she watched him

take in the rumpled sofa and Rupert stepping quickly away from her. Ed's face was
blotched with anger. "So this is why you
didn't want to come to Devon, is it? So you
could use our home as a love nest? How
dare you? Just as well I got back early."

Carla's body went hot and cold and hot
again. "No. You've got it wrong."

But Ed's voice overrode hers as he turned
to Rupert. "Get out. *Now.*"

Stunned, Carla watched Rupert leave. He
should have stayed, she told herself. Stood
up for himself. "How dare *you*?" she yelled,
quivering with anger. "I was doing nothing
wrong. And now you have embarrassed me
in front of my friend."

He would tell her to leave now, she told
herself. She'd have nowhere to live. No
hope of getting what she wanted.

Yet instead, he crumpled, falling down to
the ground at her feet. "I'm sorry, Carla. I
really am. But it's been a hell of a weekend.
You should have been there. You could have
calmed Tom down. He was awful. Do you
know what his current obsession is? Some
computer game that keeps him up all night
so he barely sleeps. When we tried to take it
away from him, he went stark raving mad.
We argued about it. Lily's mother wanted
to let him have his way. She's so scared he'll

end up like Daniel . . ."

"Daniel? What happened to him?"

"Daniel's gone." Ed made a wild dismissive gesture with his hands. "You wouldn't think of it from the way that family talks about him. Daniel's dead!"

"I don't understand."

Ed caught her by the hand. His grip was tight. "Daniel was Lily's adopted brother. He was very disturbed — had been since childhood. Poor bugger."

Now it was her turn to hold his hand as the horrific words came spilling out. The argument Lily had had with her brother. The stables. The way they found him. Ed wasn't sure of the exact details ("Lily can't talk about it"), but one thing was clear: whatever Lily had done made her brother take his own life.

"It's like there's always this thing between us. She's never let me in." Ed collapsed in sobs on the sofa.

How awful! It wasn't fair that Ed should have to suffer for his wife's guilt. Lily treated him so badly. She didn't even look after him properly. What kind of woman didn't have dinner ready for her husband? Or went to bed long after he did? Mamma had taught her the importance of these things, no matter how outdated they may seem. "We Italian women," she would say, "are different from British wives who do not look after their men."

Yet why should she be surprised? Lily was — like many a criminal lawyer — quite cold and clinical. She was used to setting murderers and rapists free.

Somehow Carla managed to calm Ed with a friendly arm on his shoulder. Then she poured him a drink (just a touch of hot water with the whisky), and after that, even though his hand was still shaking, persuaded him to start painting.

Thank you, Rupert, she said silently as she sat in front of Ed. With any luck, everything was going to work out after all.

43
LILY

Despite my recent court losses and my own reservations, the other partners agreed to my "favor" and Carla duly started work in the middle of July. "You've got a bright girl there," said one of my colleagues by the end of the week. "She might look stunning but she's on the ball."

He spoke as though looks were a disadvantage, which, in a way, they are. If you're more than averagely attractive, especially in a profession like law, people don't always take you seriously. I'm aware that I will never be considered beautiful, even though I take pleasure in the fact that I have grown into my skin. Perhaps that's a good thing.

But Carla turns heads wherever she goes. And not just because of her face or because she is doing well at my firm. Ed's portrait of her is finally finished. After one of our weekends in Devon, for once without Carla, everything seemed to fall into place. We'd argued, and he'd left early, but sometimes I think our difficulties spur him on. When I returned, he was working on the hardest part — the eyes.

Now the painting has been accepted for a big London show in the autumn, and the national press has gotten wind of it.

Suddenly, Carla's everywhere — in women's magazines, in the *Times* art pages. And in the cocktail party invitations we begin to receive. Of course, everyone wants to know the story of how we came across her again. Or rather how *she* came across *us*. When I open one magazine, I find that Carla has managed to tell the story with barely a reference to me. She praises Ed for offering her a home after the hostel fire. Ed who is her mentor rather than me. Ed who says how wonderful she is with our son, Tom, who is in a "special school," far away in Devon. She doesn't refer to the fact that he lives with my parents.

How dare she?

"You have no right to mention Tom," I say to Carla, trying to control my voice.

We're on our way to work, walking briskly. It reminds me of the mornings when I used to see her at the bus stop with her mother.

"He is part of our private life," I continue, still hot with rage after spotting the offending article in one of the magazines put out in reception for clients.

"I'm sorry," Carla says in a tone that suggests she does not mean it. Her chin juts out. It seems more angular than usual. Almost pointy like a cat's. "But it is true, is it not?"

"He is," I say, struggling to remain composed, "in the best place for him."

She shrugs. "In Italy, we keep our family close, whatever the circumstances. It is better that way, I think."

"You are living in the UK now," I splutter, almost unable to believe her audacity. We're going into the office building now. I stop myself from saying more. But I go out on my lunch hour and buy a postcard of the Natural History Museum. *This has got a great collection of fossils,* I write. *Shall we visit it during the holidays?*

Then I post it to my son.

I feel better for a bit. Then later that day, I receive a note from one of the other partners.

Luckily this has not yet gone out to the client. One of the trainees spotted the mistake, highlighted below. Please amend.

I've made a mistake in drafting a document about a company takeover. It isn't big. But big enough. Yet the worse thing is that the "trainee," according to the initials on the correction, is our Italian guest.

Later that night, Ed turns on me. "Why were you so horrid to Carla about Tom?"

A chill washes over me. I feel like the school prefect, reprimanded by a teacher for snitching on a girl caught smoking in the loo. Why should I be blamed for something she's done? "Because Carla shouldn't have mentioned Tom or the fact that he's at a special school. He's private."

"Clearly our son is to be categorized as 'not to be opened.' Are you embarrassed by him?"

This isn't fair. "You know that's not true. Do you think *you* could work if Tom was here all the time? Do you think *you* could concentrate if he was in the studio demanding to know why paint is called paint? Or giving you every statistic imaginable on Monet or John Singer Sargent?"

Ed sits up and turns on the bedroom light. His eyes are sad. I know that my words sound selfish, and I hate myself for it. But it is horrifyingly easy for the resentment to bubble up every now and then, to burst through the carefully painted veneer of outward sainthood. I know he thinks it, too, sometimes — it's simply easier to put the blame on me.

"I just can't help thinking," says Ed slowly, mirroring the thoughts in my head, "that when you have a child like Tom, you have a duty to do the right thing. That's all."

Then he switches off the light, leaving me to thrash around all night. I practically followed Daniel around for years, trying to protect him from himself. But I cracked. I said things I shouldn't have. And that's what finally tipped my brother over the edge.

If I'm not with Tom full-time, he stands a chance of making it. My constant presence won't help him.

In fact, it might kill him.

Trying to work at home one night — thoughts colliding in my head so much that I am getting little done — I make a call.

"Lily!" Ross's deep, rich voice immediately makes me feel calmer, as though everything is going to be all right.

"I thought you were out tonight?" He sounds surprised.

My previous doubts about him begin to return. Did he want me to be out? Was he intending to speak to his old friend Ed about me?

"No. I'm in all evening."

"Sorry." His voice sounds uncertain. "I

must have got it wrong. I thought Ed said you were going to that gallery opening with him."

"He asked me but I had too much to do. Besides, it's Carla they want. You know. The painter and his subject. *The Italian Girl.*" I don't even bother hiding my irritation.

Carla looked gorgeous tonight when she left with my husband. Her bob was sleek and her makeup immaculate. No one would have guessed that she'd been slaving away over her books until half an hour before-hand.

Ed looked good, too. It wasn't just because of his new blue-striped shirt and the nicely rumpled linen jacket. It's the way he now carries himself.

Success suits him. It always did. My husband, I now realize, is one of those men who need to do well, if only for the sake of everyone around him. The whisky level hasn't gone down for a while. He's even being particularly nice to me. My husband deserves this, I tell myself, as I say good-bye to Ross after arranging a dinner in a few weeks' time. Let Ed enjoy it. Maybe Ross is jealous of Ed's change of fortunes. Or, if he is gay, maybe he's jealous of me.

August 2014

Three weeks later, I am working on an urgent case in the office. It's past ten o'clock at night. Ed is at another cocktail party. Carla is still at home. This morning, she didn't come into the office with me. "I don't feel well," she said, curled up like a kitten on her bed.

It's nearly ten o'clock — everyone else has gone home — when the phone rings on my desk. I know it's Joe before he says a word. I can sense it.

"Lily. No. Don't put the phone down. Just come."

The hairs on my arm are standing up. "Where?"

He names a hotel near the Strand.

"It's to do with your husband. I've been watching him." His voice rises urgently. "Just trying to look after you. Like I always do. Just go. Now."

I replace the receiver, trembling. As I bid good night to the security guard and slip on my coat, I tell myself that I am going straight home. That I'm not visiting this hotel to see what I should or shouldn't see.

Ed wouldn't do this. Ed wouldn't do this. The words pound over and over in my mind. But then I think of his ups and downs, the way he has blown hot and cold throughout our marriage — our rushed marriage, all for the sake of an inheritance he'd never told me about. A marriage we have stayed in because of Tom. But we've made it work. Haven't we?

As I get out of the taxi, I see a figure. No, it's a couple. She has her head on his shoulder. The girl has short hair that gleams in the lamplight. The man is tall with a slight stoop to his shoulders, the kind that comes from bending over an easel for hours at an end.

I run toward them. They stop in the street, under the lamp. He lowers his head to kiss the girl. And then he looks up.

"Lily?" says my husband, openmouthed. Then, as though he can't believe it, he says it again. "Lily?"

There's a flash of light. As if a picture has been taken.

A press card is being waved in front of me. "Mrs. Macdonald. Would you like to comment on the rumors that your husband is having an affair?"

The burning smell has died down now.

That's something. But there's a taste of unease in the air.

Have I missed my last chance?

What is she up to?

What is she planning next?

44
CARLA

Of course, the publicity for the new painting had played its part in bringing them
together. The "fairy-tale story," as one paper
put it about the artist and his muse. "The
Italian Girl Grown Up." The magazine
articles. Ed's arm around her shoulder for
the camera. The brush against her cheek —
so close to her mouth! — after a particularly
glittery cocktail party. Carla didn't even
have to try.

But nothing more physical had happened
until the night when Lily was working late
in the office (again!), and Carla was posing
for yet another portrait in the sitting room,
the window open on an unusually hot night.
Carla had purposefully worn no makeup,
knowing he preferred her like that. She
could feel the warm air making tiny beads
of sweat break out on her lip.

Suddenly Ed moved away from his easel
and walked toward her. He got down on his

knees and gently, very gently, moved a tendril of hair from her forehead. "You're the most beautiful creature I have ever seen." Then he kissed her. And she let him.

For a minute, Carla had a glimpse of the man on the plane. The one she'd dismissed on the grounds of his wedding ring. Hadn't she always told herself that she'd never get hurt like Mamma had been?

But as Carla allowed herself to be laid down on the soft sitting room carpet, she couldn't help thinking how much she'd love to have a famous artist for a boyfriend. A place of her own. Her own money. A standing that would impress even the neighbors at home, who would have to be kind to Mamma now, especially as Ed's work was soon to be exhibited in Rome.

After that, they made love whenever and wherever they could. Hotels were best, Ed said. Safer than his place.

Yet he seemed to get more satisfaction than she. Ed was not the lover Carla had imagined he would be. Naturally, she'd had some experience. At university in Italy, finally free from Nonno's rules, she would flirt with boys who were likely to take her to dinner. Sometimes she would let it go further. A new dress, perhaps, in return for a weekend in Sorrento. Always, she took precautions. "I wish to concentrate on my studies — not fall in love," she had told them all. But the truth was that she didn't want to get into trouble like Mamma had. It was the financial stability of marriage she wanted, not the role of a mistress.

And yet here she was, being just that.

"I'm going to leave Lily," Ed always promised. "I just need the right time to tell her. This is more for me than just sex."

I can help with that, Carla told herself.

One day, a few weeks after they'd started to sleep together, Carla made a call from the hotel room to the twenty-four-hour hotline of a celebrity gossip magazine while Ed was in the shower. The woman at the other end was very interested in what she had to say. Carla spoke quickly. Then she put down the phone, without giving her name.

And shortly after that, Lily found them.

It was strange. Despite everything coming together, Carla didn't feel the expected satisfaction of revenge.

Instead, she felt cheap. Dirty.

Lily's face was white under the street lamp. Her glaring eyes belonged to a wild animal. Carla was scared; Ed put his arm around her protectively, even though she

479

could feel his body shaking, too. "We love each other," he kept saying to Lily. "We want to be with each other forever."

"We couldn't help it," Carla stammered.

Lily snarled, "Of course you could." Then she began to weep, which was worse. "I've helped you so much. Is this how you repay me?"

"Repay?" Carla's voice rose into the night air and a passerby turned to look. "You were the one who should have repaid me. I heard you in Devon telling Ed that you ignored my letters from Italy."

"I —"

"Don't deny it. Don't try any of those lawyer lies on me, because I know them all myself." She was sweating now with indignation. "If you hadn't told Larry to leave my mother alone, we would have been all right."

Lily's laugh was brittle. "Is that what you really think, you silly little girl?"

"I'm not —"

"Listen to me."

For a minute, it looked as though Lily was going to grab her by the neck. "If Tony could deceive his wife, don't you think he could have deceived you and your mother as well?"

Carla had a flashback to the woman in the car with the bright lipstick.

"I did you both a favor. Trust me. Just like you've done me a favor — both of you." Then she swung around to face Ed. "If it hadn't been for Tom, I'd have left you years ago." Then she swiveled around to face Carla again. "You'll soon find out what he's like. And if you assume you're going to get any money out of this, you're mistaken."

Ed's hands tightened on hers. They were as strong as the waves of fear in her chest. "I've heard enough of this. Come on, Carla. We're going."

"No." Lily's voice was stronger than she had ever heard it. "I'm the one who's going. Do you think I really want to go back to that house, knowing that you two have probably been at it like rabbits when I've been working? Besides, it will only have to be sold now anyway. Here." She tossed the keys at Carla. "Take this set, too. I'll be in touch about my things. Just get out of my sight — both of you."

Hang on, Carla wanted to say. *This isn't how I thought it would be.* But Ed's hand had tightened so hard on hers that it almost hurt. Then he hailed a taxi and they went home. "Where will Lily go?" she asked as they opened the front door to be greeted by Lily's belongings everywhere: her white coat hanging on the hook in the hall, her heels neatly positioned by the door.

"She'll be all right," said Ed, drawing her to him. "She's tougher than she looks. Look how she had us followed."

"Really?" Carla tried to sound innocent.

"How else do you think she found us?"

But Carla could not sleep for worrying. Suppose Lily did something stupid, like jumping off a bridge? *What do you care?* Mamma might have said. Yet for some reason, she did. For the first time, Carla wondered if Lily had been right when she said she'd done them a favor in pushing Larry away.

If you think you're going to get any money out of this, you're mistaken.

All night, Carla tossed and turned. When she woke in the morning, to find Ed's head on her chest like a child in need of comfort, Carla felt another flash of misgiving.

Then he woke, smiled and stretched out in the wide bed as the sun streamed in through the cream shutters.

"Isn't this amazing?" he said, tracing her breast with his forefinger. "We were meant for each other. And now we'll be together forever."

Wasn't that what she'd wanted? But all she could think of were those gray hairs on his chest, that little bald spot in the middle of his hair and the tears on Lily's face from the night before.

The headlines came swiftly:

PAINTER LEAVES WIFE FOR
SEXY ITALIAN SITTER

ARTIST BLOTS CANVAS FOR
ITALIAN GIRL GROWN UP

"I'm definitely keeping the house," Ed told her a few days later. "I'm going to borrow some money so I can buy Lily out. She's going to leave London and set up a practice in Devon near Tom. It's the best thing for everyone."

"But will we have enough to live on?"

He held her in his arms. "Don't worry about that."

She took a deep breath. "I'm broke, Ed."

"Don't worry." He kissed the top of her head. "I will look after you now."

"But I don't have any cash."

Then he reached into his back pocket and peeled off some notes. "Is that enough?"

Her heart filled with relief. "Thank you."

Of course, she banked most of it and sent a transfer straight to Mamma.

For a few weeks, Carla's doubts began to fade. There was something special about living with a famous painter. They went to nice restaurants. They were the couple of the moment. Everyone knew them.

She didn't have to worry about paying rent or bills. Ed bought her lovely clothes. Lily *had* been lying about the money! She even managed to keep working in the London office — they could hardly sack her, it would be against the law. And thankfully Lily was no longer there.

Some people of course were cool at first. "Memories are short," Ed reassured her. And he was right; within a couple of months or so, the coldness began to thaw, especially when one of the partners left unexpectedly and everyone had something else to talk about.

As for Ed, he couldn't have been more attentive. Sometimes too much so. One day, in the post, she received a handwritten note from Rupert.

Glad to see you are doing so well.

"Who is that from?" asked Ed, reading over her shoulder.

"Just a friend from law school."

"That kid who came here?"

Uncomfortable memories of Ed finding

her and Rupert in the house came back to her.

"Yes."

Ed said nothing. But later that night when she put something in the bin, Carla found Rupert's note torn into tiny bits. "Why did you do that?" she asked him. But instead of replying, he kissed her deeply, and then began to make love to her with a passion that he had not shown for some weeks.

The shredded note was worth it, Carla told herself, as she lay gasping on the sheets. It was like it had been at the beginning, when Ed was still just enough out of her grasp for him to be exciting. And she suspected he felt the same.

There was nothing like unavailability for attraction. For the first time in ages, she thought of that caterpillar pencil case, Charlie, the one she'd stolen from another child. How she had wanted it! But then, when she'd had it, the craze had turned to something new instead. What was wrong with her, she wondered, that she always needed something more?

45
LILY

November 2014

"I can't eat it now." Tom glares at me with fury in his eyes. "You've moved the cutlery. Look!"

He points angrily at the fork that I have edged a couple of inches to the left to make room for an extra setting. I've been looking after Tom for long enough now to remember not to do that, but every now and then something slips and I forget. The results can be spectacular. Screaming. Thowing. You name it. Like now.

Crash.

Mum and I jump, grabbing each other's arms. It's not just the cutlery that has flown off the table. It's the plate next to it and a rather nice crystal wineglass that belonged to a wedding gift set from all those years ago.

After Ed and I split I couldn't help thinking how ironic it was that wedding presents could long outlast the marriage itself. That's why I chose to leave most of it behind.

But now, to my horror, I feel tears pricking my eyes.

Besides, who wants an unfaithful husband? Quality wineglasses are far more useful.

"Why did you do that?" I shout, ignoring the warning look in Mum's eyes. *Don't question Tom. Definitely don't argue with him. You won't win.* During the divorce — a "quickie," which had come through with indecent haste — Ed had claimed it was "useless" arguing with a lawyer. People like me, apparently, never listen to others.

Maybe that's where Tom gets it from — his ability to see his own point of view and no one else's.

"You touched my knife," he states bluntly, squinting through his new thick-framed black glasses. "I've told you before. I don't like that."

Bending down, I sweep up the pieces of cracked glass. "You're acting like a three-year-old," I mutter.

"Shh," soothes Mum.

Normally I don't make a fuss, but every now and then, I snap. Something usually acts as a trigger, and today I suspect it's the extra place setting at the table — a reminder of the life that ended on the night I saw Ed and Carla kissing outside the hotel on the Strand.

Strangely, after those first few raw moments, there was no anger. There still isn't, though it would almost be easier if there were. Mum says it's because I still haven't worked through my feelings yet. Maybe she's right. But if so, when *am* I going to? It's been months now since Ed and I split. Yet it still feels as raw as if it had happened yesterday.

I had spent the night at the University Women's Club, and called in sick the next day. There was no way I could face Carla, and I didn't put it past her to prance into the office as though nothing had happened.

Then my mobile had rung.

Ed.

"We need to talk," he said without the defensive tone of the previous night.

"Is Carla there?"

"No."

Hope ballooned up into my throat. Ed wanted me back. Of course he did! We had a child together. Perhaps now, in the sober light of day, Ed realized we needed to stick together for Tom's sake.

I rang the bell, feeling like a stranger on my own doorstep. Ed greeted me with a glass of whisky in his hand. It wasn't even ten o'clock.

I launched straight in. "Look, I'm hurt about Carla. But I'm prepared to forgive you for Tom's sake. Can't we start again?"

Then, rather desperately, I added, "We've done it before."

Ed patted my hand as though I was a little girl. "Come on, Lily. It's understandable that you're scared." As he spoke, there was a gleam in his eye. He was on a high, no doubt helped by the drink. Something I'd seen time and time again during our marriage. Before long it would be followed by a plunge of spirits.

You see? I know him far better than Carla. How will she cope?

"You're young enough to start again, Lily. You make a great deal more money than me and . . ."

"How can you talk about money!" I stood up and strode into the kitchen toward one of his paintings. It was a picture of the hotel we stayed at during our honeymoon. A picture he'd once helped me to copy, to show how colors could be mixed to achieve that subtle combination of blue merging into green. I can still remember his arm guiding mine, his touch thrilling mine. "Not bad," he had said, admiring my efforts. And

489

to show willing, he had actually put it on the wall. Next to his.

"We need to talk about the practicalities," he continued. "I suggest that I keep the house and buy you out."

"How?"

Ed was always hopeless when it came to money.

"I've got an exhibition coming up. Remember? You could find somewhere in town and then we can each take it in turns to go down to Devon and visit Tom at weekends . . ."

"You've got it all worked out, haven't you?" I said, appalled. "You and that Italian bitch."

Ed's face darkened. "Don't call her that. You haven't shown me any affection for years. All you care about is your work."

That wasn't fair. It's true that I was exhausted at night after work, but isn't everyone? And when I had made overtures on Sunday mornings, Ed always rolled away, declaring his back was stiff or that we would wake Carla, on the other side of the wall. How could I have been so stupid?

Once more, memories of a younger Carla came back to me: the little girl who had asked me to lie for her about that pencil case, the child whose mother was really seeing "Larry" instead of working.

Like mother, like daughter.

"What are you doing?" yelled Ed.

I hardly knew myself. Later, I vaguely recall running at the kitchen wall, toward the pair of paintings of our honeymoon hotel. Picking up his, I threw it on the floor and jumped on it. Then, pushing my way past Ed, I flew out of the house, weeping.

The following day, I received a letter — hand-delivered at work — starting divorce proceedings on the grounds of my "unreasonable behavior."

But there's something else — something I'm only now allowing myself to consider. If I'm honest, Ed and I weren't right for ages. But I couldn't leave him because of Tom. Is it possible that, unintentionally, I had ignored the signs of affection between Carla and my husband? Had I, unconsciously, *wanted* something to happen between them to give me a justified get-out-of-jail-free card from my marriage?

So maybe the "unreasonable" wasn't so unreasonable after all.

46
CARLA

Every other weekend, for some months now, Carla and Ed had gone down to Devon to see Tom. At first she had been nervous. What if the boy refused to talk to her? She genuinely felt for him: an understanding between two people who had never fit in. But when Ed had picked him up from the house — they'd decided it was better if she stayed in the car while he did this — he had come running up to her all gangly-legged and toothy with excitement. "Carla," he had said, nodding. "You're here."

She wouldn't allow herself to think of Lily, who must be waiting inside. A mother forced to give up her son to another woman for the day. She deserved it, Carla told herself. Lily had neglected Tom so that she could follow her career. She had neglected her husband, too. It was the only way Carla could cope with that little nagging voice in her head — the voice that had been reflected in the letter from her mother.

"I hope you know what you are doing, my sweet," her mother had written. "Looking back, I regret the pain I caused Larry's wife. Be very careful."

And then, one Saturday morning when she and Ed had been lying in bed, came the note through the mail slot. Luckily she got to it before him.

MARRIAGE BREAKER! YOU WILL PAY FOR THIS.

The writing was in spidery capital letters. Who had sent it? Lily? Yet somehow Carla knew it wasn't her style. Someone at work, then? Even though most were friendlier now, there were still some who talked about her predecessor with affection — how she'd started her own practice, focusing on cases where parents had children with special needs, how "she deserved to do well." This last bit had been said by Lily's old secretary with a meaningful look toward Carla.

Was it possible one of them had sent the note?

Part of Carla wanted to show Ed so he could banish her fears, tell her it was all right. But what if it stirred his conscience? Made him feel guiltier than he did already?

There were times when she often found him looking at pictures of Tom with a wistful gaze. And he was always in a difficult mood after their weekend visits. Did he regret leaving his son for her? Was it possible that he might leave her and return to Lily?

Such humiliation! She couldn't end up like Mamma.

So instead of telling Ed about the note, she ripped it into little pieces and threw them into the rubbish bin down the street.

For a few weeks after that, she felt nervous, looking over her shoulder every time she went to the office, but nothing happened.

At home, Ed's obsession with her made him clinging and controlling. "Where have you been?" he demanded one night when she came back late after sorting out an urgent contract. "I tried to ring you but there was no answer."

"I had it switched off so I could concentrate."

But when she came out of the shower that night, she found him stuffing her mobile quickly back into her bag as if he'd been checking it.

"I'm not hiding anything from you," she said, annoyed.

"Of course you're not, darling." He draped

an arm around her. "I just thought I heard it buzz. Look, you've got a text." He rolled his eyes. "Your work again."

That stifling feeling grew.

Then an important client canceled a commission for a portrait of his wife. "Apparently she disapproves of the press publicity over us," said Ed, shrugging. "Never mind. Commissions come and go. The important thing is that I've got you. You know, I never really felt I had Lily. She was always thinking of Daniel or Tom or her career." Meanwhile, bottles of wine were disappearing from the cellar at an alarming rate. "I took them into the gallery," said Ed when she questioned him about it. But later in the week, she found the bottles at the bottom of the recycling bin at the back of the house.

Carla began to feel a stirring of frustration. Was this how Lily had felt?

Then, one Sunday when Ed was out sketching, she did a great tidy-up, partly to expunge Lily's presence in the house. Ed's study was sacrosanct: no one went into it. But when she peered inside, she could see the desk was overflowing with bits of paper. Cobwebs fluttered in the corners. Dirty mugs were on every surface. Just a quick bit of rearranging wouldn't go amiss.

Underneath the half-finished sketches, she found a pile of unopened mail.

Some had "Urgent" stamped on the envelope. Others, "Open Immediately."

So she did.

Aghast, Carla sank onto Ed's chair. He owed thousands on his credit card. The mortgage hadn't been paid for two months. There was a letter giving them three more months.

"It will be all right," Ed said when she confronted him. "It's just a question of cash flow. I've got the new exhibition coming up. My agent is very optimistic. I'll sell more than enough to keep us going."

Then he looked at her disappointedly as though *she'd* been in the wrong. "Please don't go into my study again. It's not as though I've got anything to hide."

The next day, she found the letters had gone.

The exhibition opening almost distracted Carla from the doubts that were building up. It was such fun to be photographed on Ed's arm! He looked so handsome in his tuxedo. "Shall I refer to you as Mr. Macdonald's companion?" asked one of the journalists.

Ed, hovering at her shoulder, had stepped

in. "Put fiancée, would you?"

Carla started. They hadn't even discussed marriage! But Ed was speaking as though it had all been arranged.

"Why did you say that?" she asked as they walked home.

Ed's handgrip tightened. "I thought you'd be pleased."

"I am."

But she really wasn't sure. Instead, Carla thought back to the night when he'd first made love to her. She'd adored his impulsiveness then. But now it felt as though she was being treated like the child she'd been when Ed had first known her. He was making huge decisions — decisions she should have a say in, too. Did she really want to get married? It no longer seemed as important as it had been.

The following night, when she was working late at the office, Ed rang. "Have you seen the *Telegraph*?" he demanded tersely.

Carla felt a quickening of apprehension. "No."

"Then get one."

There was a copy in reception for clients. Swiftly, Carla skimmed through until she reached the arts pages.

NEW EXHIBITION DISAPPOINTS ART LOVERS

Artist Edward Macdonald fails to live up to expectations . . .

"Sorry," she said to one of the partners. "I've got to leave."

He raised his eyebrows. "You've finished the briefing?"

"Not quite. But I've got an emergency."

"We'll have another if you don't have everything ready first thing in the morning."

"I will."

When she got home, Ed was slumped on the sofa.

"It will be all right," she said, bending down to kiss him on the forehead.

"Will it? We'll have to sell the gallery. I just can't afford to keep it going anymore."

Then his arms opened and he pulled her toward him. His breath stank of whisky and his mouth was wet as he pushed her down on the sofa. "Don't, Ed, don't. It's not safe." But he continued to kiss her, and it seemed easier to let him than carry on protesting.

The following week, she received a letter from Mamma.

Cara mia,

You will not believe what has happened! Larry has left me a little money. I have only just found out — his widow fought against it but the judge ruled I should have it. My Larry changed his will at the end, apparently. It shows what a good man he was, don't you think? . . .

So her visit had achieved something after all.

Yet Carla felt physically sick. Yes, Mamma would be financially secure now, judging from the amount mentioned. So much for her mother's comment about "a little money." No wonder the widow had challenged it. But where did that leave Carla? Had she put herself into this awful position with Ed for nothing?

Perhaps it was time to get out.

47
LILY

February 2015

"He's nearly here, he's nearly here!"

Tom is pacing up and down, patting his hands on his knees as if playing the drum. The action soothes Tom, according to the experts, even if it plays havoc on everyone else's nerves.

"There's his car, Mum. There's his car!"

Ross always has this effect on him. If there was one thing that Ed and I got right, it was choosing his friend as Tom's godfather. At least, that's what I used to think. But I'm now not entirely certain about anyone. Not even myself.

It's true, however, that Ross was gratifyingly shocked when Ed walked out on me for Carla and then demanded the house. "As for 'unreasonable behavior,' that's ridiculous," he said when I'd gone around the following day, barely able to stop crying.

500

I'd shrugged, looking around at Ross's place. The washing machine door was off, lying on the side of the kitchen counter as if waiting for someone to call the repairman. The kitchen sink was stacked with several days' worth of dishes and there was a pile of newspapers on the floor by the bin. Half a bottle of Jack Daniel's sat on the side. Yet Ross himself was always impeccably dressed in a sharp suit and dapper tie. This man is full of contradictions. It occurred to me then, as it occurs to me frequently, that one never really knows a person properly. Especially ourselves.

"What grounds does he cite for this unreasonable behavior?" continued Ross.

"Always working late. Not taking holidays. That sort of thing." I gave a short laugh. "Unreasonable behavior can mean anything nowadays. I had a client who got a divorce because her husband dug up her vegetable garden without asking her permission first."

My fingers gripped the side of Ross's cream work top. Imagine if Ed's lawyers knew the truth . . . No, I tell myself, don't go there.

"What are you going to do?" asked Ross. He was coming closer now. For a minute, I thought he might try to give me a cuddle. Until then, we'd only exchanged brief kisses on the cheek. It felt odd. So I stepped backward.

"I don't know." All I could think of was the geometric pattern on the terra-cotta floor. Since last night, small details seemed big. Maybe it was the mind's way of coping.

"I've got an idea." Ross was walking toward the window now and looking outside. His flat was in Holloway; the view wasn't as pleasant as our home in Notting Hill. An *our* that would soon be a *their*.

"Get out of London. Make a fresh start. Set up your own practice in Devon so you can be on hand for Tom. I seem to remember that you and Ed talked about this before."

I winced at my husband's name. "It's a big step. What if my clients don't come with me?"

Ross's face conceded this was a possibility. "Suppose you suggest to the firm that you set up an offshoot in the southwest? Then they might encourage you to take some of their cases."

I hesitated. Leave London? Go back to the place that I swore I'd never live in again after Daniel? Yet it did make sense. It would put distance between that woman and me. And, more importantly, it would take the pressure off my parents. Tom might be at school during the week, but I couldn't expect them to carry on forever at weekends.

So even now, as I wash Tom's special knife and fork and place them back on the table under his watchful eye, I wonder how we coped in those first few weeks. The firm had been very understanding: true to Ross's suggestion, they were quite amenable to the idea of setting up a new branch. As for Tom, his challenging behavior was easier to deal with now that Ed wasn't around. Although it was odd coming back to my old room with its dusty maroon and royal blue ribbons in the desk drawer. "Just until Tom and I find our own place," I said at the beginning.

Yet once there, it seemed easier to stay — to be cocooned by my parents. Protected. Hoping that Joe Thomas would leave me in peace.

No one, I told myself, must know the truth about what happened.

The door knocker breaks into my reverie now as I stir the butternut squash soup. Devon in the winter months is much darker and colder than London, but I am slowly growing used to it. There's something about the determined way in which the tides go back and forth with reassuring regularity; it's like a comforting grandfather clock.

I've always loved the sea. Tom loves it, too. When he's home on the weekends, we spend hours walking up and down the beach, looking for driftwood. I'm becoming quite an expert on fossils now, thanks to my son. And we've found a wonderful museum in a small seaside town nearby. ("Look," gasped Tom. "A prehistorical whale tooth!") Mum has gotten him a dog, too. A small schnauzer. Tom spends hours talking to Sammy, like Daniel used to with Merlin.

Sometimes I find myself doing the same.

"He's here, he's here," crows Tom, now dancing around. He never makes this much fuss about his father coming down, I say to myself as I walk across the hall. Then again, I try to make myself scarce when Ed pays his weekend visits. Since our divorce proceedings started, our "meetings" are more of a quick nod at the front door before Ed takes Tom out for the day.

I can only imagine what those outings must be like; it's awkward enough for a single father to entertain his children. With a child like Tom, it would be even more of a challenge. How does Carla cope? I wondered. Not very well, I hope. Despite that engagement gossip piece in a tabloid that one of the partners had awkwardly shown me, there had been no announcement of a marriage date.

I am relieved about that, although annoyed with myself at the same time for such a reaction. It means, surely, that Ed isn't certain. Carla, I am convinced, would jump at the chance to have a gold ring on her finger.

"Forget him," Ross is always saying. "You're too good for him."

I know he's just being nice, but I appreciate it. Ross has become important in our new lives. Tom always loves his visits, not least because he usually arrives bearing enough gifts to suggest it's Christmas, whatever the month. My parents enjoy his company, too. "I can't understand why that man has never gotten married," Mum keeps saying.

"Hi!" He's beaming now at the doorstep, staggering under the weight of flowers and boxes. "How are my favorite friends?"

Tom frowns. "How can you have 'favorite' in the plural? If you like one person best, it has to be in the singular. You can't have more than one person as favorite because then they wouldn't be your favorite, would they?"

I tire easily of these pedantic questions, but Ross merely grins. He makes as if to rub Tom's hair, like a godfather might do to his godson, but then stops, clearly remembering that Tom hates his scalp being touched.

"Great point."

Mum appears behind me, beaming. She's taken off her apron and frowns at me, indicating I should have done the same. "Come on in. You must be starving after that drive. Supper's almost ready."

Ross gives Tom a wink. "Don't tell anyone, but I stopped off for a bite on the way down. But I'm still hungry."

Tom giggles. The conversation is a ritual, one they have every time. It's a narrative that soothes me as well as my son. Indeed, it does the same to my parents. It helps to bring normality to the house that is rarely there when it's just the three of us, all trying to rescue Tom from himself, desperately making sure that what happened to Daniel will never happen to him. It's the unspoken fear that haunts us all.

No one, unless they have a child like this, can understand. I remember once, when Tom was younger, talking to a woman in a supermarket queue. Her son — about ten with gangly limbs flying everywhere — was in a wheelchair. People made way for her. They were sympathetic when he reached out to knock the tins from the conveyor belt, sending them flying.

Although I would never wish Tom to be in a wheelchair, I can't help thinking that at least it would mean others would be understanding. When my son misbehaves in public — jumping on a wineglass in a pizzeria to see how many fragments he could "make" is one recent example — I receive stares that say, *Why can't you control your teenager?*

My research warns me that as Asperger's kids get bigger and less "cute," their meltdowns and behavior can turn others against them. The other day, there was a newspaper story about a café owner throwing an autistic-spectrum teenager out of his shop because the kid kicked up a fuss when given coffee with milk instead of black. The teen fell on the pavement and broke his arm.

I'd personally kill anyone if they hurt my son.

After dinner, Ross and I go for a walk with the dog. It's another ritual. Sometimes Tom begs to come, too, but it makes me nervous. The rocks on the edge of the beach are so high, I worry he's going to climb one and fall. Tonight, to my relief, Tom announces that he's tired. He'll have a shower in the morning — he hates baths — and if his special Man United towel isn't ready, we'll all know about it.

Difficult as he is, still I find myself thinking that I am blessed. I might not have a conventional child, but my son will never be boring. He has a constantly inquiring mind. He looks at life in a way that others don't. "Did you know that the average person produces enough saliva to fill two swimming pools during their life?" he asked me the other day.

"How are you doing?" Ross now says as we walk under the overhanging cliff, gazing out at the lights flickering from boats on the horizon.

"We're fine, thanks. Tom's school, knock on wood, seems to be happy with him, and I'm building up quite a decent client base. I've also taken up core classes at the gym to give myself 'me-time,' like you suggested."

He nods. "Good."

Something's up. I can feel it. "What about you? How is work?"

"Okay, although to be honest, I feel there has to be more to life."

"I know what you mean."

We stroll on, past a stack of deck chairs neatly piled up for the following day. Past, too, a couple arm in arm, who give us a meaningful nod. They think we're like them, I tell myself. It makes me feel like a fraud, one who needs to put Ross at ease so he doesn't think I am attracted to him. Am I? At times. But there is still something about him that I can't put my finger on.

"I really appreciate the interest you show in Tom," I begin.

"It's not just Tom I care for."

I hold my breath.

"I'm worried about you, Lily."

He takes my arm and I feel a slow warmth down my spine. At times, I tell myself that I've learned to live without Ed. Sometimes he seems like another life away. Sometimes he seems like yesterday. On those days, I want him here. Next to me.

"There's no need," I say. "I'm fine. I've moved on."

My words are so clearly a lie.

"There's something I've got to tell you," says Ross.

As he speaks, a plume of sea spray leaps up. We run ahead — him pulling me — but it catches us anyway. I'm not one of those women who look good with wet hair.

Ross takes my hand and strokes it, like a parent trying to soothe a child.

"Ed and Carla have set a wedding date."

"I'm sorry?"

Ross's face is looking down on me. How stupid of me. His expression is one of pity, not admiration.

"Ed is getting married. To Carla."

Ed. Carla. Marriage. Not just an engagement that can be broken at whim.

So she's got him. Just like she gets everything she's ever wanted.

"That's not all."

I begin to shiver from the cold and the wet and the anticipation.

"She's pregnant, Lily. Carla's expecting a child."

In a weird way, Ross's news is a relief, just as it was when I found Ed and Carla outside the hotel. The shock haunts me still. Yet at least it was living proof that I hadn't just imagined Ed's behavior toward me.

And now Ross's early warning of a definite wedding date — soon to be heralded in the gossip pages — tidies things up. Shows me that there is no chance of Ed and me ever reconciling, even if I wanted to. Which I don't.

That's the other odd thing about a long marriage ending, at least for me. However bad it was, there were also good patches. And it's those that I tend to remember. Don't ask me why. I don't dwell on the rows when Ed was moody or drunk. Or how he used to hate it because I earned far more than he did, and how he'd throw fits when I was home late from work.

No, I think of the moments in between when we'd lie on the sofa as we watched our favorite weekly drama. Or how we'd take long walks by the sea with our little boy, pausing to point out a particular shell or a crab scuttling under a rock.

The thing that really breaks my heart is that Ed now does these things with Carla. I remember reading an article once about a woman whose husband had married someone else. Two things had struck me. First, she'd been unable to say the other woman's name, only referring to her as *Her.* "It's because it sticks in my throat," she'd explained. "Makes her feel too real."

I get that.

The second was that this woman had been unable to comprehend how there was now another out there, bearing the same surname and sharing the same habits with the same man the first wife had once known intimately.

And that's exactly how I feel. There's something really odd about your husband having another wife. Carla will soon be Carla Macdonald. We will both be Mrs. Macdonald. She will be my husband's wife, because — even though Ed is technically no longer my husband — you can never really wipe away a marriage. A piece of paper is not an eraser or a bottle of correction fluid. It may legally negate the "contract" between two parties, as a lawyer might put it. But it cannot expunge the memories, the traditions, the patterns that spring up between a couple, no matter how good or bad the state of their relationship.

It hurts. Yes, it hurts to know that they, too, are building up traditions of their own. For all I know, she entwines her legs around Ed's when they watch that new series on television that everyone is talking about. Now, *they* go for long walks along the sea with my son while I hide myself away at home, telling myself that it's good for Tom to see Daddy. The thought of another woman playing "Mummy" sickens me to the core. Tom is so gullible at times, quite capable of transferring his affection. After one of their recent visits, he talked incessantly about her hair. "Why isn't yours as shiny as Carla's?" he asked me. "Why isn't everyone's hair like hers? What *makes* hair?"

The first question had run into thousands of others, like it always did with Tom. But I was still stuck on the first one. I don't want to think about Carla's hair or anything else about her.

But this — this hurts more than anything. A child of their own. A child who will be "normal," no doubt. A child who won't need watching 24-7 in case he hurts himself, or worse. A child who won't impose the same awful pressures on a marriage.

It isn't fair.

I suddenly begin to feel the anger I should have felt some time ago. Ed is the one who did wrong, yet he's come out on top here. He's found someone else. He gets to see the good bits of Tom, who is always hyper with excitement after his visits.

Nor does Ed have any of the problems that still haunt me.

Like Joe Thomas.

For a while after moving down to Devon, I was on tenterhooks in case he got in touch again. I even had to warn Mum, telling her I had a former client who had stalked me in the past and mustn't be allowed in the house at any cost if he happened to turn up.

Not surprisingly, she was worried. "But why can't you tell the police?" she asked, her voice laced with worry. "Surely they can do something about it?"

It was on the tip of my tongue to confess everything. But that wouldn't have been fair. My parents had enough on their plate.

"You'd think so, wouldn't you?" I said. "But actually there's not a lot they can do."

That was true. I'd once had a client whose ex-boyfriend had stalked her. The only way we'd managed to get a court order was to get him followed by a private detective to show that he was doing the same to other women, too. Even then, he only received a warning.

Frankly, I'm just relieved that Joe hasn't tried to get hold of us here. The thought of poor Merlin still makes me feel sick. If Joe could organize that, what else was he capable of?

Meanwhile, I am banishing my fears with work. Work, work, work. It's the only way I can get some peace, the only way to shut out the shrapnel of Ed's engagement and the stress of Tom.

When I first came down, I was worried I wouldn't have enough clients and that, after a while, the partners would decide it wasn't worth subsidizing a satellite office. But within a couple of weeks, some parents from Tom's school approached me. They were convinced that their son's epilepsy had been caused by dirty water from an old well that had gotten into the water system. It just so happened that I knew a specialist who said this was not beyond the realm of possibility. It went to court and we won damages — not a lot but enough to prove that some children's special conditions are not just "one of those things," but could have been prevented.

Then a father from Tom's school asked me to look into some hospital notes that had vanished soon after his son's birth. There had been problems, he explained. The umbilical cord had been wound tightly around his son's neck during delivery, and the consultant hadn't been available. We never found the notes (they would, no doubt, have been shredded long ago), but we did discover that the same pattern had occurred a couple of times now, all when a certain consultant had been on duty. That resulted in a class action, with other parents being given compensation as well as my client.

"You're building up quite a name for yourself, Lily," e-mailed my old boss. "Well done."

How is Carla doing? I want to ask. *Will she continue to work for you when she has the baby?* But I don't have the courage to raise the subject.

Then, one morning in June, as I am jogging along the promenade before work, I hear someone running behind me.

This isn't unusual. There are quite a lot of us six a.m. joggers and we all know each other. There's even a baggy-eyed mother who runs along with her stroller.

But intuitively, I know these steps are different. They match my speed. They slow when I slow. They speed up when I do.

"Lily," says the voice behind me, a voice I know all too well. "Please stop, Lily. I'm not going to hurt you."

48
CARLA

Carla looked down at her body in the soapy water. Her fourth bath in four days. But there was nothing else to do in the evening. And besides, it meant she could close the door and be alone for a while.

Since finding out she was pregnant, Ed had not allowed her to lift a finger at home. It was bad enough, he said, that she still insisted on going out to work. She should rest instead. They would manage somehow, despite those demands from the bank. He loved her. He would look after her.

The old Carla would have loved the attention. But life with Ed was not what she'd imagined. It wasn't just his depression over unsold paintings or bank warnings, or even his drinking. Or Tom's behavior on their custody weekends, which upset Ed and affected them, too, especially when she suggested that if Tom were "punished" more

517

often, he would improve. Nor was it the latest threatening note:

WATCH YOUR BACK.

No, it was the wedding ring on her finger that really got Carla down. If it was not for the baby, she would not have agreed to marry Ed. Ed's "care" had become too controlling. But now she was trapped by her own pregnancy. How could she allow her child to grow up without a father as she had? No child of hers was going to be "different." Look where it had gotten her.

So there had been a wedding. A small one, at her insistence. Just them and two witnesses off the street. The ceremony, she'd stipulated, had to be here, in London. If they'd done it in Italy, the sharp-eyed matrons would certainly have spotted the small bump that had already started to appear.

"I think it's sweet," one of the girls at the prenatal class had said when Carla had confided that her new husband would not let her do anything in the house. What Carla stopped herself from saying was that he wouldn't even let her put out his empties. Ed now drank far more than he would admit. It had led to a spectacular argument at an art critic's party, right in front of everyone. Later, of course, he'd apologized profusely.

"I am doing it for two," he had joked, putting his hand over Carla's own glass when she had reached for the bottle herself. "No, you mustn't. I don't care what the latest report is. These so-called medical experts change their minds all the time. Far better to play safe and avoid alcohol altogether during pregnancy."

Then he had stroked her stomach. "You're carrying my child," he said in a reverent tone. "I promise to look after you both. Not long now, my darling."

Six weeks to go. Yet each day seemed to pass so slowly. How uncomfortable she felt! How heavy. Carla could not even bear to look at herself in the mirror, even though Ed told her, with the smell of whisky on his breath, that she was beautiful. Nor could she bear the touch of his hand on her stomach so he could feel the baby move like some monster inside her.

Soaping her breasts (so huge and the nipples so dark that they were scarcely recognizable), Carla allowed her mind to wander back to when she'd bumped into Rupert soon after the wedding. "How are you?" he had asked.

They were in court at the time. She was there to support the barrister, but she found it hard to concentrate on her argument with her old friend sitting nearby. He appeared to be looking at her, too. During the break, they sought each other out. "I am . . .," she began. And then stopped. Her eyes filled with tears. "I am married to a near-bankrupt drinker. A man whose child I am expecting."

Rupert's eyes widened. "I heard you had married Ed," he said quietly. "But I didn't know about the other developments. I think we need a coffee once the case is over."

Carla hadn't meant to be so open, but it all came spilling out: Ed's controlling ways, the constant worry about money, the uncomfortable feeling of living in another woman's home.

"In the end, Lily left almost everything, even her clothes. It's as though she was trying to tell me that I couldn't replace her."

And then the final note that had arrived out of the blue, threatening her for hurting Lily.

Rupert was clearly shocked. "What did the police say?"

"I haven't told them."

"Why not?"

Her eyes welled up again. "Because then

Ed would make a fuss and not allow me back to the office. He would keep me at home, shut up like a bird, in case someone hurt me."

Rupert took her hand. "This is terrible, Carla. You can't live like this."

"I know." She stared down at the now-visible lump in her stomach. "But what can I do?"

"All kind of things. You could go —"

"No." She had interrupted him fiercely. "I cannot leave. I cannot be like my mamma. I will not allow this child to grow up without a father as I did."

Rupert dropped her hand. *Don't,* she wanted to cry. *Don't.* Then he reached into his inside jacket pocket and handed over a card. "This is my private mobile number. I've changed it since we last knew each other. Ring me anytime. I will always be there for you. My fiancée would like to meet you, too."

"Your fiancée?"

Rupert blushed. "Katie and I got engaged last month. It was a bit sudden, but we're very happy."

So that holding of hands and the flush on his face . . . Carla had gotten it all wrong. Rupert really was just being a friend. Nothing more.

That had been several weeks ago now. Carla kept the card close to her. Often she thought about ringing the number. But every time she did, a sentence came into her head. *My fiancée would like to meet you.*

Carla shivered. She had had enough of stealing other people's things. This intolerable situation was her cross to bear for snatching Lily's husband.

"Carla?" There was a persistent knocking on the bathroom door. "Darling? Are you all right in there?"

"I am fine," she said. Then she turned on the tap so she couldn't hear his reply, and lowered herself down so that her head was underwater, allowing herself to think clearly without Ed's voice hammering through the door.

49
LILY

I try to steady myself by looking out over the sea and focusing on the light of a boat moored there, bobbing on the surface of the water against the apricot sunrise.

Then I turn around.

Joe Thomas doesn't look like a former prisoner. He seems much older than he did at our last meeting, but it suits him, gives him a certain gravity. He's grown a moustache, although his hair is still short.

But one thing hasn't changed — those eyes.

"We have to talk."

A chill passes through me.

"I've got nothing to say to you."

He reaches toward me. For a minute, I think he's going to grab my arms. I step back. A jogger goes past.

Joe waits a few seconds. "I need to tell you something. Please."

He is actually begging. Momentarily, I am

523

swayed. "Not here."

Uncertainly, I lead him across the road to a group of tables and chairs outside a café with a sign that reads OPEN AT 9AM! We sit opposite each other, away from the promenade and the occasional runner. "What is it?" I say curtly.

His eyes are boring into mine.

"You don't have to worry about Carla."

At first, his words are so unexpected that it takes me a second to absorb them. When I do, I am both scared and — I have to admit — excited.

"What do you mean?"

"Your ex and Carla won't last."

My mouth is dry. "How do you know?"

"Just do."

He moves his chair closer to the table. Without looking down, I can feel our legs are almost touching. A man goes past, his dog sniffing a stray chip left in the road. To its owner, we might be any pair of runners sitting down, catching our breath, admiring the view. Or maybe we could be a pair of tourists staying at one of the hotels on the promenade, taking a stroll before breakfast.

"I know it can't be easy," says Joe. "Your husband has married someone else. And now they're having a baby."

"So what? I've moved on now."

Those eyes are peeling away my pretense. "Are you sure?"

No. Of course I'm not sure. I wish Carla had never come to this country. I wish now that I had told Francesca, all those years ago, that we couldn't possibly look after her child on the weekend while she "worked."

But that's not me. At the heart of things, I need to help people. It's my nature.

"Is that why you're here?" I ask. "To see how I am?"

"Partly." Little beads of perspiration are breaking out on his forehead. I can feel the same thing happening on my back.

"I want a paternity test, Lily. I didn't believe you last time when you said he wasn't mine, and I don't believe you now. I've been watching you, Lily, since I got out of prison."

This is ridiculous. How? Where? "Is this one of your lies again?" I say sharply.

He laughs. "Even introduced myself to Carla at Tony's funeral."

"I don't believe you. She wasn't there."

Another laugh. "Then you couldn't have been looking very closely."

He draws his chair nearer. I edge back.

"I'm not far away, Lily, when you pick up Tom from school on Friday nights. Or when you take him for walks along the beach, with

Ross." His mouth tightens.

My heart leaps into my throat. Surely he wouldn't . . . "And just how have you been spying like this without us noticing?" I snap. Fear is making me angry.

"Spying?" He seems to consider the word. "I'm no James Bond, but you learn things inside. I even paid one of my contacts to do a check on you when I was thinking of hiring you. I wanted to see if you were up to the job."

There's a flash from the past. That feeling, when I was newly married, of being followed on the way back from the bus stop. My shock when Joe had known I'd just gotten married.

Could it be true? Or is this just the dreams of a fantasist? But then how to explain his knowing so much about me? About Tom. About Ross.

"Tom looks like I did as a kid, Lily." Joe's face is twisted with pain. It's one of the few times I've seen him express emotion. "I've seen him. He does the same things. He doesn't like it when things aren't ordered. I know he's mine. I've given you time because of your divorce, but I deserve to know. Don't you think?"

I'd see his point of view if I wasn't so scared of him. If he wasn't a killer.

A pair of joggers run past on the other side of the road. I see them every day. Mr. and Mrs. Newlywed, I call them to myself. Joe observes me watching them.

"Are you lonely, Lily?"

This change of tack throws me. My eyes suddenly blur. Of course I'm lonely. It's so unfair that Ed has found happiness whereas I am destined to be alone. Who else would want to take on a child like Tom?

"You don't have to be on your own, you know." Joe's hands suddenly take mine. They are warm. Firm.

"I've always loved you, Lily. In my own way."

The raw loneliness inside me screams in my ears. I'd like to say I don't know what I'm doing, but I do.

I lean toward him. Let his hands pull me toward him.

Let him lower his lips to my neck. Feel his breath against me. Making my body burn with desire.

A jogger appears in the far distance by the lifeboat station. I jerk back. Joe's eyes snap open. I leap to my feet, appalled by what I have just done. As I do so, a key falls out of my pocket. It's one I always carry, even though I no longer have use for it. The key to my old house with Ed. If you are attacked, I once learned at a self-defense course, you should jab someone in the eye to give you time to run. A key is always good, the instructor said, or else a finger. It's a piece of advice that has stayed with me, whether in London or running along the promenade in the early morning.

Joe bends down to pick it up.

This is a murderer before me. A man who should have been convicted of killing his girlfriend. And that's the nub of it. Of course Joe is bad, yet he also has shades of not so bad.

I like to think I am good. Still, there's no getting away from it — I have also done wrong. Not just a wrong that affects me. But one that touches Ed, too. And, more importantly, Tom.

And as I run back across the road toward the promenade, the sea now washing smoothly against the pebbles, I finally allow my mind to go back to that evening after the case.

Forget the pain in my chest, making it hard to breathe.

It's nothing, compared with the agony of waiting.

My body is tense. Stiff with apprehension.

I can hear her now. She's coming.

50
CARLA

The pains started the following day, when Carla was in the office, going through her mail. There was always work to be done, thank goodness. A letter, a contract, a phone call, a meeting with counsel. Anything to block out the image of Ed waiting for her at home, his eye on the clock, his hand on the bottle.

"Got another one here," announced Lily's old secretary, popping her head around the door. "Just been delivered by hand." Carla's heart quickened, although there was no need. Many letters were hand-delivered. Couriers were nothing out of the ordinary. Yet she could see as she took the envelope that her name hadn't been typed, but written by hand in spidery capital letters. She opened it.

YOU AND YOUR CHILD WILL PAY.

Carla felt the baby launch another kick, far bigger this time. "Who dropped this off?" she heard herself say in a strangled voice.

The woman had made it clear that she didn't care for Lily's successor. "A motorbike rider. Didn't say which company he was with." Flouncing off, she left the door wide open.

Getting up to shut it, Carla suddenly felt a trickle of water running down her legs.

How embarrassing! She had wet herself. Was this what her body had come to? Stuffing the letter in her bag, she scuttled past a partner in the corridor and dived into the ladies. To her horror, the same secretary was there, drying her hands.

The woman gasped. "Have your waters broken?"

Of course, she knew that waters breaking was a sign of labor. But the teacher of her prenatal class had described it as more of a flood than a trickle.

"This happened to me, too, with my second," said the woman. Her tone was grudgingly kind. "Sit down while I call the ambulance."

Carla felt as though the walls were coming toward her. "But it's too early. I'm not due for another six weeks."

"Even more need to get you to the hospital." The woman was already on her mobile. "Ambulance, please. Urgent." Then she turned around to Carla. "Shall I call Ed? I've still got his number in Lily's old address book."

Lily . . . Ed . . . would they never go away? Was she destined to be trapped forever in this marriage of three?

"I am sorry," she called out as the ambulance sped its way through the streets.

"No need to apologize, love," said the voice next to her. "It's our job."

It's not you I'm apologizing to, she tried to say. *It's the baby who's coming into this terrible mess we've created. Go back. Go back to where you came from so you are safe.* But strange pains had started in her belly. Wave after wave of pain, each one beginning almost as soon as its predecessor had finished.

"We need to slow her down," said another voice.

The urgent yet calm tone reminded Carla of the time she had been taken to the hospital as a child. *You could have died,* the doctor had told her strictly at the time, as if she — not her mother — was responsible for failing to react to her symptoms fast enough. Maybe she was dying now. Perhaps that would be best. What kind of life would the baby have with parents who were already fighting before it was born?

"Carla, can you hear me?" The first voice was hovering over her. "We're just going to give you a little injection to try and keep baby inside for a bit longer. All right?"

And then everything went black.

51

LILY

"Let's go for a walk," Joe said after we'd won the appeal, all those years ago. Such innocent words.

We began to stroll across the Heath, breathing in the cool night air after the tension of the court.

"Do you remember," he said, his eyes straight ahead, "when our hands touched in the prison?"

How could I forget?

"You know," he continued, without waiting for an answer, "there are very few people in this world whom I can bear to touch. I've always been like that, even as a child."

And then I found his hand taking mine as we continued to walk into the dark, leaving the pub lit up behind us.

Of course, I should have withdrawn it. Made my excuses and gone home, right there and then. But I was on a high after our victory. And a low because of Ed. I had to face it. My new husband wasn't interested in me. He and Davina had been much better suited. It was her he should have married, not me.

There was something else, too. What Joe had said about being able to touch me. I was flattered. Why not? This was a man whom I believed had been wrongfully imprisoned. A man who was to be pitied and also admired — not the least because he had decided not to press for financial compensation. Nothing, he had told the court, would bring back his "poor" girlfriend, Sarah Evans. All he wanted was justice. And his freedom.

"You're crying," Joe said when I found my hand squeezing his in return.

And that was when I had told him. I'd let down my guard and confided in him about my marriage. I'd like to say it was because I don't normally drink a double on an empty stomach. I'd like to say it was because of the flush of success at winning my first big case. But the truth is that Joe was someone I could talk to.

And of course there was also that one thing that you can't impose rules or laws upon, that physical energy that had sizzled between us. The electricity that should never exist between prisoner and lawyer. Except

Joe was no longer a prisoner. He was a free man.

We were both free to do what we pleased.

I can't even say it was rape, although I did attempt to resist for a few seconds. All I knew was that suddenly I was lost. I didn't even try to pretend to myself it was love, because it was far better. Why? Because love is too fragile and can be broken too easily. Lust is brasher, immediately gratifying. Hadn't my past taught me that all too well?

As Joe had pushed me roughly to the ground and unbuttoned my blouse, I remembered how "wrong" and "lust" could give you an inexplicable million-volt charge that was like nothing else. It was so strong that it made you melt and burn at the same time. It's an exhilarating feeling when someone gives you permission to break all rules — especially when that person is yourself.

"Quick," said Joe, soon after we'd finished. "Someone's coming."

I scrambled to my feet.

Only then, when I saw the disgusted look on the face of the approaching dog walker, did I feel the shame I should have felt before — shame that might have saved me from this situation had I felt it sooner.

"Go away," I said, my fingers trembling

over my buttons. "Go away and never come back."

Then I ran. I ran across the Heath, aware that I must have looked a mess. I ran to the tube, pressing myself against other sweaty bodies, conscious that I smelled of sex. I was desperate to get back home for a shower. A long, hot shower to wash Joe Thomas away.

"We must celebrate!" Ed said when I got in. "Open a bottle." His face tightened. "Then we can have that talk you've been promising."

The very sight of my husband's face had filled me with such guilt that I insisted on going out for that bottle, just to get away.

Then there was the argument with Tony and Francesca outside in the corridor. I was so hard on my colleague because I felt sorry for his poor wife. But had I lashed out at Tony because I recognized my own frailties in him?

The following night when I couldn't put off that talk with Ed anymore, I sat in the bathroom and tried to decide whether to leave him or not.

If I opened on a page with an odd number, I'd leave.

If it was even, I'd stay.

Page seventy-three.

The page showed a picture of a happy family sitting around the table. The picture and the print swam before my eyes. Sunday suppers and normal life — the kind that my parents and I should have had, and the kind that Ed and I could still have if we stopped lying.

I don't have to take the odd number fate has given me, just as Daniel often rejected the heads. "You know what you want, before the coin comes down," he used to say. "That's why it's such a great way to make a decision."

And I knew that despite Ed's behavior and mine, I still loved my husband. Joe had been lust. I shouldn't have let myself go so far. Ed was my chance at doing something right.

Sometimes you have to do something wrong before you can make things right.

So I came out of that bathroom and took Ed's hand, leading him to our bed, just in case Joe's tiny seed was already growing inside me. The following month I found I was pregnant with a child I knew in my heart might belong to either man.

52
CARLA

"Carla? Can you hear me?"

It seemed like only a few minutes since someone in the ambulance had asked her the same question. But this was a different voice. This was Ed's.

"It's all right, Carla. I'm here now. And we've got a beautiful baby girl."

A girl? Please, no. If she had a girl it meant she might make the same mistakes that she and Mamma had. It would never end.

"She's very tiny, Carla. Just three pounds three ounces. But they say she should be completely fine."

How was this possible? She couldn't even remember giving birth. Ed was lying.

His face was coming into view. He was bending over her, kissing her cheek. His touch made her skin crawl. "You gave us all a terrible fright, darling."

"It wasn't my fault," she managed to say.

There was an edge to his voice. "I could

have lost you both."

"What happened?" she murmured.

"Baby decided to come early." This voice was different. Carla tried to turn around to see where it was coming from, but everything hurt. "Just as well for us that she did. You had a low-lying placenta, dear, so we had to give you an emergency Cesarean. Caused quite a stir, you did! Would you like to see your baby now?"

What baby? Carla couldn't see one. She couldn't hear one either. She knew it. Something had gone horribly wrong.

"Intensive Care is just around the corner, dear." A nurse in green uniform came into focus now. "Legs still a bit wobbly, are they? Let's ease you into this wheelchair, shall we? That's the way."

"Is it healthy?" asked Carla faintly.

"*She*," said Ed firmly, "is a fighter." But Carla saw the uncertain look he gave the nurse. Something wasn't right. She just knew it.

"Here we are, dear."

That was a baby? Carla stared at the incubator. Its skin was so pale and translucent that it reminded her of a dead baby bird she had once found outside the old flat when they had lived near Lily and Ed. ("Leave it alone," Mamma had squealed, before walking her briskly on to the bus stop.)

This *thing* was not much bigger than the width of Ed's hand, and tubes were sprouting out of it. Its eyes were closed.

"She's on oxygen at the moment, dear," said the nurse gently. "Hopefully she'll be able to breathe for herself in the next few weeks."

Weeks?

"I'm afraid you won't be able to pick her up for some time, but you can talk to her."

"Babies can hear when you do that," Ed butted in. He sounded so knowledgeable and smug. "We used to talk to Tom all the time."

"But how can it hear if it's so ill?"

"You'd be surprised, dear. You can go home in a few days — the surgeon did a nice clean job, although you'll need to rest and not lift anything heavy. You can visit baby every afternoon and evening." There was a little sigh. "We used to have a special place for parents to stay over, but I'm afraid that went with the cuts."

Scarcely hearing, Carla continued to stare at the rat. Its puffed-up little stomach was rising and falling with a strange regularity. The rest of it could hardly be seen with the mask and tubes. This was her punishment!

This was what she got for taking another woman's husband. And now she was going to be truly trapped — far more than before. How could she go back to work? Ed had already been against that idea, but it would be impossible if her child was sick.

Furiously, she turned on Ed. "Why did you get me pregnant?"

"There, there," said the nurse, patting her shoulder. "You'd be surprised how many of my ladies say that. But you'll change your mind when you get to know her better."

Ed was staring at her with a shocked look on his face. "Come on, Carla. You've got to be strong for our little girl."

But this thing didn't look like a girl — or a human for that matter. "I don't want to see it," she said, hearing her own voice rise in hysteria. "Take it away. I want my mother. Why isn't she here? Get me the phone. Now. I need to speak to her."

"Carla —"

"No! Stop being so controlling. Give me your mobile."

Ed and the nurse were exchanging looks. What was going on?

"Carla, darling, listen." He put his arm around her. "I didn't want to tell you until you felt stronger. But your grandmother rang when you were in labor. I am afraid your mother has been ill."

Carla stiffened. "How ill?"

"She's been treated for cancer for some time now. Your mother didn't stay with an aunt that Christmas. She was actually in the hospital. I'm afraid she's been in and out since then, too."

Her mouth went dry. "Cancer?" She felt cold and sick with shock. "But she is better now? Please tell me that. She is coming over to see her granddaughter? She has to!"

Ed tried to hold her but she pushed him away. "Tell me. *Tell me.*"

His eyes were wet with tears. So, too, were the nurse's.

"I'm afraid your mother died, Carla. Just after you gave birth."

53
LILY

Back on the promenade I race away from Joe, seagulls screaming overhead. It's only then that I realize something so obvious that I wonder why I haven't thought of it before. If I can prove that Tom *isn't* Ed's child, I can surely stop him from having access. He doesn't need to know who the real father is.

And, more important, I can prevent my husband's wife from doing the same.

It would be one small way to claw back some control of my life.

But if Joe's DNA matches, then my child would have a murderer for a father.

In the distance, a small boat bobs up and down on the waves.

That's when another idea comes to me. One far better than the last.

Mamma had taken her last breath without her by her side? "But I never said good-bye," she sobbed on the phone to Nonna.

Her grandmother was weeping, too. "She didn't want to upset you." In the back-ground, she could hear deep howls of male grief.

Nonno. He cared after all?

It transpired that they had all hidden it from her. Only now did the signs add up. Mamma's gaunt appearance before Carla had left Italy. Her frail voice over the phone. Her insistence that letters were better than expensive phone calls. Her promise that she would come over to England when the baby was born but at the moment she was "busy."

And now, on top of the grief, she had to cope with this scrap. This thing.

You'll feel different when you're able to hold her. That's what Ed and the nurses kept say-ing. But when they finally placed her daughter in her arms, there was a high-pitched electronic sound. "It's all right, dear," the nurse said. "It just means baby isn't ready to come off the oxygen yet."

It was all so scary. How could she possibly take it home if it couldn't breathe on its own?

"These things take time," said the young doctor briskly.

"I keep telling her that," said Ed authoritatively. Once more, Carla felt like a child who got everything wrong each time she opened her mouth.

If only Mamma were here to help. She would know what to do.

Sometimes Carla thought they had taken her real baby away. The rat didn't look anything like her or Ed. Even worse, they had been told that premature babies often had some "developmental issues" that might not, according to the consultant, be apparent until later. How was she going to stand the uncertainty?

Five weeks later, when Carla was paying another of her reluctant daily visits to the NICU, she found a crowd of people around the incubator. This was not uncommon. Medical students were constantly being brought in to admire the smallest baby that had been born this year in the hospital. But an alarm was ringing and the screen next to the incubator was bleeping madly.

"We've been trying to get hold of you," babbled a nurse. "But your husband and you both have your phones off. Have you thought of a name?"

Everyone had been asking her that ever since the rat had been born. But Carla had turned down all Ed's suggestions during pregnancy, as if in denial at being pregnant at all. Now this thing was here, she still didn't want to name it. That would mean acknowledging that it was here to stay.

"You might like to have her baptized," said the nurse tensely. She was holding a form. "It says here that you are Catholic. The priest is here if you would like to talk to him."

"I don't understand . . ."

"My dear." A stout young man with a white clerical collar grasped both her hands as though they were intimate friends. "The nurse is trying to tell you that your daughter has taken a turn for the worse. Shall we ensure that she is prepared for the eternal life that is waiting for her?"

The rat was going to die? Wouldn't that be the answer to all her problems? Yes. No.

"Everything is going wrong," she sobbed.

"My dear, sometimes God's plans aren't always what we expect."

"Would you like to hold her, dear?"

No. She might drop it.

One of the doctors nodded to the nurse. The rat with all its tubes was placed in her arms. A pair of small beady eyes stared up at her. A strangely long, almost aristocratic nose. And then Carla saw it — a tiny red hair on an otherwise bald scalp. "Poppy," she whispered. "She's called Poppy. Poppy Francesca."

Miraculously, Poppy "turned the corner," as they put it, during the night.

"You should have consulted me before you named her," Ed said when he finally turned up, his breath reeking of whisky.

"I would have if you'd been there," she retorted, without taking her eyes off her daughter, who was now back in the incubator.

"I was selling a painting, actually."

"Never mind," said the nurse. "If you ask me, Poppy got what she needed. A cuddle from her mummy. Of course the doctors would say it was their skills that sorted out those lungs of hers, but there's a lot to be said for love. For what it's worth, I think her name is wonderful. We haven't had a

Poppy in a long time."

"I suppose it is rather distinctive," added Ed grudgingly. "Funny how the color skips a generation, isn't it? My grandfather was auburn, you know."

Incredibly, in the following month, Poppy's health improved considerably. But at the same time, that flash of love Carla had experienced during that drama — yes, love! — waned. In its place was fear. *No,* Carla wanted to say, when they talked about Poppy being "nearly ready" to come home. How would she cope on her own with a baby as fragile as this?

"I know it's hard for you, but we'll be fine," Ed said as he cradled their daughter against his chest. It was all right for him. He knew what to do with a baby. But she was hopeless. And with Mamma gone, it felt as though half of her was missing. She should never have left her to come to this horrible country.

"Just the baby blues," said the health visitor when she came to visit and found Carla in floods of tears. "It's very natural, especially after a tricky birth. Do let us know, though, if it continues."

Natural? It was a complete and utter mess. On the one hand, Carla was terrified of leaving her daughter alone in case she stopped breathing. Yet if she did — what an awful thought! — she would be free from this terrible, overwhelming responsibility.

If only she could get some sleep, she might be all right. But Poppy "catnapped" rather than slept for the two or three hours that the baby books described. Every time Carla managed to close her eyes, Poppy was yelling again. It was like being on a twenty-four-hour flight without any refueling stops. Day after day. Week after week.

"She needs to gain more weight," said the health visitor.

Once more, Carla could see in Ed's face that she was a failure. Poppy's startlingly blue eyes followed her everywhere as a double reproach.

"Have you taken her to Mother and Babies yet?" asked the health visitor on another occasion.

Luckily, Ed was in the gallery that time. "Yes," she lied.

But the truth was that Carla was too scared Poppy might catch something from one of the other babies in the group.

Had Mamma felt like this? If only she could ask her . . .

Meanwhile, she and Ed were about to lose their home. The bank was running out of patience, and they would repossess next month if it wasn't sold. That's what the letters to Ed said. The ones that she had found in his artist's bag, which he had failed to show her.

But she didn't want to risk another row. When Ed got into a mood, he scared her, particularly now that he was drinking even more than before. His eyes would go red and his body would shake as if it wasn't his own. He even started talking about getting full-time custody of Tom.

"I couldn't cope," she'd protested.

"Have some sympathy, Carla. He's my son and I want him with us."

Where had the old Ed gone? Yet he was softness itself when it came to calming Poppy, whose lungs now worked full-time, day and night.

"Get some rest," Ed would say in a way that suggested it pleased him that Poppy responded to him and not her.

But Carla couldn't sleep. Instead she tossed and turned and thought about what might have happened if she and Mamma had never had the misfortune of living next to Lily and Ed.

It sometimes takes time to bond with a baby. That was another sentence from one of those baby books that lined the shelves from when Tom had been born. But every time Carla picked up this tiny scrap to feed it or change its nappy, she felt a terrible, overwhelming sense of panic.

Her initial terror that this child would die had now been replaced by another worry. Who was writing those notes? And would that person really try to harm them?

YOU AND YOUR CHILD WILL PAY.

"Maybe," Carla told the child as it sucked greedily, "it's one of Lily's friends who wants revenge on her behalf. We can't trust anyone."

"She keeps having bad dreams," she overheard Ed tell the health visitor who'd been called out to check up on her. She always listened outside the door when they thought she'd gone back to bed.

"Giving birth is a traumatic event, you know," came the crisp reply. "She's entitled to a few nightmares."

Nightmares? They had no idea of the turmoil churning in her head. She needed another plan. But what? There was no way out. Just an endless blackness ahead that swallowed her up, threatening to suffocate her. A woman in the paper the other day had suffocated her baby. She'd gotten ten years. It would have been more if she hadn't had postnatal depression. But Carla didn't have that. Ed said it was a myth. Lily had been fine when she had had Tom. When you have a baby you just have to accept that life has changed — and then get on with it.

This meant doing things his way.

"I've cooked us a chicken." Ed took her by the elbow and steered her toward the table. "It will do you good. Come on, Carla. You know this is your favorite."

Eat? How could she eat?

He poured himself another glass of wine.

"Haven't you had enough?" she snapped.

"What are you going to do about it, then? Hit me again, like you did in front of Tom that time?"

"I didn't hit you." Carla wished he'd stop going on about it. She'd only reached out to stop him from opening another bottle, at the same time as he'd turned toward her. God knows one of them needed to be sane while they looked after Ed and Lily's son.

"I'm going to have another bloody drink, if only to celebrate my birthday. That's right. You'd forgotten, hadn't you?"

No wonder he was cross. But Poppy took up all her time. She couldn't remember everything!

She went to the sink, pulling on her washing-up gloves, shaking with fear and rage.

"Don't wash up those pans before we've eaten. I've told you. I'll do it myself later."

She ran the hot water, furiously squirting soap into the bowl.

Her heart fell at the sound of the knock on the door. The man next door again? He had already complained about the rows.

"You."

Surely Ed wouldn't speak that rudely to their neighbor?

"Rupert!" Carla felt her face flushing as she turned around to face him.

"Forgive me for just calling in, but I found myself in the area."

He held out a beautifully wrapped present: silver paper with curly ribbons.

Carla began to sweat with fear and excitement and terror and hope, all mixed up in an impossible way.

"May I see her? It's a little girl, isn't it?"

"Yes," said Ed crisply. "But actually we're about to eat so —"

"She's just here," cut in Carla.

Holy mother of God. Her husband was staring at Rupert's red hair.

Surely he wouldn't be thinking . . .

Rupert's face softened. "Isn't she lovely? I hadn't realized how small they are. Is —"

"I said we're about to eat."

Flustered, Carla tried to peel off her

washing-up gloves but they wouldn't come.

"Would you like to stay?" The invitation tumbled out of her mouth. *Please,* she wanted to say. *Please. I need you. When you've gone, Ed will say something. There'll be another row . . .*

"I think," said Rupert with a glance at Ed's dark face, "I should go. Katie — my fiancée — will be waiting for me." So she was still around. All her hopes, all her desperate, crazy ideas that she'd had when Rupert rang the bell, came crashing down.

"Fiancée?" scoffed Ed, barely waiting for the door to close on their visitor. "I'll bet. How many times has that kid been around here?"

His voice made Poppy stir in her porta-crib at the far end of the kitchen.

"What do you mean?"

Ed's face was close now. "I saw you blush when he came in. I saw how you tried to speak normally." Spit was flying out of his mouth. "He has the same color hair as our daughter. If she *is* our daughter."

"Don't be so ridiculous. You know your father had red hair. You yourself have commented on how it often skips a generation."

He had her wrists now, squeezing them hard. "How very convenient! But we both know what your morals are like."

555

Struggling, she spat back, "And what about yours? You didn't mind leaving your wife for me, did you?"

"And you didn't mind tempting me away from her."

What happened next? What happened next? How many times was she to be asked that in the next few days, the next few weeks, the next few months.

All Carla knew was this: it was sudden.

All she cared to remember was this.

There was a scream. Poppy from the portacrib. Another scream. Her own as Ed began to shake her by the shoulders.

The carving knife. The green carving knife. Another possession Lily had left behind.

A terrible, body-shaking groan.

Blood.

And then she was running. Running across the park with all those thoughts running up and down and side to side.

I hate him. I hate him.

Mamma! Where are you?

If only they could start all over again.

55
LILY

October 2015
"A man has been found stabbed to death in West London. It is thought that . . ."

Then Tom's shout drowns out the radio. "You've got to do it first, Mum! I've told you before."

How stupid of me. I know perfectly well that Tom needs me to buckle up my seat belt before he does his. Precisely four seconds before him, actually. He times it with his watch. It's another of his rituals. One that, on a normal day, is surely not too difficult to follow.

But for some reason I am feeling wobbly today. Perhaps I'm still tired after being in London yesterday. Perhaps it's the impending meeting with Tom's headmistress about the recent "incident." Perhaps it's because I've got a particularly tricky appointment with an NHS official this afternoon, concerning another set of lost notes following the birth of an oxygen-deprived child. Or, perhaps, it's because I am infuriated by Ed's latest declaration that he wants full custody of our son.

I start the engine, telling myself that there are plenty of men who live in that part of London. Stabbings happen every day. There is no reason — none at all — why it should be someone I know. But my skin has begun to form goose pimples of its own accord. At the T-junction, I take a left and then stop — over the line — just in time to allow a motorbike, which is surely going too fast, to go before me.

"That motorcyclist could have died if you hadn't stopped," comments Tom in a matter-of-fact tone.

Thanks.

"He could have been left with only part of his brain, like Stephen," he continues. "Did you know that your skin weighs twice as much as your brain?"

He's probably right. Tom usually is. But it's Stephen I'm thinking of — the boy who has just joined Tom's class. His stroller had been hit by a lorry when he was just under a year old. The driver had been having a heart attack at the time. No one could blame him. Not even Stephen, who is quite happy in his own world. Not even his parents, who are devout Christians and claim it is their "challenge" in life. It puts the rest of us to shame.

Including Ed. How on earth does he think he can ask for sole custody? He can barely make his father-son weekends, and often cancels at the last minute. It's happened more and more since Carla had the baby. She hasn't been well, apparently.

"Look out," says Tom sharply, at the same time as the lorry's horn on the other side of the road honks loudly.

What's happening to me? It's not just the wet autumn leaves that made me skid just then. I'm completely losing my concentration. But when your husband's wife has just had a child, it does things to you. Until then, Ed and I had shared something (or rather someone) that neither of us had done with anyone else. It had created a bond that couldn't be broken. But now he'll be lying next to Carla, his arm around her. They will be looking at their baby — a girl, Ross tells me — with the kind of awe that Ed and I had when we first gazed at Tom. Ed will be telling her, as he told me, that she has been so brave. And he will be promising, as he did me, that he will be the best father he can possibly be.

At night, he would get up when the baby

cried out. He would — I can see it so clearly! — feed his new baby daughter at night so Carla can sleep and look just as beautiful as she did before the birth. And he would be drawing them, sketching furiously as they slept, his charcoal sweeping over the page with love and tenderness.

It's so unfair. I've always yearned for a daughter to dress up, take shopping, share confidences with. But Ed didn't want us to have more children after Tom's diagnosis.

Concentrate. We're nearly at the school now. Tom, who has been pretty calm up until now considering the trouble he's in, appears distressed. I can always tell from the way he pulls out hairs from his arm. I selected one of them for the DNA test, some time ago.

I pull into the car park and face him. My son. My boy. My special boy, whom I would defend to my last breath. "We've been through this before, Tom," I say, looking him straight in the eyes and speaking slowly and calmly like the consultant advised. "We have to explain to Mrs. Brown exactly why you hit Stephen."

Tom's face is set. Rebellious. Unrepentant. "I told you. He kicked my gym shoes out of line."

"But he didn't mean to."

"I don't care. He still did it. No one is allowed to touch my things."

Don't I know it. It means I have to buy lots of spares for when the originals are inevitably at some point rejected. Spare shoes. Spare jumpers. Spare hairbrushes.

I lean across to switch off the radio. Please God, I pray. Don't let them give Tom another warning. My finger hovers over the off button on the radio, but something makes me pause. It's been half an hour since the last news announcement. In a minute, it will be time for another.

"A man has been found stabbed to death in his West London home," says the presenter again, almost chirpily. "A woman has been arrested in connection with the murder."

It's at this moment that my phone rings.

"You can't get that." Tom taps his watch. "We're already thirty seconds late."

Caller Unknown.

I normally get this on the few occasions that Ed (or occasionally Carla) has rung to make arrangements about Tom's weekends. Ed started withholding his number when phoning me some months ago, perhaps because I'd sometimes ignored his calls. If it's urgent, I tell myself, Ed — or whoever else it is — will ring again. Then I gather my notes, even though I've already primed myself, and walk across the playground with my son, who has got hold of my phone and is fiddling with it. At any other time I'd try to get it off him. But I'm too focused on the meeting ahead.

"Thank you for coming in," says Mrs. Brown.

Her face is kind, but she's rather frumpy-looking. One of those women who wear knee-length wooly dresses with flat ankle boots, I observe as I watch Tom positioning his chair so it's in a line with mine. She claims to be an expert in Asperger's syndrome, but at times I have the feeling she doesn't get Tom because she addresses him with emotion-driven questions. Not a great idea, as I've found out to my cost.

"I'd like to launch straight in, if that's all right," she begins. "Tom, perhaps you'd like to tell me again why you hit Stephen even though we don't tolerate violence in this school."

Tom stares at her as if she's stupid. "I've already explained. He kicked my gym shoes out of line."

Did I say Tom doesn't do emotion? Yet his eyes are welling up and his neck is going blotchy. Moving things in Tom's book is against the law. His law. Tom's Law, which only few understand.

The head is taking notes. I do the same. Our pens are competing. My son versus this poorly dressed woman.

"But that doesn't excuse hitting someone."

"Carla hit Dad the other week. He wanted another drink and she was telling him not to."

There's a silence. Our pens stop moving at the same time.

"Who is Carla?" asks the head in a dangerously neutral voice.

"My husband's wife," I hear myself say.

The head raises her eyebrows. They need plucking, I notice. They're gray and bushy.

"I mean, my ex-husband's wife," I add. It still feels odd to say it. How can someone else be Ed's wife? How is it possible that the child we used to know is now wearing his ring? Sharing his bed?

Mrs. Brown's voice is deceptively gentle. "Do you find it difficult, Tom, now that your father is married to someone else?"

I rise to my feet, my hand on my son's shoulder. "I'm not sure you should be asking questions like this. Not without an educational psychologist."

Her eyes are locking with mine. I can see

that behind the frumpy skirt and the boots there is a will of steel. I should have seen that before. Was I not frumpy once?

Suddenly a dog barks. At first I don't understand. But then I remember Tom fiddling with my phone at the playground. He must have changed the ringtone. Again. This time it sounds like a Baskerville hound.

Ross.

Mrs. Brown's eyes are disapproving. Tom is tipping his chair in deep anxiety.

"Sorry," I say, fumbling to switch it off, but somehow I press the speakerphone button instead.

"Lily?"

"May I ring you back?" I make an apologetic face at the head and turn it off speakerphone. "I'm in a meeting."

"Not really."

My mouth goes dry. Something's happened, I know it.

"I'm afraid I've got some bad news."

Tell me, I want to say. But the words won't come out. Mrs. Brown is staring. Tom's chair is about to fall.

"It's Ed. There's no easy way of saying this, I'm afraid. He's dead. He's been murdered."

"Dead?" I repeat out loud.

Tom's chair is back on the ground but his

564

right index finger is digging around his teeth. It's a sign of stress.

"Murdered?" I whisper.

"Yes."

Then the radio announcement comes back to me. The one in the car when Tom and I were parking.

A man has been found stabbed to death in his West London home . . .

No. *No.* People on the radio bear no relation to people in real life. Victims of crashes on the motorway or stabbings in Stockwell, they all belong to other families. Not to mine. Not my husband who isn't my husband anymore.

"Carla has been arrested." Ross sounds like he can't believe it either.

And then, once more, the radio announcement continues in my head. *A woman has been arrested in connection with the murder.*

Tom is tugging at my sleeve now. "Why is your face funny, Mum?"

"In a minute, Tom."

Cupping the phone, I turn away from Mrs. Brown and my son. "She . . . *she* did it?" I whisper, my words falling out around themselves.

I can sense Ross nodding. See him now standing there. Trying to hold himself together.

"She's in a police cell. But that's not all."

What? I want to say. What else can possibly have happened?

"Carla wants to see you, Lily."

There's a strange sound.

As though someone has just sat on the floor, heaving a big sigh.

If I didn't know her better, I'd think it was a "giving up" kind of sigh.

Listen, I try to say. *Maybe we can sort this out together.* But my words won't come out.

I don't have enough breath to speak.

What if I'm dead by the time they find me?

Will they work out what really happened?

56
CARLA

No comment.

That's what you told your clients to say when they were arrested. It was one of the few parts of criminal law that had stuck.

"No comment," she repeated. It was becoming a refrain — a tune that accompanied the pulse that was beating on both sides of her head.

"Tell me what happened," said a voice. It was a woman's voice, coming from a dark blue uniform sitting opposite her at the desk. But she must not look at her. If she did, she might say something she should not.

Breathe deeply.

No comment.

Inside her head, the events of the last few hours rolled over and over again like a film repeated in quick succession.

Rupert's visit.

Ed yelling.

A knife.

Blood.

Poppy screaming.

Ed groaning.

A face.

A man's face.

Then running.

The sudden realization that she'd left Poppy behind. Mamma's voice in her head.

Telling her to get rid of the gloves.

A hand on hers.

Sirens.

Handcuffs.

People staring.

The shame of the police car.

No comment.

A mattress.

Morning.

A desk.

A sharp voice on the other side.

No comment.

Relief.

Someone who might believe her side of the story.

Only then did she lift her face, staring at the woman across the desk. She had a mole in the middle of her right cheek. It stood out like a third eye.

Carla addressed herself to the mole. Find someone's weak points, the bits that made them different — it was what the bullies had done to her at school. So it was only fair that she did the same to others. It was how you won.

"It's my right to see a solicitor," Carla said firmly to the mole. "Here's the number. They'll find her."

"Her?" said the voice.

"Lily Macdonald."

The woman looked down at the paperwork on the desk.

"Same surname as yours?"

Carla nodded. "Yes. Same surname." And then, as if someone else was moving her lips, she added, "My husband's wife. The first one."

57
LILY

"Sugar? Sellotape? Sharp implements? Chewing gum?"

What happened to the crisps? Maybe chewing gum has been used as bribes here instead. Or, perhaps, it can be employed for other purposes. It's been a while since I've visited a client in a police cell. Since leaving London, my work has revolved around parents like me, whose lives have been torn apart by trying to provide for their "special needs" children. There are so many out there, trying to battle the system. They need help. Those who don't get what they're entitled to from the system. Not only babies who are damaged at birth and whose hospital notes then "disappear," but children like Tom, whose loved ones have to fight to make sure they go to the right school and who, in the meantime, struggle for support.

Cases involving murder or theft or bankruptcy or money laundering — all of which

I dealt with at the London practice — now seem a long time ago.

But here I am, showing proof of identity to the policewoman at the desk. I'm still not sure why I *am* here, and not at home with Tom. (Mrs. Brown has given him a week off school in view of "the circumstances.") Why I've left Mum to console him. (Although Tom has been remarkably matter-of-fact, asking questions like, "What will happen to Dad's brain now that he is dead?") I'm not sure why I'm in a police station, about to see my husband's wife.

A great deal has happened since that night in London when I found Carla and my husband outside the hotel. The divorce. Ross's news that Carla was expecting. Their daughter's birth. Ed's death. It sounds so unreal that I have to think it all through again.

The timescale is neat. Agonizingly so. Almost as if the whole thing had been planned with one of those clever little fertility charts that tell you when you're most likely to conceive. Or maybe with one of Ross's actuary graphs that predict average life expectancy. Birth. Death. Two opposites that have more in common than we realize. Both are beginnings. Both are ends.

And that is, I suddenly realize, exactly why

I am here. I'm not here because of Carla's demand. No, I'm here because I want to look her in the eye — want to ask why she did it — want to tell her that she's ruined three lives, that she's a bitch. A bitch who had her eye on my husband from the minute she saw him.

Yes, I wanted Ed to be punished, but I never meant this. I grieve for that sandy-haired man who took me by the hand at the party all those years ago. I can't believe he is dead. Or that it took his death to show me that I still — dammit — feel something for him. Of course he behaved badly. But we'd been married for so long. Brought up a child together. It glues you to each other for life. And beyond.

There was a woman at my old office who came in red-eyed one morning. "Her ex-husband has died," one of the secretaries had whispered. Back then I couldn't under-stand why she was so upset. But now I do. The fact that you no longer have a right to grieve for someone you once shared your life with makes the pain even worse.

We go down a flight of stone stairs that make my high heels ring out. When I first started visiting police stations, cells were no more than a stained mattress on the ground,

573

a window slatted across with iron bars and — if you were lucky — a plastic cup of water.

This cell has a window without bars. A watercooler. Sitting on the bed, swinging her legs and looking for all the world like a bored model waiting her turn on the catwalk, is Carla. I say "model," yet her hair is matted. Her usually glossy lips are pale. She smells of sweat.

"I didn't do it." Her voice is low, husky.

"Thank you for coming, Lily," I say, as if I'm reminding a sulky teenager of her manners. "Thank you for driving all the way up from Devon to see the woman who murdered my husband."

She tilts her face in a challenging manner. "I've told you." Her eyes are on mine. Her voice is more confident than it was a second ago. "There's been a mistake. I didn't do it."

I laugh out loud. She sounds for all the world like the child I first knew. The little Italian girl with the big brown eyes and innocent smile. *Mummy is at work. The pencil case belongs to me.*

Lies. All lies.

My anger bubbles up, spitting itself out of my mouth. "Surely you don't really expect me to believe that?"

She shrugs, as if I've suggested she's taken the wrong turn on a road. "It's true."

"Then who did do it?"

Another shrug, followed by an examination of each one of her nails as she speaks. "How should I know? I think I saw someone — a man."

A prickle of unease runs through me. Is this one of her stories again?

I sit forward on the edge of my chair. "Carla, my husband is dead. Tom is distraught because his father has been murdered."

Then she looks up with that same cool, catlike look. "You're wrong."

A beat of hope springs up inside. Ed isn't dead? Someone, somewhere, has got it all wrong?

"He's not your husband anymore. He's mine."

I make a *pah* noise. "I was married to him for fifteen years. We've brought up a child together."

For a minute, I stop, remembering the paternity test. Then I continue. "You were a plaything. A nothing. You were with him for the blink of an eye. That's no marriage."

"It is in the eyes of the law. And you're forgetting something. We, too, have a child." Her fists clench by her side. "They've sent my daughter to foster parents. I need you to help me get her back."

I try to bury a small stirring of sympathy. "A baby," I spit. "You'd only just started. You haven't had to go through what I have. Haven't had to give up everything to look after a demanding child while Ed —"

"Ha!" Carla breaks in furiously. "Don't be so self-righteous. I've paid my dues, too. Ed wasn't an easy man to live with. The drinking, the lies, the mood swings, the jealousy, the so-called artistic temperament . . ."

So he was the same to her, too? I feel a shot of pleasure. Yet when it comes from her mouth, I find myself wanting to defend him. *He was under pressure . . .*

Carla shudders. "He was so controlling. And he was a bastard to you, too. So why should you care?"

This isn't a word I care for, but I find myself nodding. Then I stop. Time to be professional. "Controlling?" I repeat. "Is that why you killed him?"

She leans forward now. Her hands are clenched into two small balls. I can smell her breath. Minty. "Someone was there. I told you. I saw a man."

"Well, that's convenient. What exactly did this *man* look like?"

"Can't remember."

She sits back now, supported by the wall, crossing her legs on the bed. Cool. Too cool. "I shouldn't be here. By the way, do you have a hairbrush on you?"

A hairbrush? Seriously?

"I shouldn't be here either," I say, getting to my feet. It's true. I should be at the hospital, in the morgue, identifying my husband instead of allowing Ross to do it.

"No. Please. Stay."

Her hand reaches out and catches mine. It's cold. Stone cold. I try to pull it back, but it is clutching mine, as if we have just met at a dinner party and discovered we have a mutual friend.

"I need you, Lily. I want you to be my lawyer."

"Are you insane? Why should I help you? You stole my husband."

"Exactly. But if you defend me, it's a message to the rest of the world that even the woman I wronged believes I didn't kill Ed. The barrister that you pick will trust you. And you're a good person. You have a reputation for saving the underdog."

Her eyes flicker. "And that's what I am now." Gone is the confident young woman. The latchkey kid is back.

But I'm still getting my head around all this. "Let's say you are telling the truth.

What's in it for me? Why should I help you — the woman who ruined my family?"

"Because you lost all those defense cases before you moved out of London." Grown-up Carla now steps in. "You might be doing all right with negligence cases. But this is a chance to prove you can do it again with a murder."

She looks at me like she knows she's hit a nerve.

"Please, Lily. Do it for Poppy if you can't do it for me."

"Who?"

"My child. Our child."

I hadn't known her name. Deliberately. I'd asked Ross not to tell me. It made her less real.

"If I go to prison, I'll lose my daughter." Carla's eyes fill with tears. "I . . . I didn't feel well for a time. I didn't know how to be a mother . . . I wasn't a great mother. But now my own mother is dead."

I hadn't known that. "I'm so sorry," I murmur. "How?"

"Cancer."

Carla lifts her big brown eyes to mine. "I miss her so much! I can't let Poppy miss me like that. Please, Lily. You're a mother. Help me."

"Maybe," I say, feeling an almost pleasurable harshness coming out of my mouth, "foster care is the best place for her."

Her eyes bore into mine. "You don't mean that, Lily. I know you don't."

She's right. Damn her. This is a baby we're talking about — a baby who will be screaming with anguish because she can't smell her mother. Children, however old they are, need their parents.

"But I'm not sure I believe that you're innocent."

"You have to." Carla's hands are tightening even more firmly around my wrist. She's a small girl again, and I am the older woman. It's as if her life is inextricably bound to mine and, however hard I try to shake her off, she's always there.

I run my hands through my hair. "How do you know I wouldn't put up a poor defense? To make sure you're convicted to get back at you."

Her eyes are trusting. "Because you're too moral for that. And because you're also ambitious. Think about it, Lily. You could go down in history as the lawyer who helped acquit your husband's new wife."

It bears, I must say, a certain ring to it. And yet there are numerous holes in this argument, so many flaws in the defense. I also don't care for the fact that Carla keeps using my name. It's a legal technique to get a client onside. And she knows it.

"There's still the small matter of who murdered Ed if you didn't do it."

Even as I say the words, they don't feel true. My husband — because that's how I still see him — can't really be gone. He'll be at home. My old home. Sketching. Breathing.

Carla's grip is strong for one so small. I'm still trying to shrug it off, but she's determined, it seems, to hang on to me as if I am a life ring. "Ed was up to his eyes in debt. I don't think the money was always borrowed from official places. Maybe someone wanted it back. Surely the police could find out. And I saw that man at the door. Someone must have seen something."

She seems so certain.

"There's something else, too. I've been receiving anonymous notes." Carla's eyes are locked on mine. "The last one said something bad would happen to me and Poppy because of what I'd done to you."

I go hot, then cold.

"Have you kept it?"

"For a time. Then I tore it up because I was scared Ed might go mad. But I'd recognize the handwriting."

Handwriting?

A paralyzing chill crawls down the length of my body, eating it up, inch by inch.

"You can't afford me." I'm clutching at straws now. "I can't do it for free. My firm will need to charge you."

Those eyes now glint. She can tell she's winning me over. Suddenly I know what she's going to say before she says it. "Ed's sketches! The ones he gave me as a child. They're worth something now. I will sell them to prove my innocence!"

It tastes, I have to admit, of the most delicious irony.

58
CARLA

Of course, Carla told herself, she hadn't meant all that stuff about needing Poppy and getting her back. That was just to get Lily onside.

For the first time in months, she was finally feeling more like her old self. With Ed gone, she was no longer a child who did everything wrong. She no longer had Poppy's screams ringing in her ears day and night: a painful reminder, as if she needed one, that if it hadn't been for getting pregnant, she would still be free. Without the child, she was sleeping better, although her dreams were still punctuated by Mamma. Sometimes she would sit bolt upright in the night, convinced her mother was still alive. Then she would remember. If only, she sobbed, hot tears streaming down her face, she could have been with Mamma at the end.

Meanwhile, she had to convince the judge

that she was innocent.

Now, as Lily prepared for the bail hearing — to determine whether her client had to wait in prison until her case was tried — Carla tried to remember the murder cases she'd covered at law school.

"Surely all I have to do is plead 'not guilty,' " she protested to Lily in the police cell.

"It's not as simple as that." Lily glanced at her notes. "The judge will look at the evidence — like the front and back doors, which don't look as though they've been forced — and then decide if you pose a risk."

"A risk?" she pouted. "Who am I going to hurt?"

"That's the point, Carla. The judge doesn't know you from Adam. For all he knows, you're a husband killer. It's unusual to get bail for a murder charge. But not impossible."

Lily was getting frustrated. Carla could see that. Better not push it, she told herself. She'd been amazed, frankly, when Lily had agreed to take her on. And she was lucky — or so Lily told her — that the bail hearing was happening so fast.

When she saw the judge, he would surely see she was no murderer. Lily had brought in some shampoo, a hair dryer and a hair-brush, too, although it was one of those thin wand designs instead of her usual paddle brush. Lily had also lent her a dull brown calf-length skirt, even though Carla had specifically described the one she'd wanted from her own wardrobe. "This one is more demure," Lily had told her brusquely. "It all makes a difference."

She was trying, Carla had to concede that. What was it that had swayed her? The "Ed was a bastard" bit? The baby bit? Or the argument that taking on her case would help Lily's career?

Maybe some of each.

It would have been easier, though, if Lily had been nicer to her instead of being all brusque and cold. Cold . . . Ed's body would be cold now. It didn't seem possible. None of this seemed possible. Any minute now, she'd wake up at home. Not the "home" that had once belonged to Lily and Ed. But her real home.

Italy.

Sunshine streaming in through the shutters, the sounds of children walking past on the way to school; the old man from next door grumbling about the tourists, and Mamma. Beautiful Mamma, calling her in that singsong voice. "Carla! Carla!"

584

"Carla Giuliana Macdonald. Do you plead guilty or not guilty?"

Were they really in front of the judge already? Carla looked around the courtroom.

They were all looking at her now. Everyone seemed far away, and then too close. The room was swaying. The rail in front of her in the defense box was slippery from the sweat on her hands, and there was a loud ringing in her ears. "Not guilty," she managed.

The first thing Carla saw when she opened her eyes was Lily. Lily in a smart navy suit that could have been black unless you were looking closely.

"Well done," Lily said.

It was difficult to know if she was being sarcastic or not.

Carla looked around to give herself time. They weren't in a police cell, or the court. They were in a room that looked a bit like an office.

"You managed to get the judge's sympathy with that rather dramatic faint. Luckily for you, your grandfather put up the bail."

Nonno? Carla began to sweat again. "He knows of this?"

"The news is all over the place. The press is having a field day. They're outside the court right now. Waiting for us, cameras at the ready."

Lily's eyes were bright. Glazed like an animal's, although Carla could not work out if she was in search of prey or being hunted herself. The thought made her uneasy. " 'Ménage à trois in the courtroom,' they're calling it. They got wind of the fact that we shared a husband." There was a hoarse laugh. "I'd like to say it was at different times, but there was some overlap, wasn't there?"

"I'm sorry."

"Did you say something?" Lily was standing over her like a teacher. "I didn't quite catch that. Would you mind saying that again?"

"I said I'm sorry."

Lily put her head to one side. "And you really think that a simple apology wipes the slate clean, that it atones for the wreckage of my marriage and the effect on my son?"

"It wasn't easy being married to Ed."

"If you go on like that, you'll make everyone think you *did* kill Ed — including me." Lily's tone was sharp, but Carla could tell she'd hit a nerve. It was a start. Slow but sure, employment law had taught her that. Begin by befriending the other side. Especially if it was really your own side . . .

"Right. Let's get going, shall we? Look straight ahead when we go out and don't, whatever you do, say anything to anyone. Ready?"

Lily strode ahead confidently as they followed the police officer across the lobby and into the street. At first Carla thought the sun was strong. But then, when she put down her hand, she could see the flashes. Cameras. A sea of faces. Voices calling out.

"Carla, is it true that your solicitor used to be married to your husband?"

"Carla, who do you think killed your husband if you didn't?"

"Lily, why have you taken on your ex-husband's wife? Have you always been friends?"

Carla started as Lily grabbed her arm. Firmly. Painfully. "In the car. Now."

Somehow they made their way through, down the steps and into the silver car waiting at the bottom.

"You've got it all organized," Carla said with grudging admiration. Lily was in the front, her face turned to the side, looking out at the sea of people. Then she seemed to freeze.

"What?" Carla asked.

Lily went pink. "Nothing." Swiftly, she turned around so her back was facing Carla.

Lily had seen something, Carla told herself. Or someone. Who? She tried to look herself, but the car had moved on, swiftly gliding through the traffic leaving London.

It would be best, Lily told her as they drove, if she came to stay with her in Devon. It would be quieter there, away from the crowds. They could work on the case together. They could, if she wanted, even apply to have Poppy living with them.

"You would do that for me? Have Ed's child living with us?"

Carla's heart sank. Poppy with her blue, all-seeing eyes was the last person she needed.

"Sure. It's not her fault."

Lily had it all worked out.

At least, she thought she did.

59
LILY

I have to admit that Carla's fears are not unfounded. It would be easy to take on my husband's wife's case and put up such an obviously weak defense that she would go down.

But that's not the way to do it.

"Let me make this perfectly clear," I say to her as we sit in my parents' sitting room overlooking the sea. She's curled up in my chair, the pink velvet one that has been mine since childhood. Yet it suits Carla perfectly. You'd think, to look at her, that she's on holiday. Stretching back in the sunlight that pours through the picture windows, acting as though she is a guest while preparing for the case. My mother cannot believe I have brought down the woman who stole my husband. I explain that a client is a client and that I think she is innocent.

"You need to tell me everything," I continue. "No holding back. In return, I will do my best to defend you."

She narrows her eyes. "How do I know that? Suppose you really want me to lose?"

"If you're worried about that, why did you ask me to represent you?"

"I told you. Because you knew what Ed was like and because people trust you."

Ed. Once more, his name gives me a pang. How is it possible to care for someone who had hurt you so badly?

"And I'm telling you, Carla, that if I take a case on, I put everything into it." I pause, staring out across the sea. There's a stream of yachts like a row of bobbing ducks. The sailing club always goes out on a Saturday afternoon. Tom's down there on the promenade, right now, with Mum. Poppy, too, in the old Silver Cross stroller that Mum's dug out from the attic. In fact, she's one of the reasons I'm doing this.

I don't want to like Ed's child, I really don't. But from the minute I saw her with her cute red hair and my husband's stubby fingers, I felt something tug at me. This was the daughter we should have had together. This was the child who might have come along if we hadn't had our hands full with Tom.

It helps that Poppy bears little resemblance to her mother. Odd, too, that the child screams every time Carla picks her up. And that Carla winces every time she holds her daughter.

"Of course I'll tell you everything." Carla's voice cuts into my thoughts. "Why wouldn't I?"

"Because most people are hiding something," I snap.

"I wouldn't." Her eyes meet mine in a deadlock. "I'm telling you the truth."

I'm telling you the truth. Wasn't that what Joe Thomas had said when I'd first met him? Joe, who'd been in the crowd outside the court after Carla's case. Watching me.

My gaze returns to the sea. In the distance, I can see the red cliffs. Large chunks have been falling into the sea in the last few years. People have been losing their back gardens.

Far worse to lose a husband. It doesn't matter that Ed was married to this woman after me. I was his first wife. I came before her.

"I once had a client who lied to me." I half laugh. "Others have probably done the same, but I know this one did because he told me after the case. It was an appeal. He'd already served a few years in prison, but I got him off. And then he told me that he had done it after all."

Carla is staring at me. "Did he go back to prison?"

I shake my head. "He should have. But I couldn't do anything because of double jeopardy. He couldn't be retried for the same offense."

The phone rings. It's the barrister I've been waiting to hear from. I've decided to act as his junior counsel rather than be totally in charge. As I told Carla, not all judges are keen on solicitors defending murder trials.

We speak briefly and then I put the phone down, turning to Carla. "Looks like we've got to get a move on. The case has been brought forward. We've got just over two months to prepare."

"Like I said, I trust you, Lily. You were always the best in the practice." Carla stretches out, artfully crossing one slim leg over the other as though flaunting her body in front of me.

"Why have you brought her here?" my mother keeps asking. "I don't understand."

Of course, it's not just because of Poppy with her gummy smile. It's because I want to make Carla suffer. I want her to live in a house surrounded by photographs of Ed and me, photographs that I once stored and have now rehung.

I want her to live with her husband's ex-wife, to hear me talk about times when she wasn't there. I want her to feel my parents' disapproving glares.

But most of all, I want her to know what it's like to live with Tom, whose life changed forever when she stole his father.

And it's working. I can see that in Carla's eyes. For as much as I'd like to believe "the Italian Girl grown up" is bad through and through, I suspect that she's capable of feeling as much guilt as you and me.

60
CARLA

April 2016

"So tell me, Carla. What exactly do you remember from the night that Ed Macdonald was murdered?"

Carla knew exactly what to say. Hadn't she and Lily gone over it again and again in the library for weeks on end, while Lily's mother cared for Poppy?

The prosecution barrister, who had just asked her this question, was staring at her with icy disdain. The journalists outside had, she was certain, already branded her as guilty. Glancing up at the gallery, she spotted a woman with long dark curls. *Mamma!* she nearly called out.

But then the woman turned and Carla could see that it was not her mother after all. "You often get complete strangers coming in to see a case," Lily had told her. "They are simply curious."

Strangely, it had been Lily's mother ("Call

me Jeannie") who had helped her through her grief during her stay in Devon. "I know what it is to have experienced loss," she had said after her initially cool welcome. "But you must remember that you are a mother yourself now. We mothers have to be strong."

Thanks to Jeannie, Carla had also learned that the noise of the vacuum cleaner could sometimes stop Poppy's terrible crying, and that babies were much tougher than she had thought. "You're only nervous about picking her up because she was so small and sickly at the beginning," Jeannie had said. "But Poppy's really thriving now, isn't she? What a lovely smile!"

Tom had helped, too. This big lumbering stepson of hers, who asked strange questions and did odd things, was mesmerized by Poppy. At first Carla had been scared he might hurt her, but then his clumsy attempts at spooning mouthfuls of mush into her mouth, Poppy giggling all the time, made Carla realize that babies really were hardier than they looked.

They'd all shown her such kindness — incredible really, considering she had stolen Lily's husband. "They felt Ed should have behaved more responsibly," Lily had said curtly one day.

Now Carla took another look at the gallery. She'd never been introduced to Ed's family. "We don't have much to do with each other anymore," he had once said. But, perhaps, he was embarrassed about leaving his wife and son. Either way, she had no idea whether they were here. Maybe they were the ones at the front who were staring at her.

Holding herself even straighter, Carla turned away. But inside she was frozen with fear. Who would look after Poppy if she went to prison? Nonno and Nonna were too old. They were too frail to even come to the hearing. "We both love you very much," her grandmother had written. "Your grandfather may not show it because he is proud. But we know you cannot have committed this terrible crime. You will be set free."

Would she? For the first time, Carla began to wonder if she had made the right choice in hiring Lily. It had felt clever at the time, but now she was here, in the dock, the doubts were crowding in. Lily once had a reputation for being one of the best. But she was out of practice. And what about the barrister she'd chosen? Lily was constantly passing notes to him, indicating that he hadn't always said something he should have, or had omitted something else. She would have liked Lily to be the lead barrister, but it was better, Lily had told her, that she acted as junior counsel. The very fact that she was handling her case at all had caused a flurry of interest in both the press and the court. Even the judge had questioned it at the beginning of the proceedings. "I believe you are representing your first husband's wife," he had said. "Couldn't this be construed as a conflict of interest?"

Lily had warned her this might happen. And she had clearly been ready for the question. "Not at all, My Lord. My client specifically asked me to represent her. She felt we shared common ground."

There had been a ripple of laughter through the gallery at this. But it wasn't funny. It was true.

Back to the prosecution's question. What *did* she remember from the night Ed was murdered?

"I've already said in my statement."

There was a frown from Lily's direction. "Always be respectful," she had said. "Be prepared to go over and over the facts."

Carla gathered herself. "I'm sorry. It's just that I am so tired."

She flashed a smile — one of her best — at a young man in the jury who had been eyeing her up since the trial began. He was on her side. "Dress soberly," Lily had said. But Carla had been unable to bring herself to wear the awful outfit that had been presented to her. Instead, she had insisted on wearing a chic jacket and her favorite figure-hugging black skirt.

"Is it possible to sit down while I am giving evidence?" The judge gave a brief nod. Thank goodness he was a man. She stood more chance of getting him onside, too, providing she played her cards right.

"Ed and I were at home together. He was drunk again." Her eyes closed. "He began yelling at me. Insisting that our baby wasn't his . . ." Her eyes brimmed with tears.

"And *was* he the father of your child?"

Carla's chin jerked up. "Of course. I loved my husband. I would never have been unfaithful to him. I will take a DNA test, if you like, to prove it."

The prosecution was walking up and down. "But is it not true that on the night of the murder, your former boyfriend Rupert Harris paid you a visit at home? Were you thinking of leaving your husband for him?"

Carla was so shocked that for a minute she couldn't speak. Her own barrister seemed taken aback, too. He was a young man who kept looking at his notes as if nervous of forgetting something. But according to Lily, he was "just right for the job."

"No," she finally managed to say. "Rupert was just a friend from college. Besides, I knew he had just gotten engaged."

The horrid prosecution barrister raised his eyebrows as if to indicate that he doubted whether this would put her off. "Please tell us what happened next, Mrs. Macdonald."

She glanced at the jury. There was a woman with a pinched face sitting next to the sympathetic-looking young man. Carla addressed herself to her. "Ed was shouting at me. He began to shake my shoulders. His fingers were hurting me. I was so scared . . ." She paused and pressed her hand to her chest. "I pushed him away, but he fell against the wall. He was drunk. He couldn't balance properly. His head began to bleed and I felt terrible. So I tried to stem the blood with a cloth. But he pushed me away again. He was furious. I was absolutely terrified." Then she put her hand on the rail as if to steady herself. They had to believe her. They had to.

"That was when he picked up the carving knife, the one he'd just used to carve the chicken."

She clutched at her throat, as if he was brandishing it in front of her right now. "I thought he was going to kill me."

The court was deathly quiet.

"Then I heard the door open . . ."

"Are you sure?"

"Per certo."

"In English, please, Mrs. Macdonald."

"Sorry. I am certain."

Carla wet her lips. This was the tricky bit, Lily had warned. The part that the jury might not be sympathetic to. "I ran out to the hallway. There was a man standing there. I didn't know what was happening. I thought he wanted to hurt me, too. I was so scared." A sob escaped through her lips. "Then I panicked and ran."

The prosecutor's face was impassive. Blank. "Can you describe this man?"

"I'll try." Carla's voice trembled. "He was quite tall with dark hair and brown eyes — I can't remember much more, I wish I could!"

"So do we all, Mrs. Macdonald."

What Carla didn't say — Lily had advised her not to, as she said it would muddy the waters — was that the more she thought about it, the more she felt that she remembered him from somewhere.

"Did you take your baby with you when you made this *desperate* run?"

That wasn't fair. He knew she hadn't.

"No," whispered Carla, and collapsed into sobs. There were disapproving murmurings among the jury.

This wasn't good. Somehow she had to make them understand what she had gone through. Forcing herself, Carla lifted her tearstained face.

"I had postnatal depression after my baby was born. I told my barrister that." A large sob escaped her mouth. "And my mother died in Italy of cancer on the very day I gave birth. I didn't even have a chance to say good-bye. I know I shouldn't have run off and left Poppy behind. But I just wasn't thinking straight . . ."

Carla had her head in her hands, yet her fingers were open wide enough for her to look at the jury. Instead of disdain or disbelief, the woman with the pinched face was weeping quietly into a tissue. Was it possible that she had had similar troubles?

Carefully, she started speaking again through her tears. "It was wet and cold. I wanted to go back for my baby, but I thought I heard footsteps behind me in the park. So I ran into a pub for help. Someone called the police, but they arrested me! For his murder . . ." Great sobs were coming out of her mouth now. Huge, hysterical gulps. There were murmurs of sympathy from the jury.

"I think," said the judge softly, "we should take a break here."

She had done well, the barrister had told her, his face looking flushed with excitement. Very well. The jury looked as though they were on her side. Mind you, you could never tell.

The trial went on and on. "Six days," Lily had predicted. Right now it was on its tenth.

The worst, after her own testimony, had been when Rupert was called. "Yes, I did care for Carla once upon a time," he had told the court. "But now I am happily married. My wife was my fiancée when I called in with a present for Carla and Ed's new baby. I was surprised by the tense atmosphere. Ed had clearly been drinking and didn't make me feel welcome, so I left after a few minutes." He spoke rapidly, flashing nervous glances up to a girl with blond hair in the gallery. He couldn't be too nice about her, in case his wife thought he really had been having an affair with her. She was thankful when he finally left the stand, shooting her an apologetic glance.

An expert witness had then pointed out

that the small amount of blood on Carla's clothes did not prove that she had hurt Ed, that it was more likely to have been from the head injury that her husband had sustained from falling when she'd pushed him away in self-defense — a fact backed up by the autopsy findings. Nor were there any fingerprints on the knife, apart from Ed's. It was from a sharp new knife set, which he had discouraged her from using because she might hurt herself. "Far better," he'd insisted, "that I handle all the knives myself." (Another example of his controlling ways.)

Carla's head began to whirl. An expert on bereavement. Another on postnatal depression and the link with the strain of a premature birth. Both were used by the prosecution to claim Carla might have behaved unpredictably. Her defense cross-examined them, claiming this would be why her memories were so unclear. Her barrister, who thankfully seemed to grow in confidence as the days passed, called an art dealer who spoke about Ed's "reputation for being up and down." A medical report on his drinking. A statement from the bank about his debts. Photographs of the terrible gash on Ed's body. The carving knife. She felt numb. As though all this was happening to someone else.

■ ■ ■ ■

Now, finally, they had finished. As they sat
waiting for the verdict in a room nearby,
Lily was very quiet. The barrister had gone
outside to make a phone call.

How was it possible that her entire future
could be decided by a group of strangers?
Carla's knee began to jerk up and down.

"The jury's back." It was the barrister, his
face taut. "It was quick. We're being called
in."

61
LILY

I've lost count now of the verdicts I have waited for. Sometimes I think it's like waiting for a pregnancy test. Or maybe a DNA test.

You tell yourself that you have done your best, and you hope that it goes in your favor. But you also warn yourself that this might not happen. You try to prepare yourself, argue that it isn't the end of the world if the result isn't what you want. Yet at the same time, you know that's not true.

A lost case means you've let yourself down. And, more important, others, too.

Under normal circumstances, I wouldn't have been keen on this barrister. He was very young. Some might also say he was relatively inexperienced. But as I told Carla, some juries are put off by an all-guns-blazing, confident, strutting QC (otherwise known as Queen's Counsel). My man endeared himself to me when he had said we needed to go softly. "Our defense is that there is only circumstantial evidence," he'd pointed out, flushing madly — he was one of those types, like me, who blush easily. "Nothing firm. No witnesses seeing Carla do anything other than run through the park. No incriminating fingerprints on the knife. She saw an intruder at the door."

"But there's no proof of that," I butted in. The barrister had flushed. "Carla is a beautiful woman. I wouldn't mind betting that the men on the jury will believe her. That at least would give us a fifty-fifty chance." Of course, that was when I should have told him about the envelope I'd received soon after Carla's arrest. The one with the familiar spidery writing which, the office night porter told me, had been handed in very early one morning.

Naturally I knew what the envelope contained. A tip-off. Hadn't Joe already told me in a phone call that morning?

"I want to help you, Lily."

I'd nearly put the phone down there and then. "I told you, Joe. Don't get in touch with me again. I did what you wanted — had the paternity test done — and now it's over. There's nothing left between us."

"I love you, Lily, but I don't believe you had the test at all." His voice was deep, sending tremors through me. "You're just scared. I get that. I really do. I can tell from your voice that you haven't looked at that envelope I sent you. It will help you in the case. Open it. Fast. For old times' sake."

Old times' sake? He spoke as though we had a past. Which of course we did. Can you imagine the headlines? "Solicitor has sex with the bath killer." It would destroy my family and career.

"Tom isn't yours, Joe."

"And I told you I don't believe you, Lily. I love you."

I wanted to be sick. A murderer was in love with me? I slammed down the phone. Made sure the envelope was hidden in a drawer. I should have torn it up there and then, but it's sitting there. It's my insurance — my plan B.

But right now I'm waiting to hear what the jury is about to say. Carla is shaking. Her terror gives me pleasure. There is nothing she can do now. No one she can sleep with to get her way.

She can't even blame me. No one could deny that I have done my best legally, hand on heart, to get her off. I even took her into my home to coach her for the defense. Together we have succeeded in blackening Ed's name so that everyone thinks the man

I married was a drunk and a philanderer. You see? I am not as good as I look.

The whole court is taut, waiting.

"Do you have a verdict?"

The foreman's mouth is opening. My palms are sweating. I swear I can feel Ed by my side tugging at my sleeve. When I turn, I realize I've snagged my navy silk jacket on the bench.

"Not guilty."

I don't believe it.

There are gasps from the gallery, and a baby crying. Poppy? No. It's another child — spectators sometimes bring in their children, goodness knows why. Meanwhile Carla is collapsing, and a policeman is helping her to her feet. The barrister shoots me a smug *We did it* look. People are congratulating me. One of the detectives is speaking urgently to a colleague. I feel a twinge of misgiving. They'll be on the hunt for the real killer now. But up in the gallery I see someone else.

A tall, clean-shaven man with short hair. He's staring down at me. Wearing a moss-green tweed jacket with a light beige suede collar, turned upward. And then he disappears.

The phone rings the moment I get back into

the office.

"Why didn't you use my evidence?" Joe Thomas's voice is gravelly with disappointment.

I open the drawer and take out the envelope. It is still sealed. How many times had I thought about opening it? It would have made my job easier. I knew that. Joe has never gotten things wrong before. As he's pointed out on many an occasion, I wouldn't have gotten this far in my career without his help.

"It's my insurance," I say.

"Insurance? I don't get it."

"In case the verdict wasn't what I hoped for." As I speak, I think about Carla and how she barely thanked me after the trial, with her chin tilted upward as if being acquitted was no more than her right.

"You can't use it now," he adds reproachfully. "The trial is over. The police will already be looking for someone else to pin Ed's murder on."

I wince. Even now, I miss Ed. My mind keeps going back to the better bits of our marriage.

Then my memory returns to that early morning jog on the promenade when Joe asked for a paternity test. I had felt particularly vulnerable back then. I was angry at

Ed for having his cake and eating it, too, and jealous of Carla for seeing my son on their visiting weekends. And I was confused about still feeling drawn to Joe.

And for the first time since it happened, I allow myself to think about the key. The one that I was carrying, as always, for self-defense. The key that fell out of my pocket. The one that Joe picked up.

And didn't give back.

"It's from the house," I said bitterly at the time. "The house Carla has now taken along with my husband, and my son, who seems to think she's wonderful."

"I could teach her a lesson," Joe said quietly.

I felt a tremor of fear — and yes, of excitement, too. "I wouldn't want her hurt. Or him."

"Just scared, perhaps."

"Maybe," I find myself saying.

That's when I ran over the road, toward the sea, stunned by my own actions. Had I really just allowed myself to break the law? In one brief, crazy moment, I'd just given a criminal carte blanche to break into the house where Ed and Carla lived.

Aiding and abetting, they call it.

I raced back to the café table, panting madly, but Joe had disappeared.

As time went by and nothing happened, I felt safer. The longer I heard nothing from Joe, the easier it was to put the DNA test out of my head. Maybe he'd decided not to do anything after all. Maybe they'd changed the locks. But then came the shocking news of Ed's murder. When Ross called me at Tom's school, I initially presumed Carla was guilty, as did the rest of the world.

But then she told me about the door opening and a man standing there. And the notes.

That's why I took her on as a client. I needed to make sure that she went down, because if she didn't, the police might track down the real murderer.

Joe.

He'd tell them I'd given him the key.

I would get sent to prison.

I'd lose Tom.

Even though he isn't easy, this is unthinkable.

I would do anything. Anything for my son who needs me to protect him from the rest of the world. Suddenly I had to work out the toughest defense strategy of my life. How to make Carla lose without making it look as though I hadn't tried.

Put up such a poor defense that she would go down?

But that wasn't the way to do it.

Wasn't that what I'd told myself when Carla had first asked me to take on the case? And it was true. I had to be far more subtle than that. I needed to use reverse psychology.

Why hadn't I taken on the case myself without any help? Not because a judge might not like a solicitor in charge, as I told Carla, but because they'd trust me more if I brought in someone else. Besides, the judges know me, know my style — if I'd put up a weak defense, they'd have instantly known and accused me of conflict of interest.

My husband's wife.

Far cleverer to choose a young, nervous barrister who would get it wrong for me. I told Carla that a jury didn't always like a confident, strutting QC. That is sometimes true. But not always. Yet — just my luck — they did indeed warm to my fumbling, gauche brief, and that in turn made him grow in confidence. By then it was too late to lose.

I also suspected that if I insisted on her wearing "dull" clothes, Carla wouldn't be able to do it because she's so vain. I was right. But this backfired, too. It was clear from the look on the jurors' faces — both men and women — that they admired her style.

Why didn't they see Carla as I did? A manipulative child who had grown into a manipulative, husband-stealing woman.

"You shouldn't have done it," I now say down the line to Joe. My voice is cracked with disbelief. Shock. Self-recrimination.

Joe's voice, in contrast, is cool. "I got the impression you didn't care for Ed anymore."

"You said you'd frighten Carla." I'm whispering now. "Not kill my husband."

"Ex-husband," corrects Joe. "And who says that I did kill him? Open the envelope. Go on."

My hands do what my mind tells them not to do. Inside is a sealed plastic bag.

Inside that is a pair of gloves. Washing-up gloves.

Blue. Small. They have blood on them. Blood and earth.

I gasp.

"Now do you get it?" says Joe.

I can't believe it. "Carla did it after all?"

"Who else?" He sounds smug. Pleased.

"How did you get them?"

"I'd been sniffing around their place for a while, checking it out."

"What were you going to do?" I whispered.

"Wasn't sure. Never am until these things happen."

These things?

A picture of poor Sarah flashes into my head.

"I was there that evening. Some young bloke came out. Looked upset, he did. I listened at the door and heard one hell of an argument going on. Reckoned it might provide the distraction I needed. So I went in."

With *my* key!

"There she was, in front of me, wearing a pair of washing-up gloves covered in blood. Almost as shocked to see me as I was to see her. I ran out after her. I watched her toss the gloves into some shrubbery opposite the house. Rather than carry on chasing her, I picked up the gloves so you could use them, for evidence. Except that you didn't." No, I hadn't. I'd wanted to do this on my own, without the help of a criminal.

"So what's next?" Joe's voice forces me back to practicalities. "The trial's over, Lily. Your client's won. But we both know that she's guilty. And now the police will be looking for someone else. Me."

"Will you tell them about us?" My voice comes out as a whimper.

"That depends." His voice is steady.

Threatening. "Not if you tell me what the paternity test really said."

"I did tell you. You're not the father."

"And I don't believe you." His voice hardens. "I want another one, Lily. Or else . . ."

His voice trails away. But the implication is clear.

"Are you blackmailing me?"

"You could call it that."

I put the phone down, my hand shaking. Joe isn't just a murderer. He's desperate, dangerous.

And he's not the only one.

What should I do now? Then I feel something inside one of the gloves.

It's a key. One that I definitely recognize.

If I was in my right mind, I'd go straight to the police and hand over the gloves.

But instead I'm going to pay a visit.

To my husband's wife.

62
CARLA

Carla was packing. Fast. Furious. Not the red stilettos. She'd wear them instead. Her favorite perfume, too, for luck. First she'd go to the hotel, for that exclusive interview she'd promised to the newspaper. The advance would go toward her new future.

She was free. Free!

It was all working out. Far better than she could have thought. Poor, naive Lily. Convinced that the rest of the world was good if only she could make it so. Carla almost felt sorry for her. Then again, she deserved it.

Lily needed to learn a lesson.

The jury had believed her. Yet there were elements that had indeed been true. Ed, drunk with wine and jealousy, grabbing the knife. Her, pushing him away. Him, falling against the wall and hitting his head. Blood. Then getting up and coming at her again. Her, grabbing the knife in self-defense and lashing out. The knife in Ed's thigh. It had just stayed there, sticking out of the flesh with its green handle.

Then she was running, throwing the gloves in the bushes as she went.

If only she could have confessed in court. Self-defense. For that's what it had been. But people knew they had argued — look how Ed had spoken to her at the last party in front of everyone. Suppose the jury had not believed her? It was far better to talk about the intruder. The other thing that had been true. The man at the door, whom she had rushed past.

Thank you for being there, whoever you were, she thought. *It meant we could blame you for all the blood. All the horror.*

The only way to cope was to blank it out, to tell herself it had happened as she'd said in court. She would go to the States with Poppy, and rebuild their lives away from prying Italian and English eyes. She'd give up law, too. She had had more than enough of that.

"You."

Carla jumped. "Lily? How did you get in?"

Lily tossed a key up and down in the palm of her hand as though teasing her. "I still had this. It *was* my house once. Remember? Before you stole it and my husband from me. You should have changed the locks,

Carla. You and Ed."

Carla began to shake. "You still had the key?" she repeated.

Lily smiled. "That's right. I gave it to a friend. He's the man you saw at the door. He saw you throw away your bloody gloves. And he kept them for evidence."

"You're lying!"

"No." Lily's voice was cool. "I'm not."

LILY

I hold the gloves up now in their plastic bag. "See? When they are analyzed, the DNA will show Ed's blood. Much more of it than was on your clothes. And they have earth on them, too, from where you tried to hide them. Looks suspicious, doesn't it?"

"You can't do that." Carla is laughing. "You can't use them. The trial is over."

"You don't really keep up with criminal law, do you, Carla? Employment is your specialty, I seem to remember. Well, the law has been changed. Some years ago, in fact. Way after the case I told you about — on purpose, by the way. Double jeopardy doesn't always apply now, especially when there's new evidence. Like fresh DNA. All I have to do is hand these gloves over to the police, then you will be tried again. And this time you will go down for life."

She's still smirking. "If you're so sure, why haven't you gone to the police already?"

I'm already beginning to think I've made a mistake there. "Because I wanted to see you face-to-face first. To tell you what I really think of you." My eyes are wet. "Poor Ed. He didn't deserve to be murdered. You're going to pay for this, Carla, if it's the last thing I do . . ."

That's when she runs at me, her eyes blazing like an animal's. Her push is much stronger than her frame might suggest. I push her back. Then I lose my balance and trip over the spindle-backed mahogany kitchen chair that I once bought at auction and then left behind when I moved out.

I put up my hands to protect myself, the key and gloves flying into the air.

I'm dimly aware of the following:

Flash of metal.

Thunder in my ears.

"This is the five o'clock news."

The radio, chirping merrily from the pine dresser, laden with photographs (holidays, graduation, wedding); a pretty blue and pink plate; and a quarter bottle of Jack Daniel's on the second shelf, partially hidden by a birthday card.

The pain, when it comes, is so acute that it can't be real.

A quick succession of questions race through my head. What will happen to Tom when I am gone? Who will understand him? How will Mum and Dad cope with another child gone?

Above me, on the wall, is a picture of a small white house in Italy with purple bougainvillea climbing up it. A honeymoon memento.

The one which Ed helped me to paint. I had already destroyed his version. How ironic that mine should survive. The question is, will I do the same?

And here I still am, an hour later, slumped against the wall. My limbs completely numb. Bleeding and waiting. The blood is still streaming from my head, from where I hit the wall. My chest is throbbing. Am I having a heart attack? My silver honeymoon bracelet, which — despite any reasoning — I still wear every day, is cutting into my wrist because of the way I have fallen. And my ankle, which had been throbbing quietly, is now agony.

Still, at least the smell of smoke is getting fainter. It had been rubbery. Rather like a tire burning. The gloves?

If Carla has destroyed them, there will be no evidence.

And if Joe tells the truth about the key, I might go down instead.

CARLA

That last push from Lily had sent her reeling against the kitchen counter. A saucer had fallen off the side, smashing on the floor. She hadn't been hurt, just stunned by the push but not badly enough to stop her pushing Lily back. There had been a hollow crack as Lily crashed against the wall.

Vaguely, Carla remembered staggering over to the sink and trying to get rid of the gloves. *Incriminating evidence.* How often had she read that phrase in files at work? Essential to get rid of.

They wouldn't burn properly, so she'd chopped them up into little bits and flushed them down the toilet. Then she'd slumped in the hall, below one of Ed's rough charcoal studies for the original *Italian Girl*.

It seemed a fitting place to stop. Her body might not be injured. But her mind seemed to have had enough.

From where she was lying, Carla could

hear Lily groaning. So much blood. Almost as much as when Ed had hit his head . . .

If it wasn't for the fact that her legs didn't feel like her own, Carla might have gotten up to help Lily. She'd had time to think now after that initial shock of seeing those bloody gloves. Strangely, she didn't hate the woman for trying to turn her in. In fact, if she'd been in her position, she might have done exactly the same.

All her life she'd wanted things that had belonged to other people. The caterpillar case. Nicer clothes. A father. Even her mother had belonged to Larry when she was a child. And, of course, Ed. Until she'd finally got him and saw what he was really like.

She hadn't, Carla reminded herself, meant to hurt Ed. All she'd been doing was trying to defend herself. She'd had such a fright when the knife went into his thigh. How easily the blade had slipped in!

I deserve to be caught, Carla told herself. *It's gone too far.* Then her eye rested on a photograph of Ed and Tom on the bookcase near her. Father and son had their arms around each other, grinning out of the frame.

Poppy.

How would her daughter manage without

her? Mothers needed to protect their children. Now she could see why Mamma had pretended that Carla's father was dead in the early days. And why, later, she had hidden her cancer. How could she let Poppy suffer by having a mother in prison? As a child, Carla had thought it was bad enough having a mother with a strange accent who was always at work. But this was going to be far worse. Poppy would be Different with a capital *D* from the others in her class when she went to school. No doubt about that.

She had to force her shocked body to get up and leave, if only for Poppy's sake. Reality began to kick in. She'd hung around long enough now. It was time to take a few things. Ed's grandmother's ring might fetch a bit and see them through a few weeks.

There was a moan.

She didn't, Carla told herself, really want Lily to die, especially now that she'd gotten rid of the gloves. All she'd done was push her, although that crack had sounded bad. Yet she couldn't help her either. She had to look out for herself. Maybe when she got out of the house, she could go to a phone box and make an anonymous call to say that a woman was hurt.

"Lily?"

Footsteps. Someone was coming toward her, through the front door. With a shock, Carla realized Lily must have left it open.

"Where is my Lily? What have you done to her?"

Carla stared up as fear caught in her throat. It was him! The man who had broken in through the door that night. Something about those black eyes stirred a more distant memory. That stranger at Tony's funeral!

He ran past her now toward Lily. "It's all right, my darling. I'm here." She couldn't hear Lily's reply.

She could hear his footsteps coming back now. She could see the glint of metal in his hands.

"You hurt her!" he was screaming. "You hurt Lily!"

The last thing she could remember hearing was the rush of wind as the blade came down to meet her.

63
LILY

It took me a long time to get better. Not so much physically but mentally. It still seems impossible that any of it happened.

When you realize you're not dying after all, you feel an initial gust of euphoria. "You were so lucky," everyone kept saying. "Someone must've been looking after you" was another favorite phrase.

And you believe it. You honestly do. You look out through the hospital window and see people walking, ambulances arriving, patients in wheelchairs, others on crutches, heads bowed, others laughing with relief. And you know that this is the real world — the one where lives are saved, instead of the one outside where the bad people try to take lives away.

Then, when you're out in that real world again, that's when the doubts come crowding back in. That's when you start to think. If I hadn't married Ed . . . if my boss hadn't put me in charge of Joe's appeal when I was too young and inexperienced . . . if I hadn't allowed my feelings to take over . . . if we hadn't met Carla and her mother . . . if I hadn't had that drink with Joe in Hampstead . . . if I hadn't dropped my key . . . if I hadn't defended Carla . . . if I hadn't opened that envelope . . .

"You mustn't think about the ifs," says Ross. He's been one of my regular visitors at home back in Devon, where I've been since they discharged me. There will always be a scar on the side of my head from my fall against the wall, although it might not show so much when my hair grows back. My cracked ribs (hence the agonizing pain in my chest) have mended now. But my wrist is still acting up, and I no longer wear the honeymoon bracelet that was caught between me and the wall when I fell over. My ankle, which broke as I went down, is "coming along."

"Ifs will drive you mad," he continues. "You did your best, Lily. You really did. And if you made a few mistakes along the way, well, that's life."

Mum comes into the room with a tray of coffee for our visitor and hears the end of the last sentence. She catches my eye and then looks away. But it's too late. I know what she's thinking. If I'm really going to heal, I have to tell the truth. The very last part of my story. The bit I never told my husband, or the grief counselor the hospital encouraged me to see.

Ross is a good friend. I owe it to him. And, maybe more importantly, I owe it to myself.

I was eleven when my parents took on Daniel. It wasn't the first time they'd brought children into the house. Remember that little brother and sister who Dad kept saying I was going to have? Only later did I find out that Mum had had one miscarriage after another. So my parents turned to fostering to give me "company."

Of course, it was brilliant of them to do it, but it didn't feel like that at the time.

Some of the kids were all right. Others weren't. There were times when I'd come back from school to find Mum playing with a three-year-old. I'd want to talk to her about my day, but she would be too busy. The social worker would be coming to do a check. Or she had to take the child to the doctor because he or she had a wheezy chest.

I wouldn't have minded except that they weren't real brothers and sisters. They took my parents away from me. And they made me feel different. My friends at school thought it was weird that my socially aware parents took in one kid after another, looking after them for anything from a few days to a year before they'd go away and others would replace them.

"You're going to have a full-time brother," my father announced one morning. I remember it well. We were eating boiled eggs at the time, in our house in London — a trim, neat, semi-detached house with pebbledash. Nothing bigger, even though my mother's family were quite well off, because that didn't suit my parents' socialist principles. "He's had a rough start to life," my mother said. "Poor little thing had parents who were . . . well, who did bad things. So sometimes he behaves badly, too. He's been in and out of foster homes, but now we're going to adopt him. Give him a proper home." She gave me a comforting hug. "And you can help, too, Lily, by being a kind big sister. You must look after him with us."

And then Daniel arrived.

I was eleven. He was a year younger but looked older with his tall, lanky stance and a wild mass of tousled black hair. In hindsight, my parents could have thought more carefully. But they wanted to make a difference — to take the child no one else would. Later I found that Daniel's mother had been a prostitute, addicted to heroin although he used to claim she was a trapeze artist in a circus. His father was in prison for a drug-induced double murder.

From the minute he arrived, Daniel began to push the boundaries. No, he wouldn't go to school. No, he wouldn't come home when he'd promised. No, he hadn't stolen money from Mum's purse. Didn't we trust him?

In fact, there was only one person whom Daniel trusted.

"You," says Ross quietly. I glance out the window onto the lawn where Tom is playing croquet with my father. He throws his mallet in the air with joy when he gets the ball through the hoop, just as Daniel used to. He stamps his foot on the ground when he misses a shot. At times, the similarities are extraordinary, even though there is no blood relation. Both challenging. Both more dear to me than I can say.

"Yes," I say softly. "Daniel trusted me. For some reason, he latched on to me. Adored me. But I let him down."

Ross's hand is holding mine. Firmly. Comfortingly. I think of how Ross helped me through Ed's betrayals. And I know that just as Daniel trusted me, so I can trust Ross. I won't just tell him the half version of Daniel's death that I told Joe at the pub. Or the version I gave Ed where I left out a vital scene.

I will tell Ross the whole truth.

It was the other girls at school who started it. They all fancied my adopted brother. He was so good-looking: so tall, with that mop of hair and slightly lopsided, endearing smile. How he made everyone laugh! Daniel specialized in playing the classroom fool. He would answer back. Make fun of the teachers. The more he got told off, the worse he became. He started stealing other kids' money and then swearing blind it wasn't him.

When Mum's dad died, she inherited the house in Devon. It would be a fresh start for my brother, my parents said when I kicked up a fuss about leaving my old school. And it was. Daniel and I loved our new home. Such a novelty to live by the sea!

I pause for a moment and look out the window again at the waves, lashing against the rocks on the far side of the bay.

My parents did everything they could to make Daniel happy. They got him Merlin and took on a rescue dog at the same time.

They ignored bad behavior because they believed in "positive praise." They bought him the new jacket he wanted when I'd not been allowed a fluffy blue jumper I'd had my eye on.

"I was chosen by them," Daniel would announce proudly at times.

But during his blacker moments, the mask would slip. "I don't want to be different, Lily," he'd say. "I want to be like you. Like everyone else."

Daniel wasn't the only one to be confused. Sometimes I was jealous of the attention that my parents piled on him. At other times, I was overwhelmed with love for my new brother, grateful that I finally had the company I had craved. But every now and then, something would occur that made me wonder what would have happened if they'd chosen someone else.

Of course, Daniel still got into trouble, just like he had in London. It was the same old things. Lying about homework. Lying about where he'd been. I'd cover up for him. It was what a sister did. Once a shop-keeper ran out after us, insisting that Daniel had stolen a bag of sweets.

"He wouldn't do that," I insisted.

But when we were allowed to leave, Daniel took the packet out of his sock.

I went back to the shop, explaining that there had been a misunderstanding. And Daniel swore never to do it again.

His childhood — and mine — were peppered with similar incidents.

Later, when he'd just turned fifteen, a local girl claimed he'd slept with her. It was all over school.

"It's not true," he laughed when I asked him about it. "Why would I want to do that? She's a slut. Anyway, there's only one girl I want."

"Who?" I asked teasingly.

His face closed down as if someone had drawn a curtain across it. "Not saying."

But then, one day, I had my first date.

I stop, my cheeks flushing. "It was one of the boys from the local school. All my friends had been asked out by now. But they were prettier than me. Slimmer."

My mother was excited for me. "What are you going to wear?"

Daniel was furious. He wouldn't talk to me. And when I finally came downstairs after spending ages getting ready, my brother informed me that the boy had called to say he couldn't make it. Later, I found out that Daniel had stood outside the front door, waiting for him, and then lied. Told him that I didn't want to go out after all.

Ross gently interrupts. "Didn't you wonder if . . ." His voice trails off.

"No. I know it sounds silly, but I just thought it was Daniel being difficult again. Causing trouble the way he always did." I take a deep breath. "But then his arm started to 'accidentally' brush mine. We had these long conversations, late at night. And one evening, when we went down to the stables to feed Merlin, he kissed me."

I close my eyes. Even now I can remember that kiss. It was like no other. Never, ever have I been kissed like that. The knowledge that it was wrong only added to the excitement. That's right, I wanted him to. Deep down, I realized I'd always wanted him to do this. That I'd been jealous of that other girl he was said to have slept with. But when I finally drew away, I was overcome with shame.

"It's all right," Daniel said, his breath heavy and his voice thick. "We're not related. We can do what we want." But it wasn't all right. And we knew it. Before long, the kissing grew more adventurous. Even as I speak, I can still recall the illicit thrill.

Mum began to notice something. "I might have got this wrong," she said, her cheeks burning. "But do be careful, won't you?

Daniel might not be your blood brother. But don't forget he's your adopted brother."

I was mortified, and sickened by myself. So I did what a lot of people do when they are accused of something: I threw it back. "How can you think such filthy thoughts?" I yelled.

Mum went beetroot, but she held her ground. "Are you sure you're telling me the truth about Daniel?"

"Of course I'm sure. How can you be so disgusting?" Her words scared me. By then I had turned eighteen. Daniel was seventeen. We hadn't "done it," as my school friends called it. But we were close. Perilously close.

At times, my love for Daniel was so overwhelming that I could barely breathe when I sat opposite him at breakfast. Yet at other times, I could barely stand to be in the same room as him. Both feelings that I was to have later, toward Joe.

And that's the nub of it, you see. Because of Daniel, I was unable to feel attracted to a man unless it was wrong. That's why I was so drawn to Joe. And that's why my honeymoon had been a disaster. Why I always found it difficult with Ed.

"Then," I continue falteringly, "the same boy from school asked me out again. (I'd explained there'd been a misunderstanding over the previous date.) This time, I wouldn't let Daniel stop me. It was my way to break free." I close my eyes, shutting out my bedroom with its posters on the wall; the desk with my homework littered over it; my brother with his furious eyes as he took in the clingy top I had put on for the date. A glittery silver one that showed my curves . . .

"You don't have to tell me," says Ross, sensing my distress.

"I need to."

So I make myself describe how Daniel went mad. How jealous he was of this boy. How he said I'd never be able to stop doing what he and I had been doing. How he called me terrible names.

Whore.

Slut.

Fatty.

That no one else would ever want me.

And how I then said those fateful words.

I wish you had never been born.

Daniel went very quiet then. Just stared at me for what seemed like ages and then left the room. Dabbing on foundation to cover my tears, I flew down the stairs.

I stop. Compose myself before I continue with the final part of the story.

On my way out, Mum caught me. "You look nice," she said, casting an eye over my top. "But you'll need your coat. It's cold outside."

I'd been so desperate to leave that I'd forgotten. Now I grabbed it from the rack.

Her voice quivered. "Are you going out with Daniel?"

"No." I spat the word at her, flushing hotly as though I was telling a lie. "I'm meeting someone else."

Her color was as high as mine. "Promise?" she said.

"Of course I promise. Daniel's . . . he's somewhere else."

This is the difficult bit. The bit that is so hard to say that the words choke my throat. But I have to. I've reached the end of the road. If I don't do it now, I will never be able to do it.

Ross is holding my hand. I take a deep breath.

"When I came back — early, as it happens, as the date hadn't been a great success — Mum was hysterical. They'd found a note from Daniel. It said, 'I don't want to live anymore.' Did I know anything? Where might he have gone? That's when it came to me. He'd have gone to our place. Our special place."

Ross squeezes my hand as the words stream out of my heart.

"He was hanging in his red jacket from the stable rafters with Merlin nuzzling his feet. And do you know what was on the frozen ground?"

Ross shakes his head.

"My doll. My old doll. The one I used to carry everywhere with me. Amelia. He must have gone back to the house to get it from my room and write the note. And I know why. Amelia would have made him feel I was with him at the end . . ."

As I speak, I get a glimpse of Carla as a child, questioning me about my doll in the taxi when I'd taken her home from the hospital. "Do you still have her?" she'd asked.

"No," I'd told her. It was true.

I'd asked them to put her in Daniel's coffin.

Grief at allowing myself to remember is now overwhelming me. It chokes my throat. Makes my breath come out in small, desperate gasps. I see my father, sobbing and unable to believe what his eyes showed him all too clearly. I see my mother, clasping her arms around her body and rocking back and forth on the ground, repeating the same phrase over and over: *There's got to be a mistake . . .*

I turn to Ross. "Don't you see? It was my fault. If I hadn't gone out with that boy from school, Daniel wouldn't have killed himself. That's why I never allowed myself to date anyone else. Not until the millennium when my father told me it was time to move on."

"When you met Ed," says Ross quietly.

"Exactly. That's why I became a lawyer, too. Not just to put the world to rights, but to put myself to rights. I wanted to make sure I never made a mistake again."

I stop.

"And then," prompted Ross softly.

"Then I met Joe Thomas."

64
LILY

Dear Lily,

I am truly sorry for everything. I did things I should not have done. And I did not do things that they said I did. Either way, I am paying for them . . .

That's right, there's a postscript to this story.

No one knows how Carla survived. The extent of Joe Thomas's wrath was horrific. One member of the jury had to be carried out when she saw the photographs.

One thing is sure. The Italian Girl will never look the same. Gone is the beautiful skin. Instead, it is a mass of scars. One eye will never open again. The mouth droops slightly on one side. Only the glossy dark hair remains.

Life is a long time. Especially when beauty is no longer on your side.

CRIME OF PASSION
EX-CON AND HIS LAWYER IN
MURDER PUZZLE
ARTIST'S WIDOW EMBROILED IN
KILLER SCANDAL

The headlines went on for days. There had to be two trials, of course. One for Joe. And one for Carla.

Luckily for her, Carla found a new white knight. Her real father. A man who had had nothing to do with Carla previously because he had a family of his own. But when his children left home and he got divorced, he hired an investigator to trace his daughter. By that point she was in Italy. He decided not to take it any further then, but he was sentimental enough to buy the portrait that his man had cleverly discovered in a small London gallery. *The Italian Girl,* it was called. But the accompanying paperwork had named the sitter.

Carla Cavoletti.

For a time, the portrait sufficed. But then, when he read about Carla's first trial and heard about Francesca's death, his conscience finally kicked in. He put up the bail money. Forced Carla's grandfather to keep it a secret, to say it was his money.

Then, after she was convicted for assaulting me and for Ed's murder, he had the guts to step in openly. To reveal himself. The papers had another field day.

ITALIAN GIRL'S FATHER PROMISES TO CARE FOR GRANDDAUGHTER

Glad as I was for Poppy and her little gummy smile, being looked after by family while her mother serves her time, I try not to think about any of this as I go about my daily life.

I've had enough of the law now. My new family consultancy practice has boomed. Tom is years ahead with his mathematical skills, apparently, but still has tantrums if his shoes are moved from their proper place. I have to remind myself that, according to the experts, I ought to use the word *meltdown* rather than *tantrum,* because the latter denotes a certain willfulness. I also have to remind myself that Tom honestly can't help it. I am no longer so anxious. Gone is the fear that I might "kill" my son by doing or saying something that might tip him over the edge as I had done with Daniel.

Alice, his new school friend, has helped. We all like Alice. She has issues similar to my son's. She understands him. Perhaps one day they'll be more than friends. The other weekend, I took them both up to London to the Natural History Museum. I had to drag them out at closing time. "We could stay here forever," said Alice, tucking her hand into Tom's.

Meanwhile, there's Mum and Dad, who are getting older and talking about selling the house. And Ross, of course. Ross, who has become a regular visitor to the house. Never imposing. Never pushing. But often there, even after my confession.

Like today, when he brought me the letter from Carla. I take a deep breath and read the rest of it.

. . . I am writing to say that I am to get married again as soon as Rupert's divorce is through. The wedding will be in prison, but it does not matter. Rupert does not mind that my face is different.

He loves Poppy as if she was his own. (She is not.) My solicitor says that Life does not always mean a life sentence.

Please forgive me.

I hope you can find it in your heart to wish me happiness.

Yours,
Carla

I put down the letter on the grass. It flaps

in the wind and then blows away. I make no attempt to chase after it. It means nothing. Carla always was a good liar. Yet there's something still nagging at me. Something isn't quite right . . .

"Chewing gum, Sellotape, scissors, sharp implements?"

I'm back in prison. It's a different one from the last time. And I'm not wearing my lawyer hat. I'm a visitor.

"Hands up, please."

I'm being searched thoroughly.

Now a dog is walking past with his handler. He pays no attention to me but sits silently next to the girl behind. She is led away. Apparently that's how sniffer dogs work. They don't bark or growl. They simply sit.

"Why are you here?"

I'm sitting when Joe Thomas comes in. He's thinner. He is looking at me stonily. I should be scared, but I'm not. There are plenty of people around us.

"I want to know exactly what happened."

He sits back in his chair, tipping it, and laughs. "I told you. Told everyone at the trial."

I allow my mind to go back to the time when Carla was convicted of assaulting me

644

and murdering Ed, back to the trial a few days later, when Joe was sent down for his assault of Carla. And for being an accessory to Ed's murder.

Unbelievable, isn't it?

But that's what happened. Joe stood up in court, at Carla's trial, and said that he had met her at Tony's funeral and that they'd stayed in touch. Later, he swore that Carla, aware of his criminal background, had hired him as a hit man, promising payment when Ed's life insurance came through. They'd agreed that he would come around on a certain evening. But when he had gotten there, she had been in a terrible state — and he had soon seen why. Carla had already stabbed Ed herself. In the thigh. Then she'd run, leaving him, Joe, to take the blame.

Carla vehemently denied this. Instinctively I felt it didn't ring true either. I didn't really see Carla as the type to hire a hit man.

But the prosecuting barrister was good. Very good. The persistent questioning finally made Carla break down and admit that, yes, she had plunged the knife into Ed. He'd picked it up first, she had sobbed. She thought he was going to hurt her out of jealousy over Rupert. It was self-defense. But she definitely hadn't hired Joe as a hit man. That bit was a lie.

It didn't wash with the new jury. The untruths she'd already told made certain of that.

I'd been terrified that Joe would implicate me. But as soon as he said that about Carla hiring him, I knew he was doing it to protect me. I suppose the key should have been another clue. The one he posted back to me, inside Carla's washing-up gloves. At the time, I thought he was encouraging me to take my revenge.

Now I wonder if he was giving me a "get out of jail free" card.

Joe explained his presence at Carla's house after her acquittal by saying he went there to demand his money. And that he'd found Carla hurting me.

But I know differently, of course. He'd come back because of me. Joe must have suspected I would go to see Carla after opening the envelope with the washing-up gloves inside. He wanted to make sure I was all right.

I'm painfully aware that if he'd told the truth about any of this, I'd be in prison, too.

But that's the problem with lies. As I said at the beginning, they start small. And then they multiply. So that the white lies become as black as the real thing. Yet his lie has saved me.

Amazingly the jury believed Joe. It helped that, on the night of Ed's murder, there wasn't any sign of a forced entry. So it made sense that Carla had let him in voluntarily.

Life, he got, for conspiring to murder Ed and for his assault of Carla. The same as Carla got for murdering Ed. The same that Joe should have gotten for poor Sarah Evans.

You could say it was justice, but I'm not so sure. That's why I'm here.

"I know you weren't telling the truth. I want to know what really happened."

He grins. Like we're playing a game, just as we had at the beginning when he made me work out the water figures.

"Touch me." His voice is so low that I barely hear it. Then he says it again. "Touch me and then I'll tell you."

I glance around. The officers with their folded arms. Women talking urgently to their partners opposite. Couples not talking.

"I can't."

"Look." He's staring straight at me. "Look to your right."

The woman next to me has her foot up, in between her partner's legs.

"I won't do that." I'm flushing.

"Then I won't tell you." This is blackmail.

I look again. The officer nearest me is making her way to the offending table. She's not looking at us.

"Quickly," he says.

My heart starts to speed up just as it had on the promenade when Joe took my key. A wave of desire starts to seep through the lower part of my body, even though I try to crush it.

Then the stables flash into my mind. Daniel with his limp neck. Amelia, my doll, lying on the ground below my brother. And Merlin with a puzzled expression on his all-knowing, dear old face. Killed by Sarah Evans's murderer — or as good as — in an attempt to scare me.

It's a wake-up call. A distinct prod back to sanity.

"No," I say firmly, my feet still on the ground. "No. I won't. I'm through with all these games, Joe. They're over."

A brief look of disappointment shoots across his face, followed by an *if that's the way you want it* shrug.

He makes as if to stand, and then appears to change his mind.

"Okay. You're lucky. I'm feeling generous today. I'll still give you a clue."

"I told you." I almost thump the table. "No more games."

"But this one, Lily, is in your interest. It will give you peace. Trust me." His smile chills me to my bones. "Watch my finger. Carefully."

He is tracing a number on the tabletop. There's a zero. And then a five. And then, I think, a six.

"I don't get it." Tears are pricking my eyes. I feel sick. Visiting time is almost over. I thought I might get closure coming here, but I haven't. Instead I'm trying to get sense out of a madman.

"Look again."

Zero. Definitely.

Five. Or so it seems.

Six.

056.

"Five minutes," barks the officer behind me.

Joe darts his eyes toward the clock. Is that a clue?

Try, I tell myself. Think about this puzzle like your son does, see it from another angle.

"I don't know," I sob. "I don't know."

Other inmates are beginning to look. Joe sees it, too. He's speaking. Slowly. Quietly. Like a parent soothing a child.

"Then I'll tell you. It means nothing.

Sometimes we see clues in things that are not there. The simple truth, Lily, is that you're a good person, deep down. But you were weak that night. Hurt. Scared. That's why you let me take the key. I knew that if I did something terrible using it, you'd never be able to forgive yourself. Well, now you can. So I meant it when I said that I didn't have to use the key. That's why I posted it back to you."

There's a glimmer of hope inside me. "Honestly?"

I realize for the first time that I don't really know this man. I never did. Yes, he may look similar to Daniel. Speak like him. But he isn't Daniel. He's a killer. And a liar.

He grins. "It's true. When I rescued you, it wasn't the first time I'd gone to your old house. I'd been there before on the night of Ed's murder. The truth is that I planned to get rid of him for you. He'd hurt you too much. I could see that. So he had to go."

I shudder at his reasoning.

"I was going to break down the door or maybe smash a window. But when I arrived, the door was already open. Carla was on her way out when I got there. I decided to push past and deal with your ex. I didn't need to use your key at all."

The relief is overwhelming in one way. Yet

I am also horrified that Joe killed Ed for me.

"But why say you were hired as a hit man?" I whisper.

Another grin. "I knew I would get convicted for my assault on Carla, so I figured I might as well try to take her down with me."

"But it meant you got a longer sentence."

"Yeah. Well." He shrugs. Joe looks embarrassed. "Let's just call it my penultimate act of love for the woman I could never have."

"Penultimate?" I whisper.

"Yes. And this is the final one." He leans closer. "Carla was convicted for killing Ed because she plunged the knife into him. Wasn't she?"

I nod.

"But the knife was found on the ground."

I think back to the questions in court when this very point had been raised. Yes, Carla had said at last. She had knifed Ed. She couldn't remember what had happened next. It was all such a muddle . . .

"When I went around that night, Lily, the knife was still sticking in Ed's leg." Joe is speaking very slowly. Very deliberately. "The silly woman had just left it there. You're not meant to pull a knife out without the right medical knowledge. Did you know that? It can cause far more damage."

I can hardly breathe.

"I went back. After I saw Carla drop the gloves, I returned to your house. I needed to find out if there was anything that could incriminate me. I waited outside behind a hedge for a few minutes, but no one seemed to have noticed the door being ajar. That's the great thing about those big houses. They're set back from the street. Perfect targets for burglars."

He says this so flippantly that I can barely disguise a shudder.

"I went in. Couldn't resist a look at him. Then I realized he was still breathing. I kept thinking about how much he had hurt you. So I did it. I yanked out the knife. Blood shot out. He made this weird gurgling noise . . ."

I look away, choked with distress.

"Then I scarpered. Later, I burned my clothes and gloves — I'd brought my own, of course. And waited for the police to track me down. I was quite prepared to go to prison — it would have been worth it in return for getting rid of your husband." He gave a wry smile. "I couldn't believe it when she was arrested. And then I heard you were defending her. For a while I thought you were playing the system. Trying to make her look innocent but using that bumbling brief to discredit the case and make sure she got sent down. I sent you Carla's gloves to help you. But because, as it turns out, you didn't use them, she got off."

"So you really killed Ed," I say slowly.

"You could say that all three of us did." His black eyes are trained on me firmly and squarely. "Carla and I both wielded the knife. But the right verdict would have been reached if you had used my evidence in the case. So you bear responsibility, too."

I wince again.

Joe is stretching out his hands to me now. I hesitate. Then I allow the tip of my finger to touch his. Just briefly. Much as I might try to fight it, Joe and I will always be bound together because of our shared history. He may have been in prison when we first met while I was on the outside — just dipping my toes into this new, scary world of double-locked doors, long corridors and prison guards. But because I was trying to get him out of there, it had felt like us against the rest of the world.

Add our one stupid tryst on the Heath, Tom's birth, Ed's murder, Carla's conviction. You can see why the lines between right and wrong have become so blurred.

"I love you," he says with those black eyes

focused firmly on mine. "I love you because you understand me."

Daniel used to say the same.

"I can't say the same but . . ." I begin.

"I know." Joe's grip tightens on my hand. "You don't have to explain."

I tug it away.

"You've more strength than you realize, Lily." Joe seems almost amused. Then his face saddens. "Take care of my boy."

I think of Tom's wonderful drawings — especially of fossils. The way he only has to look at a mollusk or starfish for it to appear on paper. It's a new skill — one that I didn't know he possessed until a new art teacher, fresh from college, appeared at his school. It's amazing what a difference a supportive teacher can make. Someone who really understands a child with (and without) Asperger's syndrome.

Gifts like that are usually inherited. Or so the teacher says.

Joe is still looking at me. "I've been thinking about it. I don't want another DNA test — if indeed you took one in the first place. I need to pretend that Tom is mine. It will help me to keep going. And don't worry about me. It's only right that I should be back here in prison."

"Time!"

Joe drops my hand. I feel a quick sense of inexplicable loss, followed by an overwhelming wave of freedom.

Then Joe's voice changes. "Don't come back, Lily." He's looking at me as if memorizing every part of my face. "Don't come and visit me again. It wouldn't be fair. On either of us. We both need to move forward now. But you have to promise me one thing."

"What?" I whisper.

Those black eyes lock with mine for one last time. "Have a great life. You deserve it."

Is he being sarcastic? I leave the prison, not knowing if he'd been genuine or not. But then again, could anyone really know a man like Joe Thomas?

EPILOGUE

Summer 2017

MARRIAGES

The wedding between Lily Macdonald and Ross Edwards took place quietly on 12 July . . .

"Happy?" asks Ross as we walk back to the house after the church blessing.

Yes — Ross and I. It happened so naturally that I wondered why it hadn't done so before.

"Some might say I haven't led a blameless life," he'd told me before anything really happened between us. "Nothing illegal. Well, not really. But I did something stupid a long time ago which has haunted me ever since."

"Stop," I say, placing a finger against his lips. "Everyone is entitled to his secrets."

"No," he says. "I want our relationship to be totally honest." He looks away for a moment as though trying to compose himself. Then he faces me again, watching my eyes as he speaks. "When I was seventeen, my friend Nick got a car for his birthday. He drove a whole crowd of us out of town to celebrate at a club that had just opened. He hadn't been drinking but . . . well, the rest of us had. We all got noisy and began to punch and tickle him when he was at the wheel."

There's a silence. I suspect (with dread in my heart) that I know what's coming but I also know that I have to let Ross tell me in his own time.

"Nick took a bend too fast and . . . and hit a tree. He died instantly. The rest of us were all right."

"Were you prosecuted?" I ask shakily.

"Only the boys who actually tickled and punched him." He puts his head in his hands. "I wasn't one of them but I had joined in the shouting and singing which would have also distracted him."

"And you told the court that?"

He lifts his head. His eyes are red. "No. The others kept quiet, too. We . . . well, we let the other boys take the whole blame."

I could say that the accident wasn't really his fault but I knew Ross wouldn't believe that. Nor did I.

He carries on, flatly. "After that, I became a bit of a recluse. I concentrated on school-work and became addicted to figures. They didn't carry emotion. They were clear. A simple 'right' or 'wrong'. It's also why I never had a long-term girlfriend. I didn't feel I deserved any happiness."

Just like me, after Daniel.

Ross is taking my hand now. "But then I met you. And even though you belonged to Ed, something clicked. I sensed you'd understand." His voice quickens. "Did you feel the same?"

I hesitate, thinking how I'd always felt there was something behind Ross's upbeat appearance. Only now do I realize why. He'd been damaged, too. And was trying to hide it.

"I do now," I say honestly.

His face is transformed. It's a picture of utter relief. And love. "I will tell you one thing. I will always be faithful to you. And I'll look after Tom as if he was my own."

That's good enough for me. I don't want to know the details. I've had enough to cope with. But I am secretly grateful that Ross is no saint. It evens out the balance between us.

Meanwhile, Mum is wearing a rose silk suit and a delirious expression on her face.

Tom, who refused to wear his new jacket because he didn't "like the feel" of the material, is holding hands with Alice. My son looks just like Ed did at that age, according to the photo albums my former mother-in-law left me when she died. I feel more confident about caring for Tom now. No longer do I fear that I might tip him over the edge, as I did Daniel.

Meanwhile, Dad is overseeing the barbecue.

We could be just another couple getting married in midlife. There are plenty of us. Carla isn't the only one to be getting married in prison. So, apparently, is Joe. There was a picture of his bride-to-be in the paper. I recognized her instantly as my old secretary who had announced her engagement so excitedly in the office. The one with the sparkling diamond on her left hand. *He put the ring in the Christmas pudding! I almost swallowed it.*

So she had been Joe's source! All the time he claimed to have an obsession for me, he was playing her, too. And she had apparently decided she still loved him, despite his being a murderer.

Proof, if any, that I need to move on. Ahead is a clean slate. I make a promise every day to let go of the past.

Yet the guilt still sometimes comes back to haunt me in the form of thrashing nightmares. If I told the police what Joe had told me about pulling out the knife, it is possible that Carla might have her sentence reduced. But Joe is unpredictable, I know that. And if the case is reopened, there is the possibility that Joe might tell the court about the key and claim that I as good as hired him, as he previously claimed Carla had done.

It's a scenario I can't even consider. How would Tom cope without me? How would I cope without him?

So Carla remains in prison for my son's sake.

None of this sits easily on my shoulders, trust me.

Since Ross and I have gotten together, I've done a lot of thinking. He's helped me to forgive my younger self for my relationship with Daniel. I can see now that I made mistakes because I was young and vulnerable. Daniel made me feel good about myself at a time when I was bullied at school for being fat. Yet, ironically, as Ross has gently pointed out, my adopted brother was a bully himself. "It's sometimes difficult to see that at the time," he told me kindly. "Especially when you love someone. His difficult childhood, before your parents adopted him, couldn't have helped either."

Ross has also helped me come to terms with my behavior on the Heath that night, after I'd won Joe's appeal. "You were on a high after the case," he said. "You thought you had no future with Ed. Joe reminded you of Daniel." Ross is a good man. He always sees the best in people. But I still haven't been able to tell him about Joe's final confession. How Carla didn't hire him. How Joe pulled out the knife that made Ed bleed to death. I suspect that Ross would tell me I had a moral responsibility to report that, whatever the consequences.

When I feel in need of justifying myself, I remind myself of that piece of advice I was given by one of my tutors at law school. "Believe it or not, some criminals will get away with it. Some will go to prison for crimes they didn't commit. And a certain percentage of those 'innocents' will have gotten away with other offenses before. So you could say it balances out in the end."

Maybe she was right. Joe should have gone to prison for Sarah. Instead he's there for Carla and Ed. Carla shouldn't have been fully blamed for Ed's death. Perhaps her sentence is her punishment for murdering my marriage, for wanting something that wasn't hers to take.

Anyway, Carla's sentence might be life, but as her lawyer quite rightly pointed out, it doesn't mean that nowadays. She'll be out before she's old.

"Ready?" asks Ross. Gallantly, he sweeps me up into his arms, to carry me over the doorstep of the barn conversion that Mum and Dad have just had built on their grounds to give us some privacy.

As everyone throws confetti and shouts out good wishes, I silently vow that with Ross's help, my life will be different from now on.

"I love you," he says before gently bringing his lips down on mine.

I love him, too. Yet strangely, part of me still misses Ed. It's the little things that I remember. Ed liked his tea weak, with a quick dunk of the tea bag. He knew I liked my Rice Krispies without milk. Small nuggets of understanding like this, built up over the years, create an inescapable bond.

Did I do the right thing about the paternity test? My mind goes back to when I had watched those boats bobbing on the water and had a new idea. In other words, not have the test at all. Surely this was one occasion where ignorance was bliss? After all, how would I cope if the results showed that my son had a murderer for a father? What if this made me love him less? But in the end, I chose not to have the DNA test done at all. I would rather live with the uncertainty than take the risk of discovering that Joe's cold, calculating, evil blood flowed in my son's veins.

The fact is that Ed brought up Tom as though he was his (even though he had no reason to believe otherwise). And now Ross has promised to do the same. "I will always be there for him, Lily. And for you."

Yet I cannot completely banish my doubts. Am I putting my head in the sand about Tom and also Ross? Do I deserve either of them? Can I be forgiven for my own actions?

So many questions without answers! But we all have layers of good and bad inside us. Of truth and deceit. However much we deny it.

Now as Ross and I prepare to slice the wedding cake with all our friends and family around and Tom by my side, there is one indisputable fact.

I'm no longer Mrs. Ed Macdonald.

I'm my new husband's wife.

For better.

Or for worse.

After all, who knows what lies ahead?

ABOUT THE AUTHOR

Jane Corry is a writer and journalist and has spent time as the writer in residence of a high-security prison for men — an experience that helped inspire *My Husband's Wife*, her debut thriller. Corry runs regular writing workshops and speaks at literary festivals worldwide, including The Women's Fiction Festival in Matera, Italy. Until recently, she was a tutor in creative writing at Oxford University.